ALL ENEMIES FOREIGN AND DOMESTIC

— MATT ROBBINS —

For Carla, my wife and friend.

I want to thank my military and law enforcement advisors: Adam Chute (who took one for the team), Andre Barnard ("South Africa's Son"—thanks for the knife), Mickey Sims (who reminds us to always keep fighting).

Thank you to the men and women in uniform who sacrifice body and mind.

To Gloria Lawrenson: your editing and advice were an invaluable treasure.

To Marina Hofman: thank you for your prayers, patience, and professionalism.

ALL ENEMIES—FOREIGN AND DOMESTIC

Copyright ©2024 Matt Robbins

978-1-998815-23-4 Soft Cover
978-1-998815-24-1 E-book

Printed in Canada

Published by:
Castle Quay Books
Tel: (416) 573-3249
E-mail: info@castlequaybooks.com | www.castlequaybooks.com

Edited by Marina Hofman Willard PhD
Cover and book interior design by Burst Impressions

Library and Archives Canada Cataloguing in Publication
Title: All enemies foreign and domestic / Matt Robbins.
Names: Robbins, Matt, author.
Identifiers: Canadiana (print) 20240333438 | Canadiana (ebook) 20240333454 | ISBN 9781998815234
  (softcover) | ISBN 9781998815241 (EPUB)
Subjects: LCGFT: Survival fiction. | LCGFT: Novels.
Classification: LCC PS8635.O123 A79 2024 | DDC C813/.6—dc23

CASTLE QUAY BOOKS

PROLOGUE

The old man was wrapped in a tattered blanket; hunched over a small fire. A light breeze sifted through the ashes and carried with it a sharp chill, testifying to the lateness of the season. He puffed gently on an ancient pipe, a study in concentration. The deep lines that wore their paths through his weathered, brown face told the stories of a difficult life. Yet there was an intelligent, thoughtful pattern that carried with it a certain sternness, when still. Only his eyes still sparkled with youthful excitement. He could sense what was coming.

Not twenty meters behind him, just up the hill, a silent, lithe figure waited—eyes fixed on the old Indian. There was a flash of sunlight on a blade, and then ever so gently the figure moved forward soundlessly through the underbrush. He had chosen this route, as it was the most difficult and the least likely to be expected. He had covered the last hundred meters in just over one hour, making every step count. Soon he would be within striking distance.

He wore heavy wool socks and could feel each root and pebble beneath his feet. He stepped silently around a shrub, his foot coming down gently, feeling a twig. He shifted it slightly away, setting it down carefully. Confident of the new footing, he leaned forward. A rock grated and rolled underfoot. For a moment his heart sank.

"Come to the fire, Lance." The deep voice was casual in tone.

Lance would understand, years later, this was a voice that had a powerful influence on the most powerful people in the nation.

The boy straightened up and came forward, his head bowed slightly in shame. He was twelve years old and was wearing nothing but those wool socks, a breechcloth, and a leather scabbard, to which he returned the knife. His disheveled hair was light brown, almost blond in color. His sinewy, muscular form already showed the promise of the powerful man he would become.

The old man gestured for him to sit, and he complied. There was a long moment of silence as the old one stared thoughtfully into the few coals that remained in the fire. Finally, he spoke. "Do you understand what defeated you today?" he asked frankly.

Lance knew the question was rhetorical, so he waited.

"Before you or I ever set foot on this earth, there has been a cycle of seasons, that no man has dominion over. They will remain even when you and

I have gone on ahead. When we come across these forces of nature, we then understand our own limits. We must always measure ourselves against the weather. But the weather shows no favorites. It has no malicious intent. It is simply a factor that is." He paused briefly.

"What defeated you today was not the weather; it was your assessment of it. Had you been patient and taken more care, you would not have frozen to death."

He took another drag on the pipe and looked up. The sternness was gone, and his face lit up with a smile, which in turn brought a smile to the young boy's face. Lance took a special pride in the fact that his companion spoke to him like a man—directly and with respect. There was a love and warmth from him that he had always known.

"Why did you choose the hill to approach?" He wondered aloud, half musing.

Lance shrugged. "I figured you sat with your back to it, believing you didn't need to cover that spot. I also figured you wouldn't expect me to try from there."

He looked at Lance with a long appraisal and decided the boy needed a small victory here. He would never lie to make him feel better. He spoke honestly. "I didn't. I've never seen any youngster as good as you are. I would say, Lance, there are very few grown men who could have done better."

A broad smile broke out on Lance's face. Praise and encouragement always flowed easily from this man. "Grandpa," the boy started, "are you gonna be staying for dinner?"

"I am not. I have work that I must attend to. But I do want to see your brother before I leave."

"He's over in Lone Prairie picking up some parts for that old truck he's been fixing." Lance was proud of his older brother, who seemed to be able to fix anything that had an engine, and that old truck was just about finished.

"I'll be back next week, and we will try again," Grandpa said. "And I will see Kyle then." He added, "You know, Lance, I'm not your grandfather—I'm your great-uncle."

"I know! But you're Grandpa to me!"

Uncle chuckled slightly at that. His face once again brightened. "It's time for me to go," he said. "My aide is coming."

A moment later, a massive man stood on the edge of the clearing.

Every time Lance was in this man's presence, he was in awe of his great size. He was just as amazed that he never heard his approach despite that great bulk. He wore a navy-blue suit with a crisp white shirt, black tie, and black sunglasses. Lance had never seen him smile.

"Time to go, Senator," the man said. Removing his sunglasses, he came to the fire … still not a sound.

"Lance, how did you do today?" he asked, offering his hand.

Lance reached up, looking him in the eye as he had been taught. His hand disappeared into the other's. His grip was firm as he shook—the pride of a man swelling up in his breast. It was a true honor to be treated as someone deserving a handshake.

"I was doing really good—but I blew it with only a few feet to go." Lance was enthusiastic.

"Ah," he gave a guttural grunt. "Don't do that again."

Lance realized that no better advice could have been given.

The senator rose, carefully folded the blanket, and tucked it under his arm.

"I'm ready, Ross," he said. "Lance, put out the fire, will you? Tell Kyle I will see him next week, and I want to ride in that jalopy when it's ready."

With that they were gone, and Lance was alone.

1

Six Months Ago

Kyle Coolidge was just about to wrap up the workday in his garage when a pickup truck rolled up to the service bay.

"You still open?" the stranger inquired.

Kyle needed to get home to pack, but he also hated to leave someone stranded with car troubles, especially on a long weekend. Lone Prairie was off the beaten path.

"What seems to be the trouble?" It was his way to defer to the need at hand. It was also, he reflected, the way he had built a solid business these last five years. This service station and repair shop represented his entire life's investment. He had heard other business owners grumble about their businesses, but Kyle loved what he did. He was also making a good living and was building a life for himself and Rachel.

"Not sure," the stranger replied, "she's overheating." His manner was abrupt, almost confrontational.

"Pop the hood," Kyle instructed. Something about this man's manner put him on alert.

"Start it up," he said sharply, realizing that his prejudicial feeling was affecting his attitude, and he checked it immediately.

The engine came to life. Looking into the driver's window, he saw that the temperature gauge was already high and climbing. The warning light was also on. Kyle tapped on the thermostat housing with a ball-peen hammer, and a moment later, the stranger, with a triumphant tone said, "It's going down. Looks like you fixed it."

"Not quite," Kyle replied. "The thermostat was stuck in the closed position so the coolant's not passing through. Pretty common."

"Well, can you fix it?" Again, that sharp edge to the stranger's voice.

"I don't have the part." Kyle neglected to mention that he could call Frank, the owner of the parts store, and he would probably come back into town, open the store, and likely have the part in stock. But that would take an hour, and he had promised Rachel he'd be home right after work so they could leave for his mother's. He didn't want to be late, and Rachel didn't like traveling at night.

"I'll tell you what—let's give it fifteen minutes to cool down. I can take the thermostat out, and you can go without it."

"Will that work?" The stranger's eyes narrowed.

There it was again—that testiness. Kyle decided he wanted to be rid of this man quickly.

"Sure it will—your heater won't work, but you don't need it this time of year. I can replace it after the long weekend if you're going to be staying in town?"

"Nope," the stranger, muttered. "Just passing through."

Kyle felt relief. He turned the release valve and heard it hiss as the steam pushed past the seal. "If you want," he suggested, "there is an automatic coffee machine and a restroom inside. Help yourself. This won't take too long."

The stranger nodded and went inside to wait.

———— • ————

It has been said that our lives turn, not on the huge dramatic things, but on the incidentals. The seemingly innocent little things—a right turn here, a change of mind there. This small stop at a lonely little town turned out to be the catalyst for a chain of events that unleashed forces no one could have foreseen. As always, it is the little things.

Kyle had a slight scowl on his face. The hoses were still hot after twenty minutes. He kept glancing at his watch. Rachel will not be happy.

Deciding he could wait no longer; he loosened the bolts on the housing slowly—a little worried he'd scald himself if there was still hot water in the lines. He worked on both bolts taking a few turns on each side, one at a time. Within moments, there was another short spit of steam, and the housing was off. He lifted the thermostat out and threw it in the garbage.

After resealing the housing with a silicone bead and putting everything back together, he looked at his watch and grimaced. A half hour! He topped up the coolant and hopped into the truck to start it up. The gauge was reading normal, so this was mission accomplished.

What Kyle didn't notice, in the rush, was the big yellow envelope on the passenger side of the bench seat. When he jumped in, the envelope slid toward him, and when he jumped out again, the momentum pulled it out with him, spilling its contents onto the pavement. Kyle cursed under his breath and quickly stuffed the contents back into the envelope and carefully put it back on the seat.

He went into the office, to find the stranger looking intently at his phone.

"All done!" Kyle said. "On the house!"

"Really?" The stranger seemed genuinely surprised.

"Yeah, it's no problem." Kyle really needed to get going.

The stranger gave him a suspicious sideways glance. Clearly he saw that Kyle was trying to rush off. As the old proverb says, "The guilty flee, when no man pursueth."

"Okay, thanks," he said, still trying to get a read on Kyle. He had a take-out cup with his coffee in it. He held it up, looked Kyle in the eye, and said, "And thanks for the coffee." With that he walked out, got in his truck, and drove away.

Kyle felt like the air in the room warmed up as soon as the stranger left. "That," he said out loud, "is a very dangerous man!"

Locking up the shop, he jumped in his car and called Rachel to explain. Their home was only a half hour away and with luck they would be on the road within another half hour. But there was no avoiding it—the last hour of driving would be in the dark. Hopefully, Rachel would just fall asleep, as was her habit.

When Kyle pulled up to the house, he could see suitcases on the doorstep, and he frowned a little.

"Rachel!" he called as he hopped out of the car and approached her. "What have you been doing? You know the doctor said to take it easy, right?"

Rachel appeared in the doorway. Her presence still gave him a little start. She was taller than most women at five-ten and had beautiful auburn hair and deep brown eyes, rimmed with long, dark lashes. Slim and athletic, she always kept herself fit. The summer dress that she was wearing did nothing to hide the late stages of her pregnancy.

"You look beautiful," he said with sincerity.

"Don't think that flattery will buy you any mercy from me, Mr. Coolidge!" She glared at him with feigned intensity.

He reached around her waist, drawing her close to him. "Why would I adjust my strategy when it's worked so many times in the past?" His eyes were wide and innocent.

"Why, Mr. Coolidge, what kinda woman do you take me fo'?" she said, with a playful hint of southern drawl as she pushed away from him.

"Not a woman," he corrected, "a lady." He said the last with great respect and bowed in a grand gesture.

They came close, and he kissed her firmly on her slightly parted lips. He then reached down and gently rubbed her belly. "And how's my son doing today?"

"Son? A little presumptuous, wouldn't you say?"

"Nope," he declared. "That's my son you're carrying, Mrs. Coolidge. And I love you all the more for it."

Many people would have taken this as false gallantry. But Rachel knew better. This was the Coolidge way. To be regal in speech and deed. It was one of the things that made her fall in love with him.

"Well, let's get going!" He started putting the suitcases in the car. One was very heavy. She had lugged it down the stairs one step at a time, and he picked it up like it was a woman's valise and tossed it into the trunk.

He was a powerful man that she had never seen sick. Not even a cold in the twelve years she had known him.

He was working at the garage when her parents first moved to town. They had decided that the country life would be more suited to them in their retirement and bought a nice house on some acreage just out of the municipality. Rachel came to visit them during her breaks when she was in college.

It was during one of these visits that she met Kyle at a dinner party a friend hosted. If there was no such thing as love at first sight, she was a fool. The moment they were introduced, she knew in her heart this was the man for her. He was six years older than her and seemed so much surer and more confident than the "men" she went to school with. Despite his physical and mental toughness, she never felt—even for a single moment—anything but love and protection from him. Not a moment of fear, insecurity, or intimidation.

Yet she had seen ferocity in him on one occasion. It was at a dance. A persistent would-be dance partner grabbed hold of her and tried to pull her out onto the dance floor, and instantly Kyle was at her side. He clamped down with an iron grip on the other man's wrist. The fellow let out a half scream and released his hold on her. He'd had too much to drink and staggered a little out the door without looking back and without a word.

Rachel's best friend, who worked at the clinic, told her a few days later that they had put a cast on the man's arm.

———— • ————

They were looking forward to seeing Katherine, Kyle's mother. Even though they lived only a four-hour drive away, with the business and Rachel's work at the preschool, it was hard to get away. The business was now doing well, and Kyle had hired Clarence, a master technician, who moved his family to Lone Prairie for a lifestyle change.

So they were making the time now. With the baby coming, Katherine had insisted they come for a visit. She had items, kept for years, that she wanted to give them. And in fairness, they were overdue for a visit.

It was not a good thing to try the patience of Miss Katherine. She was a serious woman, who loved her family and had accepted Rachel instantly. They had many long and intimate talks and had become close. More like friends than in-laws.

A few drops of rain began to spatter as they were loading the last of their luggage into the car. Kyle had decided he could go for the weekend visit with a small duffel bag, a spare set of clothes, and a toothbrush—and felt like he had overpacked. Rachel, on the other hand, to put it politely, was prepared for every eventuality. He was sure that he would need half the fuel if he traveled by himself without all her luggage. But what would be the fun in that?

The sky was darkening rapidly. As they pulled out of the drive, he could see the worry in her eyes.

"Maybe the storm will be short-lived," he said, trying to alleviate her concern.

She nodded nervously. Placing a pillow between the seat and the window she stretched out, tilted her seat back, and reclined her head to get some rest. Kyle was still hoping she would sleep.

Kyle was speaking, and that brought Rachel out of a daydream.

"I think he's finished. Maybe he can settle down now."

"What? What are you talking about?"

He pursed his lips. "Where did you check out to?" He laughed. "Lance. Miss Katherine said he's been discharged, and he's coming home."

Lance was a mystery to Rachel. She had seen him briefly at Christmas dinners and on the few occasions he was home on leave. She knew how important his family was to him because he always made the effort to see them. The visits were always short and on short notice.

Everything about Lance made you take notice of him. Like Kyle, he was strikingly handsome. He was shorter than Kyle's six feet, two inches. But he was a solid mass of lean muscle and even in casual movements around the house, he had the grace of a wild animal. There was a quiet, cool assuredness about him that put you at ease. But there was also a wall—a strange aloofness that kept you at arm's length. It was never anything you could put your finger on. He was always kind, always pleasant, and very encouraging to Kyle. He didn't use profanity, or the rough language of the soldier, but you could only get so close. And somehow he would always deftly steer the conversation away from himself.

She'd asked Kyle about it a few times, and he'd explained, "That's just his way. Even before Father died, Lance was a reserved kid. But it became more pronounced afterwards, and I suspect it's just his character. He was eight when Father passed, and I think he took it pretty hard. But our uncle Joseph started coming around to spend time with us—said he was fulfilling an oath to our grandfather. His visits made all the difference to Lance. They would spend hours, and occasionally days, together in the woods. Uncle Joseph was a United States senator. He'd been raised on Indigenous land along with our grandfather. They were considered half-bloods. Their father before them was of the Anglo-Saxon tribes, and their great-grandmother was a full-blooded Indian, or of the First Nations, as they say these days."

———— • ————

Rachel knew how much Kyle looked forward to seeing Lance and how much he worried whenever he left. Lance never spoke about the military—just snippets, a comment here and there. Nothing definitive. He didn't really look like a soldier to her. Not the crew-cut and clean-shaven look you would typically expect.

"It will be nice to see him, then." With a mischievous grin, she added, "We could throw a party while he's home."

"Oh boy, here we go!" Kyle reacted. "The matchmaker up to her tricks!"

"Last time he was here, he started quite a stir with the women at the preschool. The mothers, single or not, were asking a lot of questions and asking for introductions," she reminded him.

Kyle knew better than to get in the middle of these schemes. It never ended well. And the thrill for the women was the romance and the chase.

He'd heard that Lance had an off-and-on-again thing with one of the girls from the fitness club back home. The rest of his love life, like everything else about Lance was a mystery. It was no surprise when Lance enlisted nor when he rose through the ranks quickly. However, when he began breaking off contact for long periods, Kyle suspected it was for secret operations.On one of his visits, they were having a beer on the deck of their mother's home, and Kyle asked Lance about it.

He replied, "You're my brother, and I trust you implicitly, and I will tell you the truth about anything you ask me. But before you do, I would ask that you respect me … and not ask. As you know, once a word is spoken, it can never be retrieved."

Kyle raised his beer. "To honor and respect." With that, their bottles clanked for the cheer.

That was the last time Kyle asked.

2

The world of Clifford Bellamy was a relatively simple one. He took pleasure in money, casual relationships, and little else. He was utterly without conscience. He simply lacked the ability to experience empathy. He could not remember a time in his life when he had felt sorry for someone else. Or when he had imagined what their experiences were like.

He had been bred for the world in which he existed. He did not lack intelligence—quite the contrary: he was brilliant and cunning. He saw human emotions and reactions almost like an outsider, observing from a distance with a bird's-eye view. Even from an early age, he probed and exploited the tendencies in others that did not encumber him. He was cold and calculating and had the knack of understanding why people did what they did. His observations and calculations gave him a distinct advantage in most interactions. He saw pity as pitiful and mercy as weakness.

His mind was now on his interaction with the mechanic; trying to fit him into one of the many personality types he had catalogued. He was not having much luck. Kyle—his name was on the door of the garage with an after-hours number—had a quality about him that sent a flicker of caution through Clifford's mind. He recognized him as a man of strength, but it was more than that. He had a rare, almost familiar quality that Clifford just couldn't seem to place.

He sensed he was mistaken about the man's character. There were two red flags. One—Kyle had grown nervous after working on the truck. And two— who works without accepting pay? Why had his attitude changed so rapidly?

Suddenly a thought crept into his mind, a stark possibility that chilled him. He quickly pulled the truck over to the side of the road, his heart thudding in his chest. He reached for the envelope on the seat, and there it was—a distinct greasy thumbprint on the top corner.

One emotion Clifford was not immune to was fear. He felt it wash over him then. Everything we have worked for and planned so carefully is compromised. How could I have been so careless? Suddenly another thought hit him. Maybe the mechanic just moved the envelope over on the seat? He carefully reached inside and pulled out the contents. He had placed those papers in there himself and knew instantly they had been put back differently, hastily, sloppily. He swore bitterly. The key was missing!

With a sudden urge, he wheeled the truck around on the highway and drove back towards the garage. He hoped he could resolve the issue before he had to call it in. He would need to know if Kyle had told anyone about what he had seen. He would also need to know what he planned on doing with the key. The odds were that Kyle wouldn't have a clue what it was for, but you never could be sure.

He pictured Kyle again in his mind's eye and recoiled slightly at the idea that he would need to extract information from a man like him.

Back at the garage, he pulled up to the front door and got out. He read the two names: Kyle Coolidge 204-915-8007 and Clarence Peterson 204-915-8716.

Clifford opened Facebook on his iPhone and typed in "Kyle Coolidge Lone Prairie". Sure enough, his profile came up. Clifford felt a surge of satisfaction when he saw Rachel's lovely smile in the picture. A quick scroll through the photos made clear the nature of their relationship, and he realized that finding leverage on Kyle would be simple indeed.

A quick Google search revealed their address. Entering it into Maps, he got back in the truck. As he did so, his eye caught something yellow in the fold of the seat where it met the backrest. It was the key! He stared at it for a moment, hardly believing his luck. Maybe Kyle had just moved the envelope as he was getting in or out of the truck. Either way, he had seen the contents and could not be allowed to tell anyone, even casually. The risk was too great.

Clifford made the cold decision that it would be simpler to just eliminate him. Once he had tied up that loose end, he would call it in, and everything would be on track again.

When Clifford arrived at the address, he immediately recognized Kyle's Dodge Challenger from the garage, having admired it when he first pulled up to the service station. Kyle was now loading suitcases into the trunk, so Clifford continued up the road and waited. Having been in this situation many times, he would be patient. People operated in patterns, and he had learned those patterns. He would pick a spot from which to strike.

Clifford killed with precision. Methodical in his approach, he always gave himself plenty of time to put his plans into action. Now however, without the luxury of time, he must act quickly. Because it was not his way to rush, he contemplated for a few moments in a half-meditative state.

The luggage! They were going on a trip somewhere.

As they pulled out of the driveway, it began to rain lightly.

Clifford made up his mind. He would follow them and wait for an opportunity.

———•———

Kyle grinned. Rachel was sleeping and would be less likely to pay attention to the approaching storm. They had only been driving for an hour. He was looking forward to seeing his mother and Lance. It would be great to have everybody together again. Deep in thought, Kyle did not notice the headlights behind him. He was feeling satisfied and confident. They were winding along a twisting canyon wall for several miles before the interstate. Once there, he could step on it a bit and make up some time. Kyle looked over at Rachel, and a peace settled over him. Soon their child would be born, and a new adventure would begin.

I'm going to be some poor kid's dad. The thought made him chuckle out loud, causing Rachel to stir, mumbling something in her sleep. He'd best stay quiet.

Lost in his thoughts, he didn't notice that the lights behind him were closing in. The radio was quietly playing "For Bobbie" by John Denver. It was one of those perfect, surreal moments. All was good in the world.

With a start, Kyle realized the truck was starting to pass, and its engine roared in his left ear. Suddenly the truck swerved sideways towards them. Kyle took his foot off the accelerator and steered to the right, trying to avoid a collision. He was an experienced driver and was careful not to oversteer.

However, it is the little things …. Sometimes the forces of time and chance simply conspire against you.

Earlier in the week, a construction crew had left some sand on the shoulder. Kyle's right front tire caught that sand and lost traction, and the Challenger smashed through the guard rail.

In a stark moment of clarity, time and space were suspended, and Kyle knew with certainty that they would die. With incredible presence of mind, he reached down and unbuckled his seat belt, milliseconds before the car's hundred-foot fall ended in shattered glass and mangled steel.

There was a blinding burst of light, and he saw the spirit of his son and then his wife streak upwards like meteors in reverse. He could still hear the music on the radio playing, "I'll walk in the rain by your side …."

Rising above the crash scene, he could see that one wheel was still spinning. Then the liquid light was moving all around him.

Kyle, Rachel, and their unborn son all perished in one violent moment to the sound of gasps of shock from somewhere beyond the ether.

——— • ———

Clifford wheeled his truck around at a pull-out only a few hundred meters away, grimly satisfied. Ever alert for danger, he had remembered this stretch of road from a few days earlier and timed his approach perfectly. There had been no contact between the vehicles. No one would see this as anything but an accident. The rain was pounding hard now, drumming an aggressive paradiddle on his roof. He slowed as he drove past the spot. Although he couldn't see the car below, he was sure no one could have survived. He drove away into the coming night completely without conscience or guilt.

Picturing Kyle again, he felt as though he had been victorious over a formidable enemy. Why was that? He did not know the man and normally would not have given him a second thought. However, something had been nagging him since he first met Kyle, and he still could not put his finger on it. There was something familiar about the man.

Am I intimidated by Kyle? He dismissed the thought out of hand. He feared no man. He could be extremely careful but was always supremely confident in himself.

He had succeeded again, which reinforced his contempt for others and bolstered his own sense of indestructibility—a dangerous attitude for someone in his line of work.

3

Lance Coolidge was brewing a cup of coffee. He had gone to sleep at midnight and was up at five. This had been his habit for years. He had no idea how much sleep he needed, but he always seemed to do fine on five hours. He used his hand grinder on the coffee beans so as not to wake his mother. She had been sleeping fitfully since the accident. She had tried to stay strong and positive, but the ordeal had added some years to her face. He had always seen her as a vibrant young woman, but there was fatigue there now, and fine creases grew slowly deeper around her eyes.

He found himself thinking about Kyle a lot, and he had to admit he missed his strong, confident older brother. He had become a bit of a fatalist since joining the military and seeing the righteous die while the evil lived on, and he could find no greater purpose or pattern in any of it. Death comes to everyone, even the evil, eventually. There had been times when he might have given the odd "sinner" a nudge down the road to eternity. But usually it came down to a conflict of interest where each party fought for what they believed in or a way of life they wished to preserve. It was the way of things. This he understood fully.

A lot of people think of the soldier as an idealist, but often you fought just to survive, or you fought for the brothers around you. Of course, the broader political objective was a motivator, but one fought on long past the point where that illusion held sway. It then simply became your job and a matter of duty. Well, he was done with all that now and had been for almost seven months. Among the pangs he felt when thinking about Kyle was the longing for what would never be. He had hoped to reconnect with his brother and get back to a normal life—whatever that meant.

The kettle began to boil, so he turned it off and waited—a practice he'd picked up from a coffee shop owner in Laos. He'd told Lance there was a perfect temperature to brew coffee, and the boiling point was not it. After a few minutes he poured the steaming water through his AeroPress. No cream or sugar, just as Mother Nature intended it. For a rough-and-tumble soldier, he had only a few particular tastes, and the perfect cup of coffee was one of them.

This peculiarity of his had become almost legendary back at the base after one incident. His team was out on a prolonged reconnaissance mission deep into the White Mountains on the Afghan-Pakistani border. Just after dawn they had strayed (on purpose) into Pakistan and ran into a small group of Taliban fighters sitting around a small, smokeless fire in a tiny recess, almost hidden in a grove of pine trees, one of a thousand such places tucked into that mountain range.

The Afghans were just as surprised as Lance's group but with one big difference. Lance's team had weapons at the ready, and the others were caught flatfooted; they had them cold. There were only six men in that group. They looked on their enemy with undisguised hatred, knowing what would come next, but not one of them flinched. They froze and watched Lance, the only one moving.

He saw an old Coleman pot percolating on the fire. Lance was no longer surprised at the number of American- and Canadian-made products in use there. He picked up the pot and poured its contents onto the ground. Then he rummaged in his pack and pulled out his coffee grinder and some Guatemalan beans. Both parties watched in silent curiosity. When he achieved the consistency he was after, he poured it into the brew basket, refilled the water from his canteen, and waited. The tension began to seep out of the air, and one of the Afghans smiled slightly. Lance's men never wavered, holding their guns steady. But now they were not pointed at anyone in particular.

When the coffee was brewed, Lance poured the Afghans half a cup each and did the same for his men. He made the universal gesture for cheers, and everyone did the same. They sat there in the beautiful morning sun on a mountainside in the middle of nowhere, enemies on all sides, and enjoyed a perfect cup of coffee together.

As Lance and his men rose and began to back away from the camp, one of the Afghans got up slowly and stood at attention, made a slow salute and held it there. The rest of the Afghan men rose and did the same. Lance was genuinely touched by their honour and snapped a sharp salute back as they retreated through the trees.

None of his men said much, but he sensed them looking at him curiously throughout the rest of the day. Word of the encounter went through the base like wildfire. Lance had won the hearts of many of his comrades. And he now had the nickname "Coffee". As nicknames go, it could've been a lot worse. He was certain that name would have stuck had the events of another day not overshadowed the camaraderie he'd won with the Coleman percolator.

———— • ————

Lance glanced in the mirror as he went by. He was barefooted, wearing only a pair of track pants. At twenty-nine, he had spent eleven years in the military. At five feet, eleven inches, he was of average height, and he weighed two hundred and five pounds. His weight never seemed to fluctuate, and people always guessed him to be about 25 pounds lighter. He was lean, every muscle sharp and defined against his taut skin. His movements had the grace of a ballet dancer. He could not remember being sick a day in his life and was constantly on the move and busy with something. He had shoulder-length brownish-blond hair and sharp green eyes. He had let his hair grow since coming home. Even in the military, it had not been short, because that would have been a hindrance to the job. He had been told on many occasions how handsome he was and supposed it was true but took little pride in that—it was his physical prowess that gave him his self-confidence.

It was late fall, his favourite time of year. Walking quietly through the living room, he grabbed one of the heavy wool blankets from the sofa. Then he opened the door to the balcony. Old habits die hard. He was careful not to silhouette himself and let his eyes adjust to the dark before stepping out into the crisp morning air. There was no tangible conscious thought behind his actions, no stress to make him alert. His routines were as deeply ingrained as any of the habitual expedient behaviours we all develop. Lance stood silently, soaking in the cool air. It was still pitch black with only a small light on inside. The sky was clear, and the stars were out.

Wrapping the blanket around himself, he curled up on the big, padded chair and listened to the night sounds, sipping on his coffee. He understood how different he was from most people. Embracing the darkness like an old friend, his senses were alert and attuned to the feelings that only other people of the night understood—people like the long-haul trucker, the night shift worker, those with nocturnal occupations. A forlorn longing often surrounded him on nights like this—a longing for something undefined, maybe—a place to belong or someone or something to belong to? It always left him feeling like something was lacking in his life, but it was just out of reach. Thankfully, the morning light always chased the feeling away.

After several cups of coffee and his morning meditation, he heard his mother stir. His heart went out to her; she had lost a dearly loved husband and now a son, daughter, and grandchild. Women felt things on a deeper level than men, and this made loss even more poignant. In a way, men should envy women. They are more authentic and real about their feelings, and that authenticity actually allows them to heal more fully. Some wounds are too deep to ever heal completely, but over time, one learns to compartmentalize, cope, and move forward.

The eastern sky was graying, and Lance went inside to say good morning. He had been worried about leaving his mother alone and asked if he could stay at the old house for a while—knowing she would never refuse him, and certain she guessed his intentions.

She was pouring herself a cup of coffee when he came into the kitchen.

"Good morning," she said in her usual bright tone.

"Morning," he said, a deep admiration in his heart for her.

"Can I make you some breakfast, Lance?"

Lance glanced at the clock, thinking about the things he wanted to get done today. It didn't go unnoticed. "Sure, why not," he said with a grin.

She was already cracking the eggs.

"So are you going hunting?" she asked casually.

"I haven't decided yet," he replied.

"Lance," she started. "You have been pacing around this place like a caged animal. You have fixed everything from creaking doors to fence posts and then some. You're going to drive me crazy. Besides, I have some plans of my own."

"Oh?" He lifted an eyebrow.

"Yes, I'm going to Florida to visit May in Panama City. I want to help after the storm, and frankly I need to get away. I'm getting cabin fever here."

Lance thought about his aunt May. The woman was a going concern— always working on a project or volunteering for this or that. She was always trying to rope people in, enlist them to help or volunteer. And she drove "hell-bent for leather," as the saying goes.

"Promise me you won't get into a car with her behind the wheel." Lance took a gulp of his coffee.

"Oh, hush with that kind of talk. We haven't seen her in years. She may have mellowed by now," his mom responded good-naturedly.

"Not likely," Lance responded, smiling. He was enjoying the banter, and it was good to see the spark still in her eyes. He peered at her over his cup. "Are you sure, Mom?"

"Yes, I'm sure," she said honestly. "I need to get outside of myself and stop dwelling on the accident. I miss your brother every day, but I can be of some use down there, and you can stop watching over me like a night nurse."

They both laughed at that.

"All right." His tone was resigned.

After breakfast, Lance went back out on the deck. The sun was just touching the valley, revealing the autumn leaves in full display. The sight was breathtaking. Hues of yellow, red, and gold blended into a smattering of green that was still holding on. A slightly pungent fragrance wafted on the cool morning breeze. This was the end of the cycle for another year.

It was hard to believe that all this beauty and majesty was a precursor to the death of millions of living things. Their sacrifice as they fell to the earth, becoming part of the soil, would contribute to the new life that was sure to follow next spring.

Lance thought, I hope when I go out it's with that kind of sacrifice and glory.

He never tired of this view—you could see for miles down towards town. The house was nestled on the front of a great high hanging valley that was naturally fenced on three sides by steep, seemingly impenetrable walls. Looks were deceiving, though, as there were three ways out the valley, but you had to know where to look. The house stood just back from a precipice. A small stream fed by a spring further up wandered through the property and then off down the gap towards town, losing itself as it ducked away underground only to reappear again. Eventually, it disappeared completely into the earth, making its way to worlds unknown. Behind the house and into the valley was a hundred acres of natural pasture with groves of aspen scattered about. Here and there, the pasture made forays into a great stand of old-growth timber, mostly fir and pine. That in turn was brought up short by those towering cliffs that stood like eternal sentinels. A long road made its way up through the gap that led to the homestead.

From the front deck, one could sight several points on the road, and with a pair of binoculars (always handy), you could spot someone approaching. It was like his father to build this way—a clear line of fire from the front and several escape routes in the back. Although his father had never described it in that way, as Lance grew up, he began to see the military genius of this layout. His father was not a military man but was always cautious and prepared.

The natural beauty of this place would have been reason enough to build here. He remembered again, his mother telling the story of how they would come to this place when they were dating. They would ride on horseback up the road, which was little more than a widened game trail at the time. This was where they would dream and make plans for the future. It was on one of those visits that Mr. Coolidge (as she often referred to him) had proposed. She recounted the story with delight and with as much romance as she could muster.

Sitting on a blanket by the spring, her mind was drifting as aimlessly as the clouds above them. "Katherine," he said gently. Suddenly, he was kneeling in front of her, holding out a tiny box containing his grandmother's diamond wedding ring. "Would you do me the honour of becoming my wife?"

She almost giggled at the formality of his words, but the look in his eyes made her catch her breath.

"Yes!" she blurted out her reply almost too quickly.

He laughed as he drew her to him, placing the ring on her finger. Somehow, he'd sized it correctly.

"I promise to always take care of you," he said earnestly and then added that to see her smile would be "the greatest aim" of his life.

Katherine swore that he had never failed in that promise.

"I have one more surprise for you," he said, a mischievous glint in his eye. Taking her by the hand, he led her to the viewpoint where they could see down the gap, back towards the town.

"The first time I brought you here, you said this was about the most beautiful view you had ever seen. How would you like to see this view every day?"

"Uh … what do you mean?" She was genuinely puzzled by this odd question.

Reaching into his pack, he pulled out a folder. Holding it up, he explained, "This contains the deed to this property, and I … we own it! I bought it for you as a wedding gift. All I can say is I'm sure glad you said yes." His face broke into a huge smile.

She could not believe that he had made this already perfect day even better.

"I don't understand—how did you manage this?"

"Now that you are going to be my wife, you'll just have to get used to my mysterious ways," he replied.

How many times had they heard that story as boys? Lance had lost count. She would exaggerate a kissing scene in the story, and the boys would pretend to be disgusted, even though secretly, they relished the love their parents had for each other.

———— • ————

Later that morning, Lance fired up his Jeep. The familiar pang of loss hit him once again. Kyle had rebuilt the engine, and now it always started up right away. Over the years, when Lance was away, Kyle had instructed their mom to start it every few weeks so it would not acquire any "lot rot", as he referred to it. It turns out that vehicles are like people—you gotta keep them moving to keep them in good working order. The difference was, the harder you work your body, the better it performs. Not so with vehicles.

Better designer? he wondered.

The thought came unbidden into his mind, but he shrugged it off. These deep philosophical questions were imposing themselves on him with greater frequency these days, and he liked it not one bit.

Lance, he would tell himself, there is no great purpose or reason to life. You've seen enough to know that.

Yet that nagging feeling seemed to stick with him. He chalked it up to a bit of boredom mixed with PTSD.

It was a crisp morning, but he didn't feel like putting the top on the Jeep, so instead, he turned up the heater and headed for town. The wind was cold in his hair, while his feet were overheating. First world problems, he mused.

Even though he had told his mom he wasn't sure, Lance knew he was going hunting, especially now that she had freed him from responsibility to her for the time being. Part of his reason for going into town was to get some food for the trip and to buy a few odds and ends he would need to round out his gear.

The local hardware store was typical of those you find in small towns. It had a surprising variety in stock and could order just about anything else you might need. There were had some incredibly obscure items way back in the stockroom as well. Amazon was probably eating away some of their business, but the locals still seemed to like the in-person touch. In the spirit of entrepreneurship, the owner, Ben Roussel, had purchased two cargo vans and was doing local and regional deliveries in order to stay competitive in a changing marketplace. The store was still a hub of activity in the area.

Ben, who had been the owner for as long as Lance could remember, greeted him as he walked in. "Howdy Lance, can I help you find anything?"

"As a matter of fact, I'm looking for some hundred-grain broadheads and some fletching if you have any."

"Sure thing." Ben went into the archery case behind the counter. "How many would you like?" His back was turned.

"I'd like a dozen broadheads and enough fletching to make a dozen arrows or so."

"You got it," Ben said with a slight smile.

"I'll look around a bit," Lance said. "There are a few other things I want."

He found a flint and steel set that had a magnesium coating, some Vaseline and some cotton balls. He also located some fishing line and few bare hooks. Gathering up the gear was almost as much fun as the hunting itself.

So many of the "modern" camping and hunting items seemed foolish to Lance. Things like microfibre towels and plastic cutlery sets were ridiculous in his opinion. One thing he did want was some scent shield. A bowhunter needs every advantage to get within range of big game.

After some small talk with Ben, Lance paid for his order and walked across the street to the pharmacy to replenish his first-aid kit. Gauze pads and bandages were at the top of the list. He also added an antacid and some cough drops to the basket he had commandeered. He found a suture kit, which was something he really wanted. There were no doctors up in the mountains, and if he was injured, he would have to rely only on himself. Out of habit, he put a box of condoms in the basket as well. In a pinch, he could use them as a bladder to carry water; there were other non-sexual uses as well.

Where he was going there would be no women, so that was not a consideration. Besides, he was close to swearing off women altogether. He compared them all to his mother, and they always came up short. These days, he wasn't much of a companion for the ladies. They always seemed to have a million questions about things they had no damn business asking about.

His final stop was the service station to top up the Jeep. On a whim, he filled up his spare jerrycan, which he kept strapped to the outside of the Jeep in the back.

He hadn't been to town in about a week, so he decided to go into the pub for lunch. The place was buzzing with activity. One of the best places in town for that kind of food, it had become a popular spot.

It was a little dimmer inside the first set of doors and out of habit he took a moment to let his eyes adjust before walking in. Country music mixed with a hum of voices greeted him.

He scanned the room, noting the faces. Most people enter a room and look for a place to sit or a friendly face. Lance always scanned the room for trouble first.

His gaze came to rest on Cindy McKinnon. She was with a man he had never seen before. Cindy and Lance had dated now and then. Never anything serious, but since he had come home, they had gone out a few times, picking up where they had left off. She had broken it off after only a few dates, citing his inability to have a "real" relationship. She was frustrated by his lack of transparency when she asked about his life in the military. She said he was "emotionally unavailable"—a term he guessed she had come across in a ladies' magazine. In his estimation, she had never really matured past her teen years. He figured his experiences in the military and the life he had led out in the world had given him a broader perspective than most people, and to be fair, she just hadn't travelled much, if at all. They were definitely not a good match. They both knew it, but sometimes it's hard to let go of youthful fantasies. Thoughts of her had helped him through some long nights on patrol and times of loneliness, thirst, and hunger.

She looked up, and her eyes hardened.

He turned his back and walked over to the bar. Ordering a steak sandwich, he idly glanced at the football game on the big screen just overhead. He really had very little interest in sports since he'd stopped playing himself. In fact, he realized he couldn't name a single player anymore. He appreciated their skill level, but finding three hours to sit still for a football game just wasn't his thing. The Super Bowl parties at the base always had a dual purpose: to keep everyone entertained, and it was a great excuse to get together.

Lance pretended not to notice when Cindy and her man-friend walked past him out of the pub.

A few minutes later, he paid for his meal and made his retreat as well. Outside, the guy was having a smoke and for some reason that just pissed off Lance. Before he had time to formulate the thought fully, he was speaking. "Didn't take you long to move on, did it?" His tone was hard and flat.

Her nostrils flared and he realized too late that he had just displayed the same level of maturity that he had been critical of in her. He did not want this woman, but like a kid with a toy in a sandbox, he didn't want anyone else to have her either.

"What I do and who I see is none of your damn business." She was vibrating with anger.

Lance could see no dignified way out of the hole he had dug and was trying to formulate a retort when the guy stepped forward belligerently. "What the hell is your problem, buddy?" He was coming to her rescue.

The hot moment had passed for Lance, but now he was left with an awkward situation to handle. He took a purposeful step back, hoping to defuse things. The guy took this as a sign of weakness and closed the space between them. Lance could see what was coming but was powerless to stop it. The stranger reached out and shoved him.

Most people don't realize that a reflex response doesn't go to your brain for validation or verification. Instead, the signal goes to your spinal cord and then travels back, converting that energy into action. And if the motions have been trained extensively, they have become muscle memory and happen of their own volition. Lance impulsively grabbed the guy by his wrist, twisting sideways while pushing his elbow in the same direction. For Lance, the motion was effortless. The aikido movement caused the stranger's body to follow the angle of his twisted shoulder and wrist, and he tumbled over in a somersault. This left him on the ground stunned, but relatively unharmed.

"Lance, stop it!" Cindy shouted, and several passersby turned to look.

Lance was thoroughly embarrassed. The stranger jumped to his feet, fire in his eyes, his fists balled and ready for action. It was clear by how he held himself he was no fighter. Lance knew men, and he could tell that although this man wanted no further confrontation, he was still angry. He knew it was up to him to resolve this in a way that would preserve this guy's dignity.

He held his hands up, palms forward in the universal nonaggressive posture. "I'm done if you are," he offered.

There was relief in the stranger's eyes.

Cindy interrupted, "Now that you have introduced yourself to my cousin, perhaps I can go get my mother, and you can slap her around a bit." Her voice was full of contempt.

"I guess I had that coming," Lance replied, looking sheepish. He turned to Cindy's cousin. "Sorry, friend. No hard feelings?" Not waiting for his reply, he did the walk of shame to his Jeep and sat in the driver's seat for a moment before driving away. "What was I thinking?" he muttered under his breath.

Maybe I am emotionally unavailable, he thought to himself. He knew in his heart that this was not true. In fact, his emotions were very real and very raw. But sometimes things are pressing so deep down that no words can draw them out—they are the unspeakable utterances of the soul.

Lance had never spent much time dwelling on mistakes. He believed in moving forward and mitigating weaknesses. However, he found himself doing more and more self-analysis these days. It was odd that he couldn't shake these deep feelings of self-doubt. It was one of the reasons he had left the military.

His unit had been charged with some of the country's most sensitive missions—incursions behind enemy lines as well as working covertly inside the borders of allied countries.

The most troubling missions for Lance were those where the enemies were his fellow citizens. Threats to national security, he discovered, came in all shapes and sizes.

Lance had always been definitive in his decision-making and rarely hesitated or wavered. The problem was that in hindsight, some of those decisions now seemed amoral. His conscience had been pricked, and his belief system was now somewhat shaken.

———— • ————

At the height of the violence between the Mexican drug cartels, there had been several attacks on American citizens as far north as Phoenix, not to mention the forty-two hundred murders in Juarez in one year. The situation had spiralled completely out of control, and the brutal turf war was taking lives at an alarming rate. The US had tried to stay out of it, but when it spilled over into its backyard, it was time to act. The word came down that some of the cartel leaders had to go—an unmistakable but untraceable message from the top.

In response, the military presence had been increased at Fort Bliss—an ironic name, for the staging grounds were anything but peace. Then, one by one, key members of the cartels began turning up dead. At first, the assumption was that the deaths were gang related. But the sophisticated nature of the dispatches, the lack of anyone claiming responsibility, and the in-your-face, bravado-laden comments meant something else was at play.

Then rumours surfaced that special forces were at work in northern Mexico. It turned out that the cartels had resources and ideas of their own and had bribed a US official inside the military. Special forces had been caught in a firefight on some leaked intel, which put the operations on hold. There was no way the US government was going to take the risk of its soldiers being exposed doing special ops on a neighbour and ally.

The word went out that the US would put a soldier every ten feet on the border, and no business would be done there, period. That strategy worked; there was never another identifiable cartel-ordered hit in the US again. The murder rate in Juarez plummeted to less than that of Detroit, a dubious distinction indeed.

An unexpected consequence of the strategy was that a notorious gang known as MS-13 filled the vacuum left by the cartels on the US side of the border. They were a different animal altogether, utilizing some of the same brutal tactics as the cartels. Where things got foggy was that they were mostly American citizens and as such were under constitutional protection.

The military decided to clean up its own mess and began making some of the MS-13 leadership disappear. That created an ethical problem for Lance, who had tremendous respect for law and order and the constitution. The orders came with the reminder that he was responsible to deal with "all enemies foreign and domestic".

At the time, he had justified his involvement by recognizing that Wyatt Earp and his brothers had been bound by the same second amendment constraints as he was. Yet they forced people to surrender their guns when in town, forcefully rooting out organized crime in their territories. If you were honest about it, some of their constitutional rights had been trampled. Lance understood that kind of thinking had the potential to lead down the slippery slope to tyranny.

The job was eventually passed off to local law enforcement and as a result, their progress ground to a standstill amid the legal process. The drug war put a tremendous amount of pressure on the western states and all the way up into British Columbia, Canada, where the Hells Angels had a stranglehold on the drug trade. They were facing pressure from several incursions into their territory from rival groups.

Maybe the Canadian government preferred the devil they knew, or maybe it went deeper than that …. But they offered their help, and Lance found himself working alongside Joint Task Force Two, or JTF-2, Canada's version of the US Navy SEALs.

While the US maintained command and control, the JTF-2 boys executed orders as crisply as any soldiers he had ever worked with, although they sometimes had a ruthless way of getting things done.

He had worked with them in Afghanistan and again unofficially in Iraq. They were a small force, but as General Schwarzkopf acknowledged during Desert Storm, while they were only 5 percent of the fighting force, they did 20 percent of the fighting. They were pure fighting men and some of the bravest he'd ever met.

They had a great military tradition that they were proud of, even if no one was going to make a movie or write a book about them. Still, there was something very troubling about foreign soldiers operating on American soil, taking the lives of US citizens. Lance was glad when that short foray ended and they went home. As soldiers do, they had forged a strong bond and on more than one occasion had each other's back. These men had become his brothers-in-arms, and blood spilled is some of the thickest. They had strict no-contact orders, and consequently, they didn't keep in touch, becoming ghosts of a time best forgotten.

The ways of war and politics were growing more unsettling for Lance. His last tour in the Middle East had really tested his mental and emotional capacities, and things were beginning to surface that he felt ill equipped to comprehend or deal with. At times, it was just a swirl of emotion that he could not really identify.

The deaths of Kyle and his family had created a space for these pent-up emotions to ooze out. He had practiced meditation while in south Asia, and at times it helped bring him back to center.

As he drove home from town, the peculiar feeling that something unidentifiable was missing came over him once again.

4

On the outskirts of town, a car was pulled over on the side of the road, hood up.

Triggered, Lance swung wide. In his mind he clearly heard an explosion, and he reflexively stomped the gas pedal to the floor. He heard gunfire and screams, and his vision suddenly clouded over.

He pulled sharply to the shoulder and threw the clutch into neutral. His breath was coming in short shallow gasps, and despite the chill, he was sweating. "Damn," he whispered, realizing he was sitting on the side of the road in Montana with birds chirping in his ear, the flashback fading away.

A car with the hood up was a common way the Taliban used to set a roadside bomb, an IED or "improvised explosive device". They had been effective and devastating. He waited a few minutes until his mind was under control and his heart had stopped racing before continuing on.

The day had warmed up considerably, and he turned the heater off. He loved the drive through the gap towards the house. Here and there you would catch a glimpse of the big house way up on the bench.

If the sun was at the right angle, the light would reflect off the windows. The road was a series of twists and turns and in several places the canopy almost covered it completely. This time of year, with the leaves swirling and the sun glinting, it was spectacular. He breathed the crisp autumn air deeply, feeling immediately grateful and happy to be alive.

For a PTSD sufferer you sure handle it well, he thought. There was no denying it: he loved life.

As he pulled up to the house, he noticed Marie's car in the driveway. Marie was a beautiful woman of about forty who had been housekeeping for Miss Katherine for several years. He thought it was strange that she was there, since today wasn't one of her cleaning days.

He found her at the table with Miss Katherine. "How was town?" she asked.

He deftly avoided the topic. "What's up, ladies? Are we changing the schedule?"

He had directed his question to Marie, but Katherine responded. "Marie is going to stay at the house while I'm in Florida," she said cheerfully.

"You got me pegged, huh?" Lance said, grinning.

"I know you're heading into the mountains to go hunting—that's for certain. So Marie will be here to water the plants and care for the animals in the meantime."

"I love being in this house," Marie cut in, "and it will be a nice break for me as well."

"When are you leaving?" Lance asked his mom a bit more seriously.

"I want to coordinate that with you," she replied.

Lance thought for a moment. "How about Thursday?"

"Okay, Thursday it is. Marie, does that work for you?"

"Absolutely," she replied.

"Great," Katherine said, "it's settled then. Marie has offered to give me a ride to the airport. I've also explained everything she needs to do while we are away."

She turned to Marie. "You have a spare key already. If I know Lance, he will be gone by 6 a.m. Sound about right?" she asked without looking at him.

Lance snapped to attention with a sharp salute. "On your orders, commander," he said jokingly.

She always looked at him critically when he mimicked anything military. He was sure she did not like the fact that he had chosen that career, though she respected him for it and would never have said anything negative about it. In a way, it had stolen a part of him, an innocence she had cherished, and she was afraid it was gone for forever.

After Marie left, Miss Katharine asked for a few minutes of his time. He recognized the familiar wistful look in her eyes and knew that she would miss him.

"Where are you planning to go hunting?" she asked.

"Up in the Anzac mountains." He could sense what was coming.

"Good, can you take care of some business in Lone Prairie while you're there?"

"Yes, of course, what is it?"

"We need the signed papers for the sale of the garage"—she hesitated briefly—"and Rachel's parents need to sign their copies as well so the house can be sold."

"Okay." Lance knew she had been handling the probate and their affairs. It had become clear that in their grief, the Freemonts were unable to cope with these details. Lance looked at his mother and once again was amazed by her strength.

"Make sure you say hello, and give them my love," she added.

"I will," Lance promised. For him this was a solemn oath.

The subject of town did not come up again and Lance was glad for it. He was sure the gossip would reach her eventually, but he wanted it to be after her trip. By then he hoped the minor event would have blown over. With so little excitement in a small town, anything could make front-page news—not that there'd been a newspaper in ten-odd years.

———— • ————

In the workshop, Lance took out his bow case and gave it the once-over. First, he tested the draw weight on a scale. He had rigged it with a wire hook on the bottom that he could hang the string from. Seventy-eight pounds. He tightened the limbs up slightly and tested it several more times until he had the tuning at an even 80 pounds draw weight. Eighty pounds was a heavy draw weight, but he had conditioned himself to raise the bow to the shooting position and draw the string back without any gyrations or unnecessary movements.

He imagined he was in the high mountains, the sun just cresting the eastern ridges, a giant bull moose charging out of the trees at his call. "We have a date with destiny, old boy," he said aloud.

He waxed the string and then secured the Allen key to the balancer with a piece of electrical tape.

Lance prepared several arrows to his personal draw length and glued in the inserts that he would screw the broad heads into.

Once the arrow is released, a lot can happen even in the forty-to-fifty-yard range. He had seen deer "jump the string" at that distance, which was almost beyond belief. Consequently, he left as little to chance as possible.

Lance wiped the bow down with a damp rag and carefully popped the arrows into the quiver on the side of the bow. It held eight arrows in all. The rest he stored in the bow case, handling the bow as if it were a precious treasure. His final act before putting it away was to tie a piece of dental floss with a down feather onto it. As long as it wasn't snowing or raining, this allowed the hunter to pick up wind direction and stay downwind to avoid detection.

———— • ————

The anticipation of the hunt was always exciting, and Lance loved the high mountains, the fresh air, and the crystal-clear water from a fast-running stream. For him, the excitement was just as much about being out in nature as it was about the hunt itself. For as long as he could remember, he had always felt more like himself outdoors than anywhere else. The wilderness had a way of removing the pretentiousness of life.

As a teenager, he had once spent a week by himself in the woods. It was then that he first made friends with the night. It had forced him to come to terms with himself, to really understand who he was, and it sharpened his perceptions of others at the same time. When he returned home after that week, he was suddenly able to see through the masks people wore.

For him, the first impression was powerful. People attempt to project their narrative onto your psyche. No matter how hard he'd resist, eventually he'd accept their story as reality. It seemed unavoidable. But now a free mind allowed him to make unfettered judgements and assess his perceptions. That was what being in the wilderness did for him.

Lance's ability to accurately read people came across as a form of extra-sensory perception. It was impressive that he often understood people more accurately than they would have believed possible. He had used this ability to impress more than one girl over the years. Women seem to love a mysterious man and more importantly, one who understands them—a winning combination. Often, he perceived their pain and found himself full of empathy. He once shared these perceptions with a young lady, and she accused him of violating her privacy. After that, he decided to never explore the darker, deeper side again.

His next order of business was to repack. He had a specific set of items he carried with him at all times. His influence had changed some of the equipment soldiers carried in the field. It was challenging to find items that were vital, strong, and yet light at the same time. An item with multiple applications made its way up the value scale quickly. An exception to this rule was the Swiss Army knife. No wonder they hadn't been in a war in two hundred years. That thing was the most "versatile", useless tool he had ever come across. Lance valued mobility above all else and would forgo quantity for quality every time. He restocked his first-aid kit with the bandages he had purchased and replaced the suture thread he had used up. His use for it was nothing too dramatic.

On his last tour, he had made a basic shelter out of an old wool blanket. He'd used the thread to sew up a tear to keep the rain out. Still, it had been a miserable night as he woke up soaked and the repair was of minor benefit.

He was of the opinion that people often learn more from their failures than their victories. He figured this was because good judgement was the result of experience, and experience was usually the result of bad judgement. This allowed him to shake off defeat, placing it in the category of a lesson learned. It became an important part of his personal philosophy, and he rarely made the same mistake twice. In battle, you don't have the luxury of mistakes. You get the test, then you get the lesson. It was the opposite of college life.

He took out the cotton balls and rolled them liberally in the Vaseline. He made a dozen of these and carefully placed them into a ziplock bag. They needed to stay dry. He also opened the box of condoms and put several into the zippered pocket of his hunting pants.

The camo pack had a fleece exterior that would make very little noise as he was sneaking through the woods, scraping up against the odd branch here and there. He made a mental note of what was where. He had packed and repacked it so many times he could find anything he needed with his eyes closed. Of course, that was not necessary because the headlamp, lighter, and candle were in the front compartment.

He checked his 1911 .45-calibre pistol, cleaned it, and put it in its holster. He didn't expect he'd need it, but up in grizzly country he wasn't taking any chances. He knew that a couple of well-placed rounds would put just about anything down.

His plan was to drive his Jeep to a place he had been a few times—a natural gravel cove just off an old logging road. He had scouted it out one summer and decided to use it as home base. It was comfortable because it would keep him out of the wind. It got cold up there this time of year.

The metal carrying rack on top of the Jeep would hold the wall tent, axe, saw, and foldout table. The little woodstove would fit in the back of the Jeep, along with his sleeping bag and the rest of his gear. He could buy food and fuel again in Lone Prairie since his shopping trip to town had been cut short.

He had absolutely no worries about going into the mountains on his own, but he would leave a map of where he was planning to be and his schedule at the sheriff's office. This practice had saved many people from death. Sometimes when you got into trouble, it took very little help to get you out.

Lance had become disconnected from the community while away, and people had moved on with their lives, so he really didn't have anyone he could ask to go with him. If he was honest, he was looking forward to this time to be alone anyway.

———— • ————

That evening his mother was doing some packing of her own. She had two large suitcases, a smaller carry-on, and her purse. She was going for two weeks, but she had packed enough for two months. Women! Lance mused.

The phone rang, and Katherine answered in a cheerful tone, "Hello."

Then he heard her say, "Uncle Joe! How are you?" The other end of the conversation was unintelligible, but he could fill in the blanks.

After a few minutes she said, "Yes, he is here," and handed the phone off to Lance.

"Hello, Grandpa," Lance said, elated to have the chance to talk to him. "Are you calling me from your landline?" he asked deviously.

Joseph absolutely hated cell phones. In his opinion, they were nothing more than "glorified walkie-talkies," designed to distract and track the masses.

His tone deepened now, taking on a less playful tone. "How are you?"

Lance knew this wasn't a formality, but a serious question. "Hmmm, I'm a bit lost," Lance replied and then continued, "I need to get centered. I've been taking some time at home keeping Miss Katherine company. By the way, I wanted to thank you for your guidance at the hearing. I was out of my element there."

"You handled yourself like a professional," Joseph said. "You could have a future in politics if you wanted to," he added.

Lance laughed. "No offence, but I think I've had my fill of politicians and politics."

His uncle chuckled. "None taken, son—you held up well under that grilling." And then he added in his no-nonsense tone, "Those senators had no business or moral authority asking questions and passing judgements. But that is how the system works. As Churchill said, 'Democracy is not a very good system of government, but it's the best we've got.' Which reminds me, can I ask you a question, son?"

"Of course," Lance replied without hesitation.

"What is the difference between a technical truth and a moral or ethical truth?"

Lance paused for only a second because he was pretty sure he understood the source of this query. "I suppose the one is a truth without any context or without expounding and the other includes the periphery details."

After a moment Grandpa asked, "Can you give me an example of this contrast?"

"I believe you have one …," Lance said.

"That's what I thought. Those damn cell phones really are a problem. Landlines aren't much better."

Lance accepted this as a veiled message to keep the conversation vague.

"You know Lance, a soldier does his duty, but a man considers his actions. There are times when these two constructs collide. That is one of the fundamental paradoxes of the trade. It is why we permit soldiers to disobey illegal orders. Which construct gains dominance has a great deal to do with what is inside of the man. In my position, I have access to a tremendous amount of information. Many of the things I learn come by word of mouth, a word here and a whisper there. I have a fair picture of some things, and with others it's foggy with limited details."

His voice rang with a poetry that Lance always appreciated. He also admired his grandfather's ability to say something pointed that to a casual listener would seem benign.

"Some things are better left buried," he replied.

"Lance," Joseph persisted, "when you bury something while it's still alive, it tries to crawl out of the grave."

Lance didn't have a response to that. He felt the truth of it in his heart.

Grandpa continued, "There is a passage in the Bible that says, 'Make your bodies a living sacrifice.' It's the same challenge. How can you leave a living thing on the altar? It naturally wants to crawl off."

Uncle Joseph knew more Bible than anyone he had ever met.

"Then I guess it is a strange request," Lance replied. "Why not just kill it and make the sacrifice then? I hope this is a metaphor?"

"Because then it would be dead! What makes it holy is where it is, not what it is."

Lance was lost—Joseph's lessons of the earth, the sky, and nature he could understand, but these exchanges left him confused.

"Don't try to bury something while it's still alive," he said, rephrasing his point.

That Lance understood, and he interjected, "A person can go by the rules and still make wrong decisions. How do you find a context for that or justify such things?"

"There are times when we must forgive ourselves so we can move on." Joseph didn't wait for a response. "These are things to meditate on. They are the substance of life. Only the heart can understand them. We can talk of them again another time."

There was a slight pause, and then Joseph asked, "When are you going hunting?"

"Day after tomorrow." Lance was relieved the conversation had taken a turn. "How did you know?"

"Because it's where I would expect you to be," he replied and added, "You have done an honourable thing caring for your mother."

"She's a trouper," Lance said. "I'm not sure how much help I have been."

"She might not have survived this blow if not for you."

Although Lance could not imagine that, it was not his way to disrespect or argue with Joseph. When he spoke, you listened. He could not remember there ever being error or fault in any of Joseph's advice or teaching. Often the heroes of youth are eventually exposed for the flawed humans they are, but Uncle Joseph had remained a steadfast beacon of light.

5

After the call, Lance thought about the technical truth he had provided the Armed Services Committee. He had taken a particular grilling from Senator Wallace. The man was relentless and was making a name for himself. He could smell blood in the water but couldn't find its source, and Lance wasn't about to help him out.

There had been unaccounted expenditures, and it was rumoured that money had been funnelled to a special ops program, running illegal missions in the Middle East. They had found the accounting irregularities but not how the money had been spent. The trail led to special forces but then went cold. Lance had been issued a subpoena to testify, both because he was a team leader and because there were coincidental deployments of his teams at the same time as the money disappeared.

Normally a low-level officer would never have been brought before a Senate hearing, but Lance had the misfortune of being related to Joseph Coolidge. Wallace was doing his level best to discredit him. He suspected that Joseph knew very well where that money went. His strategy was to squeeze Lance in order to get to his uncle. Lance wondered whether Joseph knew anything.

All the queries were centered on his Afghanistan and Iraq missions. Lance answered all those questions as vaguely as possible. He purposely omitted dates and details about his team sizes, hoping to raise their suspicions that he was hiding something there. He never lied about anything; he simply didn't volunteer information until and unless a specific question was asked. He answered questions in the tense they were asked. Do you know? is slightly different than Did you know? And Lance slipped through every language loophole he could find. The prep work Uncle Joseph's staff had done with him had made all the difference.

Their best piece of advice was to pause, think, and then answer the question. In the end, he denied any knowledge of monies being spent illegally. He denied knowledge of covert ops in the Middle East. One of the questions included the phrase "over there". He took a deep breath on that one. It wasn't "anywhere". So he was able to answer those questions "technically" with the truth.

Senator Wallace had grown frustrated and combative. His instincts told him something was there, but he couldn't pinpoint it. He was a cunning and malicious enemy, who took politics to the extreme. This was how it was now in a polarized nation. Most politicians were out not only to win but to destroy their adversaries. "War is politics by other means" had been flipped on its head and was now, "Politics is war by other means."

———— • ————

The next day, Lance woke up in a dark and angry mood. He was reliving his interrogation before the Senate committee all over again. Truth is one of the greatest casualties of war, he decided. Truth, there it was again—the nagging sense that something was missing. Is there actual truth? It is true—he loves his mother. It is true—he is alive and breathing the fresh air of freedom.

If there is no truth, there can be no justice. The thought washed over him, sending a cool shaft of reason through his mind. The flip side of that realization means that an assault on truth perverts justice … Doesn't that also mean that truth by definition is exclusive, and the law of non-contradiction must apply as some philosophers suggest? In other words, either something is true or it's not? Therefore, everything that is not the whole truth is a lie or an error. This line of thinking was getting him nowhere, and he really wanted to finish packing for the trip.

The temperature had taken a decided turn south, and the chill was heavy in the air. Throwing away the rest of his coffee, he returned to the house. He took a deep breath, attempting to abort an oncoming panic attack. It was vexing that he was experiencing the emotions of a nightmare while still awake—a horrible dream from which he could not shake himself.

———— • ————

In the shower, he stood under the cold water for as long as he could stand it. He shivered, and his breath came in short gasps that he could not seem to control. He felt like he was losing his mind. He turned off the water and wrapped himself in a towel. There was no steam on the mirror, and he stared hard, searching for visible evidence of the turmoil within. He looked normal.

He forced himself to recall the meditation and breathing techniques he had learned in the East. He knew he needed to put them into practice now. He began by taking a deep breath through his nose for a count of five … and exhaled through his mouth for a full count of ten. The hold in between was important. He repeated this cycle several times and went to his "happy place"—a spot under the pines on the edge of a gentle brook on a sunny spring day.

Slowly the symptoms subsided. Part of the technique was to forget about the attack. It's not easy to concentrate on not concentrating about something. It was a matter of interrupting your pattern of thinking and making yourself wilfully forget something. Lance had learned that the best way to wilfully forget something was to replace that thought with something else.

The same principle applied to dealing with panic attacks. He decided he would not dwell on them for the rest of the day, further compounding the effects. He was getting better, and the attacks were becoming less frequent. They could be a few minutes long or more, and they were always a mad few minutes while he reloaded the program.

This attack was brought on by too many philosophical thoughts, he decided.

Another response he had to the darkness that sometimes invaded his soul was a cold indifference to the world around him, but underneath his cold indifference was a molten core of churning rage. When the darkness was upon him, he feared himself, knowing it was a force that must always be kept in check. He was thankful that this had not occurred during his encounter with Cindy's cousin. He tried to reserve that level of darkness for his deadliest enemies, because it brought with it a reckless superiority that at times led to audacious behaviour.

———— • ————

He was feeling considerably better by the time Miss Katherine began stirring in the kitchen. Taking one last look in the mirror, he whispered to himself. "You're one messed-up dude. Let them see you now, tough guy."

He came into the kitchen dressed and ready for the day. "My turn to cook."

Katherine didn't argue. She moved to the other side of the island and perched on one of the stools. He started cracking eggs for an omelette. She sat there silently watching him, and her very presence comforted him.

When the meal was ready, they sat opposite each other, eating quietly, comfortable with each other even in silence. After a few moments, they began chatting casually about a few of the things she wanted to improve upon in the spring. They also discussed the weather he was expecting for the hunt as well as some of his preparations.

It was a good morning. His mother was an intuitive woman. While she might not have been aware of all his struggles, she was wise enough to know when it was time to have a chill conversation.

———— • ————

Eventually, she disappeared down the hall to get ready for the day, and he went out to check the oil and fluid levels in the Jeep and the air pressure in all the tires, including the spare. He loaded the table, tent, axe, and chain saw onto the roof carrier. He decided to take an extra spare tire, and the twenty-litre jerry-can would give him almost an extra tank of gas. He would get a few containers of water when he fuelled up in Lone Prairie.

Of all the knives in his pack, his favourite and most comfortable was his combat knife. It was not standard issue. Bob Lay, a private knife maker and friend of his father's, had custom-made it for him. He had known Bob since he was a kid. Naively, he'd drawn the design on a piece of paper, thinking it would be a simple matter for Bob to forge the knife.

Later, comparing it with other knives he came across, he began to understand the intricacies of knife making. It dawned on him what had been created for him. It was a six-inch blade boxed design with a traditional edge up to the point and there it tapered back a full three inches at the top of the blade, with a second razor sharp edge. It could cut both ways. Behind the top blade close to the hilt were the saw teeth. Lining up the carbon and steel in unity had been challenging, and the result was a true work of art.

Bob had engraved the formula on the base of the handle. The blade, handle, and hilt were forged from one piece of steel. There were no finger grips, but it was perfectly balanced so that holding it was secure and comfortable. The handle was encased in polished cherry wood. When turned in the sun, it had a three-dimensional effect. Bob said that the wood had been lathed from stress wood, where limbs of the tree met the trunk. He said you could get the same effect from burlwood—the strongest and densest part of the tree.

Lance had wrapped the handle in Paracord, and it was easy to hold on to, even if your hands were sweaty ... or bloody. It also made it easy to shift the knife from one hand to the other on the fly.

Tinkering away the rest of the morning, he grew more excited and restless as the day wore on. He hooked up the small utility trailer to the Jeep. There was no way he would be able to bring a moose back in the Jeep. There was lots of space for more gear in the trailer, but he decided against it, with one exception: his plastic sleigh. Isaac Newton taught that it was nine times the work to lift a thing than to drag it. It was even easier on snow. With that thought, he threw his snowshoes in as well. Finally, he drove the ATV into the trailer and cinched it down.

By midafternoon he was packed and ready to go. His stomach was beginning to remind him that he'd skipped lunch, and he was making a sandwich when Katherine came back into the kitchen. "Hungry?" he asked.

"No, thank you, I'm still full of that omelette."

"Whatever happened with you and Cindy?" she asked.

He glanced at her sideways. Had she heard something? Judging from her tone, he thought it unlikely. Besides, it wasn't her style to beat around the bush.

"Ahh … you know she's a vegetarian." He kept his voice as neutral as he could.

"And that's a problem why, exactly?" she replied.

"Me great hunter!" He thumped his chest.

"You're impossible." She sounded disgusted.

Lance laughed.

"You know Lance, it's not good for a man to be alone," she said, quoting a favourite Bible verse. "When you find the right girl, you hold on tight and don't let go. Life is meant to be shared—that's what gives it meaning."

"Yes ma'am, I will, but I have some sorting out to do before I invite any-one into my life." It was as close to transparency as he could get.

"When you find the right one, the timing won't matter," she replied mat-ter-of-factly.

At first, he didn't respond. He was on thin ice, and he knew it.

"Where I'm going there won't be any girls to find," he said. Winking at her the way he remembered his father used to do, he added, "Keeps a man out of trouble."

She scoffed playfully, but in the intricacies of human interactions, he was at a deficit and preferred the enemies he could face head-on.

———— • ————

Morning found him in his usual perch on the deck, sipping his favourite blend of Guatemalan coffee. He'd woken an hour earlier than usual, full of anticipa-tion for the day. Checking and rechecking his gear, he was confident that little had been left to chance. In the wilderness the right gear was everything.

Katherine had woken early as well and was buzzing about the house with last-minute preparations. Lance was anxious to be on his way but showed no signs as they waited for Marie to show up.

After a breakfast of bacon and eggs, he was finishing his third cup of cof-fee when the glint of light from an approaching car appeared down the valley. He went inside and grabbed his mother's suitcases, placing them outside the front door.

"She will be here in about five," he called out.

Miss Katherine came out of the bedroom in her travelling clothes. She was wearing a pair of dark slacks, a grey sweater, and some subtle make-up. She looked fresh and beautiful. Lance casually stated, "You may need a bodyguard to keep the suitors away." She smiled at the compliment but did not respond.

"You sure you didn't forget anything?" he said in a mocking tone, eyeing her luggage.

With equal innocence she quoted him: "The right gear is everything … and," she added, "I don't need a truck and trailer for my stuff."

"Touché," he said with a smile.

Marie had pulled up, so Lance carried the suitcases to the car, and she popped the trunk. After loading them, he greeted Marie warmly and embraced his mother, holding on for an extra moment. "Say hello to Auntie for me," he reminded her, "and enjoy your trip."

"I will," she promised.

With one last sweet smile and a wave, they were off. Lance stood for a moment in the frigid morning air. The house was suddenly silent. Lance realized that he had a habit of being the last one to leave. It was his way of making sure that everyone else had gone on ahead safely. He felt the secret forlorn freedom. Would he always be alone? he wondered.

6

The eastern horizon was beginning to grey, informing him that morning was nigh and the time had come to leave. He locked up the house, even though it would only be a few hours before Marie returned.

With the turn of the key, the Jeep roared to life, and after one last review of his mental list, he headed towards town.

Lance hit the McDonald's drive-thru for a coffee before pointing the rig north. The sun was just coming up. It streamed in the passenger window, flickering through the trees and adding a magical quality to the morning. The satellite radio provided some background travelling music. As the soulful rhythm of Willy Nelson's "Always on My Mind" played, Lance relaxed, barely noticing the passage of time.

A couple hours later, he was brought back to the moment as the Jeep climbed through the winding pass where Kyle and Rachel had died. He was focused on the road, anticipating the spot with dread. Slowing his pace, he unknowingly stopped at the same pull-out that the killer had used after his terrible deed was done.

Lance put the Jeep in neutral and sat there for a moment. He understood that he couldn't stop here every time he went by, but still it drew him. He imagined all kinds of scenarios in which they had come upon foul play. But he told himself he was looking to blame someone for what had been nothing more than a tragic accident. Still, he wished for something that would give it meaning or someone to hold accountable.

Even as he understood this, the analytical side of him couldn't shake the facts. Yes, there had been a rainstorm that night, but Kyle had driven that road at least a hundred times; he was one of the best drivers Lance knew. Since Rachel was a nervous traveller, he knew Kyle would have been extra cautious.

The most puzzling factor of all was Kyle's seat belt—he was emphatic about their use. Is it possible this was a clue he left for me? He was an unusually clear-thinking man, but could anyone have the presence of mind to take such action, with death just a breath away? It didn't seem likely, but Lance left the possibility open in his mind as he walked the short distance to the accident scene.

He could clearly differentiate the section of guard rail that had been replaced. Scrape marks were visible at the edge of the asphalt and on the quartz outcropping, where the wrecker had winched the car up.

Lance stood there trying to recreate that fateful evening in his mind. The rain coming down, limited visibility, the couple settling in for the trip, and then what? The sheriff assumed that Kyle had simply fallen asleep. No skid marks to indicate that he had even tried to slow down. It just didn't make any sense to Lance.

He allowed his mind to create alternative theories. What would cause someone to drive straight through a barrier? Evasive action? An animal on the road? Possible, but the only animals on these cliff faces were mountain goats. That was extremely unlikely at night, in the rain. The sheriff had said that some sand left behind by a construction crew had affected the traction of the car.

Lance turned it over and over again in his mind. Evasive action would explain the no-braking issue. Had an oncoming car come into their lane? It was possible, but why had Kyle not braked? Lance shuddered as a thought intruded into his mind: What if someone pulled alongside them and forced them off the road?

Lance held this theory up as the second most likely. On a hunch, he walked up and down the southbound lane looking for debris in the ditch—something that might prove some sort of contact had occurred. There were a fair number of items: candy wrappers, coffee cups, plastic jugs, and a hubcap. There was a reflector lens, but it turned out to be from a bicycle. So unless they were run off the road by a mountain bike, there was no evidence here to support his theory.

Walking back to the pull-out, he quickly inspected the tie-downs and the trailer hitch. It was beginning to settle in that this was exactly what it appeared to be—a tragic accident. Other than road rage, he could think of no motive for someone to harm a young couple. If Kyle had had that kind of enemy, he would have told Lance.

Unless—the thought came to him suddenly—someone wants to get to me through my brother! He dismissed that idea immediately. It had been six months, and by now someone would have claimed responsibility if that was the case. It looked like it was time for him to start putting the accident behind him.

This trip would go a long way towards accomplishing that. It was his nature to freewheel ideas when he was up against a problem or challenge. He noticed that the ideas came more rapidly and with more creativity if he was on the move. Driving was good, but walking opened up his mind in ways little else could.

7

Cathy Short was not what most people would consider an attractive woman. She wore baggy clothing and peered out from behind a veil of long mousy hair. She was slightly stooped, even though she was just thirty-five years old. This hunching was subconscious on her part, an attempt to make herself small and ordinary, but her squeaky, nasally voice had the opposite effect.

She had lived in Lone Prairie most of her life, always on the fringe. She was intelligent, hardworking, and good at her job. Her unique sense of humour was just off enough that people didn't get her. She became one of those socially awkward souls among us who don't fit in. As a result, her insecurities piled up, and she increasingly withdrew from society.

While it was not in her nature to court danger or trouble, right now she was scared to death, and she had no idea where to turn. She was just a few weeks into a new clerical job at the sheriff's office.

Her ex-boss had started the trouble, coming to her unexpectedly one day about six months ago. His voice was shaking. "Cathy, can you do me a favour?" He had never sounded like this before, nor had he ever made a personal request of her.

She had a little crush on him even though he was a widower fifteen years her senior. She hesitated, having mixed feelings about personal requests and hoping it was and was not of a romantic nature.

She decided to take a risk and answered with an unqualified "Yes."

"Just a minute," he said nervously, scurrying into his office and returning with a large yellow envelope and a flash drive, which he pushed into her hands. "If anything ever happens to me, I want you to give these to an old friend of mine."

Her heart sank. "Is this your will?" she asked, real concern in her voice. "Are you sick, Gerald?"

"No, no, nothing like that," he said, not looking her directly in the eyes. "It's just something of a personal nature that needs to go to a particular person if … you know … the worst happens."

She was relieved that he wasn't dying.

He was talking again. "I want you to commit this to memory and never tell a soul."

She nodded her agreement.

"The combination of my safe and the name of the woman I want these to go to—"

"Woman?" Cathy felt a slight pang in her breast.

"She is the wife of an old acquaintance, and it's imperative that she gets this if, if …," he stammered, and his voice trailed off.

Wife of a friend? she thought. Cathy was on a rolling tide of emotions. Suddenly, the conversation had taken a decidedly upward swing.

He looked at her earnestly. "Can you do that for me, Cathy?"

"Of course, I will," she replied emphatically.

"Thank you so much." He seemed relieved.

Obviously, this was a burden to him somehow, and she was impressed that he'd given her his trust and the combination to his safe!

While she didn't believe anything bad was going to happen to him, over the next few days, she noticed that something was clearly worrying him. Things eventually went back to relative normal, and she forgot all about the strange conversation.

Then, one day a few weeks later, Gerald didn't show up for work. He had never missed a day, and she began to get nervous, calling his home and cell phone several times. Both went to voicemail.

He had never mentioned any children, and she didn't know what else to do, so she called the sheriff's office. They agreed to send someone around to his house for a welfare check. When the sheriff's deputy came in less than an hour later, she knew it was bad news.

"A heart attack." His body had been found behind the treadmill, which was still running on high.

Cathy was stunned.

After the deputy left, she started sobbing, devastated that he was gone. But her grief soon turned to fear as their strange conversation came back to her. She panicked, remembering her solemn promise to him, but now she shrunk back from it. She had so many questions. What am I getting into? Why did he think his life was in danger? What was in the envelope and on that flash drive?

Whatever it was, Cathy decided it was not worth risking her life for. A twinge of guilt lingered for the rest of the afternoon. She had promised, after all. She went into his office several times, eyeing the safe beneath his desk.

Suddenly she had an idea. Opening the safe, she took out the flash drive. She did not want to know what was on it. Fumbling around in her desk, she found a spare drive. Trembling, she inserted Gerald's flash drive into her tower. The one file that was on it was large but to her relief it provided no hint as to its contents.

Dragging the C-CUD file to the desktop, she then transferred it to her thumb drive. It took only a couple of minutes, but they were excruciating.

She was sure that at any moment someone would walk in, and God only knew what would happen.

———— • ————

Cathy was remembering that fateful day. Why had she panicked and resigned so suddenly? Had her sudden resignation alerted the men that she suspected were now watching her? She hoped that by staying unemployed for a while people would assume she left because of stress or grief. Realizing her naivety in hindsight, she cursed herself for having been such a fool.

———— • ————

Clifford Bellamy had planned the morning meticulously as always. He saw the opportunity in Gerald's pattern of living. People just couldn't help themselves. Clifford respected that Gerald was an early riser, who, after a light carb snack, would spend thirty minutes or so on the treadmill.

He would have to act soon. People just couldn't hold on to secrets for very long. He suspected that the records would be in his possession and that he had started putting the pieces together. He knew it was only a matter of time. Gerald's job was to understand what he was looking at. It was important to find out what Gerald knew, retrieve the documents, and move on from this boring little town.

———— • ————

Clifford's interrogation of Gerald had been efficient and brutal. He was taking an antidepressant, Clifford noted with satisfaction. It's amazing what a man will tell you at gunpoint, especially when he is led to believe that cooperation can save him. The files were in a safe in the office—both the documents and a copy on a flash drive. Gerald said he had just started connecting the dots and didn't have much more than a working theory. Under interrogation, he swore he hadn't told anyone else and that he knew precious little that he could have shared.

Clifford decided he believed him.

Gerald was begging for his life when he put the pistol to his head. "Please!" he begged. "For god's sake, don't shoot me!" His inhalations were shallow gasps and he was sweating from the strain.

"Okay," Clifford said, lowering the gun. "Shoot yourself!" He hissed the order.

"What? No, please, no!" Gerald wailed.

Clifford held out a needle. Gerald blinked, not understanding.

"Shoot up the heroin, or take a bullet; it's your choice."

Gerald was blinking rapidly now. "Probably fentanyl!" he blurted, on the edge of hysteria.

"No, I promise it's not fentanyl." Clifford's eyes held a malicious gleam.

Shaking, Gerald took the needle and without hesitation plunged it into his bare thigh, emptying the contents into his leg. He felt a sudden surge of energy, and with it, the fog and fear left his mind.

Clifford reached over, turned the treadmill on, and said quietly, "Now, run!" The gun came up again, and Gerald stumbled onto the treadmill.

"Faster!" He urged Gerald on. "Faster, man!"

His legs were pumping as fast as they could go when the sharp pain hit him, and he collapsed.

There was no fentanyl in the needle and no heroin either. No one was likely to believe this upstanding citizen they had known for most of their lives had suddenly become an addict. No, it was simply ephedrine. A large dose could be fatal all by itself, but combined with an antidepressant, it was deadly. The autopsy would show that his heart simply gave out during his daily workout.

Clifford retrieved the needle and wiped the fleck of blood from his leg. He checked for a pulse, knowing there would be none. With that, he simply slid out the back door, leaving everything in the house as it was. He walked to the park a few blocks away where his truck was hidden and drove off.

Tonight, he would go to Gerald's office, break into the safe and retrieve the documents. His plan was to leave town immediately afterwards. He knew more than a little about safes.

The office closed at four and he would be waiting.

If it hadn't been for the car trouble and that nosey mechanic, it would have worked out just like that. He broke into the office right after it was closed, making short work of the safe and ransacking the place. He needed to make it look like a run-of-the-mill burglary. No doubt some locals would be rounded up first. The suspicion would be that someone had taken advantage of Gerald's death, breaking in before anyone could retrieve his valuables. It would take a few days to sort out, and by then he'd be long gone.

He checked both computers to make sure the file wasn't on them as well and uploaded a key log program to monitor any suspicious activity.

The IT people had assured him nothing out of the ordinary was happening on those computers. He scanned their emails and left only after he was satisfied that he had all the documents and no copies remained. He was in the office all of twenty minutes and was just a few minutes down the road when the truck began to overheat.

———— • ————

Now, six months later, here was Clifford on strict orders, back in this jerkwater town. At first, he decided it wasn't unusual for someone to make a career change. The timing didn't seem suspect to him, but then IT realized that Cathy had resigned just days after Gerald's death. Typical of IT guys, they found this pattern to be "unusual". Clifford still didn't think it amounted to much. If she knew anything, he was sure it would have come out by now. However, he also knew the importance of being thorough, and they could ill afford any problems at this stage.

He was paired with Roger Corker, his now and again partner. Roger was his subordinate, but like most men in their line of work, he was independent. If a choice had to be made Roger would do what he thought was right. In the meantime, he was amicable, and Clifford tolerated him. Besides, Roger was clean and efficient and didn't need to be told something twice. Obviously, the boss was doubling up to be safe, but Clifford worried that maybe he wasn't trusted, and they were keeping an eye on him.

Their orders were to check Cathy's home computer and go through her house to see if there was any evidence that she knew about the operation. Part of Cathy's regular routine was to walk her small dog in the evenings. They used that window of opportunity to let themselves into her house. Taking their time, they did a thorough sweep, including checking her computer. It was password protected—"Bailey" her dog's name. When will people learn? Her history was benign and there were no suspicious files. He found two thumb drives, which he carefully inspected. Nothing! They were in and out in less than twenty minutes.

———— • ————

What they had no way of knowing was that Cathy had cut her walk short. Had they been in the house for five minutes longer, they would have been discovered. When they were back in the car, Roger commented, "Boring as hell. That's one sad, lonely life she's living. Not even any porn on the computer."

Clifford looked at him dismissively. "Who cares?" he said.

Roger held his peace. Clifford was in one of his moods, and it was best not to prod him.

———— • ————

It was the thumb drive that tipped Cathy off. You know how sometimes you think something is out of place, but you can't be sure? It was that kind of a moment for her. She opened her desk drawer that evening to get a pencil and noticed that her retractable thumb drive was in the open position. She picked it up and examined it carefully. She was a creature of habit, meticulous, and quite certain she had retracted that drive the last time she'd used it weeks ago.

Her suspicions had already been raised at the grocery store earlier in the day. One of two unfamiliar men had been watching her in the produce aisle. Instead of diverting his eyes, he pretended to be looking past her, but she had clearly caught his gaze. This was a small town, and she knew just about everyone. Unless they were new to town, these two were not from Lone Prairie. Even though it was a popular spot for backcountry hikers, it was getting late in the season, and they weren't dressed for the outdoors.

She cast a quick glance about the room. Carrying the baseball bat she kept for protection, Cathy walked from room to room in her small house. Nothing appeared to be out of order. Accepting that there was a possibility she might have left the drive unretracted, she tried to concentrate on a crossword puzzle, but as the evening wore on, her anxiety increased.

She decided she would take the thumb drive with Gerald's file to work tomorrow. She would tell the sheriff about their conversation, and it would be out of her hands. She'd been working there for several weeks and was just beginning to feel like she fit in.

She vacillated between two thoughts. She wondered if having the drive in her possession would cause problems with her new employer. On the other hand, it might turn out there was nothing to it, and she'd come across as grandiose. Experience had conditioned her to weigh all the potential reactions from others to her behaviour. She decided she would be casual about it all and let them come to their own conclusions. She wanted it out of her hands. Coming to this decision brought her an immediate sense of relief.

The thought that she was denying a friend's final request was nagging at her. Going to the freezer, she retrieved the roast she'd wrapped it in. Triple sealed in ziplock bags and rolled into the roast, it had been safely stored in her freezer all these months. She put it on a plate on top of one of the heating vents and closed the door to the room so Bailey couldn't get at it.

The same day that Gerald died, Kyle and Rachel Coolidge had lost their lives in an accident. When Cathy heard about their deaths, she was even more terrified because the person she was supposed to get the flash drive to was Katherine Coolidge. Cathy had quickly found out that Kyle was Katherine's son. He'd been the owner of one of the two garages in town. Although Cathy had very little to interaction with Kyle, she remembered him as a polite, friendly man. She decided it had to be more than a coincidence that these interrelated people had all died on the same day. Memories of their fateful conversation played over and over in her mind. She forced herself to breathe. Tomorrow she would be rid of the memory stick, and this period of her life would be over.

Cathy slept fitfully that night. In the morning, she retrieved the flash drive from the bloody bag and placed it in a small envelope in her purse for safe-keeping. Not one to waste a perfectly good roast, she put it in the Crockpot with a few vegetables and turned it on low.

8

"You want to break into a jail?" Clifford was incredulous.

"We have to make sure she's got nothing, and then we can put this thing to bed."

"No!" Clifford was adamant. "Activity breeds activity. We keep an eye on her for a day or two more, and then we can leave …." His voice trailed off.

There she was, just like clockwork.

Roger laughed. "This chick needs to get out more."

They were far enough away from the sheriff's office to be unobserved, watching her through a set of Vortex binoculars. She was getting out of her silver VW Golf. Clifford focused in on Cathy's face. She was looking around nervously and at one point stared directly at him. Her gaze was so intense, a less experienced person would have reacted.

"That's new," Clifford mumbled, thinking out loud.

"What's that?" Roger asked.

"She looks all nervous and suspicious this morning. Did you forget to do something?" Clifford asked.

Roger grunted his disapproval at this comment.

They had been there for several hours, taking turns watching the building. Alarm bells were going off for Clifford, the student of human nature.

Roger on the other hand, had expressed his boredom, alternating between drinking coffee and catnapping. A few vehicles had come and gone but for the most part, it was a sleepy little town and very little of it arrested his attention.

It's just about time for Cathy to take her lunch, Clifford thought.

Then a Jeep with a trailer pulled up to the station. A man got out and stretched. Through the binoculars, Clifford could see his face. Something about this man was familiar. As he stretched, his eyes scanned from side to side, taking in the surroundings. He had a shadow of a beard and dishevelled shoulder-length hair. A reckless look about him, Clifford thought. Finally, his eyes came to rest on their truck parked on a side street, about two hundred yards away. The street was on a slight angle from the sheriff station and was a designated parking area. Their truck wouldn't look out of place, and they had a clear unobstructed view of the building. This time when his eyes came to rest on their position something inside of Clifford gave a start and he sub-consciously lowered the binoculars. Something about the man was definitely familiar. Embarrassed by his own reaction, he looked over at Roger, but he was oblivious.

———— • ————

Lance had noticed the pickup and thought he'd detected some movement inside, but at this distance he couldn't be sure. After years of conditioning, he automatically evaluated his surroundings at all times. He couldn't have willed himself to do otherwise. He saw the truck, appreciated its position, and decided that if he were to watch the place, he'd use that exact spot. The assessment was made, but no conclusions were drawn. This was simply the observation of a skilled tactician, and then his mind moved on. He turned away and walked into the station.

Lance stopped just inside the door and looked around. It was a typical police station; a front counter with some public service announcements and wanted and missing person posters. There was not much activity—just a couple of deputies and a young clerical type of woman at a desk in the back. In a single sweeping glance, he took it all in. The young deputy with a round friendly face got up from his desk to meet Lance at the counter as he approached.

"Howdy." His tone matched his demeanour. "What can I do for you?" His nametag read "Barton."

"I'm heading into the mountains north of here to go hunting for a few weeks and thought I'd check in and out," Lance said, then continued, "I'm going solo, so I thought it wise to let local law enforcement know in case I get into trouble." He smiled reassuringly.

The young officer looked at him carefully. "Not a good idea to go off traipsing around in the woods by yourself."

"Understood," Lance replied patiently. "Nevertheless, because I am, I thought it best to check in."

"Okay …," the deputy said in an it's-your-funeral sort of tone. He pulled out a notepad from under the counter. "The truth is," he said, "very few people do check in, and every once in a while, we lose a mountain biker, hiker, or hunter, and most of the time it's family that comes around asking when it's already too late."

Lance didn't respond to that.

The deputy's pen rested on the pad. "Your name?"

"Lance Coolidge," he said.

At his name, the young clerk's head snapped up and she stared at him for a moment from across the room. Lance noted her reaction from the corner of his eye and wondered at it.

"Where will you be going?" asked the deputy.

"Up into the Anzac range, just north of the Sukunka River where the road spurs off to the right; there's a natural gravel deposit at seventy-five k"—he corrected himself instantly—"I mean forty-six and a half miles up. The logging companies excavated it to build the road, and it's a natural camping spot. That will be my base, and I'll be hunting on foot from there. No more than a twenty-mile radius."

The young deputy was concise with his notes, carefully writing down the landmarks and distances. He looked up when he had finished.

"How long will you be up there, Mr. Coolidge?" He looked a bit worried now. "That's a very remote area and the weather can change quickly this time of year in those mountains; it wouldn't take much for you to get snowed in." He continued, "There's a sour gas plant about twenty miles from where the road spurs, but there's very little activity now that it's starting to freeze up. There won't be much help if you get into trouble."

"I will keep an eye on the weather," Lance assured him, "and I do have a four-by-four Jeep, so I should make out just fine. Two weeks." He was definitive.

"Two weeks by yourself?" Barton was incredulous.

"Uh-huh," Lance answered.

The young woman got up from her desk, clutching her purse. "I'm going for lunch," she announced abruptly in a nasally voice and pushed through a swinging gate that separated the public from the work area.

Deputy Barton didn't notice her strange reaction or at least didn't appear to.

After a bit more of a lecture, Lance supplied his licence plate number, the year and colour of the Jeep, and his cell number, and they made small talk about the area and the hunting conditions.

Then Lance casually asked, "So who's the gal that just left?"

Barton's eyes widened in surprise. "Why do you ask?"

"Just curious," he said smiling.

Barton was having trouble with that one, thinking about how plain she was. "Her name is Cathy Short, but if you're looking to meet a girl, there is a great pub here, and Thursday is karaoke night. The place is usually full, and there are always a few single women there." Barton found it hard to believe he was giving dating advice to this well-built, handsome guy.

"How long has she worked here?" Lance persisted.

Barton decided that everyone has their own tastes, and chuckled, remembering a funny saying. Beauty is in the eye of the beer holder. "She's only been here for a few weeks, but in fairness I really can't share personal information about a sheriff's department employee."

Lance decided to let it go. He'd ask Clarence when he stopped at the garage in a bit.

"Fair enough," he replied. "I respect that."

———— • ————

All morning, Cathy had been waiting for the right opportunity to bring up the flash drive with one of the deputies. She'd made up her mind to approach Deputy Barton because he was always nice. But every time she was close to getting up the nerve to broach the subject, she imagined how absurd and silly her story would sound.

She was running out of courage and opportunities when Lance walked in. When she heard his name, she couldn't believe it. What a world of coincidences she lived in! She made her decision on the spot—he was her best course of action.

There had been some talk around town about Kyle's "hot" younger brother. There could be no doubt that this was him. This plan would allow her to keep her word to Gerald. Once in the parking lot, Cathy noted that the Jeep was the only vehicle. Looking around quickly, she opened the driver's door and slipped the envelope under the seat. She would sneak a look at his cell number later from the notes and make an anonymous call—suggesting he look under the seat for the envelope and then her part would finally be over.

———— • ————

"What the hell was that?" Clifford brought the binoculars up to his eyes. Cathy was walking off in the direction of the cafe where she usually had lunch.

Roger looked up from his cell phone. "What was what?" He asked.

"I think she just opened the door of that Jeep."

"Shit," Roger hissed. "Are you sure?"

"No, I'm not sure." Clifford's tone was caustic. "But when I looked up, I think she had just closed the door. She definitely walked around it and there was no need to do that. The cafe she eats at is in the opposite direction. So is her house." He started the car.

"What are you thinking?" Roger asked.

"Let's take a quick peek in the Jeep. Maybe my eyes are playing tricks on me," he said, even though he was certain they were not.

Lance was just exiting the station as Clifford and Roger pulled into the parking lot. Realizing who he was, they simply pulled on through without stopping. For the moment, they had missed their opportunity. It was a casual maneuver that normally would not have raised suspicion.

Lance decided the truck looked very much like the one he had noticed parked up the street earlier. He stared after the dark older Chevy with two occupants and out-of-state plates. He wondered only for a moment why they hadn't stopped. A shortcut perhaps? Small towns often spawn questionable driving behaviours, and that was as far as his mind took the matter, deciding it was inconsequential.

9

Lance's next stop was the garage to see Clarence. He walked in on a testy conversation. In a matter-of-fact way, a woman was telling Clarence that without a working truck she wouldn't be able to feed her stock. She reminded him that he'd promised it would be ready today.

Clarence cleared his throat. "As I said, I don't have any control over back-ordered parts. The supplier assured me it would be here Monday or Tuesday at the latest. That means the worst-case scenario is it will be ready by the end of business on Wednesday."

Lance had entered quietly and was next in line. He noticed that the woman's loose-fitting jeans and oversized sweater did little to hide her shapely figure. Her long, wispy honey-coloured hair was flecked with golden highlights. He was caught off guard by a thread of excitement coursing through his body.

She was speaking again, and her frustration was evident. "Well, I guess there's nothing I can do but wait. I don't mean to be rude, but this has been a year of setbacks." Her tone was almost apologetic.

Clarence had made one of the cardinal errors in business—he had over-promised and underdelivered. The gap between expectation and reality is generally called disappointment.

"I will do my best to have it ready Tuesday," he offered, potentially making it even worse if the order was further delayed.

"Fine, please call me one way or the other!" She turned to go and saw Lance standing behind her. Her stoic gaze made no adjustment because of his presence.

She had the most amazing green eyes, and the angry storm in them made them even more attractive. She was possibly the most beautiful woman he had ever seen. She was looking him directly in the eye. He tried to speak. Instead, he just continued to stare.

Before he could form a word, she shifted from one foot to the other. "Do you mind?"

He realized he was blocking the door. "Oh, I'm sorry, miss …," he stammered.

She didn't respond, and when he moved out of the way, she walked past him and out the door without looking back.

Lance stared after her. He'd always held the interest of the opposite sex, but here was the first woman in a long time that he had any interest in, and she'd simply ignored him. Worse for his ego was that she hadn't even seemed to notice him.

Finally, he turned his attention to Clarence, who was still somewhat flustered, nervously adjusting work orders on the counter. "Still like retail?"

This brought a smile to Clarence's face. "I'm just a dumb mechanic," he said humbly. "How are you, Lance?" He held out his hand.

Lance wrung it with friendly emotion. "Who was that?" He asked, not hiding his interest.

"That," Clarence replied dryly, "is Lynette Craig. She runs her family's ranch north of here."

"I may have to look her up in a few weeks when I get back from hunting," Lance said.

"Yah, she seemed super interested in you," Clarence replied, poking fun at him.

"Ouch, the truth hurts." Their banter was good-natured. Then Lance turned more serious. "For your sake, I hope that part comes in next week."

"That's for sure. She's not just beautiful. There's no nonsense with her; she's all business. I wish you luck. Several of the local guys have asked her out, but she turned them all down flat. Add to that her big brother, and I'd say she's a tough nut to crack."

"Brother?" Lance asked.

"Yup. Big guy … maybe six three or four. He'd weigh a good two-forty. All muscle. The family bought that spread five or six years back. She lost both her parents the first year, and she's been running the place on her own until her brother showed up about a year ago. He warned a few of the lads off. So love and Miss Craig have been in a standoff."

Lance was thinking about how he could bring that standoff to an end when Clarence interrupted him. "Did you bring the paperwork?" he asked.

"I sure did. Kyle expressly indicated in his will that you were to get the first right of refusal to buy the place. Now my mother and I both know you want to be fair and that you think the price is too low—"

"Way too low," Clarence started, but Lance cut him off.

"Now listen, you came along when Kyle needed help, you helped him grow the business, and this is what he wanted, so no arguments."

Their generosity was overwhelming, and Clarence choked up a little. "Okay … and thank you. Make sure your mother knows how much I appreciate this."

"She knows," Lance assured him. Across the counter over a cup of coffee, they reviewed the documents. Clarence signed in the appropriate places, and Lance left him a copy. This was the way business was supposed to be done between two trustworthy parties, both interested in the fairness of the process.

"My lawyer is holding the money in trust, and he can transfer the funds as soon as I get him the paperwork."

"Sounds good."

"Would you mind mailing our copy back to Mother's place after the Freemonts sign? I'm going to be in the woods for a week or two."

"Of course," Clarence replied. "No problem at all."

Lance hesitated for a moment. "Clarence, did anything unusual happen around the time of my brother's death?" He knew he should "let sleeping dogs lie", as the saying went. Yet he was still struggling internally with the whole affair.

"Not that I can think of. Why?" Clarence replied sincerely.

"Ah it's probably just me. I keep wondering how they could crash on a road Kyle knew so well, and to top it off, he wasn't wearing his seat belt."

Clarence was surprised. "First I've heard about that. It's weird, since he wouldn't even let you ride around with him if you didn't put yours on. Maybe that's how the accident happened—he took it off to reach for something and lost control?"

That made so much sense! Why hadn't Lance thought of that? Because, he reflected, I am looking for someone to blame. "I guess we'll never know," he conceded.

As he was about to leave, Clarence remembered something. "The thermostat," he said suddenly. "It was the long weekend, and I left early but we had already kicked out the last job, and I had dumped all the garbage cans while Kyle was wrapping up the paperwork. When I came in on Tuesday, I noticed a thermostat in the garbage. There was no work order, so I wondered where it came from."

Lance was a bit lost. "Are you saying Kyle did some work after you left? For who?"

"I have no idea, but you asked if I had noticed anything unusual …. It's probably nothing."

"You're probably right," he concluded. "But it would be nice to know who the last person was who interacted with him before he died."

Clarence nodded in agreement.

"Good luck, Clarence," Lance said as he walked out the door.

The new piece of information had seated itself front and center in his mind. He needed to know who that last customer was. He walked back inside. "Sorry," he said. "Could you tell what kind of vehicle the thermostat would have come from?"

"Hmmm …." Clarence thought for a moment before replying. "I had wondered the same thing myself. An older model GMC or Chevrolet—and a big engine, a V8. Probably a pickup truck."

Immediately a picture flashed through Lance's mind—the truck in the sheriff's parking lot. But he discounted it almost immediately. After all, there were millions of trucks on the road, and that visit to the garage was more than six months ago.

10

L ance was dreading his next stop, but he'd promised his mother. A little bit of discomfort would not dissuade him from his duty. Even so, he sat in the Jeep for a few minutes outside Peter and Beverly Freemont's home, steeling himself. *Why do I struggle so much with this part of life?* He also realized he'd forgotten to ask Clarence about Cathy Short. He'd revisit that when he got back into town.

At his knock, there was movement inside the home, and Rachel's father, Peter, opened the door. They had not seen each other since the funerals. There was a new weariness in his eyes, but his smile was genuine.

"Lance, come in," Peter said warmly, wrapping Lance's hands in both of his. "Bev!" he called down the hall. "Lance is here."

Lance was saddened when he saw Beverly Freemont. She shuffled down the hall in her pyjamas, her hair in a bun with more than a few wisps hanging at odd angles. "Hello, Lance," she said woodenly.

"Hello, Mrs. Freemont, it's good to see you," he lied, walking over and awkwardly giving her a hug. Her arms came up about halfway but made it no farther. "That's from Miss Katherine," he said, stepping back.

She gave him a half-hearted smile but said nothing.

In an effort to change the mood of the room, Peter offered Lance a coffee.

He readily accepted, but with the first sip, he knew it was instant. Lance, the coffee snob, hid his disappointment, drinking it eagerly and doing his best to carry the conversation. It was a struggle. He told them that the sale of the service station was almost complete.

Peter looked at him weakly. "Thanks Lance. We couldn't ...." His voice trailed off.

Lance instinctively put his hand on Peter's arm. "I know," he said simply. "As we agreed, the proceeds of the sale will go towards a scholarship in Rachel's name for one deserving child a year to attend the Montessori school she had taught at."

"That's a fine thing you've done," Peter said. Beverly was lost in her own thoughts, in another world.

"It was Katherine's doing," he said honestly. "She wanted to honour them in a meaningful way. Their work can carry on with the spirit and passion they both had."

Lance lingered as long as he could but eventually indicated it was time to leave. He was relieved when Beverly initiated the hug this time.

Peter escorted him to the door. "She needs more time," he said, adding, "I hope you can understand. We are so thankful for you and Katherine. Our faith is carrying us through, but it's been hard."

Lance nodded, not sure there was anything else to say. He was thankful they had faith and on a basic level he wished he had some of his own.

He was thankful the deed was done, but a little ashamed that he was glad to be gone from the Freemont home. Grief lurked in every corner and made it hard to keep his own at bay. He shook off the darkness.

———— • ————

"Never go grocery shopping when you're hungry" is wise advice, Lance thought as he finished up the last of his errands. He was getting hungry, and everything was starting to look appetizing. He had fueled up at the service station, filling an extra jerrycan with premium for the ATV. With that, the final preparations for his trip were complete.

He needed to eat something. Despite the deputy's advice, he would avoid the pub and opt instead for Kelly's Bistro. The quiet cafe served an excellent lasagne, which he loved. He was hoping he would run into Lynnette Craig. Was she still in town? It was just after six when he entered the cafe, and of course she wasn't there. He was momentarily deflated, but he reminded himself that he still had the lasagne to look forward to.

He'd been seated for only a few minutes when the door opened, and Lynette walked in. Is there such a thing as love at first sight? Lance wondered as he watched her standing at the front of the cafe. Lance didn't know, but what he did know was that she was the girl for him. There was something in him beyond sexual attraction that reached out to her. He could not explain it. As she waited to be seated, their eyes met and held for a few seconds, and she crossed to where he sat. He rose to meet her.

Lynnette noticed that he had paid her the respect of coming to his feet and was surprised by the gesture.

"How do you do?" he offered her his hand.

He was expecting a firm cowgirl handshake, but she extended her hand more like a lady of the Victorian court might—palm down. He slid his hand under hers and instinctively almost kissed it but caught himself.

"I would like to apologize for my behaviour earlier," she said in a conciliatory tone.

He acted as if he didn't understand. "Apologize? For what?" he asked innocently.

"I'm afraid I was a bit rude at the garage earlier today. I'd like to believe it was out of character."

"Don't mention it," he replied, brushing it off with a gesture. "Are you dining alone?" he ventured.

She laughed playfully. "Yes, I'm dining alone ... if that's what this is." She glanced around the plain room.

Lance was over his shyness now. "I'm a connoisseur of fine coffee and lasagne," he said, "and the lasagne here qualifies as dining, even if the decor leaves something to be desired."

Lynnette nodded in agreement.

"I am Lance Coolidge. Would you do me the honour of your company?" he asked gallantly.

She looked at him from under her long eyelashes. "Lynette Craig," she replied politely. "I'm pleased to make your acquaintance, Mr. Coolidge."

He pulled out a chair. She wasn't sure if his manners were for show, but it was refreshing nonetheless.

"It would be my pleasure," she answered as he slid the chair under her.

"What's wrong with your truck?" he asked, keeping the conversation relevant. He took in everything about her—the movement of her head, the way her chin came up proudly, and the gentleness of her eyes. He wanted to reach out and touch her.

"It's the alternator," she said. "How hard is that?" she complained. "You'd think it would be overnight delivery. I could probably order it on Amazon, for crying out loud." She was passionate, but the anger was gone.

They talked casually about the town, and she asked what he was doing in Lone Prairie. He didn't want to get into the details surrounding Kyle's estate, so he told her about the hunting trip instead. What he didn't know was that she'd already put two and two together. She knew Kyle very well and ascertained this was his brother. She didn't want to pry so she didn't broach the subject, assuming he'd bring it up if he wanted to talk about it.

After a while, she asked him how long he'd been out of the service. The question caught him off guard and his eyes narrowed suspiciously. "What makes you ask that?"

She immediately regretted asking, realizing she might have crossed a boundary. "I think I know the look," she replied confidently. "Both my father and my brother served."

Lance decided her intuition deserved to be rewarded, and maybe he was a fool, but for some reason he trusted her.

"About eight months," he told her.

Lynette didn't say anything, but she doubted his hair had grown that long in eight months. Special forces! she concluded but kept the thought to herself. "How long were you in the military?" she asked, genuinely interested.

"Too long," he replied, his eyes clouding over slightly.

Lynette felt a connection she was having trouble defining.

"Forgetting what is behind, we press on to what is ahead," Lance said out of nowhere.

Leaning back in her chair, she appraised him with an amused look on her face. "You're a Bible-reading man, Mr. Coolidge?"

He was once again caught off guard and shifted uncomfortably in his seat. "No ... is that from the Bible?" He was surprised. He was thinking hard now, trying to place the memory. "I must have heard it somewhere." He shrugged.

Was that disappointment on her face?

"My father used to say that it's faith that makes sense of life, when life doesn't make sense," she volunteered, adding gently, "He was a Bible-reading man, and I guess I picked up some of his ways."

"My father as well ... and my uncle," Lance responded. "I don't want to sound shallow, but I just sort of live life."

After a slight pause, she asked, "And how is that going?"

Was there a conspiracy afoot? He was trained to identify distinctive patterns, and for the last few months he had sensed a certain direction, almost as if he was being herded down a trail.

Lynette waited as he gathered his thoughts.

He shrugged again. "I've seen good men die and bad men live. Some of it's just the luck of the draw." He added, "If there is a deeper meaning or purpose, I haven't seen it."

"So you believe it's just in the regular course of human existence that we are here enjoying a meal and having this conversation?" she asked, her green eyes fixed on his.

There was something so familiar about her and so intoxicating, he could believe they were meant to meet. Am I being a fool? He raised his glass. "Here's to destiny."

She lifted hers up and gently touched it to his. "To destiny." She looked at him carefully from under those long lashes and took a sip.

Their conversation continued over dinner and then comfortably carried on into the evening. She shared more about her faith, her plans, and her dreams for the ranch. It turned out it was a massive spread—a great deal of it still in bush and timber, but there was also plenty of natural grassland and cleared hayfields. The property also sported a few small lakes and several streams and springs.

Lance in turn talked about his mother and the untimely death of Kyle and his pregnant wife. He also shared some light stories about military life. They talked and laughed until the last of the other patrons had left.

The owner of the bistro came by their table. "I don't want to rush you two, "she said kindly, "but just to give you a heads-up, we are closing in about fifteen minutes. It takes me about a half hour to clean up after that."

Lance looked up at the clock and realized it was almost nine. Where have the last three hours gone? He had never talked so much in his life.

Lynette's phone buzzed with an incoming text. She picked it up and typed a quick response. "They are closing, and my ride is here," she announced.

Lance felt a pang of disappointment that the evening was coming to a close.

"Lynette, I'd like to see you again," he said emphatically. "May I call you in a few weeks when I get back from my hunting trip?"

A few weeks? He's not exactly clingy, she thought to herself, liking his independent spirit. "I'd like that," she replied.

Just then the door to the cafe opened, and a monster of a man stepped in. Their eyes locked. This had to be her brother, and he was even bigger than Lance had expected. Not just in sheer size, but also in the presence he brought into the room. Lance saw him a moment before he saw them. Out of habit, he had chosen a seat that allowed him to watch the door. He held himself, waiting. Her brother strode towards them. He reminded Lance of a bull moose or a grizzly bear, supremely confident because there was nothing bigger or more dangerous in the environment.

Lynette watched Lance closely to see how he would react to her brother and saw none of the usual signs of fear. He was simply evaluating him. She was pleased.

"How do you do?" Lance was polite.

"This is my brother, Daryl. Daryl, this is Lance Coolidge."

Lance offered his hand, and Daryl took it. There was no bravado in his grip, no dominant squeeze, no one-upmanship. He simply squeezed once as some strong men are apt to do and said, "Nice to meet you." Turning his attention to Lynette he asked, "Ready to go?"

Lynette got up and reached for her purse. Lance raised a hand. "My treat."

"Again, thank you, Mr. Coolidge." There was a hint of grace in her slight bow.

"Please call me Lance," he said, wishing he could hug her.

"Thank you, Lance," she replied, adding, "Clarence has my number."

Daryl looked puzzled for a moment, and then they were gone.

The air seemed to have been sucked out of the room after she had left.

———— • ————

Lynette got into the car and buckled her seat belt. They drove in silence for a few minutes.

"Nothing to say?" she asked, breaking the silence.

Daryl waited a full minute, a stoic expression on his face, then spoke. "You know I don't believe as you do, but if I did have foresight, I would say our lives just became more complicated."

She waited in silence. She had never heard him speak like this before.

"What do you mean by that?" she said finally.

"I see trouble and death with this man, but when I saw you together, I knew."

"Knew what?"

"I knew that my duty to you would soon be done."

A spattering of rain fell lightly on the windshield as they drove the rest of the way home in silence.

11

The air, light and breezy, lent itself to the gentleness that had touched his soul. Lance took a deep breath and felt the wind tug loosely at his hair. Normally, he would have been cautious and careful, checking his surroundings like a guard on sentry duty. Instead, he was overcome by a feeling of euphoria.

How is this possible? Lynette was consuming his thoughts. He knew this was a dangerous place to be and cautioned himself not to let his guard down, even for a moment. It is the curse of those who have known combat to never completely relax. At certain moments in her presence, he had felt a complete release, and it bothered him, even while it drew him into its sacred rest.

The moon had clawed its way up through a thick blanket of clouds on the horizon, casting a ghostly pale onto the street as he got into the Jeep. He fumbled briefly with the keys, hesitating before inserting them into the ignition. He looked up to the moon and counted it a lucky omen, for it would illuminate his way.

He had to resist the sudden urge to drive straight towards her home. The thought occurred to him that, from this day forward, any road that took him away from Lynette Craig was a road that was taking him away from where he was meant to be—away from home. He pushed the thought away. He told himself he was thinking like a lovesick high school kid. The memory of her gentle voice, her fragrance, the direct gaze of her beautiful face, and their easy conversation lingered long into the evening.

He had booked a room at one of only three motels in the community. It was a nondescript sort of place in the shape of an open-ended rectangle with two rows of rooms facing each other, with a parking lot in between. There were thousands just like it around the world.

The owner was bleary-eyed, showing evidence of the toll such an occupation takes on a person. He was large around the middle with bushy eyebrows. His spectacles were resting on his forehead, and his breathing was laboured as he filled out the paperwork. His dark brown eyes were friendly, with a mischievous twinkle.

"Numba seven," he said, placing the key on the counter. "Dey's fresh towels on the bed and extra pillows in da closet."

"Thanks," Lance said. Seven … what is it about that number? The Seventh Calvary … 77 in my licence plate … born on the seventh day of the seventh month … my driver's licence ends in 777. That number dogged him everywhere.

"Noticed yer gear …." Eyebrows was speaking. "Going huntin'?"

"Yeah." Lance acknowledged the question casually.

"Used to do a lot of huntin' myself, but my knees are 'bout wore out now … hard for me to get around."

"Tough … you must miss it?" Lance decided his knees were only part of his issues. His overall health looked questionable.

"I sure do," he said with a surge of energy. "But the missus don't care much for wild meat, and my boy done moved away to the city fer work, so I ain't had much moteevation of late."

For a moment, Lance was tempted to invite him along but knew that would be a terrible idea, so instead he said, "We all go through phases, I guess."

"I reckon." Eyebrows looked off into some distant memory for a moment.

Lance picked up the key and tipped it forward in a gesture of gratitude. "Thanks," he said and headed back out to the parking lot.

There were a couple of trucks and a few cars parked for the night. One of the trucks that had caught his eye was a camouflaged F-350 loaded down with two ATVs. It was parked in front of a room at the other end of the building. The door was open, casting a beam of light on a couple of men outside having a beer. One drew on a cigarette. Their talk was rough but friendly, peaking only to be broken by laughter.

Lance was taking in the scene as one of them looked in his direction. He knew it would take a few seconds for the others' eyes to adjust to the darkness. He turned the key and entered his room.

It was as one would expect from such a place. There was a bed with a nightstand, a cheap lamp from Walmart sitting on it. Under the large front window was a desk with a matching lamp. Off to the right was the bathroom. To his surprise, it had a full bath with a tub and shower. The decor was simple, but the place was neat and clean.

He unloaded some of his gear, locked up the Jeep, and got ready to settle in for the night. The two hunters had done the same and were now inside their room. He drew the curtains closed and began to fill the tub for a bath.

He returned a text from his mother. She had arrived safely and wanted to know how things had gone with the Freemonts and Clarence. He gave her a short, concise report. With the time change, she wouldn't see his response until tomorrow. Several times, he tried in vain to explain meeting Lynette and finally gave up. He was having trouble articulating how he was feeling.

———— • ————

After the close encounter at the sheriff's office, Clifford did some calculating. Did I see what I thought I saw? Did Cathy Short open the door of the stranger's Jeep? If so, for what purpose? Did she put something in there? Or were my eyes playing tricks on me? He wasn't certain, but he needed to make a decision—follow Lance and search his Jeep, or find out directly from Cathy herself. Both options would broaden the circle of people involved and would need to be explained. He decided on the latter.

The odd familiarity of the stranger was bothering his subconscious. He would let it rise to the surface and work on it for a while, but the trail was cold, and he couldn't make the pieces fit. He didn't fret over it. He was just looking at it from all angles with the cold, calculating approach that was his way.

Clifford tapped idly with his index finger on the top of the steering wheel, thinking. Roger waited patiently. He had suggested they go after the girl but had left the final decision to Clifford, who was now tapping faster and faster. Suddenly, Kyle Coolidge's face flashed through his mind, and he remembered the rain tapping on the roof of his truck the night he had run them off the road. He shuddered as a sudden chill came over him.

"Someone step on your grave?" Roger quoted the old saying.

"Not mine," Clifford replied grimly.

He had it now—this stranger looked like that mechanic. Maybe a brother or a cousin. Either way, he felt a sense of satisfaction having made the connection but kept his thoughts to himself. His mind was doing some serious gymnastics—What is the connection between Cathy and this stranger? If she knew him and was going to share something with him, why had she waited so long?

It was her erratic behaviour that had drawn them back to Lone Prairie in the first place, so he could discount nothing. He decided their best course of action was to question Cathy and find out what she knew.

They waited for her to get settled into her evening before they knocked on the front door.

———— • ————

She might have expected subterfuge or a break in, but not a knock at the front door. She was completely surprised and immediately suspicious when she saw the two men standing there. The subtle smile left her face as she looked beyond them in vain for some unbidden help, but she was on her own.

"Miss Short, my name is Agent Bellamy, and this is my partner, Agent Corker." They produced their FBI credentials, and she examined them carefully, unsure of what was happening.

"May we come in?" Clifford asked.

Her mind was swirling, but her overriding emotion was something akin to relief. She hesitated only briefly before moving aside to allow them to enter. It was then she noticed they hadn't parked in her driveway. Puzzled, she became so nervous that she found herself fidgeting.

Because they had been here before, the two men made no effort to familiarise themselves with her home. Perhaps a more astute observer would have noticed their lack of interest.

"What can I do for you?" she asked, in the most confident tone she could muster.

"It's a rather delicate matter," Clifford said, not wanting to share anything she didn't already know. With luck, they could eliminate the possibility that she had any relevant information and then check the Jeep to confirm that she'd been truthful. That was the best and most likely outcome.

"We are looking into the death of your former boss. We know he may have been working on some sensitive projects, and we wanted to make sure there had been no foul play."

"Foul play?" she asked, echoing his words. "We … I thought he had a heart attack."

"We are fairly certain of that as well," Clifford assured her. "But we need to be sure; it's routine procedure. Did you notice anything suspicious or unusual about his behaviour in the days before his death?" he probed.

Cathy was struggling to answer, suddenly afraid she'd inadvertently raised suspicions.

"Miss Short, you do know it is against the law to lie to a federal agent, don't you?" Clifford said impatiently.

She sat down abruptly at the table, her breathing becoming shallow from the fear. Her mouth was dry. "I need a drink of water," she said weakly.

"Sure," Roger said, taking a glass out of the cupboard.

"There's bottled water in the fridge," she suggested.

Roger handed her a cold bottle of water from the fridge.

"Thank you," she said meekly, raising it to her lips with trembling hands.

She noticed the hard stare that Agent Bellamy was giving his partner, and then it dawned on her—he had gone straight to the cupboard where the glasses were. How is that possible?

"I'm afraid this isn't a good time for me to talk. I have someone coming over soon," she lied.

"Ain't nobody coming over—you know it, and I know it." Clifford's tone was ugly.

His sudden change sent fear coursing through her body.

"Why are you so nervous?" he badgered, taking a step towards her.

"You're scaring me!" she replied, trying to summon assertiveness into her voice.

"Why did you quit your old job, Miss Short?" Clifford was now standing over her.

Her eyes darted left and right, looking for a way out, but there wasn't any. "What do you know?" Clifford demanded sharply.

Cathy leapt off her chair and bolted towards the bathroom, but he grabbed her arm, twisting it behind her back. Her cry was muffled by his hand over her mouth. He spun her around, pushing her so hard against the wall that the picture on the opposite side crashed to the floor. The wind was knocked out of her, and Cathy struggled to breathe, with his hand still over her mouth. A terrible realization came to Cathy in that moment: they were going to kill her. She was unable to breathe!

Clifford slowly released his grip on her and put a finger up to his lips. Slowly he removed his hand from her mouth. Her breath returned in a singularly painful and elated moment.

"If you want to live, tell us what you know." It was not a question but an order.

The momentary stay gave Cathy that hope of life we all cling to. In garbled sentences, through tears, she told them everything she knew. Once they were satisfied that they had all the information, they turned as if to leave.

"One more thing," Clifford said absently.

Cathy slid down the wall, sobbing.

"What were you doing near that Jeep today?"

Why she lied, she didn't know. Perhaps it was because she had guessed the truth of her situation and somehow hoped to foil them or exact some sort of revenge.

"I don't know what you're talking about," she managed, her voice squeaking more than usual from the stress.

Clifford wrenched her onto her feet and slapped her. It was a wicked, powerful, crushing blow. "Don't lie to me!" He yelled, spittle forming at the edge of his mouth.

Her head was pounding, her ears were ringing, and she lost her resolve. "I put a copy under the seat …," she stammered. "I—I was going to call and let him know it was there, and then I would be free!" She emphasized that last word, seeing the futility of that hope now.

"Why him?" Clifford insisted, his hand raised to strike her again.

"Because his mother was a friend of Gerald's, and he was Kyle's brother," she burst out.

Shock, frustration, and anger welled up in Clifford. He had told no one about Kyle. He struck Cathy again, another ringing blow, purely out of frustration that this mousy woman had gotten so close to the mark.

"What about his brother?" he demanded.

"I don't know," Cathy swore. "I just guessed there was something suspicious about their deaths."

He raised his hand again, his eyebrows lifted in a menacing question.

"I swear that was all it was … a guess, that's all I know, I swear … I swear," she repeated between sobs and gasps.

At that, Clifford loosened his grip on her, kicking over the coffee table and then an end table with a lamp. The bulb burst with a final flash as it hit the floor. Clifford put Cathy in a choke hold. She struggled briefly, but after a few moments her lifeless body slipped to the ground, the light flickering and leaving her.

"Let's find that Jeep," Clifford snapped.

They quickly gathered some of her money and jewelry and a few other small items. They would make this look like a robbery gone wrong. Taking the back door, they left evidence of the struggle where it was. As they made their way down the path that followed the river to a moon-shadowed tree, they encountered no one. From there, they cut at a right angle to where the truck was parked.

———— • ————

After checking a few pubs, restaurants, and motels, they found the Jeep. It was parked outside of hotel room near the edge of town. They rolled up about an hour after Lance had settled in for the night. The parking lot was dimly lit, so they waited.

Not once during the three hours that they waited for the last light to go out did they mention the terrible crime they had just committed. Instead, they took turns napping and scrolling the internet.

"I'll go," Clifford said finally, putting one of Cathy's necklaces into his pocket.

He inched along the edge of the building, keeping in the shadows as much as possible. The Jeep was parked in front of room seven. Crouching low, he swiftly went to the door of the Jeep, slim-jim in hand. It would make short work of the older locking mechanism. He popped it open in seconds and quietly opened the door. The light flickered on. He had anticipated this and pushed the release button at the base of the door jamb, and it went out almost in the same instant. He pressed a piece of duct tape over it to hold it down. He turned on his small LED flashlight, gently opened the glovebox, and slid the necklace inside.

———— • ————

Lance woke up in a cold sweat, a panic attack in progress. How the hell do these come on while I'm sleeping? He slipped out of bed and, by the ambient light through the curtains, found his way to the bathroom. There he turned on the cold water, splashing some on his face. He shook his head, trying to clear it. What time is it? he wondered, feeling like he had just fallen asleep. He pulled the curtain back slightly, looking for the moon. At that moment, a light flashed in the darkness from inside his Jeep. Someone seemed to be looking under the seat.

Realizing someone was breaking into it, Lance slipped on his jeans and quietly opened the door. Probably some drug addict looking for money, he thought to himself. He decided to give him a scare and slipped out of the room.

As he came around the driver's door, three things were happening simultaneously. Clifford had spotted the edge of the envelope amongst the trash under the seat. Roger spotted Lance's approach. And the hotel owner, who had just gotten up to relieve himself for the second time that night, spotted movement in the parking lot.

"Looking for something?" Lance kept his tone cool, but a tingle of perverse delight came over him—that old desire for action and confrontation. Clifford froze in place. He was in a vulnerable position, stretched out on his belly, with his back to Lance. Slowly, he eased backward—there was nothing else he could do.

"I'm sorry," he said, trying to sound as scared as he could. "I'm just broke and looking for money. I wasn't gonna break nuttin," he added, trying to sound streetish and uneducated. Damn it! He needed to get that envelope and end this thing. Five more seconds and he'd have been clear and no one the wiser. He'd make short work of this fella, get the envelope and be gone for good.

Lance had decided to just give the guy a stern warning. He never got the chance.

From his half-crouched position, Clifford kicked viciously at Lance's shin. His heavy hiking boot caught Lance just below the knee. Had he not seen the blow coming, it would have hyperextended his knee, doing some serious damage.

While Lance couldn't avoid the kick entirely, by jerking his leg up he was able to let his knee bend naturally, minimizing the blow. It was completely reflex, but it made him take a step backwards. This gave Clifford the chance to whirl around and scramble to his feet. Both men were ready, their faces indiscernible in the moonlight.

Clifford shot out a beautiful left jab that Lance deftly slapped aside.

This is no kid stealing stereos, Lance thought.

Clifford snapped another jab that glanced off Lance's chin. He followed that up with a front push-kick that drove him back. Lance circled and put the dim light of the pole behind him. He'd had just about enough of this.

Clifford realized the value of the maneuver too late. Lance feigned a jab and looped a right hook behind it that clipped Clifford's ear, showering him in blood and causing him to stagger momentarily.

Clifford used the impetus of the blow to throw a spinning back fist that landed solidly against Lance's skull.

It didn't even slow him down. He drove forward with a quick left-right jab combo that briefly stunned his opponent. The wicked uppercut that followed snapped his head back, flooding his brain with stars and fireworks. For the first time since childhood, Clifford Bellamy found himself on his back from the blows of an adversary. He blinked and tried to shake off his disbelief and confusion about what had just happened.

Suddenly someone yelled, "Look out!"

Lance whirled around just in time to see Roger running towards them, pistol in hand.

"Back up!" the man with the pistol demanded.

Lights were coming on throughout the motel.

"You start shootin', I start shootin'."

Lance recognized the voice coming from his right as that of the hotel owner. He took in his laboured gait as he came towards the scene, shotgun in hand.

There was some distance between them now, as Lance had backed away. Roger was helping Clifford to his feet with his left hand, pistol in his right unwavering. With Clifford still swaying slightly, the two men slowly walked to their truck and then sped away.

Lance realized it was the same Chevy truck that had come through the parking lot at the sheriff's office earlier in the day.

"Y'all right, son?" Eyebrows asked.

"I am, thanks to you," Lance said. "It appears I owe you one."

Eyebrows shrugged. "Friends of your'n?"

"Not so's you'd notice," Lance said, matching his odd dialect. "Caught them breaking into my Jeep."

The hotel owner slapped his back hardily. "Boy, ya done whupped that one. Mighty purdy piece o' work." He turned towards the few patrons who had been brave enough to come outside. "All the fun's over, folks!" He bellowed. "Ya kin head back ta bed."

There were a few excited words as people straggled back to their rooms. One of the hunters gave a wave and went back inside, taking it all in stride.

Eyebrows waddled back into his office with a bit of extra energy in his gait that wasn't there before.

Next time I'll call 911 like everyone else, Lance thought to himself. He went back to the Jeep and closed the door. He locked it up again and noticed the light didn't come on. He tried the manual button on the roof but that failed as well. He decided he'd check it in the daylight.

As he went to close the door, his foot brushed up against the slim-jim. He stooped down and picked it up. Tossing it on the seat; he closed the door—one of those little things. His sixth sense was warning him that something was amiss here. What were they doing in my Jeep?

———— • ————

Clifford was cursing violently as they sped into the dark. His mind refused to accept what had just happened.

"Damn light in my eyes, lucky bastard … didn't see him take a swing … he got lucky." His voice trailed off.

Roger knew better, of course, but he wisely kept silent, knowing Clifford would not appreciate his analysis of the fight. Lance had easily overwhelmed Clifford, and Roger saw it for what it was—a masterful performance by a superior fighter. And they still didn't have the envelope! Worse, now Lance would probably be curious about what they were looking for.

Roger steered the truck over and pulled a dark cloth bag from under the seat. Opening the bag, he withdrew his burner phone and powered it up.

Clifford was dabbing the blood from his ear with a greasy rag. "What are you doing?" Clifford's voice was bland.

"I'm going to report a murder." Their eyes locked for a moment, and Clifford nodded in agreement. The phone rang five times before it was answered.

"Small towns," Roger said with contempt.

"Sheriff's department." Barton was on call.

Roger flawlessly mimicked a female voice. "Yes, I'd like to report … I heard someone screaming, I think … a bit ago. It didn't sound too good."

"What's your name?" Barton asked.

"I … I don't want to get involved."

"Involved in what? Can you at least give me your first name?"

"No … I just heard some screaming …. Maybe it's nothing."

"Hold up now, we can talk about you later. Where was it you heard this screaming?"

"I was walking along the river near the high-water marker and heard a woman screaming from inside a little grey house."

Barton caught his breath—that was Cathy's place. "What time was that?"

"Just after dark. I was out walkin' the dog … I gotta go." With that he hung up.

———— • ————

"Hello? Hello?" Barton cursed.

No sooner had he hung up than the phone was ringing again. "Hello." Barton thought the caller had had a change of heart.

"Hallo, Sheriff." It was a male voice.

"It's Deputy Barton, who's this?"

"Earl Jepson. Had some 'citement here this eve'nin'. Couple fellers got inta a tussle in my parkin' lot tonight. Reckon ya oughta know. One of 'em pulls a shooter, and I outs with Betsy, and we got us a Mex standoff."

"Betsy?" Barton asked.

"My shooter … They done plumb took off, but reckon ya oughta know."

"Anyone get hurt?" Barton asked.

"Not so's you'd notice." He reassigned the phrase Lance had used.

"Okay, I'll pop on over as soon as I check on another complaint," Barton offered.

"No hurry. Headed back ta bed m'self."

Earl hung up and for the second time in as many minutes, Barton was left holding the phone.

He quickly slipped into his uniform jacket, checked his weapon, and jumped into his cruiser. It took him all of four minutes to reach Cathy's house.

He had worked out a few scenarios in his mind on the way over. It was probably nothing, and there was probably a logical explanation for why she wasn't answering her phone.

The house was dimly lit as he pulled into the driveway. He didn't turn on his emergency lights, as there was no point in alarming the neighbors. Even though he was sure the caller was mistaken, his training and experience had taught him not to take anything for granted. Her car was in the driveway, and the hood was cold to his touch. He loosened his gun in its holster as he climbed the three steps to the porch.

He knocked on the door and paused. After a few seconds, he knocked louder. She was probably a sound sleeper. Still no response. Worried now, he pounded on the door with his fist.

"Cathy, it's Deputy Barton. Open up, it's important!"

Silence. It went against his ethics to do so, but when he twisted the knob, the door opened.

Lots of people don't lock their doors in a small town. But knowing Cathy's nervous nature, he figured it was most unlikely she wouldn't. He drew his gun, braced himself, and stepped inside.

The first thing he noticed was the mess. His weapon was out and ready as he flicked on the switch. He had been taught to squint his eyes to minimize the effect of the light, but in his heightened state he forgot, and for a split second he was blind. He grimly noted that if anyone had been in the house, that mistake could have gotten him killed. As it was, the place was silent.

Then he saw Cathy lying on the floor. He didn't need to check to know she was dead, but he got on his knees anyway and checked for a pulse. Nothing. He called the ambulance and the sheriff and started CPR. He was still doing

CPR twenty minutes later when the ambulance pulled up, sirens blasting and lights flashing. Sweat was pouring down his face.

Sheriff Hallward arrived moments later. He was a tall man of sixty, with a permanent frown on his face. His skin was leathery and his voice gravelly. He stood straight and this gave him an even more commanding presence. The paramedics had taken over CPR, but they too knew it was futile.

"I think we need to call it," one of them said.

The sheriff swore under his breath. "Doc calls it," he said matter-of-factly. "Okay, guys, clear out!" he commanded. "This is now an active crime scene. Nobody touches anything. And call Sandy!" His order was directed at Barton.

"I need pictures of everything. Find out who called this in. If we can't find that out, I want to know what cell towers the call pinged. Wake everybody up!"

Sheriff Hallward was one of those unsung leaders—a man proficient at his job—very thorough and a natural-born leader. The world of law enforcement is full of these men and women—strong, intelligent, and capable of rising to almost any set of circumstances.

He put his arm on Barton's shoulder. "Not the quiet night you were expecting, huh?" It was then Barton remembered the call from Earl. As he relayed it to Hallward, the sheriff's eyes narrowed as he considered this factor.

"Let's use our resources here. We can send Miller over to check into that tomorrow. Right now, I need everyone available, here."

Within half an hour, the neighborhood was alive with activity. Nobody was going to get any more sleep tonight.

The sheriff's phone buzzed. It was a blocked number; the transfer was from the main office number.

"Sheriff Hallward?" It was a female voice. "I saw a man in a dark-coloured Jeep driving away from that poor woman's house."

"Who is this? When was that?" The caller was gone. "What the hell is going on tonight?" he said to no one in particular, but several people looked up. "Barton! Another anonymous call … something is out of sorts here."

When Barton came closer, he explained—"This must really have people spooked."

"I don't blame them."

The sheriff was frowning but offered no reply.

———— • ————

After Roger made the call, he hung up, feeling pretty good about himself. They had circled back into town and cruised by on a side street. When they were sure the police were on the scene, he'd made the second call. Clifford was still sulking, leaning against the passenger door.

About time someone took the starch out of him. Roger was secretly pleased.

The next call would be the hard one. He dialed the number slowly. The phone rang several times before a man answered, a bit groggy.

Senator Elliot Wallace had been up late working and he hated having his sleep interrupted. "What?"

"Sir." Roger spoke quickly. He was nervous. "We've run into some problems here."

"Problems, what the hell is that supposed to mean?" Anger had replaced his grogginess.

Clifford grabbed the phone, and for the first time, he related the story about stopping to get the truck fixed and the events that unfolded—up to and including his decision to eliminate Kyle. The senator listened quietly. When he had heard everything, he sternly demanded to be put on speakerphone. Clifford complied.

"I need to know right now. Is there anything else that you two are not telling me?"

"This is the first I've heard about this other stuff." Roger was defending himself. He was well aware of the thin, deadly edge of the man he was talking to. He now remembered the "brother" comment made by Cathy Short and understood Clifford's rage.

"Is there anything else?" The senator's tone was growing sharper.

"No sir," Clifford promised.

"Okay then, this whole thing is salvageable. I want you to get that envelope back. Shoot that hick if you have to, but I want this thing done. Is that clear?" His voice was like iron now. "Or do I need to send you some help?"

"No sir, we've got this under control. I owe that Coolidge one for tonight anyway." Clifford was finding his footing in the conversation.

"Control?" Wallace was incredulous. "You call this control?" His voice trailed off. "What did you say? What name was that?"

"Coolidge, the guy who owns the Jeep," Clifford replied.

"How would you know his name?"

"Well, that was the last name of that grease monkey—Coolidge, Kyle Coolidge …. The girl said he was his brother."

"What's his plate number? I'll run it, and we'll know who we are dealing with."

Both men knew that getting a plate was very basic and that their incompetence would seem magnified, but Clifford boldly responded. "No sir, things just unfolded too quickly, and we missed it."

"You two amateurs are really something." The senator's voice was thick with contempt. "Did you get his phone number off the girl? We can get it that way."

Clifford swore silently. "No, we couldn't find it," he lied this time.

Wallace was thoroughly disgusted, fuming audibly over the phone. "The sheriff may have it—we can get it from him. I'll make sure we offer some help from the state level. I'll need to move fast on this."

"Sir, we can handle this guy—he just got lucky, that's all. No need to worry about him." Clifford was wondering about the sudden shift in the conversation.

Steel re-entered Wallace's voice. "Don't tell me what to worry about." Then he added, "Hold on the line."

———— • ————

Wallace called his secretary. "Barry, can you check on Joseph Coolidge's family members? Does he have a nephew named Kyle?" He knew his luck couldn't be this bad, but he had to be sure.

"When do you need this?" Barry asked.

"Now!" he snapped back sharply. Through the phone, he could hear Barry typing away on his laptop.

"Yes, well, he did—a nephew—died in a car accident a few months back, Kyle Coolidge."

"Did this Kyle have any extended family?" His hope was waning.

"Uh … yup. Mother Katherine and brother Lance."

"Thank you, Barry. That will be all." He hung up before Barry could respond.

His heart was pounding. How is this possible? All our meticulous planning, and one of my fiercest political opponents could soon be nosing around. Wallace knew that if Joseph even got a whiff, he would be like a dog on a bone, and God help them if he discovered Kyle's death was no accident. His mind was moving swiftly. He had muted the other phone and now hung up purposefully.

Roger called back right away.

"We got cut off," Roger responded to the senator's hello.

"You're done," the senator said flatly. "I want you two to come home—now."

"But, sir—" Clifford began to protest.

"Now!" His command left no room for argument.

"Yes sir!" Clifford said, and the senator hung up.

———— • ————

Both men had been issued a code word that indicated each was to eliminate the other. The phrase that Roger had received was, "Come home." The switch flipped in his brain, and he decided to get it over with quick. He shrugged his shoulders and reached for the bag he had gotten the cell phone from.

"What was that all about?" Roger asked.

"Beats me," Clifford replied, adding, "He sure went cold on us quick."

Roger powered down the phone and put it back in the bag. He was returning it to the spot under his seat. With the same motion he laid hold of a gun he had hidden there as well.

When he turned towards Clifford, he was staring up the barrel of Clifford's own Glock nine-mil. In that instant he knew that he was dead.

Clifford didn't speak or hesitate. He simply pulled the trigger, and the bullet caught Roger just above his left eye. The force snapped his head back against the side window, and the gun slipped from his fingers, making a dull thud as it fell to the floor.

Clifford's ears were ringing some as he opened the passenger door. They had driven just out of town and were at a pull-out in a dark area. He took Roger's wallet and his fake FBI ID and then dragged his body into the woods. Sloppy, sloppy, sloppy, he thought to himself. But there wasn't time for anything else. By midday tomorrow, the birds will have found the body, but with a little luck I'll be far away by then. He knew there was only one chance in a million he'd make it out of this alive. Momentarily, he considered blowing the whistle on the whole thing, but had no interest in spending the rest of his life in jail. Should I turn to the other side? No, he knew they would just use him as a bargaining chip. His first idea was the best one.

Driving several miles to another pull-out, he turned on the phone and hit redial. The phone rang only once before it was answered. There was silence. Clifford knew there would be a second code word that Roger would have to say to confirm the order had been executed.

After a moment, the senator spoke. "Bellamy, you're a slippery son of a bitch. What's your play? You know it's only a matter of time …. You screwed this up royally."

Clifford waited, enjoying his momentary upper hand.

"Is this where you threaten to hunt me down?"

Clifford finally spoke. "No. I'm not that stupid."

"You could have fooled me." The senator had nerves of steel.

"I'm going to do some hunting all right, but not for you. I'll get you what you want, and then we'll be even. You let my mistake go, and I'll let yours go."

"You're a fine negotiator, Bellamy, a fine negotiator. This is a win-win for me. If you get the envelope back before anyone sees it, you'll have made yourself a deal! If not, that means Coolidge will have completed the job Roger was too clumsy to." With that, Wallace laughed. "Good luck, son."

He thought about warning Clifford but knew it wouldn't help him. He had read up on Lance before the hearings and knew Clifford would be lucky to live through another run-in with him. He had bigger problems on his hands.

Clifford was no longer confident in the phone, so he powered it off and removed the SIM card, tossing them both into the darkness. He was puzzled by the senator's attitude—he spoke as though he knew who Coolidge was, but that was impossible.

Then he remembered the hearings. Maybe he just figured that because he had bested him once, he would again. He knew that at this very moment, the senator would be moving heaven and earth to retrieve that envelope—which meant Clifford's time was very short. He turned the truck around and headed back towards town with the sky on the eastern horizon showing the first hint of grey.

———— • ————

Wallace called his secretary again. "Barry, I want you to check the wire. As soon as you have a report about a murder in a small town called Lone Prairie, I want you to let me know."

The report came in about two hours later.

———— • ————

The sheriff's phone rang; this time it was the FBI. They had spoken with their senator and wanted to offer any assistance they could. Since Cathy was an employee of the state and a law enforcement employee, they were treating this as if she were an officer.

"That was quick," Hallward said as he hung up the phone. He was grateful for the offer. It was usually like pulling teeth. "Where's Miller?" he asked of no one in particular.

"You sent him to the Harvest Moon to follow up on a complaint that Earl called in last night." His lone female deputy answered his query.

"Brenda, I haven't even seen him this morning."

"Barton gave the order before he went home to get some sleep."

"Oh, I see." Hallward nodded and poured a fresh cup of coffee.

Cathy's murder had left him confused and concerned. At first glance, it seemed like a robbery gone bad. Like every community, Lone Prairie had problems associated with drug abuse and addiction. Thus far it had only been petty theft and vandalism—nothing like this. He felt sorry for her and imagined her last moments. The coroner would have to verify it, but at this point there was no evidence of sexual assault. It seemed random; there was nothing about her place that would make it a target. She lived on a well-lit street with neighbors on both sides. The lots were large and relatively quiet. The whole thing just didn't make sense. The door had not been forced, and the struggle was limited to the kitchen and living room.

Had she known her attacker? If so, it could mean that the killer was living among them.

Darren Hallward was turning these thoughts over in his mind with an increasing sense of urgency to find out who was responsible when Miller came in.

"Wild night in Lone Prairie," he offered.

If he was hoping for a response from the sheriff, Miller would be disappointed as usual. He continued, "Earl Jepson said that someone tried to break into a car in his parking lot last night, and it almost became a shoot-out." He relayed the story the way Earl had told it.

Only after he was finished did the sheriff speak. "Just like that, they drove off into the night? Were you able to talk to the victim?"

At that Miller smiled. "The way Earl tells it, this guy was hardly a victim. Handled himself very well. But no," he said a bit more seriously, "he left shortly thereafter."

"No name, no phone number, I suppose?" the sheriff asked, anticipating the answer.

"Actually, all of the above … name's Lance Coolidge. I have his address and cell phone number. I tried to call him to finish off the report, but it went straight to voicemail. Earl said he was talking about going hunting. So maybe he's out of service already."

"We've got bigger problems than chasing after some out-of-towner on a matter that seems to have resolved itself. Put it in your planner and try him every couple of days." Then, as an afterthought, he mumbled, "Coolidge … any relation to Kyle and Rachel?"

Miller shrugged.

12

After the parking lot skirmish, Lance knew wouldn't sleep, so he decided to pack everything up and get started. He was a bit concerned that if he went back to sleep, he'd be hit with another panic attack. If he got tired along the way, he would simply pull over and get some rest. It was his way to not dwell on the fight. Violence came and went in his life; he accepted it and moved on.

He had driven for about an hour and a half when he decided to pull over and take a short nap. He was well on his way up the backcountry road that was the first leg of his trip. In another three hours, he'd leave the paved road and turn off onto the Sukunka River Logging Road.

The spot he pulled out at was maintained, with an outhouse, a garbage can, and a picnic table. It was rare to see anyone this far into the mountains this time of year, and the park attendants had probably wrapped up their work for the season. After he had catnapped on and off for an hour or so, he turned the engine on to warm up. He had pulled a wool blanket over himself, but the cold air was working its way in around the corners.

Coffee cups and wrappers were underfoot because Clifford had pulled them out while looking for the envelope. Lance decided to clean them up while he had access to a garbage can. He opened the door and remembered again that the interior light was out. There was still some ambient light from the moon and stars. On his second attempt, he grasped the Slim Jim on the passenger's seat where he had tossed it and used it as a rake to gather everything up from under the seat. In doing so, he inadvertently hooked the envelope and gathered it up with all the other trash. He then took the armload over to the garbage can and tossed it all inside.

It's the little things ....

———————•———————

The air was crisp and clear as Lance drove deeper into the mountains. The sun was coming up when he finally pulled over to make his breakfast. It was a quiet little spot with just enough room for the Jeep and the trailer. There was a small meadow and beyond that the darker green of the wild bush. He lowered the tailgate of the trailer to use as a chair and table combination. Then he dug around in his gear, pulled out his Jetboil, and was soon sipping on a hot cup of coffee. The aroma of decaying leaves mixed with that of the coffee. He closed his eyes and felt the morning sun on his face.

These moments stilled his soul. He could hear the wind gently caressing the fir and pine boughs, and a small brook was chuckling quietly not far off. The stress of the previous night was melting away, and he was at peace. He decided for breakfast he would go all out and make eggs, toast, and, of course, a couple more cups of coffee. He opted to use his regular camp stove with the fuel canister from the Jetboil. His toaster was a metal coat hanger. It was an old trick—you simply bend the coat hanger in half to make two opposing triangles and then use the hook as a handle. He placed the coat hanger on the stove and balanced a piece of bread on top of it. A few minutes later, it was brown on one side, and he turned it over, pleased with himself.

He ate his meal slowly, savouring every bite. Food always tasted better out in the woods. While he ate, his thoughts were occupied by Lynette. What a woman! She had spirit, and they had made a connection. He had the feeling that she understood him already. Her father and brother were military men, so she would have first-hand experience with his kind.

Her brother Daryl seemed to be quite a man himself, not just his stature but the presence he brought into a room. He had detected no animosity from him, just a quick evaluation and caution bred of experience. He would definitely be visiting her when this trip was over. He thought now of the graceful sway of her movements.

It was not his way to go chasing after a woman. He believed that if a man is serious, he should create a life he can offer a woman and invite her into it. If pursued too eagerly, women are likely to lose interest, but if you see a spark of interest, you will pursue her with care. Being a bit mysterious probably didn't hurt a man's cause either, since women are curious by nature. Some men ignore the extent of their intuitive capacity at their own peril. A woman's ability to connect emotion and thought gives them a distinct advantage in understanding people—and in fact probably accounts for their capacity to access this intuition more readily.

Then the thought occurred to him: What do I really have to offer any woman? He was but an ex-soldier without a definitive plan for the future. Maybe he was a fool to think of her in this way. He knew deep in his being that he would need to solve these issues, whatever it took. This was the woman for him. Still, he could not ignore the turmoil he felt and the very real concerns he had. Since he was not one to shirk responsibility, he would need to start thinking seriously about the future.

When he had finished eating, he made his way across the meadow towards the stream with his dishes. It was just inside the treeline, a quiet little brook maybe two feet across and six inches deep. It ran gently over small, smooth stones. Next to an eddy was a small, sandy beach. He took a few moments to dam up the spot with some rocks, creating a pool to wash the dishes in. Without dish soap, he utilized the sand as an abrasive and had the dishes cleaned in just a few minutes.

He was just finishing up when heard a rustle in the trees, and a dainty white-tailed doe stretched an inquiring nose towards the water from the other side.

It always surprised him how curious these animals were. They seemed to know when you weren't hunting them. "The old ones" said they could feel your energy—you are all at once the naturalist and the hunter.

Lance held still, enjoying the encounter. The doe took a tentative step into the water. She was downstream and downwind but no more than ten feet separated them. Her ears were twitching in all directions.

Finally, she nuzzled into the water, taking a long drink. Sniffing the air in his direction, she pawed the ground lightly. Then, spooked, with her tail up, she darted silently into the woods. Lance was exhilarated by the moment and found himself looking skyward.

He wanted to share this exhilarating moment with someone. But who am I going to talk to? God? What God? Nope! I have seen too much go wrong in this world to believe there was a guiding benevolent force behind it. Good people died, and bad people all too often lived on. There was no fairness in any of it. All I can count on is myself—my own speed, skill, cunning, and hopefully some luck if I want to survive in this world.

That's what the freedom of the woods can do for you, he decided. It was a safe place to ponder difficult life questions and come to your own honest conclusions.

He repacked his mess kit and started out again. With a fresh cup of coffee, he made his way deeper into the mountains. Finally, after several hours of driving, he made it to the turn-off.

It was already eleven, and he still needed to set up camp at the spot he had chosen. He preferred to have everything ready before dark. He checked his cell phone again, but there hadn't been a signal since before he'd stopped for breakfast, and there wasn't one now. He pulled over to check everything one last time. From here on, the road would be unpaved and unpredictable.

Lance topped up his fuel from one of the jerrycans and checked the tires on both the Jeep and the trailer. Everything was secure. The first few miles were graded, and he moved along well.

The sun flickered through the trees like an old film reel. He drove absent-mindedly, letting his thoughts wander. Suddenly he remembered Clarence mentioning the thermostat in the trash can the weekend Kyle was killed. Did Kyle have a last-minute customer, or had he found it just lying around?

Lance knew that because the shop was kept spotless, the second option was unlikely; besides, Clarence would have remembered doing the job earlier in the day. Whoever that customer was, he or she was one of the last people to see Kyle alive.

Then he remembered something else Clarence had told him. It was from a GMC or Chevy V8. The Chevy truck from last night flashed through his mind. But how could there be a connection between the altercation last night and Kyle's death six months ago? It's not logical. Was it a coincidence? His life experience had taught him not to trust coincidences. Still, the connection was tenuous at best. The thieves hadn't fit the typical profile of those who break into cars to feed their drug habit—or for that matter, any other profile he could think of. But the thought kept returning again and again. He decided he would search for that truck and its owners when his trip was over.

———— • ————

Senator Wallace's mind was in high gear. He had always been quick and decisive but rarely rash. He needed to deal with the suggestion that an old adversary's family might have discovered their secret, however unlikely. He knew with certainty that he must tread lightly. Somehow, he needed to have Lance eliminated and retrieve that envelope.

An idea crept into his cunning mind, and the more he thought about it, the more he liked it. What if I leverage Cathy's murder to put suspicion on Lance? That could be the pretext for sending "The Boys" to go in and get him. We can't trust local law enforcement to go after a man that dangerous.

Wallace would need to act quickly and to keep it as far away from Joseph's desk as possible.

Senator Wallace did not realize the extent to which circumstances had already lined themselves up to make Lance's culpability logical.

His first call was to an old ally at the state FBI—Byron Crown. He kept the conversation professional and brief. They were to send an agent to Lone Prairie to aid the investigation into the murder of a state law enforcement employee. He made it clear he was to be kept abreast of any information that became available as well as how the investigation was going. Crown never questioned Wallace. He had a good thing going and no intention of rocking the boat. He dispatched one of his best investigators to the scene—Geraldine Lombard, a seasoned veteran with thirteen years on the force.

She arrived at Lone Prairie the next day and presented herself to Sheriff Hallward. The sheriff said he appreciated the help. Even so, warning bells were going off. After all, he'd never been offered this level of assistance before.

"Why did this catch the interest of the FBI?" he asked Geraldine.

She simply responded with what she was told—"State law enforcement employee," she said matter-of-factly, which was her nature. She never considered the motivation behind her assignment. She was here to do a job at the behest of her boss, who had relayed to her in confidence that this was a matter important to the senator.

Hallward laid out for her, as best as he could, the facts as they currently stood. The break-in appeared to be a robbery. Cathy was either at home or had stumbled upon the burglar. A struggle ensued, and she was killed. There was an anonymous tip of a Jeep leaving the scene—a woman's voice, but unknown identity.

Barton was back now, well rested, and alert. "You know something, boss? A hunter came in to let us know where he'd be hunting and when he'd be back … Good lookin' fella. He was driving a Jeep." He paused and then his head came up sharply. "You know what? He was asking after Cathy like he had some interest in her!"

A moment of silence hung heavily in the air. "That would be too easy," Hallward said.

"I even suggested he hit the local watering hole if he was looking for a girl. Not to be critical, but Cathy wasn't exactly …." His voice trailed off. "I have his info."

Barton walked to the counter and retrieved the notebook. "Lance Coolidge." Triumph was in his voice. "Brother to Kyle!"

"What?" Hallward was incredulous. "Kyle was one of the finest men I've ever known."

"No accounting for family," Barton reminded him.

The sheriff was doing his own thinking. He called Miller and turned on his speaker.

"Hello, Sheriff," Miller answered.

"Miller, what was the name of that guy who got in the altercation at the Harvest Moon the other night?" He held his breath.

"Ahhh, Coolidge. Lance Coolidge. They had his name on the register."

Everyone in the room looked at each other.

"Do they have a record of what he was driving?"

"Yup, give me a sec."

They heard him paging through his notepad. "Ninety-six Jeep YJ. You want the licence plate?"

"Yes."

"PBH777."

And just like that the pieces fell together. They had a prime suspect.

"What could possibly be the connection here?" The sheriff was a contemplative man.

"Trouble follows some people," Barton volunteered.

"Too easy." The sheriff thought aloud. "Too easy."

"Too easy is right." Barton held up the book. "We pretty much have his exact location."

"Take no action," Geraldine warned, "until I've had a chance to contact my superiors."

———— • ————

That afternoon Geraldine logged her report. She then called her boss to relay the information personally. Even she was impressed by how the day's events had unfolded. But that's what happens when you get everyone in the same room, communicating, and working together. She had seen this before. Most criminals have no idea about the forces stacked against them. Not the least of which are the voluminous mistakes they make along the way. They may have been committing crimes of various kinds for most of their lives, but law enforcement had generations of skills and intelligence at their disposal. Add to that computers, modern communications, forensics, facial recognition, and AI, unheard of in times past.

Her report was immediately passed on to Wallace as per his instructions. He received it with delight. This was beyond anything he could have hoped for and all the pretext he needed to take charge of the investigation and order the arrest of Lance Coolidge. This would be a significant blow to the Coolidge family.

"Sanctimonious bastard—serves him right." He hissed the thought out loud. Pausing for a moment, he weighed Joseph's potential response. He was under no illusion about the shitstorm this course of action might start. However, it must be done, or they risked exposure and the loss of billions of dollars.

He thought of Lance, sitting in those hearings. That he had been well coached was obvious. But there was something that troubled Wallace— Lance's quiet confidence.

Wallace shook off the feeling. He had just the right person to handle a situation like this.

"Barry!" He snapped at his ever-loyal secretary. "Call Brad and set up a meeting for tomorrow. No matter where he is or what he's doing, I need him here! Is that understood?"

Barry nodded and left to make the call.

13

B rad Akron had earned the nickname BA. His time in the special forces
had been marked by action and heroism. He had received several commendations for bravery and earned a reputation for being extremely cool
under fire. He spoke Russian and Spanish in addition to his native English.

He had learned Russian from his grandmother, with whom he had spent
countless childhood days. The Spanish he had picked up living near the border. He did a little low-level dealing and quickly learned the value of a sharp
mind and a still tongue.

Growing up in southeast Texas, he fought his way through school, and had
several run-ins with the law as a teenager. His dad was an alcoholic whom he
hadn't seen since he was four years old. His grandmother, the only person he
was ever close to, died when he was thirteen.

His mother worked as a waitress to put food on the table and paraded a
steady stream of boyfriends through his life. Most were short-term; others
hung around for a time. None took an interest in Brad. To them, he was nothing more than an inconvenience.

When Brad was fifteen, one of those boyfriends decided to display his
manhood by hitting his mother. When he came in the door to find her crying
with a welt forming on her cheek, all the ugliness and pain that had built up
through the years came up and caught in his throat. He felt rage as he had
never felt it before. He was one of those rare individuals whose rage becomes
a cold burning thing. It left him smoldering, beneath a cool veneer.

Without saying a word and with stark clarity, he went after the boyfriend,
intent on destruction. He was close to his final height of six feet, but at only
one hundred and sixty pounds, was lanky and awkward.

He caught up with the man at the local pub, where he knew he would be.
As Brad walked into the bar, the manager stepped out to stop him, as he was
clearly under age. Brad straight-armed him out of the way. With two more
steps, he was on the boyfriend. This mature man outweighed Brad by sixty
pounds and had reached his full strength. At the last moment, he saw Brad in
the mirror, turned toward him, and started to say something belligerent.

There is a time for talking and a time for fighting, and the boyfriend
missed the cue. Brad caught him with a solid punch to his midsection, in the

middle of the first word. The punch drove the wind out of him, and when his jaw dropped open to gasp for air, a sweeping left shattered it.

He would have fallen had Brad not grabbed hold of him and held him up against the bar. He drove two more solid rights to his ribs and then head-butted him, flattening his nose. He slumped against the bar and slid sideways to the floor. The action was so quick and so vicious, no one in the pub reacted. The manager stood in stunned silence. Even Brad was surprised. Never before had he felt such power and confidence. He glared around the room, daring anyone to challenge him, mistaking their fear for respect as their eyes refused to meet his.

He took the boyfriend's beer and downed it, slamming the glass on the bar as he had seen it done in a movie. It tasted horrible, and he felt like he was going to vomit, but he made a good show of it and swaggered out into the street. His life was now on a new and deadly trajectory.

When he found out the next day that his mother had gone to visit her boyfriend in the hospital, Brad grabbed a few things from his dingy little room and left. That was the last time he saw his mother. To this day, he didn't know if she was dead or alive, and he didn't care.

He was running—just ahead of the law and out of options when he saw the advertisement for the Marines. He met with a friendly recruitment officer and signed up, taking immediately to the discipline of the forces. It was as though the routine was something he had been craving his whole life.

He moved up through the ranks quickly, becoming skilled in all small arms and hand-to-hand combat, favouring the blade. He led his first team at twenty-four and seconded as the linguistics specialist, learning Farsi quickly. He was a natural leader, and the men liked and respected him. He was utterly ruthless in battle—in his world, you fought to win. No matter what, this was the primary goal of any mission. He would skirt the rules of engagement if necessary and wasn't above taking things into his own hands if he felt like the objective was at risk.

In this way, he was the ultimate soldier, a weapon to be wielded with deadly proficiency. However, it wasn't idealism that was behind his intense drive. It was pride. He simply wanted—no, needed to be known as the baddest man around. Even though he feigned indifference, he secretly loved his nickname.

Brad also had plans of his own, aware he was being used to meet the ends of powerful men. He waited and watched for the right opportunity. When it came, it was from an entirely unexpected source.

After a particularly messy mission, one of his commanders summoned him and informed him that he could be facing a court martial for an unauthorised kill. The commander had read Brad right though. When it was suggested he do a few "favours" that could keep him out of trouble and earn him "something extra", Brad accepted without question.

Shortly thereafter, he was reassigned to destroy some poppy fields owned by the Taliban. This was official US policy in order to cut off the Taliban's money supply. Brad handpicked three men he had been carefully cultivating for just such a time as this. They had openly discussed looking for opportunities and had sworn an oath of secrecy to one another.

They attacked just after dark, burning the first field to the ground. Intel was sparse, but the commander had a local source who knew where the heroin was stored. The resistance had been heavy, as expected, and Brad's team broke off and raided the storehouse nearby, burning it down as well. Loading fifty kilograms of heroin into a Humvee, they left it in the maintenance yard back at the base. What happened to it after that was none of Brad's concern.

From that time forward, his team was always assigned under the same commander, and they all started making money. They did three tours together, and by the time they were done, they had each amassed a small fortune.

When he returned to the States, Brad was introduced to a money manager who worked with returning vets. He helped him with a sophisticated approach to managing his finances, and soon he had several bank accounts in various countries around the world. He even had a Crypto account with a credit card from which he could draw funds.

He never knew the back end—and frankly, he didn't care to know. As long as the money hit his account, he was happy.

———— • ————

One night, Brad met Senator Wallace in an arranged meeting. He was being awarded the medal for bravery, and the senator was doing the honours. He invited Brad to meet him privately for a drink. Never one to miss an opportunity, he readily accepted.

He was guided to a hotel room in DC by a Secret Service agent. The conversation started with congratulations and small talk. Brad could tell the senator had something else on his mind, but he waited patiently, curious as to what it could be.

"I could use a man like you," the senator finally said.

"How so, sir?" Brad kept it formal.

Wallace flashed the smile that had just helped him get elected to his second term.

———— • ————

Their work together turned out to be even more lucrative than what he had been doing in the Marines. Brad and his team worked as an independent security force, moving around the Middle East in relative freedom. They moved high-value prisoners, transported guns and drugs, and on two occasions, even performed night raids into Mexico, assassinating key cartel leadership. This systematically ensured that their suppliers of meth and cocaine were handpicked and rooted out any and all competition.

Being hypercompetitive by nature, Brad paid close attention to stories about the men in the service that he considered to be his competition. He had heard of Lance "Coffee" Coolidge more than once, and he had also heard the nickname that he'd gotten from the Afghans—"Arwa Rue ... The Ghost Spirit". The stories of his exploits always bothered Brad a little. It was as though Lance was born under a lucky star. Opportunities to stand out had always presented themselves—like having a coffee with the Taliban in the mountains. Brad saw no sense in that. You killed the enemy, and that was that. He had trouble seeing why the men were so fascinated. He was simply jealous but would never identify it as such. To do so would have required him to admit that Lance had done something special that he hadn't or couldn't have.

On this day, he arrived at the senator's office dressed in a finely tailored suit. He had ordered it all the way from New Zealand. It was handcrafted by RJB Designs, one of the finest tailors in the world. His hair was trimmed to perfection, and he was clean-shaven.

A trained eye might spot the brutality lurking under the surface. However, to most, Brad appeared to be a man of class and grace. He had come to love and appreciate the finer things in life, and his tastes had become markedly more expensive over time.

Brad listened quietly and intently as the senator explained the mission, not revealing the exhilaration he was feeling. He could never have dreamed of a circumstance where he and Lance would meet in battle. Yet here it was. Best of all, in the end, it would be public, and he would be known as the man who had bested Lance Coolidge, doing the world a favour in the process.

Wallace made it clear that there was to be no arrest. Brad accepted the instructions with grim satisfaction.

"I have cleared the action with the State Department. I've made the case that due to his specialized skill, he should be apprehended by your team." Wallace took a deep breath and continued, "Bloody oversight BS, the committee insisted on a second insertion team."

At that Brad's head came up, and he frowned. "That could make things a bit more difficult. Who do they have in mind?"

"Romey."

Brad groaned. "Romey is by the book. We'll need to neutralize them somehow." He spun the senator's laptop around. "You have the sat feed?"

"No, not yet; I've sent the request in."

Brad looked at Geraldine's report, complete with a picture of Lance's destination. He opened Google Earth as he read the logbook from the sheriff's office. As expected, Lance's directions were concise. Once he found the camp, he scrolled back and forth and in and out for several minutes.

"Until we can get that feed, here's the plan." His mind drew up the plan as he spoke. This was his gift, and it was one of the things that made him so dangerous—the quick and decisive mind of a master tactician. "We come in from both the east and west; a chopper makes a wide sweep before dawn. We drop in here." He pointed to a spot on the north-west side of the campsite." After zooming in, he jotted down the coordinates.

"Romey's team will put down here," he decided, indicating a spot farther to the east. "That will give us about a ninety-minute advantage—all the time we need."

"That doesn't leave much room for error." Wallace was stroking his goatee.

Brad stifled his impatience. "Well sir, he doesn't suspect anything, and if we approach quietly, we may just catch him by surprise. If not, we can use a ruse to gain his confidence." He was thinking about the coffee story again and figured Lance would be willing to talk his way out of the situation.

While the senator had come to rely on Brad's knowledge and tactical skill, he felt compelled to warn him that Lance was a formidable opponent. "I've met this man; my gut says don't take him lightly."

Brad was under no illusions, and he didn't take the warning personally. "I know exactly who he is. If we make even the slightest mistake, we are all in for a bad day. Normally, I would tell you not to worry. But in this case"— Brad offered a rare smile of his own—"worrying may be the wisest course of action."

"We must get that envelope back or make sure it is destroyed. Otherwise, the whole operation will be useless," Wallace said.

"What about Bellamy?"

The senator thought for a full count of ten. "If you encounter him, kill him. He's going to want to save his own skin. Right now, he's a wild card, so we'll burn that bridge when we get to it."

"Understood." Brad got to his feet and, out of habit, almost saluted. He had some calls to make.

———— • ————

Brad's first call was to Ian Leadbeater. Everyone called him "Beats".

During his first tour, someone tried to give him the nickname wife-beater. After that, it was shortened to Beats. He was one of those guys people instinctively steered clear of. Tall and lanky, he had the awkward style of a cowboy. With sloped shoulders and a permanent sneer that made him look about as sinister as he was, he was a force to be reckoned with. Beats was a sniper, but you'd be making a mistake if you thought he wasn't much in close quarters. He was effective with a pistol or a knife, or hand-to-hand, if it came to that. Caught in the open with nowhere to hide, he had once held his breath for three minutes in a shallow pond while a dozen enemies passed slowly by.

Brad's second call was to Lee Cross, also known as "Preach". The nickname was partially due to his last name but also because he would quote Buddha, Confucius, and sometimes Christ. Anyone who was acquainted with him knew he was about as religious as Karl Marx. He was the smallest man in the group at five-eight and weighing in at 170 pounds. A ranking MMA fighter, he was deadly hand-to-hand. He had been disqualified more than once for not yielding when his opponent tapped out. In his last sanctioned fight, he broke his opponent's elbow and dislocated his shoulder—after the bell. To say Preach had a mean streak was an understatement. He was quick and always seemed to be on the move, fidgeting until the fighting began and then suddenly as cool as ice and usually taking the first shot. Brad had never met a man more eager for trouble. He was darkly handsome with a pair of black eyes that danced with a crazy light.

Lastly, Brad called Gary Van Rhymes, aka "Truck". At six-four and 260 pounds, he should have been called Tank. But with Van in his name, it all seemed to work. He was quiet and ruthless and despite his size, stealthy on the trail. Growing up on a farm, he had spent his childhood hunting and fishing. Few men knew their way around the woods like Truck. He talked slowly and came across as simple but was far from it. He had a degree in mechanical engineering from MIT and had joined up after college. Brad knew little about Truck, as he rarely talked about himself. He never spent much money as far as anyone could tell. There was an aloofness about him that at times made the other guys nervous.

Larceny was what brought the team together. They were tight and had relied on each other for their very lives more than once. There was tension between Preach and Truck from time to time, since both men were wound tight. Had it not been for Brad's dominance, they might have had more serious conflicts. All it took was a word from him as their leader to settle things down.

———— • ————

Brad laid out the situation for each of them. He didn't minimize the challenge, and each man had already heard about Lance Coolidge. His plan was simple—they would sneak in and take him out quickly. If they were spotted, they would try the direct approach—make contact with him, explaining they were on a training mission and, when the chance presented itself, kill him immediately. Each man accepted this as a matter of course, but none of them took it lightly.

They would be Insertion Team 1—IT-1.

Insertion Team 2 would consist of four men as well; Jerome Manning, "Romey", would be in command. Serving for fifteen years, he'd received commendations for bravery. He was a big man at six foot three and 220 pounds of muscle. His brow was somewhat extended, giving him a Cro-Magnon appearance. His eyes darted from side to side when he was deep in thought, but they were warm and quizzical most of the time. He was a no-nonsense leader who followed orders without question.

These last few years though, he was feeling the pull of autonomy and found himself questioning matters that had never bothered him before. Going after a decorated SEAL sounded like a bad idea. Still, he was wanted for murder, and Jerome knew how easily a man could snap. I guess the guy went native, he surmised. A streak of caution had been Romey's hallmark, and he sensed that this would be a dangerous mission.

Edwin Strong, aka "Strongman", was an African American with a teaching degree. He had taught elementary school for a few years. He was the youngest of five brothers, and if you messed with one of them, you messed with all of them. It was said that if he could get his arms around something, he could move it. Putting on exhibitions to entertain the troops, he was the current armed forces record holder for Atlas stone lifting. He was a fighting man, with only one gear—forward. During one skirmish, he had taken two bullets to the chest. His right lung full of blood, he had charged forward and throttled a man to death before collapsing. Airlifted to Frankfurt, he was hospitalized for three months, made a full recovery, and received the Purple Heart.

Theodore Mussal, "Teddy", was an average-sized man and a sniper. He was one of those men whose work ethic earned him his place. His true gift was marksmanship. Everything else he was average at. But that was the thing—he could do a little bit of everything. Languages, munitions, communications—and he could step into just about any role as a stopgap. In the age of specialization, Teddy was an anomaly. His Mideastern ancestry had been a double-edged sword. It was useful during forward deployment but also aroused suspicion. There is a lot said these days about prejudice, but he was pragmatic: The enemy for a time looked a lot like him, so from his perspective, there was no point in getting bent out of shape, and he wasn't losing any sleep over it.

Angus Redding, or "Red", rounded out Insertion Team 2. At forty-two, he was the old man of the group. He had grown up in Canada but had moved to the States when he was twenty-one, claiming his birthright, a born citizen of the USA. He had only been in the service for six years. It had taken some convincing to let him "try out", as it were. They kept telling him that thirty-six was a good age to retire, not to get started. However, his second marriage had just ended, and he was looking for a complete lifestyle change. He found it in the military and had been promoted three times in three years. A volunteer firefighter who didn't drink or smoke and had stayed fit, he passed all the physicals with flying colours. When he applied for a position with the Military Police, he was offered this position instead and the team had become his family. He chose not to think about what things would be like in five or ten years. Right now, he could still keep up.

———— • ————

Brad oversaw the briefing in his usual precise style. Even though the current satellite images were helpful, it was dense and difficult terrain any way you looked at it. A real-time satellite feed would have been nice, but the resource could not be allocated on such short notice. He finished up, asking if there were any questions.

Romey was looking at the photos, a slight scowl on his face. "It looks like your landing zone will get you there first. Do you think it's wise to leave that kind of lead time? What if he makes a break for it? With his ability … if he goes underground, this will be a long, difficult, and dangerous mission."

Brad had anticipated the concern. "Good question. To get everyone in quietly we need to drop each team off here and here," he said, indicating the locations on the satellite photos. "As we are taking lead, we will move into position first. We don't have any idea what Lance's mindset is. He's already made mistakes you wouldn't have expected from a man of his calibre. He may just come in quietly but there are no guarantees. He already has several days' head start on us, and we need to move quickly."

Romey still wasn't satisfied. "Why don't we all move out and arrive at roughly the same time?"

Brad exercised cool restraint in his reply. "We want to be sure to leave some room for error in case things are different when we hit the ground. IT1 has been given command and control of the operation, so we will do the heavy lifting. You will be there for backup primarily."

Each man in the room saw things for what they were. There was a moment of silence that was broken by Red's cool voice. "Listen, guys, we are all professionals here, and there is a reason you boys were selected to take point. I suspect you shoot first and ask questions later?"

When Brad began to protest, Red raised his hand. "Hold up! I'm not judging, I'm just acknowledging. One of our own has gone astray, and the powers that be want him arrested or dispatched. We all get that; no need to sugarcoat it. Let's just remember, we are all the same team. No bullshit."

Brad nodded in agreement. "Now that that's out of the way, we have a transport to Helena, and then we catch the red eye to hell."

A grim group of battle-hardened men checked their equipment and arms, like so many before them. They were ready to do their duty, compelled by biology, destiny, or whatever it was that brought soldiers to the battlefield.

14

Clifford Bellamy was doing some planning of his own. He had picked up enough of the conversation over his police scanner to surmise what was happening. He knew Wallace wouldn't leave much to chance. Bellamy's only hope of staying alive was to undo the damage he had created. He had already decided on a course of action when he got the word that a SWAT team was being dispatched. The local police had been ordered to stand down.

"That didn't take long," he said to himself. In a brazen act, he walked into the sheriff's office, introduced himself, and produced his FBI credentials.

"More help from the Feds?" Hallward was sure he'd seen this man around town, but he couldn't place it.

Luckily for Clifford, his lie filled in that gap. "I've been in this area from time to time as part of a task force. We are watching a potential drug route through here to Canada, keeping an eye on the biker gangs."

The sheriff knew it had long been a suspected route. The logging roads went in every direction, and many of them were lonely and isolated.

"You run into one of them bikers?" The sheriff indicated Clifford's cut ear.

"No, stupidest thing you ever saw. I pulled over to take a leak just off the road and while I was ducking under a tree, I smacked my head." He stayed on course. "My superiors were just asking for a bit of background info in case things overlap."

Hallward outlined the situation for him and finally got around to the location where Lance was camping.

"Kind of glad it's out of my hands," Hallward finished.

Bellamy produced his business card and handed it to the sheriff. "Let me know if there is anything we can do."

The radio came to life. "Sheriff!" It was Miller, his voice animated. "I need some backup at the Bridge Creek pull-out. A trucker waved me down—we've got a dead body here. A male. He's been shot."

The sheriff swore bitterly. "What the hell …. Is it Coolidge, you think?"

"Doesn't match the description. I'd say no."

"Okay, you know the drill. Don't touch anything. I'll be there shortly." The sheriff shook his head. "This used to be a quiet little town," he told Bellamy.

Bellamy was a study in confidence. While he was surprised they had found Roger's body so quickly, there was no reason for him to worry. The fact that he was at the office when the call came in was a stroke of luck, as it would draw suspicion away from him.

"Duty calls," Hallward said, grabbing his hat.

"Of course. Again, if there is anything we can do, just call me."

"Thanks." Hallward was out the door.

———— • ————

Bellamy hurried to his truck, fueled up, grabbed some snacks, and headed toward the Harvest Moon. Making short work of the flimsy lock, he double-checked the room Lance had stayed in but came up empty.

A few hours later, he arrived at the same rest stop where Lance had taken a nap, only a few feet from where he'd unknowingly tossed the envelope into the garbage. A half hour later, not knowing the country, Clifford took a wrong turn on one of the many back roads.

———— • ————

The insertion teams arrived in Lone Prairie late in the day and were met by Agent Lombard and Sheriff Hallward. Lombard viewed the group with a critical eye. She saw them for what they were—soldiers single-minded about their task and killers, when the circumstances dictated. They were taken to an empty rental home on the edge of town where they were fed and caught a few hours' sleep.

Sheriff Hallward caught Geraldine's eye. "What are we dealing with here?" he asked, sensing the overkill.

"A killer to catch a killer, I suppose … let's just let them do their job."

Hallward didn't like it one bit. It was his job to keep the peace in this little town, and all of this seemed to be getting out of hand. Hell, he mused. Barton could probably go up and talk with the guy and ask him to come in. He was a firm believer in innocent until proven guilty, and none of this sat well with him. As an experienced law enforcement officer, he knew the danger of information gaps. However, it was out of his hands, and he hoped it would soon be over.

———— • ————

When Lance set up his camp late that first afternoon under a clear blue sky. He had no idea of the storm brewing behind him.

He raised the wall tent inside the gravel pit out of the wind. The Jeep and trailer he parked sideways in the gap. After spending part of the afternoon cutting wood, he piled it next to the stove inside the tent. He was already beginning to feel the bite of the evening air. The northern nights were cold and long this time of year.

Loving the physical work, Lance worked for several hours before taking a break. Afterwards, he filled up the twenty-litre jug at the spring he had found. He had plenty of bottled water, but this water was cold and sweet, and he decided it would be good for coffee and cooking. He fashioned a makeshift porch out of a canvas tarp extended from the tent and created a firepit from some large stones.

Just as it was getting dark, he made a fire and pulled his foldout chair close. He also lit a fire in the stove inside the tent, deciding on a cup of hot chocolate and a light snack before bed. As he sat by the fire staring at the stars, the northern lights began to dance in the sky. A deep green glow crackled and moved like the wind through a field of wheat—absolutely awe-inspiring.

He remembered a legend his uncle Joseph had told him. The old ones believed that the northern lights were the souls of dead children, dancing in the sky.

Once again Lance found himself contemplating a higher meaning to life. Is there a God? And if there is, why doesn't he intervene and make things right? Tonight, he permitted himself the luxury of contemplating these things fully, fairly, and honestly.

Is this because of Lynette? Probably. She was so sure of herself and confident in her beliefs but not preachy or desperate to make her point—just a quiet faith that left him with a deep longing. Wouldn't Joseph like to hear that I'm contemplating these things! He smiled at the thought.

Joseph was all the father a boy could have asked for. "God works in mysterious ways," he always said.

The northern lights had settled down and were resting now—the little ones had made their appearance and then disappeared just as quickly. The stars hung low in the sky, and he felt as though he could reach out and touch them. The wind stirred the fire, and he drew his coat tightly around him. The cocoa tasted good, and it warmed him, reminding him of his childhood. He let the fire burn down to coals before retreating to the tent. Folding up the chair, he placed it under the porch, having sat on wet chairs too many times to have missed that lesson.

The fire in the stove was down to coals, so he added some more wood and turned the damper down. An oxygen-starved fire will burn for hours this way. The tent would be comfortable as long as the fire kept burning.

He lay for at least an hour on top of his sleeping bag, continuing his mental discussions about life, God, and faith. His mind kept recreating a vision of

Lynette—her raised chin and gentle laughter, and the sway of her hips as she moved. At some point, he drifted off.

———— • ————

Awakening suddenly, Lance checked his watch. Three thirty-seven. The fire was down to coals again, and the temperature inside the tent had dropped several degrees. After restocking the stove, he slipped into his sleeping bag and was soon asleep again.

The wind picked up, ruffling the tent. The moon slipped in and out from behind fast-moving clouds. Somewhere off in the distance an owl made its haunting call.

Lance was up before dawn. His Browning LED lamp cast a decent light throughout the tent. Stoking the fire, he soon had a pot of water on to boil for coffee. Taking a long drink of the ice-cold spring water, he could feel its coolness as it went down. After digging out his cast-iron skillet, he made a hearty breakfast of eggs, sausages, and toasted bagels.

After two cups of coffee, he pulled out his bow case. There were a dozen arrows fitted with broadheads and three with the claw-like Judo points for birds. With a little luck, he could supplement his food stock with some wild chickens—or grouse as they were called in these parts. They were a lean bird but excellent eating and chock-full of protein. He found if you seared the bird first and cooked it at low heat, it would remain moist.

He double-checked the tips of his arrows to ensure they were tight. He had waxed the string again, doing a few test draws with an arrow on the string. The modern bows were accurate and deadly, well below the eighty-pound draw weight. He was able to pull it back comfortably and opted for a hooked release. This allowed him to get into action a split second sooner. With practice, he had learned to do it by feel, so that he didn't have to take his eyes off the animal.

———— • ————

He dressed quickly, slipping on his shoulder holster, and checked the .45 as he shrugged on his fleece jacket. He strapped the bow onto his pack. Although he had a sling for it, he preferred to carry it in his hand so it was ready for use. He would make the transfer as soon as there was enough light to hunt. He shouldered his pack, drawing the straps in tight.

Though he was confident in his ability to guesstimate distances up to one hundred yards, he attached a range finder to his belt. Lastly, he strapped his knife—his constant companion of many years—to his waist.

It was still dark when Lance stepped out of the tent. Out of habit, he killed the light and let his eyes adjust to the dark before making a move. Checking his watch, it was just past six. The moon had set, leaving only a slight glow in the west.

The trail he intended to follow started only a few metres past the spring and headed in a northerly direction. It looked well used and might have even been a logging caterpillar push in the distant past. His map indicated a lake or swamp about three miles in. He would need to cross a small creek just before he got to the lake. It looked like another stream flowed out of the other end of the lake as well. He decided he would move at a slow pace, listening as he went. There was still an hour and a half before light, and he loved the feeling of the early morning.

After about ten minutes, the trail closed in, choked with alder bush. He was confident now that this was an old logging path. The alder was patchy, and he was in and out of it as he moved along the trail. Whenever it widened, he paused to listen. He could hear the cries of a pack of coyotes somewhere off in the distance.

After about forty-five minutes, the sky was showing grey. Whatever the plan had been for this road, the idea had been abandoned. The light of day revealed an old growth forest of pine, elm, and spruce. Here and there it was so well spaced it looked like a manicured park. It would then transition into a gnarled and tangled mess of thick growth.

In the full light of day, he began to hear the distant sound of running water. That had to be the first stream he had seen on the map. He paused to take a drink from the bottle tucked into the net sleeve on the side of his pack. He drank it all at once; he would refill it at the stream.

The sound of the water grew louder as he neared the stream. Where the trail intersected it, the bank dropped away a good fifteen feet. A clear dark pool of water below had eddied against a log jam. Looking across the stream, he saw the far bank was much lower and that the trail continued towards the lake. In the distance, it looked like the trees gave way to a more open space—the lake or at least the beginning of the muskeg on its outer banks.

These wet meadows were the perfect home for moose. They could get down into the willows and burning almost no calories, feed for weeks at a time, packing on some serious weight for the winter months ahead. The rut would now be in full swing, and the moose would have little else on their minds for the next three weeks or so. This was one of the most intense mating rituals on the planet, such focused drive made them easily distracted and thus vulnerable to a man with a gun or bow and a bit of know-how.

The cows only went into estrus for about twenty-four hours in the whole year, so they gathered around a dominant bull. If he wanted to pass on his genes, he needed to fight off all other suitors—and there were plenty of rivals.

When a cow was ready, the bull needed to be Johnny-on-the spot or miss his chance. It was a grueling period during which the males were harried and exhausted, and truly only the strongest were successful.

The stream was more like a river; up and downstream, it was a raging torrent in both directions. Lance knew there would be no crossing here. There must have been some early snows up in the high peaks that were melting and swelling the streams.

He decided to head back to camp and review the maps again. He would hunt some of the clearings closer to camp and maybe drive the roads farther up before dark to see if he could catch one on the road.

Before leaving, he decided to try a call. He cupped his hands, covered his nose, and made the long nasally call of a cow: "Aaaaawwwwyyyyh, aaaaaw-wwyyyyh."

He waited quietly. Moments later, he heard a faint call echoing back towards him. He felt the familiar excitement stirring. He hesitated to leave but knew he would have to find a good place to cross. If he was going to harvest a moose this deep into the woods, he needed a plan to get it out as well.

He recalled the story of a young guy who'd gone up to Alaska to live off the land and had starved to death because he couldn't get back across a swollen river. It turned out, there was a cable cart just downstream a few miles that he could have used to escape. Knowledge is power.

What was his name? McCandless, he recalled.

No, he would make a good plan first. Lance had no need to hurry back to camp so he took his time, pausing often to listen, rest, and occasionally nibble on a snack. He was finding that inner rhythm and peace that nature and seclusion provide. The day began to warm up some, and he took his turtleneck off and stuffed it into his pack. There was a lot of moose sign, but most of it was old.

Back at camp, he did a few odd jobs and made lunch and a hot cup of black coffee. It was a clear day, and he stood looking at the high peaks, sipping on his coffee. Some of them towered up ten thousand feet, holding glaciers and earning their keep as an important part of the life cycle in these high mountain ranges. The stillness of this place held his attention—a special kind of quiet, the mountains standing silently, guarding an ancient mystery. It was humbling to know that year after year, century after century, they remained. Long after he was gone, even long after the last person that knew his name was gone, the mountains would remain.

Not until I've left my mark.

Lance donned his pack after lunch and headed south down the main road. He wanted to check out some swamps and clearings he had spotted on the drive in. After walking for almost a mile, he found a game trail that intersected the road. On an impulse, he followed it. For a couple hundred yards, the trail led through some old-growth timber, which then petered out, giving way to some smaller trees, willows, and shrubs. Here and there he caught glimpses of a swamp or small lake off to the right. The trail was heading in that direction, so he stuck to it. The closer he got to the lake, the softer the ground was, and when he paused to listen, water seeped up to the top of his hunting boots.

Something was moving in the brush about fifty yards ahead. His field of view was twenty yards at best. In the narrow space between two rows of brush, he couldn't really go left or right.

Moose, he decided, due to the thrashing noise he heard. His fingers tested the nock of the arrow to make sure it was securely on the string. His heart was beating slowly, and he was taking short, quiet breaths. A moose early in the hunt would certainly be nice and would take the pressure off.

A moment later, a bear cub scampered into view. The wind was such that it could not pick up his scent. Lance realized right away this was a grizzly cub. He could tell by its light brown colour and stubby face. It was small—so this year's cub. He glanced around carefully scanning for the mother.

There are few things on this earth more dangerous than a mama grizzly protecting her cubs. "Unless it was a fool," Joseph had often quoted. "Better to meet a bear with her cubs, than a fool in his folly."

Lance reached under his jacket and slid out the .45. He didn't want to harm the bear, but neither did he want to be the fool, caught off guard. A few moments later the sow came into view. Her head snapped up—the wind had changed! He could feel it now breathing on the back of his neck. Mama bear stood up on her hind legs sniffing the air and woofed at him. The cub had disappeared, and he dared not take his eyes off her even for a second. He knew she could cover that distance in a flash.

Many people give advice on how to respond to this type of showdown with a grizzly. Lance decided he would resort to experience. He brought his gun to the ready position and started speaking low and quiet.

"Hey, Mama," he said, "looks like we've got us a good ol' Mexican stand-off here. I got nowhere to go, and I can't outrun you, so keep your distance."

She snapped her teeth in a menacing manner, her eyes flat and lifeless.

"Come on now," he continued. "This could end badly for one or both of us."

She came back down on all fours taking an aggressive step forward, her head swaying from side to side.

Lance dropped his bow and chambered a round. At the sound, she woofed again, spun around, and ran off into the brush.

Lance remained steady and alert in case she had a change of heart. After a few minutes, he heard a distinctive crack several hundred metres away. He let out a long cleansing breath and started to back away. "That was close," he said aloud.

Over the years, he had noticed that animals seem to be able to judge your intentions. There is something about the energy you give off that lets them know when you've made up your mind to take action. Just as the doe near the stream had been relatively relaxed, this bear chose to retreat instead of attack. She might have heard the sound of a gun being cocked before. But in his estimation, it was just as likely that she had sensed the change in him.

His father had told a story about a bear that climbed onto the deck at his childhood home and was looking in the window while his parents were eating breakfast. His dad opened the door slightly and yelled at the bear. It just looked up at him casually and didn't move. He opened the door a bit wider and yelled even louder. Still no movement from the bear. He retrieved his shotgun, realizing he had a nuisance bear on his hands. This time when he opened the door, the bear took off like a shot. He was up and over the deck rail and disappeared into the woods. What had changed? Only his father's intentions and somehow that bear knew the difference. Men can be like that, he reflected. When you stood your ground and decided you would fight if need be, that change in attitude combined with your confidence would often cause them to stand down. And for those who didn't—well, at least you were ready.

———— • ————

Lance spent most of the afternoon walking clear-cuts and sneaking up on beaver ponds, hoping to catch a moose feeding or drinking. He found more sign but nothing very fresh. He had covered several miles when the sun started making a dash for the horizon. It had been an excellent day.

As he had worked his way up or down small streams, he took time for long drinks of mountain water and snacked on energy bars. It felt as though he was the only person on earth. You would rarely see anyone up here in open season, let alone bow season. He found himself in a meditative state as he inched along. Time ceased to have meaning—he was living in the moment, breathing the crisp mountain air, and taking in the vistas of meandering valleys. He felt relaxed and alive as the cares of the world melted away.

He made the main road just as the moon was rising on the horizon. After ten minutes, he fished out his headlamp for the rest of the trek. He was always surprised by how little distance he covered while bowhunting. There just wasn't any point in hurrying, not when you needed to get close to your quarry. He kept Mama Bear in his consciousness—he would need to remain alert with grizzlies around.

It took him forty-five minutes to get back to camp. He turned on the lantern, lit a fire in the stove, and put some water on to boil. He moved to the table under the makeshift porch where his camp stove was set up and made a hearty dinner of stew. After several cups of coffee and a good bit of water, he went into the tent. He hadn't realized how much colder it had become—the contrast from the outside was marked. Checking his watch, he was surprised that it was only a few minutes past eight.

Placing the lamp near his bed, he pulled out a book he had brought along: The Abolition of Man, by CS Lewis. It had been on his mother's bookstand.

"Of course" was her response when he asked to borrow it. Coincidence? he wondered. First I borrow this book, then I meet Lynette.

He remained skeptical of the book written by a converted atheist but thought he might as well hear some of the arguments from the other side. The fact that Lynette had appeared in his life spurred him on, as he wanted to be able to communicate with her in a meaningful way.

Reading and rereading the first couple of chapters, he was having a hard time with the context. In his opinion, it would have been easier for the reader to grasp if Lewis had named the book he was critiquing. But once he decided to go with it, the book began to flow, and he was able to get the gist of it. Still, when he finally put it down, the author's purpose continued to elude him.

He slipped it into the pocket of his jacket with the intention of reading some more tomorrow while waiting for a moose to present itself. He had to admit there were some concepts and ideas that he hadn't considered before but that made him uneasy. He decided that if the book didn't start to make more sense in the next few chapters, it probably didn't deserve his attention.

———— • ————

At a sudden burst of gunfire and an agonized scream, Lance bolted erect in his bed. The residual hum of a helicopter faded into his subconscious from whence it had been conjured. He was in a cold sweat, his breath coming in shallow, fearful grabs.

A helicopter … the sound was unmistakable. It was a Chinook, but is it real or part of my dream? Good sense told him it was just part of a dream, but a deeper instinct was trying to push the idea forward. Whatever the case, it was gone now. He listened intently but heard nothing further. He checked his watch. Twenty past four.

The temperature had plummeted since he'd gone to sleep. He shivered as the cool air passed over his sweaty body, and he slithered back inside his sleeping bag, the warmth enveloping him instantly. Then came that age-old argument. Do you stay in your sleeping bag, or do you get up and coax the flames back to life? He settled on the former. For a moment, he considered the water bottles under his bed. By morning, they would be frozen. He reached under the cot and found the case, extracting a bottle. It sloshed around, already half frozen. Finding one of his wool socks in the bottom of his sleeping bag, he slid the bottle inside and kicked it back down to the bottom of the bag. At least he would have one unfrozen bottle to drink and make coffee with. He focused on keeping his toes away from the freezing bottle and was soon sleeping again.

———— • ————

Five kilometres to the west, Insertion Team 2 (IT-2) led by Jerome Manning had just been dropped. In the east, Brad Akron and IT-1 had been in position for about fifteen minutes. Both had been dropped far enough away to avoid alerting Lance.

The situation was good, if not ideal. To approach from both directions with the higher mountains to the north and road access to the south meant they would most likely drive him towards one group or the other. There was always the possibility that he would simply surrender. Most of the time when push comes to shove, a man will save his own life above all else. This was a desperate, dangerous man with a murder hanging over his head, so they'd best not count on his surrender.

Romey was thinking about these factors when suddenly Red was by his side. He was reminded again of the quality of men he worked with. Not too many men could approach without detection as he had just done.

"Almost time, boss," he said quietly. "Sounds like we may be grabbing an old Lobo by the shorties here, eh?" The last syllable attested to his Canadian upbringing. A moment later, he continued, "It almost goes against the grain, coming after one of our own, right here in Montana, USA."

Romey's shrug went unseen in the darkness. "Just doing our jobs, that's all. Must be an hombre yonder, though, or they wouldn't have sent us here, so keep alert and stay quiet." He checked his watch. "Let's roll." With that they moved out silently, each man grim and determined.

———— • ————

IT-1 began moving thirty seconds later. The ground phase of Operation Coye-Wolf was under way.

Brad had looked at the topos and satellite photos and knew his approach would allow their team to arrive well before Romey's. By the time they got on scene, it would be over, and Coolidge would already be dead.

———— • ————

Lance catnapped his way through the next hour, in and out of consciousness until he finally decided it was time to make the move. He got up and dressed quickly. It was definitely colder this morning, and he was shivering as he got dressed. He had paused briefly, testing the coldness of the air, before getting dressed. He figured it was ten or twelve degrees below freezing. The fire was out, so he started a new one. After he had it going, he crouched down, holding his hands to the warmth and rubbing them together.

Soon it began to warm up in the tent, and he took his jacket off. The last thing he wanted to do was to start sweating and then have the moisture freeze next to his skin when he got outside. Coffee in hand, he thought about today's hunt.

Lance noted a spot on the map upstream where the river widened and appeared to be quite shallow. The trail led north, and the river intersected it, roughly at an east-to-west angle. The spot he was looking for was about five hundred yards east. He had taken some screen shots from Google Earth, but knowing full well that the images could be deceiving, he decided it was worth a try. If he could cross the river and make his way back to where the road continued on the other side, he would have access to that valley and the lakes and ponds within it. There had been no indication of recent activity; most likely no one had been there for years. With no hunting pressure, his odds would go way up. If he ended up getting a moose, he would quarter it, bring it out on his packboard, and ford the river. He might even be able to clear some of the trail and get the ATV close. It would be a lot of work, but it would be well worth it if he could get a big ol' bull with his bow and arrow.

After breakfast, Lance rechecked his gear. It's the little things .... He took his Swiss flint and steel out of his pack and slipped it into his pocket. On a secondary impulse, he changed his mind. Since it had a cord attached, he hung it around his neck, tucking it into his jacket. The .45 slid smoothly from its holster. After checking it, he returned it to its place. Old habits die hard, and out of necessity, Lance had become a creature of some useful habits. He checked his watch: 6:32—time to get moving. It would be light enough to shoot within the hour.

After preparing lunch, he shrugged on his pack and did a test pull on the bow string to ensure the cold hadn't bound the fibers. Turning out the light, he stepped into the darkness. The stars were still faintly winking. There was no wind; the smoke from the chimney lifted lazily into the morning air. He stopped for a long drink at the spring, letting its coolness seep into him. Because it was still early, he decided to make time and stepped out at a good pace.

———— • ————

Earlier, IT-1 had run into the same snag that Lance had the day before—not anticipating the depth and force of the stream. They had dropped north of the creek near a pond—a good spot because it was open and relatively dry. Their plan was to ford the creek and make their way down the same trail Lance had just come up. They were not expecting an encounter in the dark. They had checked the maps and decided to try at that same spot east of the old road. The team had moved off silently and had made a few hundred yards, with Leadbeater lagging behind, as was his assignment. They had cast about for a short time, trying to find a place to cross, and it had eaten up some of their lead on IT-2.

Not wanting to be left out of things, Romey had set a blistering pace and was closing the distance fast.

When Lance stepped out to the edge of the drop-off above the river, Beats just happened to be looking in that direction. Lance had materialized like a ghost, and the stories about this man came back to him instantly. He shuddered involuntarily, raised his rifle slowly, and peered through the scope. It was low light, and he didn't want to kill the wrong man. At that moment, Lance was looking away and his face wasn't visible. Beats held his breath. Finally, after a long moment, Lance turned towards him, and Beats was sure. Even though Lance was looking right at him, Beats figured his position would be invisible. He adjusted his aim for a heart shot. It was just over two hundred yards, and at this distance he would not miss.

Lance caught the slight movement, and his years of training and conditioning kicked in. Something in his subconscious responded before his conscious mind could evaluate what was happening. Instinctively, he dropped to his knees, but it was too late. With stark clarity, he saw the muzzle blast and felt a searing pain stab him. As he fell, the bank gave way, and the water rushed towards him. A thousand ice picks stabbed through him as he splashed down. He instinctively gasped and some of the icy water got into his lungs. For a moment, all was still and quiet. Then he heard what sounded like the roar of a freight train. He had the sensation of being carried in a blanket by a tribe of Indians. The sound was actually rocks being ground and pushed by the raging current.

As he was carried downstream, Lance had a desperate fear that he would be ground to powder under the same force. He was holding his breath now—and that spoonful of cold water in his lungs as they were convulsing to expel it. He slammed against something that sent a dull pain through his ribs. He groped, reaching out to take at least one stroke. Suddenly the shoulder strap of his pack was hung up on something, holding him under. In a desperate panic, he wrenched himself free from the pack and shot to the surface. He had been carried downstream to the first bend in the river. Just as he made it to the surface, he collided hard with a small log. He hit it head on—square in the chest and instantly he coughed the water out of his lungs. Maniacal hands grasped at his legs, and unable to maintain his grip on the slippery log, Lance was pulled under again. Barely managing a shallow gulp of air before he was forced down, a terrible tornado of bubbles accompanied by a deafening roar surrounded him. Cold hands clutched him in a witch's embrace, pulling him deeper into the cold.

Beats had watched him go down and into the water. He was always amazed at how quickly a bullet could change a man from a walking, talking person to—well, nothing at all. He realized in that moment that he had just taken out one of their finest military heroes. He had no qualms about the circumstances, no bravado that they had not met on equal terms or any of that parade-ground honor BS. This was the way it is at any given moment; the circumstances dictate the terms, and the victor is usually the one who acts first and decisively.

After hearing the shot, the first man back was Truck. He was moving low, rifle up, scanning the area. Their eyes met and Beats waved him in, shushing him with his finger to his mouth. With sign language, he indicated that he had made the shot and gave the thumbs-up gesture. Within moments, the team was gathered. Brad, who had been on lead was the last one to arrive. In a whisper, Beats explained what had happened. He did not embellish or exaggerate—just gave a simple explanation. The tension drained from the group as the sun was coming up, bright on the horizon.

Brad slapped Beats on the back. "Well done, buddy. Let's go retrieve the body. Keep a steady eye, boys, and stay alert." At two hundred yards, Brad knew there was simply no chance Beats had missed. Beats replaced the round in his clip and retrieved the spent casing from the ground. He had the unusual habit of marking his bullets with a small "B". He loaded his own and didn't like anyone messing with his bullets.

From the edge of a pool, they surveyed the bank on the far side of the river. Scuff marks indicated where Lance had gone in, and Brad breathed a further sigh of relief as this validated Beats' account. He scanned downriver, looking for some evidence of the body or gear, but couldn't see anything. His eyes followed the river for over a hundred metres, where it then took a sharp left turn.

Brad indicated the scuff marks with a casual gesture. "Pretty sure he didn't go back that way."

They all laughed in unison.

"Oh, how the mighty have fallen," Preach quoted.

This brought a subdued silence, as though each man was momentarily reflecting on his own mortality. They began a slow march down the river, with Brad at the water's edge. Moving in a pattern perpendicular to the stream, ten yards apart, guns at the ready. They were looking for tracks or disturbed vegetation, anything that might indicate that he had somehow made it out of the water. As professionals, they took nothing for granted.

However, even the best trained find it challenging to overcome a predetermined mindset. They were convinced that Lance was dead and that they would find his body downstream at the water's edge. They had moved no more than thirty yards when Brad raised a fist indicating they stop. He waved the men in, pointing at something in about six feet of water on the edge of a darker, deeper part of the river. It was a bow. Beats nodded, remembering seeing it in his hand.

"Should we fish it out?" Preach asked.

It was a good twenty feet from shore, and the current was moving swiftly, even though the water here was not all that deep.

"Yes, we need everything we can find," Brad answered.

Without hesitation, Preach began to undress. He fished a pair of water shoes from his pack. The temperature had not risen, even though the sun had been up for a while. He stood there naked, and he might as well have been standing on a beach in the Caribbean for all the effect the frigid temperatures were having on him.

"Looks like it's colder than we thought." Truck broke his usual silence.

Preach shot him a sharp glare. "You want to take the swim?" He took an aggressive step forward.

Truck chuckled, taunting the smaller man. Preach turned, waded into the water, took a deep breath, and plunged in. With a few strokes, he was at the bow. He grabbed onto it, surprised by the strength of the current as it was trying to carry him away. With a few more kicks, his free hand touched gravel, and he was able to stand up. He walked back upstream and dropped the bow at their feet—several arrows were still in the quiver. Brad had a towel waiting in hand. He indicated for Preach to turn around and he began vigorously drying him down. Preach took the towel to complete the task himself. He dressed and started to warm up within moments. Not once did he complain or shiver; he was a tough man, and they all knew it.

Brad took one of the arrows from the quiver and walked back to the spot where the shot had been taken from. He javelin-threw it a few yards and into the ground. It was unlikely that a lot of questions would be asked but still .... A crazed murderer might just throw an arrow at an unsuspecting officer attempting to arrest him in the course of his duty. He made his way back to the group.

"We let someone else find that if necessary." For a few moments nobody said anything, but they all understood.

"Yup, crazy mother, must've spotted me from up there and took his chance," Beats said.

Brad finally got on his radio and called Romey. "IT-2, this is IT-1. Wolf is down. I repeat, Wolf is down." No response.

Brad waited a few seconds, puzzled. "IT-2 this is IT-1. Do you copy?" Still no reply.

Finally, after another minute, Romey spoke, "IT-1 we have eyes on."

As a group they turned, as Romey and his team filtered out of the brush on the far side of the river. He was holding the radio up, waving it.

"Shit." Preach breathed the word, both surprised and embarrassed. "That hasn't happened to us before. How long have they been there?" He glanced back toward where Brad had thrown the arrow.

Brad seemed unfazed. "Well trained, I'd say."

Brad spoke on the radio, giving a brief account of the events while Romey listened without comment. "Let's grid-out on both sides, keeping eyes-on and work our way downstream. He couldn't have gone far." The orders were simple.

Romey tucked the radio back into his belt, and his eyes met Red's.

"That's a long shot for a bow," Red said simply. Romey was thinking the same thing—there was no accounting for human nature.

Eight of the best trained, most dangerous men on the planet began a methodical search. Each man was alert, knowing the mission was not complete until they found Lance's body.

———— • ————

Under the surface and out of sight, Lance's pack clung to a claw-like branch bobbing up and down as the small force moved quietly past. Just a few feet beyond the pack, under twenty feet of water, something metallic was jammed into the gravel, reflecting the dull bit of light that reached it. It was a 1911 .45 caliber pistol, which would not be seen again by human eyes for almost two hundred years.

———— • ————

IT-1 and IT-2 searched for most of the morning. When the first few snowflakes extended their cold fingers to Brad's brow, it made him frown. A snowfall was the last thing they needed. If it picked up, they would lose any tracks left behind.

As they walked, Brad grew more and more certain that Lance was dead. Just around the first sharp bend in the river were a series of minor rapids, with snags and deadheads here and there, jammed in place from years of flooding and settling. A half mile beyond that, the river narrowed and flowed into a forty-foot waterfall. Brad knew from experience how deadly a waterfall could be. He had once helped recover a body trapped in just such a spot, where the water had spun it around and held it under, like the heavy-duty cycle on a washing machine. Every bit of hair had been churned off—even the eyebrows and eyelashes were gone. Combined with the bloating, it was a gruesome sight.

Between the cold water and the bullet, the odds were one in a million that he had survived. He estimated that soaking wet in these frigid temperatures, a man would have at best, half an hour.

Damn it! We need to find his body—nothing less would suffice. The stakes were just too high. Ideally, they would find the envelope on his person, or at the very least, in the Jeep. The search was hampered by a snarl of underbrush that clung to the side of the river. They had to work their way around the waterfall and made another five hundred yards before the snow really began to fall. It was coming down so hard that they were having trouble seeing the fourth man out in their skirmish line. When it closed in even more, Brad ordered a halt, glancing at his watch: 12:31 p.m. He led them into a small clearing among the fir trees and made a makeshift camp. Romey's team on the opposite side were making similar arrangements.

"How far down are we going to go, boss?" Beats broke the silence.

Brad was snapping off some dead, low-hanging branches for the makings of a fire.

"We'll press on until dark and then make that decision." He had been thinking about it for the last hour or so.

"He's probably doing gymnastics under that waterfall," Preach volunteered.

"I was thinking the same thing," Brad replied. "Tomorrow we'll backtrack upstream and see if he popped out somewhere after we passed." He then ordered Preach to make his way back upstream, cross the river, find the camp, secure the Jeep, and destroy the envelope, videotaping it with his phone.

"Roger that," Preach said as he brought several large pieces of deadfall for the fire. Soon it was blazing, and their little spot was warming up. They had chosen well—it was tightly surrounded by trees with blowdowns on three sides to keep the wind out.

———•———

Every now and then a bit of snow would work its way through the "roof," hissing and spitting as it fell into the fire. They heated some water and dissolved some of their dried food rations into it. Truck used his Jetboil to make some cowboy coffee. Cowboy coffee is made by placing grounds in boiling water until it reaches the desired strength, then tossing in some cold water and letting the grounds settle.

While they sat there, Brad asked, "You know how he got his nickname?" He indicated the direction of the stream with his head.

"Yeah," Beats said. "I think everyone knows that story about catching those Taliban fighters flatfooted. The guy's an idiot. If it were me, those bastards wouldn't have lived to take a shot at ol' Derek here."

"The Taliban called him Arwa-Rue," Brad added. "Everyone thinks it's a reference to that incident because they think they are saying brew or coffee with an accent. But Arwa-Rue actually means something entirely different to them." He had their full attention. "The story goes something like this. On his second tour, Lance's unit came under heavy fire. A local scout betrayed them at the last minute, killing one of their men and retreating under cover fire to join his Taliban comrades. As you know, this wasn't as rare as one might think—it's one of the things we always worried about. I bet some of you were remembering some of those stories and wondering about Teddy."

Everyone nodded at that.

"Anyway, they were airlifted back to base, and Lance asked for a furlough. His commanding officer granted him leave, recognizing the obvious stress the loss of one of his men had put on him. One week! The military is so ... compassionate," he said mockingly.

They all looked at him knowingly, a nod here and there.

"The next day, Lance was gone. Nobody knew where. On the fifth day, he returned with that scumbag scout tied and gagged and had him put in the brig.

"A few weeks later, they captured a small village and the locals kept pointing at Lance, saying something. 'Arwa-Rue'. The men would smile, thinking they were saying brew with an accent. One of the men even commented, 'It would appear your reputation has preceded you, sir.' One of the translators finally corrected them, explaining that they were saying, 'Spirit-Ghost'. And something about a Kahffen, which sounded like coffee.

"Apparently, the translator had spoken to one of the villagers, who told a strange tale about a funeral for a village elder. As the procession bore the casket down the road, there was a thumping from inside. Startled, the casket bearers put the casket down, and the lid popped open. This American sits up in the coffin, pistol pointed at one of the villagers—the scout. 'Traitor!' he said in Farsi as he led the young man away at gunpoint.

"Assuming the American had come for revenge, the villagers gathered their weapons and began searching. They looked until dark, certain they would find the young man's dead body, or at least the body of the elder, but they found neither. Since it's Islamic tradition to bury the dead within twenty-four hours, this was a grievous insult. While they may have understood and even respected the action taken against the scout, the loss of the elder stung.

"The coffin was taken back to the home of the elder's widow. When morning broke, the widow ran into the street, waking the whole village with her wails. 'My husband is back!' It turned out the elder's body had mysteriously reappeared in the coffin, adding to his status. His new nickname was born— the man in the 'Kahffen'. When they heard Lance's men calling him 'Coffee', they assumed it was the same word."

After a moment Beats said, "Looks like a bullet can put an end to any man, even a superhero." The rest remained silent.

Truck spoke up in his low tone. "I want to see his body with my own eyes."

"Ha!" Beats was insulted. "You think I missed?"

"Didn't say that." Truck was careful. He wasn't scared of Beats, although you could easily misinterpret it as such. He simply knew when to push and when not to. This was the most important deal of his life. With this bounty, he planned to cash out and disappear forever. The arrangements had already been made, and he wasn't going to screw it up. He liked picking on Beats, but that was because he knew he could get under his skin.

"Things just happen, that's all," he said with a slight grin.

Beats scoffed at that. "Yeah, the thing that happened was, I shot him dead, and he fell into the river, and now he's snagged up somewhere upstream … downstream … either way, he's dead."

"Maybe, yeah … I guess so." Truck yawned with boredom.

Preach was delighted, seeing the big guy back up. He, like so many others, had misread Truck.

———— • ————

Meanwhile on the other side of the stream, Romey and his men were gathered close to a fire of their own. It had been a difficult morning. The first hundred metres hadn't been too bad, but as they made their way downstream, the high ground along the creek descended, and it was bushwhacking from there on out.

Their little group was subdued, each man alone with his thoughts. The spot they had chosen was a lee hollowed-out cave in the riverbank. There was plenty of fuel around, and they had a nice fire going. After that hard push first thing in the morning, they were enjoying the reprieve.

"Not a trace." Red was speaking. "He must've been pulled under somewhere, or we'd have found his body by now. Maybe he's snagged on the corners where all the driftwood ends up."

"I agree," Romey said, confidence in his voice. "Of course, it doesn't pay to be careless either."

Strongman piped up. "This is super confusing for me, boss."

"How so?" Romey asked.

"This highly trained guy kills this Cathy woman and then sticks to his original plan to go hunting. Leaves exact directions as to his whereabouts, and then runs into one of ours. Takes a low percentage shot with a bow at a man with a rifle. Then stays in the only open spot long enough for our guy to get a bead on him? Seems improbable at best."

ALL ENEMIES FOREIGN AND DOMESTIC

The group was silent for a moment.

"You think he just up and capped him?" Mussal asked, "Why would he do that?"

Strongman shrugged, "Who the hell knows. Why were they so hell-bent on getting here first? All I know is they want his scalp bad. We could've called in a chopper to check the river as we patrolled it. But instead, we're all out here with no end in sight, especially if it freezes up and the blizzard continues. Something's off here—my spidey senses are tingling."

"Red and I were having our doubts this morning as well, but we have a job to do. I for one won't lose too much sleep over a woman killer, even if the shooting wasn't up and up. This guy was a dangerous man. Beats probably just made an executive decision."

"Well, I don't like it." Strongman wasn't letting it go.

"Dead men tell no tales," Romey reminded them. "Besides, this is a sanctioned mission, and we are suckin' on the hind tit, so that's just the way she goes."

That put an end to it, or at least put an end to the conversation about it. But Romey was thinking his own thoughts as well. It wouldn't do to ignore the realities on the ground.

Red picked up his rifle and slung it over his shoulder. "I'm taking a leak," he announced, walking away from the group.

Stepping away from the shelter and the fire, he was reminded of just how cold the air was. He has to be dead! There is no way he could have survived a plunge into that cold water. Even if he had swum to shore, he couldn't go far without warming up—and we have found no trace of him.

The wind was swirling the snow around, causing intermittent breaks in visibility. He decided to climb the bank above their shelter and have a look around. He'd only been up there a few moments when he saw a shadowy figure walking at a good pace through the snowy curtain. His rifle came up instantly, but the figure disappeared behind a row of trees. He calculated the pace of the lone figure, spotting him twice in brief glimpses between the trees. Suddenly, the figure appeared in an open spot. It was Preach! He was heading upstream with all his gear on, moving at a good clip. Then as suddenly as he'd appeared, he disappeared. Puzzled, Red surveyed the rest of the area as best as he could. When he returned to the shelter, everyone was breaking camp.

"We got the call," Romey said. "We are going to resume the search."

Red reported what he had seen, and Romey too was puzzled. "What are they up to?"

———— • ————

The camp was empty. The Jeep's radiator was stone cold, and so was the stove within the wall tent.

Daryl Craig had been checking the northern range when he noticed the camp set up. It was technically on their land, and normally they couldn't have cared less. This was the northernmost point of their gigantic spread, and they didn't plan to develop it for years, if ever.

Nevertheless, they checked periodically to make sure some poor animal didn't get trapped and end up tainting the water. There were several such springs in the area. He moved quietly about the camp, curious about who was here. It was clearly a hunting camp, and the hunter, whoever he was, was alone, as there was only one cot in the tent. He circled the Jeep several times, reluctant to check the glovebox for a registration. What if he got caught? The hunter might take him for a thief and start shooting. He hesitated a moment and then checked the passenger door—it was unlocked. He opened it quickly, then the glovebox. The registration was in a large Ziploc bag. "Lance Coolidge." He frowned when he saw the necklace. He replaced the registration, closing the door tightly without slamming it. He smiled.

Wouldn't you know it, I am a prophet. He mused. He had known this man would be connected to them somehow. He was looking forward to reporting this discovery to Lynette. He began thinking about how he could casually interject the information into a conversation, as though it wasn't important.

Since the night she had met Lance, Lynette had been completely distracted, plus she had a new bounce in her step and was bubbly and friendly. It was starting to unnerve him.

He was just turning back to his truck when he heard the voice.

"Hold it right there." It was icy cold. "Turn around slowly."

Daryl did a quick calculation in his mind. Could he draw his Glock nine-mil as he turned? The tone of the man's voice warned against it. Besides, he was sure who he would see when he turned around. He turned slowly, but instead of Lance, a smaller man in full military gear stood in front of him. His rifle left no room for argument. Preach was as instinctual as an animal. He had been spooked earlier, by an eerie feeling that he was being watched. That combined with his usual nervous energy pushed him on, and he had made good time.

Nodding at the gun in Daryl's waistband, he smirked. "Good choice. Bet you thought about it, though … right, big fella?"

Daryl waited. Something wasn't right. He was trying to make sense of it, but nothing fit.

Preach knew this wasn't Coolidge, but the man's presence here was puzzling. He had an instant dislike for him, which wasn't unusual, since he had a chip on his shoulder and a particular distaste for big, powerful men. If he was ever given to introspection, which he never was, he would have recognized his own insecurity, which manifested itself as meanness.

"Who might you be, big fella?" He used the phrase again.

"Well as it happens, this is my land, and I should be asking you the questions, but you're holding the gun, so I guess you get to call the tune … for now." He let that hang in the air only a moment. "I'm Daryl Craig, and this is part of my family's ranch. Who might you be?"

Preach ignored the question and followed up with another of his own. "What are you doing here, and what were you doin' in that Jeep?"

"I'm range riding, checking to see if there was any way of ID'ing the owner. I see this is going to be a one-sided Q & A."

"Range riding?"

"Yeah, you know, checking fences, springs … or for trespassers."

"Huh." Preach half nodded and lowered his gun. "You're pretty cool. You've had a gun pointed at you before I'd say. You the law?"

"Nope, like I said, just checking the range."

"Did you find anything?"

"No," Daryl replied, not sure why he had lied. "You interrupted me."

"Don't let me stop you … carry on."

Daryl retrieved the registration from the glovebox. While he was pulling it out, he noticed the necklace again. He fingered it lightly, noting that it looked valuable. "Someone named, uh … Coolidge, Lance Coolidge."

"Know him?"

"Can't say I do." Technically, he didn't really know him.

"Count yourself lucky that it was me that came up on you and not him. I'm Captain Lee Cross. US Army."

"Nice to meet you," Daryl said but didn't offer to shake hands. "Why do you say that?"

"He's a killer. Killed a woman in Lone Prairie a few days ago. You must have heard about it, being from around here."

Daryl had heard about it, of course. It was the talk of the town. He thought he was beyond being surprised or shocked anymore. This just didn't make any sense. Daryl recognized Preach for what he was but decided to play dumb and dig for information.

"Are you part of a SWAT team or something?"

"Or something, yeah. We've been sent to bring him in for questioning. It turns out he's a well-trained soldier, so not just anyone could come and get him." He was bragging.

"We?" Daryl looked around.

"We spotted him earlier today, and the team is trailing him as we speak. Took a shot at one of our guys. Like I said, he's dangerous, and you're lucky it was me you ran into and not him."

Daryl feigned relief. "Sounds like it, for sure. Where did you spot him?"

Preach's eyes narrowed with suspicion. "Why do you want to know that?"

Daryl was on a roll now, and he lied again, detesting this little man with his big ego. However, he knew a dangerous man when he saw one and suspected his confidence wasn't all bravado.

"I know this country. Thought I might be of some help, that's all."

"No, I think we have it under control …. Thanks, though."

Odd, Daryl thought. Odd that the man is still on the loose, but they have it all under control. He is special forces, Daryl decided. He knew the type. What is going on here?

Daryl thought about his encounter with Lance. Yes, he would take some killing, that was for sure—and maybe these are the guys for the job. But why is he lying, and what is it about this that seems so wrong? He turned this over in his mind but couldn't come up with anything. He just had a gut feeling, and he was a man who always trusted his gut.

This was going to hit Lynette hard, and he was reluctant to go home and face her. This was the first man in years that she'd taken an interest in, and Daryl had liked him right away. His thoughts went to Cathy Short, and he felt deep sympathy for her. If the man's a killer, he has bought a world of trouble with men like Lee Cross after him.

Preach was speaking again. "I'm going to need you to leave the area for a while … for your own safety. We will be impounding the Jeep and cordoning off the campsite."

Daryl nodded, heading to his truck.

"Where's that spring?" Preach was giving him one last test.

Daryl pointed to where it was and drove off without waving.

Preach's eyes followed him until he was out of sight. He followed up with a thorough examination of the Jeep and trailer; nothing. The tent was neat and orderly. There wasn't a ton of gear, just the usual stuff you'd see in the camp of a seasoned hunter. He checked the stove inside and out, sleeping bag, and cot. He even examined the seams of the tent itself. He stood there, hands on his hips, thinking. Maybe Lance had stashed the envelope somewhere nearby.

It hadn't snowed as much here as by the river, so he painstakingly checked the ground and found the place Lance had used as a toilet. He walked to the spring, and nothing was out of the ordinary. He double- and triple-checked the Jeep and looked around until he was satisfied that the envelope was not at the camp. He figured if he couldn't find it, no one else could. Lifting the hood of the Jeep, he removed the main coil wire and stowed it in his pack.

He headed back down the trail, knowing they would resume the search in the morning. He was feeling a little better knowing the envelope wasn't at the camp. Within a mile, the trail reached a high enough elevation for him to make radio contact with Brad.

"Lair is empty. I repeat, lair is empty."

After a few seconds, Brad responded, "Roger that, stay put for tonight. It will be dark soon. Make another slow search of the river in the morning on your way back down, and we'll rendezvous after that."

"Ten-four," Preach replied.

He made a quick decision to work his way back to the camp and spend the night. There was no need to rough it out in the snow and cold when he didn't have to. In twenty minutes, he was back. The snow had already partially covered his tracks. After starting a fire in the stove, he tossed his own sleeping bag on the cot. He warmed up some food and ate, enjoying the silence. He was confident that Lance was dead. Even if Beats's bullet hadn't got him, the elements would have. We had best find his body and wrap this thing up tomorrow. Thinking on these things, he relaxed and was soon asleep. Aside from getting up a couple of times to restock the fire, he had an excellent sleep. He knew his night had been a lot more comfortable than the rest of the team. At that thought, he smiled to himself.

Eating a quick breakfast, followed by fifty slow push-ups to get the kinks out, he was back on the trail as soon as it was light enough to see. The snow had continued all night, and there was no evidence of his tracks from yesterday. This was a good sign. If Lance had somehow made it out of the river, there would be no tracks for him to spot.

His radio came to life as he crested a rise. "Copy?" He caught the last word and waited. It came to life again, "Preach, you copy?"

"Roger that," he replied holding his breath. Damn it, how long have they been trying to reach me?

"You on the move?" There was no indication he had made them wait.

"Yes, on the move." He was relieved.

"Good, come straight back and double-check the riverbank on your way in. I'm hoping he may have surfaced in the night."

"Okay, boss," Preach replied. They hadn't found him yet. The distant hum was growing louder. Preach had made it to the river when the chopper arrived. He made himself visible as it made a slow, low circle past him, then lumbered on downriver.

———— • ————

After slugging it out another two kilometres, Brad decided they had followed the river far enough. There were so many logjams, he was confident that the body had not made it beyond this point.

IT-2 scrambled over a natural dam, built up at a narrowing in the river. The snow had continued off and on through the afternoon and night, and now the forest was covered in a six-inch blanket of snow. The tracks of several small animals and birds and a huge set of moose tracks had been visible, but beyond that, nothing.

Brad looked up at the chopper with satisfaction. There was now a good chance they'd find the body soon.

After an initial search, the chopper began to circle farther and farther out.

When Preach rejoined the group, he handed the coil wire to Brad. "A trophy for you," he said and laughed.

Brad tucked it in a side pocket of his pack.

15

That same morning, Lynette and Daryl Craig headed into town on their way to the sheriff's office. Lynette had received the news with shock and disbelief. How was it possible that Lance could've murdered a woman he barely knew on the same day he'd been with her late into the evening? She intended to draw their attention to some obvious facts that they must have overlooked in their incompetence.

When they arrived, the entire contingent of four cruisers were in the parking lot along with a few extra vehicles. The Craigs pushed through the front door into a hum of activity and waited at the counter until Brenda finished a phone call.

"Lynette, how are you? I think this is the first time I've ever seen you here. What's your trouble?" Daryl hung back, listening to the conversation, and reading the notices on the bulletin boards.

"I'd like to speak with the sheriff." Lynette's tone was firm but kind.

"Sure," Brenda replied. "Can I let him know what it's about? We're having a very busy morning."

Lynette hesitated briefly. "I'd rather talk to the sheriff directly if that's okay. It's a rather sensitive matter."

Brenda was a bit taken back at that, showing her minor displeasure with a passive delay tactic. "All right, take a seat, and I'll let him know you're here. Like I said, we are busy this morning."

"I'd rather not take a seat." Lynette was a bit firmer and less kind this time. "Believe me, Brenda, the sheriff is going to want to talk to me."

Daryl remembered he had a pistol in his waistband, so he gestured to Lynette and went back to his truck, where he locked it in the glovebox. Going armed into a police station wasn't smart, even if it was legal.

When he returned a minute later, they were ushered into the sheriff's personal office. It was a makeshift series of glassed walls cordoning off a section of the room. But it allowed for privacy, with blinds that could be drawn on all sides and a generous amount of neat and orderly shelving.

———— • ————

Sheriff Hallward was generally a patient and methodical man. He pushed his laptop to the side to give them his full attention, but he also wanted to get back to work. He had two murders on his hands and a suspect somewhere up in the mountains with a team of soldiers chasing him down. They had promised to keep him in the loop, but it had been forty-eight hours and thus far … radio silence.

"What can I do for you?" He was looking at Lynette with no sign of impatience.

"I want to know what's going on with Lance Coolidge."

That caught Hallward off guard completely. He leaned back in his seat to collect himself. "What about him?"

"Is he really a suspect in Cathy Short's murder?"

Man, you can't keep anything a secret in a small town. "Who told you that?"

Lynette looked at Daryl, deferring to him. He quickly relayed his encounter with Lee Cross and the circumstances surrounding their meeting. Sheriff Hallward was unsure how to proceed. He didn't have a clue what was happening up there. The last thing he was expecting was intel from a citizen. As was his nature, he decided head-on was the best approach.

"Miss Craig, we do have some concerns, but right now this is an active investigation with a possible suspect on the loose." He chose his words carefully. "I can't tell you any more at this time."

"You can't or you won't?"

"That's the same thing in an active investigation, but I will tell you we've had no report about this incident with the … SWAT team member." He used Daryl's word.

"Did you meet these guys?" Daryl asked.

"As I've said, I can't really comment on that."

"Yeah, we got that," Daryl said, "but if you had, you would know it's not your typical 'SWAT team'—more of a search and destroy operation by the looks of the one I ran into."

Hallward didn't reply, instead asking what their interest was in Coolidge. He added that he was surprised they knew him.

"Our interest is personal," Lynette interjected. "He's a friend of the family." She stretched the truth a bit.

"I thought you didn't recognize his Jeep?" This question was directed at Daryl.

"He's more of a friend of mine," Lynette amended her statement.

The sheriff saw this for what it was—Lynette Craig was in love with Lance Coolidge. He had always liked her, and in their few brief encounters, she had been polite and considerate, even thanking him for his service once. He felt sad for her now.

———— • ————

"Sheriff," she implored him, "I really need to know what's going on out there." She had hoped that somehow, she could come in here and convince them that Lance, the man she had laughed and talked with, could not possibly be involved in this crime, but now she was feeling hopeless. She was beginning to realize she had nothing concrete to offer. The situation was even more complicated than she had thought. In desperation, she tried a power move.

"I'd say a manhunt taking place in the northern woods would make an interesting news story, wouldn't you?" Her comment was directed at Daryl. He picked up the meaning immediately and ran with it.

"Yes, it would … my buddy Dan is still working for the Independent … I could give him a call." There was no such person, but Hallward didn't know that.

The sheriff stared at them hard for a moment, clearly evaluating his options. Without averting his gaze, he hollered out his door. "Agent Lombard, would you come in here for a moment?"

Geraldine stepped into the doorway. "What's up?"

"I'd like to introduce you to FBI Agent Geraldine Lombard. She's here as part of a special task force looking into Cathy Short's death. Geraldine, I'd like to introduce you to Daryl and Lynette Craig. They own a ranch north of here, and they have some information to share with us."

"Oh?" Geraldine's interest was piqued. "Nice to meet you, Mr. and Mrs. Craig, is it?" She held out her hand, and Lynette rose to her feet and shook it.

"Daryl is my brother, actually."

Daryl stepped forward and shook her hand as well.

Hallward brought another chair into the office for Geraldine and closed the door firmly.

After repeating the story of his encounter with Lee Cross, Daryl asked. "Why is Lance a suspect?"

At that, Geraldine threw a questioning look at the sheriff.

"Either we talk to them, or they talk to a reporter," Hallward explained.

Geraldine didn't like that at all and liked the idea of being pressured even less.

"Or door number three is, we could have you both jailed for obstruction. How does that sound?"

"There will be none of that," Hallward snapped, showing his iron. "These are upstanding citizens. We are not kicking over the hornet's nest here, there's not enough honey to make it worthwhile." No one pointed out the mixed metaphor.

"Fine," Geraldine said tersely. "What's your connection to the suspect?"

Lynette was unsure how to answer that. How could she explain that she had only met Lance twice … on the same day? They had talked and laughed, making a powerful connection, and she was … in love with him? It was preposterous but there it was. She realized that to try and explain all of that would seem juvenile.

"He's a friend of the family," she said, reverting back to her original explanation.

"I see." Geraldine picked up on the hesitation. She decided to approach that line of questioning later if it became important. She had learned long ago that people conveyed as much by what they didn't say as by what they did—sometimes even more.

Geraldine relayed the story briefly, leaving out key details. She made it clear that Lance had shown an interest in Cathy and that he had opportunity. It was made to look like a robbery, but they didn't know what to make of the fact that several valuables had not been taken. She was watching them carefully and could see the blood draining from Lynette's face.

Daryl was thinking about the necklace in the glovebox but kept it to himself. Doubt began to creep into his mind for the first time.

Lynette's voice faltered. "Was she sexually assaulted?"

Geraldine had a moment of compassion as she suspected that Lance was more than a friend. "I can't comment on that," she replied. A part of her wanted to tell Lynette that they had ruled out sexual assault, but she knew better than to provide sensitive information that could make its way back to the suspect.

Geraldine continued, "Is there anything you can tell us that would help us locate him? Does he have a favorite spot he likes to go when he leaves camp? Anything at all, even if you think it's inconsequential. If he's innocent, maybe we can bring him in without trouble. But so far, he hasn't been acting that way."

Daryl thought again about Lee Cross. He wasn't going to play nice, and he knew it.

There wasn't much they could say. In reality, they knew very little about him.

"Not that I can think of," Lynette answered.

"If you think of something, here is my card. You can call me anytime, day or night," Geraldine said, handing it to Lynette. "I'm sorry, Miss Craig, but we have to do our job. I hope you understand."

Lynette half nodded as she rose from her chair. "We ate dinner together between six and about nine thirty that evening." She wanted to provide him an alibi for their time together at least. "We ate at Kelly's Bistro," she added.

——— • ———

When they had cleared the building, the sheriff turned his attention to Geraldine. "So far he 'hasn't acted innocent'?" he demanded, partially quoting her. "Don't keep me in the dark. This is my jurisdiction, and I will not be kept out of the loop."

When she didn't answer right away, he called Barton into his office. After a brief explanation, he ordered him to go to the camp and take pictures and video of everything. He reminded him that he was acting under his authority and that no one should interfere with his work.

"I'll head out right away, sir," Barton said.

The sheriff took his own keys off his desk and handed them to him. "Take my Bronco; there'll be some rough patches up in the high country."

Geraldine interrupted. "Doug …," she said, using his first name, "I don't think that's such a good idea if you ask me."

"I didn't ask you." He was mad now. "When you stop with the BS, I'll consider taking your advice."

His rebuke silenced her. If she were in his shoes, she'd feel the same way.

Hallward continued talking to Barton. "In and out … take your time … document everything thoroughly. There is a full survival kit in my rig. Make sure you take your gear with you. I'll expect you back by the morning, so don't delay more than you need to."

After Barton left, Hallward turned back to Geraldine. "Close my door. We need to talk. Agent Lombard, you will be long gone when this is all over. I have a job to do, and I have to look these people in the eye every day. I live here. You need to keep me in the loop. Is there something I'm missing?"

"I know only a little more than you do about Coolidge, but clearly they are taking no chances with him."

"Who is 'they'? You're FBI, and I'm the sheriff," he reminded her.

"It's looks to me like special forces going after one of their own who's gone off the reservation. I just got the call this morning … some sort of skirmish … Coolidge was shot and ended up in a river. They have a chopper, and the team is trying to recover the body."

Hallward cursed under his breath. There was going to be a lot of questions. Kyle had been well liked. And the death of his brother coming on the heels of his own was going to create a stir.

"No more secrets." It was a demand, not a request. Geraldine knew she couldn't promise, but she did anyway.

"Is there any way we can find out if this is related to drug trafficking?" He asked frankly.

"What? Why would you ask that?"

"The FBI has a long-term operation going in this area to deal with suspected drug trafficking through the northern border."

Geraldine frowned. That seemed unlikely. As a senior agent, she would have been in the loop.

Hallward reached into his drawer and pulled out Bellamy's card and tossed it onto his desk.

"I had a visit from this agent just a few days ago."

Geraldine picked up the card. It was one of theirs, all right, but she didn't recognize the name, and it was a DC number. She decided to contact this Bellamy and see if they could coordinate their efforts. She took a picture of his card.

"This is news to me," she said honestly. "I'll call him and see if there is any connection."

Hallward believed her this time. "Okay, let me know."

Geraldine went back to the desk she was using and dialed the number. It went straight to voicemail. The message seemed wrong. No emergency back-up number or name. "Agent Bellamy, this is FBI agent Lombard. I got your number from the sheriff in Lone Prairie. Give me a call when you get this message; it's urgent."

Her next call was to her boss. She asked him to check and see if there was anything of value that could be shared. She texted him the picture of Bellamy's card. He too was in the dark. He promised to look into it right away.

———— • ————

The deputies had recovered Roger's body from the pull-out where Clifford had dumped it. This was a puzzler, with no ID and nobody reported missing. The body had a tattoo that the coroner thought might have been done by hand. Maybe as a teenager—it was on the left forearm—the word love in the typical hippie style of the 1960s. No wallet was found, so a possible robbery.

Lone Prairie hadn't had a murder in years, and now they were dealing with two in the space of as many days. Could they be connected? It didn't seem likely, but Hallward didn't believe in coincidences. He would simply let the evidence lead where it may. When they recovered Lance's body, they would need to make a solid connection between him and Cathy—some physical or forensic evidence to place Lance in her house. They would treat the murders separately until the evidence proved otherwise.

Hallward called the coroner. "Gail, do you have an estimate for the time of Cathy's death?"

"Yes. Around six or seven p.m. Do you want me to explain the technicalities?"

"No need, I'm trying to put together a timeline for that evening. Thanks though."

Sheriff Hallward wanted to make sure they did their due diligence for the inquiry that was sure to follow. Cathy had left work at 4:30 and her body was discovered close to midnight. He checked Barton's notes. An unidentified woman had called, claiming to have heard screaming just after dark. So five or five thirty, this time of year. That would be outside the time of death the coroner provided. But maybe too close to call.

Hallward was delving deeper now, jotting down his thoughts and drawing a timeline on a piece of printer paper.

4:30 Leaves the office
5:30 witness hears the screaming
6 Lance has dinner with Lynette
9:30 Leaves the restaurant
12:45 Tip called in.

He tapped his ring finger idly on his desk, thinking. "Miller!" He caught his eye and waved him into his office. "Call Earl. Find out what time Coolidge checked into the Harvest Moon."

Miller came back in a few minutes. "He says it was just before ten. I asked him if he was sure and he said yup, because from ten to eleven he watches COPS." Miller smiled at the irony.

Hallward added the new info to his timeline. Unless … Coolidge left the motel … killed Cathy and then returned … it didn't fit. The fight in the parking lot was close to one a.m.—about the time the tip came in. It would be nice to talk to that witness …

"Miller! Call him back and ask if Coolidge left at any point that night."

Miller was gone again for only a few minutes before he returned. "He said he didn't think so, but that he couldn't be sure."

"Okay, thanks," Hallward said. Then he picked up the phone and called Agent Lombard in.

"Geraldine, can the FBI get a record of Coolidge's credit card purchases on the day of Cathy's death? In fact, it would be nice to trace what he was up to that whole week."

"It will take some doing, but I sure can," Geraldine said agreeably.

Maybe having the FBI around was good after all, he decided.

"While we are at it, let's pull his phone records and see what towers he pinged that day and at what time." He was doing good old-fashioned police work now.

Geraldine smiled. She opened her briefcase and produced a file. "Way ahead of you on that one. The last time he pinged a tower was the morning after Cathy's murder. He was making his way north. So that fits."

"What about the night before?"

She traced her finger down the list. "Here." She tapped the page. "He pinged a tower about two miles north of town … and sent a text to his mother in Florida just after ten p.m."

"You people scare me," he said, shaking his head in disbelief. "How long have you had this?"

"We pulled it day one," she replied.

He showed her his timeline. "Assuming our witness and the coroner are accurate, we have a major timing problem."

"That's a big if," she countered.

"Like I said, I live with these people. I'll confirm Lynette's account with Kelly at the restaurant. For now, let's say we ignore the tip and the coroner's time of death. That gives Coolidge about two and a half to three hours after dinner to go to Cathy's home, kill her, return to the motel, and get into the fight. Since it didn't ping any other towers, he would have to have left his phone at the hotel or turned it off."

"We would have been able to track it even if it was powered down," Geraldine volunteered.

Hallward shook his head again. "I'm glad you're on my side. So he would have had to leave it at the hotel then. Let me know when we have his banking records. If he made any debit or credit purchases, we will add that to the timeline. However, it's starting to feel like we are trying to shoehorn the facts into our theory."

His voice trailed off a bit as he went back to thinking. If Lance Coolidge didn't kill Cathy, then who did? He listed some unanswered questions below the timeline, starting with that one.

Who had he gotten into the fight with and why?

Who was the dead guy at the pull-out?

Who was the anonymous tip from?

Was the coroner wrong about the time of death? Unlikely ….

———— • ————

Barton called a few hours later. "Hey, boss, I'm starting to get spotty cell service, so I thought I'd check in one last time."

"Okay, be careful; the weather reports aren't looking too good."

"Will do. I'll check in when I'm back in cell service. The sat phone is charged as well, but I won't use it except in an emergency."

"Sounds good." The sheriff paused. "Barton, I'd really like to talk with Coolidge. There are quite a few gaps here. If you encounter him … take all necessary precautions, of course, but an arrest is preferable, understood?"

"Of course. Barton out."

"Be careful with the soldier boys as well—they are wound pretty tight."

Barton heard the last comment, but his affirmative reply was cut off as his service dropped again. The comment made him frown—it was strange. He had learned to trust the sheriff's judgment, so he took it to heart rather than brushing it off. The temperature gauge was holding at a chilly minus five degrees when he came to the spur road with the Sukunka River Sour Gas Plant sign. This was where the steep climb into the mountains began. It would be much colder up there.

———— • ————

After leaving the sheriff's office, Lynette and Daryl went to the bistro for a coffee and debrief.

"This makes no sense," she began. "Daryl, am I being a fool?"

"I have always trusted your intuition; it is a sixth sense for you." He paused. "This is definitely a damn mess. I think we have to face the possibility that he may be guilty."

Lynette refused to believe it. Something deep in her soul told her Lance did not do this thing. Unbidden, tears welled in her eyes, surprising her as much as they did her brother.

"Hey." He spoke softly, placing a hand on her shoulder. "I'm sorry for you, Sis ... this is a hell of a thing. You finally find a man you want, and now this. I haven't told you yet but when I was looking for his registration, there was a woman's necklace in the glovebox and a Slim Jim on the floor. There was jewelry taken from Cathy's home, and why would he have the Slim Jim? It doesn't look good for him."

She was listening intently, her hands resting palms down on the table. At this news her right hand clenched into a fist. "He's not a killer." She dropped her fist on the table passionately. "I know it's crazy." She was emphatic. "Somehow I just know it in my heart."

"Okay, okay ...." Daryl raised his hands, palms forward, in a calming gesture. "What do you want to do?" He knew she wouldn't want to just sit idly by.

"I think we should head up to the northern range, find his camp, and see if we can locate him ourselves," Lynette said, as if it was an easy thing.

He took a deep breath, calculating all the factors. "What makes you think we can find him? We have to face the fact that the special forces team may get to him long before we do; they may have already."

"Then we better get going," she said, her indomitable self-confidence returning to her voice. "We can stay at the line cabins. I doubt they have any idea about them. The main cabin is provisioned for the winter, so we can use that as a home base. As long as we have warm clothes and two or three days' food, we can stay up there for as long as we need to." She seemed to have it all planned out.

"We need to be careful we don't get in the middle of a firefight." Normally, Daryl would attack a fortress with a bucket of fire, teeth bared and a roar on his lips, but with Lynette to worry about, he was more cautious. He knew that when action was needed, it was decisiveness, a steady hand, a keen eye, and a willingness to take risks that counted. He decided to go with his gut and trust his sister's intuition and her ability to hold her own under duress. Gulping down the last of his coffee, he placed the cup carefully on the table. It had looked like a child's toy in his massive hand. He grabbed his hat and rose from the table all in one swift motion.

Lynette's heart thrilled to see him like this. He was dark, imposing, and dangerous, but not to her. She knew his big, honourable heart, and she loved him all the more for it. A part of her recognized that she was releasing a dark and terrible force upon the world. Once started, he would not deviate or shrink from his duty. God help those who ran afoul of Daryl Craig in times like these!

———— • ————

The call was from Lone Prairie. She had received lots of calls from there over the years and didn't have to think twice about answering it. Katherine Coolidge was wearing a pair of jean shorts, a light flowery blouse, and a wide-brimmed straw hat that kept the sun off her face. They had been working around the yard for a few days. The hurricane had blown down several trees, and roots were exposed, revealing sandy soil that still clung there, not knowing the war was over.

Pulling off a glove with her teeth, she said, "Hello," on the fourth ring. It was a woman's voice. She braced herself. Bad news was almost expected when you were already grieving. She realized in that instant that she'd been so absorbed in the work that she hadn't thought about the accident the whole morning.

"Mrs. Coolidge?"

"Yes, this is she."

"Mrs. Coolidge, my name is Lynette Craig, and I own a ranch near Lone Prairie. I need to talk with you about your son Lance, but I'm not sure where to start." Daryl was driving, and they were in the truck on their way back to the ranch.

"Miss Craig, I don't know who you are, but I lost my other son recently, so you'd better just come out with it. My heart can't take suspense."

Lynette started with "I'm a friend of Lance." Then as concisely as she could, she told the whole story, careful not to leave out anything important.

When Lynette finished, Katherine finally allowed herself a deep cleansing breath. "If Lance is in the woods, it's unlikely anyone will find him unless he wants to be found." She had walked into the house and was taking notes. "How well do you know my son?"

There was a definite pause, and Katherine picked up on it.

"I don't want to sound silly, but we've only met once—well, twice, really, but it was the same day. We had dinner together, and—well...."

Katherine threw her a lifeline. "Sometimes one meeting is all it takes. How did you get my number?"

"I called Clarence at the service station, and he gave it to me. Lance told me while we were at dinner that you were in Florida helping your sister."

"He did, did he? Lance usually doesn't talk much about himself. That must have been some dinner." She continued, "I'm going to make some phone calls, and then I'll be on the first plane home. Call me if there is any news, will you?"

"I will," she promised. "My brother and I were going to head up to the area and see if we can't find him ourselves. We have several small line cabins up there, and we know the area fairly well. There is not much cell reception in the mountains, though."

A mother's pride swelled up in her breast. Who is this girl that after just one meeting is willing to take this risk to help a near stranger?

"I don't want to promise too much, but we have a better chance than anyone of finding him .... After all, that's our land up there."

"Thank you, Miss Craig."

"Please, call me Lynette."

"Okay, Lynette, I need to make those calls, so I need to go. I can't thank you and your brother enough. And you need to know that most of all, your faith in Lance is not misplaced. When he is exonerated of these ridiculous accusations, 'Your faith will become sight.' I promise that with everything I am."

Lynette fully appreciated the biblical reference. She was fortified by Katherine's words, and as she hung up the phone, her gaze turned towards the mountains rising up in front of them. "We have to find him, Daryl, or that poor woman's heart will be broken beyond repair."

Daryl put a little more pressure on the accelerator. More than anyone, he had a sense of what Lance was up against. He had served in combat and understood the elements. And he was certain that if they didn't find Lance quickly, the special forces team would.

16

Joseph Coolidge was sitting in his worn leather chair when Katherine called. The chair had been a gift when he won his Senate seat the first time. If someone had told him back then he'd still be here all these years later, he would have scoffed.

Listening quietly to Katherine's telling of the events, he took studious notes in his own shorthand. He paused for a moment after she finished.

"We have to act fast ... you should get on the next plane home. Be ready to be his advocate and to speak on behalf of the family if that becomes necessary. My experience tells me that when family members step up, its hard for law enforcement or even governments to ignore them. Don't talk to the media, or anybody else for that matter. We don't need to exacerbate the situation."

After a slight pause, he took a more encouraging tone. "Remember that the wilderness is the best place for Lance. I know you have guessed at the nature of his work, and I can assure you there is no one better. I will find out what's going on from this end and put the support we need into place. Continue to pray, and I will let you know what I find out."

An hour later, Joseph knew everything about the accusations against Lance and the subsequent investigation. He had the name of the FBI agent on the ground—by all accounts, an uncorrupted and capable woman. He wasn't surprised to learn that Sheriff Hallward was still in place in Lone Prairie. They had never met, but Joseph made a point of knowing who the local authorities were. He had also discovered something else: there was no word on a SWAT team sent in to arrest Lance. In fact, there hadn't been a single SWAT unit dispatched. The usual channels had been bypassed. This meant that someone was pulling strings higher up the food chain.

He called the DOJ and spoke with the liaison to the FBI director, who offered no insight. Joseph had pressed to have the director look into it and was expecting a call back soon. He resisted the urge to storm around bullying people.

Joseph slid open a desk drawer and retrieved his pipe. This had been a no-smoking building now for almost thirty years. He tamped some tobacco into it and lit it up, puffing thoughtfully.

———— • ————

Ross had been summoned and smelled the smoke as he approached the senator's office. The bear is awake, he thought to himself.

"Come in, Ross." The beckoning came before Ross was able to knock. Why does he still surprise me after all these years? Ross made no reference to the smoking and listened quietly while Joseph brought him up to speed.

"I want you close by for a while. There is something afoot here that doesn't make sense."

Ross was almost disappointed. He was expecting to be dispatched to Lone Prairie right away. His face revealed none of his thoughts. He had learned to trust Joseph's judgment. "Do you think this is a move on the family?"

"It seems doubtful, but I know that I can be of the most help for Lance from right here, and I need to stay healthy and safe to do that. Understood?"

"Yes sir. What else can I do for you?"

"Speak to some of your friends at the Secret Service and find out if there have been any significant changes in details or if security has been beefed up in any sectors. I don't need to tell you that time is of the essence here. I need to find out who was sent in to get Lance and who authorized it."

Ross nodded with his usual lack of drama. "I'll be close by."

Joseph called his executive assistant in. Lorraine had been assigned to Joseph for the past twelve years.

"Good lord!" She exclaimed, waving her notepad to clear the air as she entered the room. She had never seen him smoke before.

"Can you keep a secret?"

She gave him a slight frown. "I'm assuming you're not talking about keeping your smoking from the surgeon general?"

He ignored that. "I need you to find out if any of my colleagues have made a trip to my home state lately or have met with delegates … that sort of thing. Any activity out of the ordinary that may have a connection with Montana. And, Lorraine, this needs to be done on the QT. Just have some conversations with your peers and see what the latest gossip is."

"Is there anything in particular I'm listening for?"

"What I'm looking for are changes in patterns and behaviours. I have a personal matter unfolding at home, and I want to make sure none of my political adversaries are meddling in our affairs. I need everything else put on hold; this is top priority."

Lorraine loved working for Joseph. He was kind and professional and lacked the arrogance of the other senators, most of whom had come and gone. She was part of his important inner circle. She started making some "social" calls immediately.

She had just left the room when Joseph's phone buzzed. It was the FBI director's office.

"What have you got for me?" he asked.

The voice on the other end responded professionally and promptly. "I have the field agent's phone number, as you requested. It looks like this investigation is priority … a lot of resources have been allocated. Other than that, it looks like standard operating procedure in a criminal investigation."

"Why the FBI? Wouldn't this usually be a local matter?"

"Yes, that is a bit unusual, but the victim worked for the local sheriff's department. It appears they called us in to help under the circumstances."

Joseph was methodically making his way through the chain of command to find a kink somewhere. This could be it, but the explanation wasn't entirely implausible.

"Thanks—and keep digging. I'll consider it a personal favour."

"Will do," the other responded.

———— • ————

Joseph's next call was to the state FBI commissioner, Byron Crown. His service record was bland. It appeared that he was patient and had been promoted slowly. He had held his current position for a number of years now. What was of interest to Joseph was that Byron had ordered Agent Lombard to the scene. Joseph intended to find out why Byron made that decision and how he had been alerted to the situation in the first place.

Cotton-mouthed panic crept into Byron's psyche when he heard that Senator Coolidge was on the phone for him. *What is this about?*

"Senator Coolidge." He feigned enthusiasm. "To what do I owe this pleasure, sir?" He specialized in butt-kissing.

"Mr. Crown," Joseph dove right in, "what is the status of the investigation into my nephew?"

Byron was genuinely shocked and immediately made the name connection, cursing himself for not putting the two together sooner. *This is what you get when the game is played at such a pace that you just can't keep up.*

He stumbled through his first few words. "Uh …what? I—I didn't make the connection until just now, to be honest." His first impulse was to cover his own ass. He had done nothing wrong; he just needed to keep Wallace's name out of it. He knew he was underwater, but he was desperately trying to process his options and protect himself. He anticipated the next few questions and was glad now he had taken some time to think and plan what he might say. The FBI's involvement, while unusual, wasn't unprecedented.

"How did you get involved with this investigation?" Joseph's voice cracked like a whip.

"That's a great question. We were notified of Miss Short's murder, and because she is a state employee, we assigned a field agent to the scene."

When it came to conversations, Joseph was always a master tactician. "Geraldine Lombard, is that correct?"

Byron's heart sank. What else does he know? "Ah, yes sir. She is one of our best and very fair, I might add." He was trying to give the impression of impartiality.

"How did you hear about it … the murder, I mean?"

Byron was relieved. This one was easy—his answer was entirely true. "We get daily reports on all major crimes, and we take special note if any government employees are involved. It's part of the Homeland Securities Act. I think it was intended that—"

"I know what the act intends, I voted in favour of it." Joseph could have added that he was one of the architects of the bill. Instead, he changed tack. Deciding on the "Columbo" maneuver, his tone became softer, easier going. "Well, thanks for your time, Mr. Crown. I don't mean to be difficult; it's just that this situation is personal, you understand?"

"Oh, yes sir, no worries. I'd feel the same way if I was in your shoes." Byron just couldn't help himself. Too many years of sucking up had formed some unconscious habits. "If there is anything else, I can do, please don't hesitate to call."

"Thanks for your time," Joseph said in a subdued tone, hoping to sound defeated.

Byron was already imagining how this new political connection might serve him, but the next question caught him off guard.

"Any word back from the SWAT team?"

Byron's dreams came crashing back to reality. He hesitated, knowing he was trapped, and Joseph read that for what it was. There is no SWAT team. Does Joseph know this as well? Or did he accept the story as presented? He tried to cover up his hesitation by pretending that he was checking. "I'm just reading the latest, and I don't see anything about that yet, sorry."

"The latest? The latest what?"

"Today's report from Agent Lombard."

"Ah, send me a copy of her reports, will you?"

Byron had been trapped again. How many times have I told my agents that less is more in a conversation? Realizing that this situation was getting out of his control and knowing that Geraldine's reports couldn't be redacted sufficiently so that the senator wouldn't become suspicious, he decided to share enough of the truth to prevent suspicion from falling on him at least.

"Senator, this isn't a typical SWAT team as far as I know. I think it's a SEAL team, sir."

It was Joseph's turn to be caught off guard. "What? How's that?"

"I was contacted by the military, and they said it was protocol because the suspect was one of their own. It fell to them to arrest him."

"So you just abdicated your responsibility, without question?" Joseph was incredulous. "My nephew is no longer an active member of the armed forces; he retired months ago."

"Ah … I didn't know. I—"

Again Joseph cut him off. "Who in the military contacted you? I want to warn you, Byron: Your career and possibly your freedom are dependent on you giving me straight answers here."

Byron was even more desperate now. He couldn't tell what Joseph knew, but Byron had to cough up a name. In the long run, it would be as damaging as telling the whole story. He desperately needed to buy some time to think.

"It was a Captain Akron. He arrived with his team shortly after the initial call."

"What else do I need to know?"

Byron had finally started to think, and it dawned on him that he wasn't just speaking to a US senator but the uncle of their prime suspect. He mustered his remaining courage.

"With all due respect, sir, we probably shouldn't even be having this conversation, as you have a personal connection to the suspect."

He braced himself for Joseph's retort and it came in the form of a warning. "That's your play, huh? Okay then. If I find out you have obstructed justice in this matter, there will be serious repercussions!"

Joseph let the threat hang in the air. "Here's my secure email. Send those field reports immediately," he demanded.

Byron scribbled the address down. One way or the other he needed to wash his hands of this whole mess. "Got it."

"We will be talking again." With that, Joseph hung up.

Byron was visibly sweating when he hung up the phone. He dabbed his brow with a tissue. His immediate reaction was to warn Wallace, but as he dialed the Washington prefix, a wave of fear swept over him. To hell with it! It is every man for himself. His survival instinct kicked in, and he decided there would be no further record of his conversations with Wallace. He had been using a private server for their emails, but decided even that wasn't safe, as Hilary Clinton could attest.

He set about deleting the emails, although he was certain that wouldn't survive a forensic investigation. Perhaps he could reduce the chances that someone would take a hard look at him.

———— • ————

Joseph knew the important thing now was to discover the motivations and orders of the SEAL team and get Lance some help. After that, he would work on unwinding the conspiracy that was beginning to materialize. One thing at a time, but he must act swiftly.

Lorraine's voice came over the speakerphone. "Director of the NSA for you, sir."

Joseph picked up the phone on the first ring. "Max, thanks for calling me back so quickly."

"No problem, Joseph. What's up? First urgent message from you since I became director."

"I don't have time to mince words. This is a top priority for me. If you don't mind, I'll skip the pleasantries?"

"Of course, go ahead."

"One of the reasons I put your name forward for director is because you're a straight shooter, and you are by the book. After Snowden blew the whistle, I knew we needed people that we could trust. But I'm in need of a favour, and we may need to colour a little outside the lines. I know it's a lot to ask—"

"Senator two things you need to know. When I got to the NSA, I realised they have never read 'the book', and as for the lines … well, we make Picasso look like a traditionalist. You still think Snowden was a traitor?"

"You're damn right I do, and one hell of a patriot! He broke the law, but so does a cop when he runs a red light to catch a bad guy. I've never claimed the system was perfect."

Max understood the paradox all too well. "What do you need?"

Joseph knew who he could trust and who he couldn't, and he trusted Max. He relayed in concise detail the situation, and when he finished, Max whistled.

"That is a rat's nest, all right. How can I help?"

"Several things right now; I need the phone, banking, and email records for Byron Crown—who has he been in communication with and who ordered the SEAL team in? Oh, and I need an electronic trail on Lance for the past week … anything that can give me some insight. And lastly, a dossier on Captain Akron."

"Done, I'll have that ready in an hour. I must tell you though, anything that's not relevant, be it personal, criminal, or otherwise, I will not be able to share."

"I would expect nothing less. Thanks, Max."

———— • ————

Although she didn't recognize the number when her cell phone buzzed, Geraldine recognized the prefix. She was sitting with the sheriff, working on the timeline together. She stepped out to answer the call.

"Hello?"

"Agent Lombard, this is Senator Coolidge. I need a few minutes."

It wasn't a request. She immediately connected the name. For a split second, she thought this might be a prank, but something in his voice erased that doubt.

"Yes sir, what can I do for you?"

"Your suspect, Lance, is my nephew. What the hell is going on over there?"

Geraldine's mind was working quickly. This was an unusual set of circumstances and an irregular conversation. "I'm just the field agent, sir; perhaps you could speak with my supervisor. I think that's protocol."

"Miss Lombard." Despite the urgency, Joseph was patient and kept his voice calm. "I appreciate the chain of command more than you know. I've already spoken to Mr. Crown, as well as the director of the FBI. Look, by all accounts, you appear to be a top agent and someone who can be relied upon. So I repeat, what is the status of your investigation?"

Geraldine was momentarily flattered; hard work and dedication were usually overlooked in a large organization, and the FBI was no exception.

Briefly and carefully, she relayed everything, including the fact that Lance had been shot, presumed dead, and they were looking for his body. She finished off by saying, "I'm sorry sir, to have to be the one to tell you this."

Joseph was silent for a moment, collecting himself. The news was a blow, but he knew better than to give up hope. The thought of losing Lance was unfathomable. He thought of Katherine and felt a sharp pang. Heads will roll over this.

"Sir, are you still there?"

Joseph came out of the fog. "Yes, I'm here." His mind had slowed now, knowing he needed to put his feelings aside for the moment. "Do you know why the local authorities called in the FBI in the first place?"

"I'm sure they didn't, sir. The sheriff was surprised by my arrival."

That didn't fit. Joseph was beginning to sense the kink he had been looking for. "Are you sure about that?"

"Yes, I'm in the station now." She stepped back into the office. Hallward looked up and saw her expression. "I can put the sheriff on speaker," she suggested.

"Who is it?" Hallward mouthed silently.

Geraldine held up a finger, indicating him to wait a moment.

"Yes, do that," Joseph instructed.

She covered the mic, but Joseph heard her anyway. "It's Senator Coolidge; Lance Coolidge is his nephew. I've brought him right up to speed." She emphasised the word right. Hallward nodded and she hit the speaker button.

"Senator Coolidge, I wish we were talking under better circumstances."

"So do I, sheriff, so do I …. It's been my experience that the closer one gets to the ground, the clearer an investigation becomes. And local law enforcement knows the people and often have the best instincts. Did you or did you not ask for the FBI's help in your investigation? I've been led to believe that is the case."

"I did not."

At this, Joseph paused. Crown! That's where this thing deviated. He could feel a slow burning anger growing in the pit of his stomach. He hated being lied to, and with Lance's life in the balance—it was inexcusable. He wouldn't have the ability to call in a SEAL team, so he had to be working with someone higher up. Someone he feared more than Joseph himself.

"Sheriff, what does your gut tell you?"

"I'm going to give it to you straight, Senator. The evidence has stacked up heavily against Lance. This is a tight community, and people here are quiet, hard-working folks, but I can assure you they will want justice to be served."

"Yes, and you have an office to keep." Joseph's comment was intended to measure Hallward's character. Was he only playing politics, or was he, as Joseph expected, a man of integrity for whom the law took priority over getting re-elected? He let the comment hang in the air.

"Look, Senator." Hallward's voice was firm. "I can understand your feelings, but I have kept my job here by doing it! Wherever the evidence leads, that's where I will take this investigation. And to top that off, Cathy Short worked for me." He stopped short of claiming she was his friend.

Joseph was pleased. He liked Hallward already. "Good to hear, but you still haven't told me what your gut says."

It was Hallward's turn to pause. "I don't like it. I have a list of unanswered questions, and this confusion at the FBI isn't helping matters. We were just looking at the timeline and the window of opportunity for Lance to have committed the murder is narrow. He has an alibi for a good portion of that evening."

"How's that?"

Hallward relayed the story about the fight at the Harvest Moon, the meeting with Lynette, and Daryl's run-in with Lee Cross.

Joseph kept Lynnette's phone call to Katherine to himself. "Sheriff, would you email me a copy of your timeline?"

"Of course. It's handwritten, so I'll take a picture with my phone and send it over shortly."

"Is there anything else unusual happening in your area? Families never want to believe the worst about their own, but in this case, I know my faith in Lance is well founded. Something must have sparked this powder keg."

"Well, in fact, we've had our second murder in as many days. And apparently the FBI has been investigating drug trafficking across the border for several months, which I wasn't aware of, so this has been an unusual week on several fronts."

"Another murder?"

Hallward relayed the scant details they had at this point.

"No suspects?" Joseph queried.

"I'm thinking the murders may be connected but the truth is it could have been a random robbery, connected to drugs or something else entirely. I'm treating it as a separate incident, but I have to be honest, I'm not a believer in coincidences.

"Nor am I," Joseph agreed. "Agent Lombard, what's the story with this drug investigation. Is that not usually a DEA issue?"

Geraldine had been listening quietly. "Yes, but often there is overlap. In fact, I tried calling this Agent Bellamy, who left his card with the sheriff. There was no answer, so I left a message. Service up here can be spotty," she added.

"It's one of the best things about that area," Joseph volunteered. "Send me a picture of his card as well, will you?"

"Will do," she replied. "I'll also type up our timeline and send it over," she said, winking at the sheriff.

"Great. Don't share this conversation with anyone, and I mean anyone. And, Sheriff, along with my email address I'm giving you my personal cell number. Call me if anything develops and as soon as there is news from your deputy. Can you do that?"

Geraldine gave a why-not shrug to the sheriff. "Sure," Hallward said.

———— • ————

Turning to the computer, Joseph brought up recent satellite photos of the area. They weren't real time but better than you would find on Google Earth. He zoomed in on the area. Lance had left precise directions to where he was going. It was preposterous to think he would carry on about his business and go exactly where he said he would if he had committed a murder.

Joseph continued to scroll through the sat photos. The most notable man-made feature in the area was the sour gas plant. Its position made it a valuable marker for orientation. He remembered well the environmental protests when they had approved the plant several years earlier. The local community was not thrilled either, as almost all the skilled labour was recruited from out of state, so it didn't even create local jobs. But they had approved the project in the push to make America energy independent.

Following the road with the cursor, he soon found the gravel pit that Lance was camping in. Joseph then surveyed the rugged and remote area in greater detail. He was able to make out the main line cabin on the Craig's ranch and guessed at its purpose. The three smaller line cabins were not discernible from these photos.

He permitted himself a few moments to think about Lance. The fact that they had not yet recovered his body was the hope Joseph would cling to. It would also be the hope he would offer Katherine. He scanned the weather reports. It was cold! He remembered the little boy and their many lessons together. Joseph was sure that whoever was out to get Lance would inevitably make one mistake: they would underestimate his tolerance of the elements. Still, if Lance is wounded …. Joseph pushed the negative thoughts aside. He needed to focus on the job at hand.

He was reaching for the phone when Lorraine came over the intercom. "NSA director again, sir."

He picked it up on the first ring. "That was quick. What have you got?"

"Lance hasn't been up to anything unusual. His electronic trail is the usual stuff: Gas, groceries, that sort of thing. He made only a couple of purchases in Lone Prairie itself."

"Was a restaurant in Lone Prairie on the list?" Joseph asked.

"Yup, Kelly's Bistro … paid for his meal at 9:14 p.m. That's not the last purchase though. It looks like a motel, The Harvest Moon, ran a room charge through the next morning and fifty-dollar incidentals hold that evening at 9:58 p.m."

Joseph was listening carefully, taking notes as they went.

"I can hear you scribbling away there. I've got this in a report I'll send over right away." The NSA director was amused by the old-school habits.

"Helps me concentrate. What about his phone records?"

"It's a small town but there are three cell towers. His phone pinged two of them." Joseph held himself waiting for what came next. The director continued, "He was not near the murder victim's house. At least his phone wasn't."

"Aha!" Joseph exclaimed. "That cinches it doesn't it?"

"Well, I don't know about that, but it all but eliminates the 9:14 to 9:58 window of opportunity."

Just then an email came in from Geraldine and Hallward. "Hang on a minute will you, Max?" Joseph murmured as he skimmed the timeline.

"Max, I'm looking at a report from the deputy on shift that night. They had an anonymous tip about a woman screaming just after dark. That's about 5:30 this time of year—within a half hour of Lance arriving at the restaurant. That means he would have had to stash his phone somewhere, drive to her house, commit the murder and then make it back to his stashed phone and go for dinner—all within about a thirty-minute window. I'd say we are approaching the improbable here if not the impossible."

Max stopped him. "Where are you getting the six o'clock time from?"

"Oh, sorry, yes, Lance had dinner with a young lady that evening. She said they were together from six to nine thirty roughly."

"Oh, that's interesting," Max responded. He had never checked to see how old Joseph Coolidge was, but if he had to guess, he'd say around ninety. He was amazed by his sharpness and clarity.

"I think we clearly have reasonable if not extraordinary doubt, that's for sure." Max continued, "I'll check that anonymous tip and find out where that call originated from."

"That would be great. Thank you."

"Now about Byron Crown. There is nothing special going on in his life. He's been at the same job for a number of years after some rapid advancement early on. He lives in a modest home and banks his pay cheque regularly. No big deposits, no luxury yacht or expensive cars. He does some contract work here and there—all vetted, all legit. He mostly provides cyber and physical perimeter security advice for independent businesses. He gets paid a little here and there but nothing that's making him rich. His most recent client had been paying him in shares and stock options. When he cashed it in, it barely paid for his time."

"Who's the client?" Joseph asked.

"ComCorp. I'm guessing you've heard of them?"

"You guess correctly—they run a sour gas plant in my district. What can you tell me about them?" Joseph's vast experience was paying off. He knew they were on to something. Did Lance see something he shouldn't have? Was he in the wrong place at the wrong time? Suddenly a thought stilled him. Has he been reactivated?

Max was speaking again. "ComCorp is a Canadian company, but they have holdings all around the world. Natural resource exploration and development, mining, oil, et cetera. It would take some time and manpower to untangle subsidiaries, umbrella corps, and the like. Crown didn't call anyone after you talked to him."

Joseph pretended not to be impressed by this real-time intel on his own activities. Too bad—he had hoped he'd spooked Crown enough that he'd flush out the others involved. "Let's leave that for now. What about the SEAL team?"

"That's bad news for Lance. Two teams were dispatched, authorized by the DND and approved by the Senate Oversight Committee. It was a necessary authorization because Lance is now a private citizen, and the operation is on American soil. Brad Akron is the most highly decorated active SEAL, and he's leading one of the teams personally. The second team looks just as capable. These guys don't fail."

He has not been reactivated then …. "Who made the request?"

Max knew this was going to sting, but he needed to give Joseph all relevant information.

"The request came from none other than Byron Crown. His point of contact was a bureaucrat on Senator Wallace's staff. It's a loosey-goosey chain of command, but according to phone records, they have had conversations on and off in the past. We don't know how they met, but it could have been at a cocktail party or some other innocuous meeting."

This stinks to the high heaven! Joseph had suspected for some time that Wallace was corrupt, but he'd always managed to stay at arm's length from trouble, using proxies to do his dirty work. He was a highly intelligent, formidable adversary. Is this Wallace's opportunity to strike a blow to me personally? He wouldn't put it past him. They stood on opposite sides of the aisle, their ideologies were diametrically opposed, and over the years, they had become bitter political adversaries.

"Thank you, Max. I'll be in touch."

"Anytime, my friend. Stay well."

———— • ————

Joseph quickly checked the timeline, scribbling the inconsistencies beside each point. Lance needed allies on the ground. On impulse, he called the FBI director's office, reaching a subordinate who he asked to check the status of the agent "Clifford Bellamy" posted near the Montana-Canadian border. After several minutes the answer came back. They had no agent by that name.

Next, Joseph replied to Hallward's email with the subject line, "Lance Innocent—Timeline Does Not Fit." He requested the pursuit and arrest to be called off immediately. He would also call, but he knew how important a paper trail would be.

His final sentence read, "Agent Clifford Bellamy does not exist! Exercise extreme caution, arrest if possible."

Then Joseph called the chairman of the Armed Services Committee, Senator Peter Ashgrave, who listened carefully as Joseph relayed the events to this point.

"Peter," Joseph said finally, "we need to call off the dogs!"

Washington was a rumor mill, Ashgrave knew, but he was appalled by the depth of information Joseph was sharing with him. These matters were always top secret and only shared with those on the committee or relevant actors. He wouldn't have believed that most of what Joseph knew had come from non-clandestine sources. The problem was that information is fluid—a liquid that seeps through the tiniest seams and cracks. Winston Churchill had famously said, "The truth is so important we surround it with a bodyguard of lies."

"It sounds like you know as much if not more than I do, Joseph. I will raise your concerns and let you know what the committee decides."

Joseph wasn't satisfied. "Peter, my nephew is innocent and being pursued like a wild animal by the best trained men in our forces. He doesn't have the time to wait for your committee to reconvene. If he's killed out there, I will move heaven and earth to ruin the careers of everyone involved."

Ashgrave didn't care for the threat and snapped back, "Maybe you've been in office too long, Coolidge. We don't alter official operations on your say so."

Joseph changed his tone to iron. "You may think this is an idle threat. I'm an old man, and you're right, the time for my departure is at hand—which means I have very little to lose." His voice was raised slightly now. "If you look at your hole card, you will see you're holding garbage. A military operation on American soil against a decorated soldier, an American citizen on trumped-up charges? This will not go well; I can assure you of that, Peter."

Ashgrave was relatively unfazed. They had followed due process; however, he knew Joseph would not relent. "I'll see what I can do."

———— • ————

Lance needed help, and there seemed to be nowhere to turn. Joseph turned the problem over again in his mind, but a solution did not present itself. Again and again, he came to the same conclusion: He would need to send Ross in. He needed him here, but Lance needed him more. At his behest, Ross returned to his office and reported to the senator. "Turns out Brad Akron has been keeping company with Wallace for some time. The Secret Service has been around during several of their meetings."

"Ross, has he got his own private little army here?"

"That's unclear," Ross replied. "However, it's possible." He continued, "I can be on a flight in the morning and be in the theater within twenty-four hours. I don't need to tell you that this is the end of the line for both of us. I don't care about myself, but you know this will be politicized, and you will be vilified."

In all the years Joseph had known him, Ross had never verbalized a thought to this extent. He could hear the sincerity and loyalty in his voice. He was more than an aide, more than a friend. He was family.

"My legacy is hardly my priority at this point. If Lance is still alive, we must do everything we can to get him out of this. I'm open to ideas ...."

"You know Romeo Dallaire?"

Joseph sat upright in his chair. "The Canadian general who was ordered out of Rwanda just before the massacres? He refused to leave at first knowing what was coming. I've heard of him of course; everybody has, but I don't know him personally. Why?"

Ross remained silent, letting Joseph think. Finally, he said, "This is all happening really close to the Canadian border." Ross rose smoothly from his chair. "I'll be around. Let me know if I need to cancel my flight."

At that Joseph smiled wryly. Of course, Ross had already booked a flight. Joseph picked up the phone again and dialed an old friend at the Canadian consulate. If the course of action he was taking was discovered, more than his legacy would be at stake, but he needed to call in a favour.

After he hung up, he decided to put some heat on Byron Crown, so he sent a freedom of information request on ComCorp.

17

Captain Ben Thompson led one of the most secretive and elite combat units on the planet—Joint Task Force Two or JTF-2—Canada's special forces. At an even six feet tall and two hundred pounds, he was lithe and moved like a panther. His father was a Cree Indian, and his mother was of Irish decent. He spoke Cree, English, French, and Spanish. He grew up on a First Nations reserve in Northern Manitoba, where he learned to track, hunt, and trap. He worked the trapline with his father and was homeschooled by his mother. She insisted on a good education, and he got it.

He completed his last two years of high school in Winnipeg, where he didn't exactly fit in and found himself in several fights. He did well enough that after a while, no one bothered him. He drifted into a boxing club at the Native Friendship Center that first year and found himself under the tutelage of Scotty McRandle. Scotty had coached several Canadian champions as well as Commonwealth Games winners. He had also been the Olympic team coach in the early eighties. For some reason, he took a liking to Ben and trained him vigorously. He had opportunities to spar with some of the old-timers that Scotty had trained.

"You're too old to start boxing," Scotty had told him. "If you'd come in when you were ten or twelve, you could've been a champion."

He won several amateur bouts handily. Carrying more of the native than the Irish in his looks, his olive-skinned face was framed by neatly trimmed black hair. The only evidence of his European heritage were his grey-blue eyes, startling against his dark skin and high cheekbones.

Ben's career in the military started when he was eighteen, right out of high school. He attended the Royal Military College in Kingston, graduating top of his class. Where he really excelled was in combat. His keen sense of tactics and natural toughness made him a dangerous soldier. He was able to flip a switch and go from calm parade-ground cadet to hunt-and-destroy killer. After years in the military, he was battle hardened and never wavered in his duty. He and Lance had worked side by side, rooting out the MS-13 element in the States. Unlike Lance, he never gave his orders a second thought. They had taken a keen liking to each other and there was an unspoken understanding between them. They anticipated each other well. In sports they call it chemistry. But as soon as their mission ended, they never communicated again.

Ben was a soldier through and through. Once his missions were over or they were called back, life went back to normal. Ben's final exercise as part of his JTF-2 training had been a night drop in an undisclosed location on foreign soil. He had no equipment, no money, and no idea where he was when he hit the ground. He had two weeks to make his way home and report to base. He came in on exactly the fourteenth day. That was because he took a three-day vacation along the way.

Wes Bass was number two in Ben's unit. Their bond went beyond a brotherhood. They worked together and took leave together, and for a time, Ben had dated Wes's sister. Ben and Wes had similar builds and similar interests, and they made a deadly team. They bought two quarter sections side by side in southern Alberta, planning to go into ranching full time when they retired from the military.

Their childhoods couldn't have been more different. Wes grew up in an affluent neighborhood in Oakville, Ontario, playing basketball and wrestling in high school. His father owned his own law firm and was somewhat mad when Wes announced he was joining the military. He tried to pull some strings to keep him out, but Wes threatened to disown his father if he didn't let it go, so finally he did.

Wes was a quick learner and deadly in a fight; his endurance was unmatched. Thriving on four hours sleep per night, he never napped and would always take the first watch, even after a grueling day. He had that strange lust for combat some men are just born with, men who usually don't make it to old age. But Wes was not reckless—it only appeared that way because once set on a course, he was quick and decisive. Both men were still active but on leave.

Wes spotted the dust cloud being stirred up off the hard-packed cold earth by Ben's old truck as it came up the long driveway. His binoculars were on the bench, under the covered porch of his modest log home. But there was no need for them. He recognized the truck and went inside to get a couple of cold beers. He was back on the porch as the truck pulled up to the house, the sound of gravel grating under the wheels. Ben deftly caught the beer that Wes tossed to him without word or warning.

Wes nodded to the bench, taking a tug on his beer. Ben dropped heavily onto it, stretched out his feet and rested them on a wooden stump. He cracked open the beer and took a long drink. It was ice cold, just the way he liked it.

Wes spoke first, "Vacation over?"

Ben nodded, taking another long drink. "This one's different," he volunteered.

"They're all different, man."

With his mouth full of beer, Ben laughed through his nose, and it came out as a sort of snort. It had become a trademark of his. "I suppose they are," he agreed. "But this one is different."

Wes waited.

"We are invading America!"

Wes took a sip and looked over his drink at his partner. He didn't appear to be joking. "Well, hell!" he exclaimed finally. "That's more like it, a real challenge. What's the gig?" Wes was fully expecting another go at MS-13.

"You remember our old buddy, Lance Coolidge? It seems like he's got himself in trouble with a couple of SEAL teams just across the border in the mountains of Montana. They say he's been wounded … maybe dead. We have been asked to go in, find him, and, if possible, bring him out."

"He'd take some killin'," Wes said, then followed up: "Asked?"

"This is a dark one. No support. Disownment in fact. If we are captured or killed, nobody is going to claim us. Real mission impossible crap … blah-blah-blah … you know."

Wes did know. "Just you and me against two SEAL teams?"

"Uh-huh."

"When do we leave?"

"After you finish your beer."

"Guess I'll take my time with it then."

———— • ————

Four hours later they were producing their Global Access cards, describing to an American border guard the camping trip they were taking. The border at Sweet Grass was chill most of the time. They picked up their ordnance at a predetermined location on the American side and were on their way. They had no illusions about this op—they knew it might well be their last. Nobody in their right mind seeks out a fight with the Navy SEALS without accepting that as a strong possibility.

———— • ————

At the same time, as Ben and Wes were crossing the border, Barton had made it to the gravel pit and was surveying the campsite. It was abandoned, but he was cautious nevertheless. He had his shotgun at the ready. First, he checked the wall tent, then the Jeep and trailer. When he was confident that there was no one about, he took out his camera and began snapping photos. When he came across the Slim Jim on the floor of the Jeep, he frowned. Vehicle B&Es

were rare around here. Most people still left their keys in the ignition of their vehicles around town.

Barton was thorough, taking several dozen pictures and bagging the Slim Jim. When he opened the glovebox his heart sank. He had seen Cathy wearing that necklace on many occasions. No one deserved to die like that, and he hated Lance for it. He found himself hoping he'd run into him somewhere along the line. After photographing the necklace, he put it in an evidence bag as well. The rest of the Jeep was clean.

Spotting the tape covering the light switch in the door jamb, he took a picture and pondered it for a while. Had Lance taped it shut so he could approach Cathy's house without being noticed? A Jeep had been spotted near the scene. But several days and nights had gone by—why had he not removed it? Maybe it was an oversight. He remembered the account of the fight in the parking lot of the Harvest Moon. Wasn't it an alleged break-in that had led to the fight? Perhaps the thief had taped the light off to not draw attention to himself and abandoned the Slim Jim when Lance caught him. Barton was trying to stay objective and let the evidence speak for itself.

It dawned on him that he'd seen none of the same tape in the Jeep or around the camp. Surely if Lance was careful enough to dispose of the tape, he would have also removed it from the switch.

Taking the necklace from the crime scene as a trophy spoke of a deeper psychosis on the part of the killer. In fact, it had the hallmarks of a serial killing, which might explain the second body they'd found. But why would he leave it in his glovebox at the same time he'd left directions to exactly where he'd be? Barton could not connect these dots. The evidence was a puzzling trail that left him feeling unsettled.

When he finished documenting the scene, he used a roll of "police line" tape to cordon off the entire area; it was getting late. He got out the sat phone and called Hallward. The connection was good, and Barton relayed what he'd seen. It surprised him that Hallward didn't seem excited about the evidence he'd found. He volunteered to find an isolated spot and spend the night, but Hallward overruled the suggestion, ordering him to come home.

———— • ————

Knowing Lance was dead or dying, the sheriff could see no reason to keep Barton up there. He would explain it to him when he got back. He added Barton's information to the growing list of inconsistencies. The necklace brought everything full circle, making Lance look guilty. Barton's theory about it and the Slim Jim was sound, however. If true, it suggested a much more sophisticated plot—a murder, a frame-up—but it was all a little too much. From experience, the sheriff knew that the most likely scenario was the most likely scenario. Damn it! He needed Lance to fill in some of these blanks. Considering the men that had gone in after him, Hallward knew that might never happen.

———— • ————

It didn't take long for word to find its way to Senator Wallace's office. He received the information that Joseph Coolidge was on the warpath with a combination of anger and perverse pleasure.

When this was over, he and his family would be disgraced, and he would be driven from office. Things would be simpler if they could recover Lance's body. He was confident that being shot and plunging into fast-moving frigid water was not survivable. With the recovery of his body and the envelope or lack thereof, they could assume it had been destroyed in the river.

The search was into its third day, and he couldn't keep the teams in there when Lance was presumed to have drowned.

He called Brad on the secure sat phone.

"Nothing yet" was the reply to his question. "How long do you want us to keep looking? He hasn't surfaced and things are freezing up tight. If he is found in the spring, there won't be much left."

Wallace relayed the information about Joseph's investigation. "One more day and we'll pull you out."

———— • ————

"Roger that." Brad palmed the antenna down. He called a halt to the search and brought both teams together. Three days of blowing snow and cold and still not a trace—no tracks, nothing. They had been up and down the river, checking every nook and cranny and every logjam and eddy.

Brad joined the men huddled around a blazing fire by the river. "Well, boys," he began, "we stick to this for one more day, and then we're pulling our freight."

Romey nodded in agreement. The group was chiselled down with varying degrees of shadow and beard that had grown in the past few days. Their hair was damp and wild. They looked like what they were—elite fighting men who got tougher as things got harder.

"I don't want tomorrow to be the kind of wrap-up day where people get lazy, so stay sharp. Act like it's day one! We've been up and down this river, and I don't see any point in going farther downstream. However, we will push downstream for the rest of today just to be safe. Tomorrow, we send two men from each team deep into the woods, post one at five hundred meters and one at a full click. Then we will make grid pattern and work our way back upstream. We'll meet where Leadbeater tapped Coolidge and make camp there tomorrow night. Then we catch our bird home the next morning. Questions?"

The orders were straightforward, and everyone moved out.

18

"Lance … Lance, they're coming." The soft voice faded away. It was like trying to catch a vapour of breath in your hand on a cold day. Lingering for a moment, then filtering away as though it had never been.

It was cold! Nothing seemed real. He had tumbled beneath the waterfall until his breath had been beaten from his body. Trying to break free from its iron grip, he had fought with every ounce of strength he had, but his strength began to fail. For the first time in his life, Lance tasted complete and utter defeat.

"Lance, they are coming!" Somehow, he was on the riverbank, clutching the smooth waterworn wall that guided the flow into that terrible chute. Lance looked up, and his head began to swirl. He clutched at the wall, even more desperately.

For a time, he was unaware of much, but slowly, rational thought began to creep in. His legs were dangling in the river; his torso and head were on the small rocky outcropping he clung to. He had no idea who had shot him or why, but he knew with desperate certainty that if he did not get warm and dry, none of that would matter. He was tempted to just lie here. There appeared to be some dry wood, higher on the ledge. Perhaps he could get a fire going. He pulled himself up until his whole body was fully on the ledge. He looked up again and could see clearly to the top. Through the fog of semi-consciousness, he realized that if his enemy came upon him here, he was a dead man.

He reached into the pile of sticks. They were dry, but he was already losing the feeling in his hands. That would not do. Without the use of his hands, he wouldn't be able to climb out of here. He felt for his knife. Amazingly, it was still there at his side. The flint around his neck was in place also. He clumsily unzipped his pocket and found the Abolition of Man. It was soaked through, of course. He appreciated the irony of the moment.

Lance focused on finding a crevice or a crack he could grasp to make his way to the top. He was in one of nature's perfect prisons—a half circle with this little ledge at its center. He couldn't see around the corner. He strained but his feet slipped, and he almost ended up back in the water. Then he remembered the voice. They're coming … a man's voice, urgent but quiet, almost a whisper. Lance knew he couldn't stay here. Whoever "they" were wanted him dead. For now, it was survive. Survive at all costs. He dared not think about his wound. The cold water had numbed the injury, and all he felt was a dull throb that seemed to keep pace with the drum of the waterfall. He gathered as many sticks as he could tuck inside his jacket. Taking one last look above, he lowered himself back into the water.

The current clutched him immediately, pulling him around the corner. He could see another smooth, rocky outcropping maybe thirty-five metres downstream, but the current would probably carry him on past. As he ducked his head underwater, his body responded by lowering his heart rate and recirculating blood back into his limbs, allowing him to regain control of his motor skills. Under the power of several tremendous strokes and kicks, his hand struck gravel. With a great heave he lay gasping on the bank.

The shelf of bedrock had been worn smooth by the current and was wet and slippery from the churning of the river. He must move immediately. The bar was barely fifteen feet across, and he was facing another smooth wall—much shorter than the one that plunged into the waterfall. Here too, he would be visible from above.

He might have used his one and only get out of jail free card and it appeared he was no better off. The ground was littered with sticks and driftwood that had been trapped during high water. This place would be a deathtrap in the spring. There was a slight crack in the wall off to the left on the upstream side of the little cove, under a natural overhang. It looked like a place to get out of the wind, and maybe it was wide enough to hide in. He decided he would let the deck play out here. He wasn't getting back into that water a third time.

As he got closer, he realized the crack was wider than it had first appeared. He backed into it until his head came up short, contacting a low shelf. For the moment, he was out of the wind. Reaching behind, he expected to feel a wall but there was nothing. Puzzled, he turned and found himself looking into a small cave, with a slight downward grade. He ducked his head and pushed his way forward. With his body now blocking most of the entrance, he couldn't see anything in front of him. His head came clear of the overhanging shelf. This caused him to lose his footing. Suddenly, he fell forward, dropping a few feet down into a lower, secondary cave. He groaned in pain, the fall reminding him again, that he'd been shot.

As his eyes adjusted to the darkness, he saw that the cave was round, hollowed out by millennia of erosion. It was only about six by six, just high enough for him to stand. The base was littered with debris—sticks and driftwood on a sandy bottom. He could hear Uncle Joseph's voice: You would not have frozen to death. The phrase kept repeating itself in his brain. He was out of the wind, and he was alive, but he was still scared. He had never been this cold. He knew his core temperature was dangerously low and that if he didn't warm up soon, he would die.

Fumbling into his jacket, he found the ziplock bag with the Vaseline-coated cotton balls. Whatever advantage he had gained from the dunk under water, the effect was lost now. His hands felt like clubs. With his elbows, he pulled some sticks into the middle of the cave. With huge effort, he pulled the leather strap to which his flint was attached from around his neck. Beating his hands together, he then slid them down inside his crotch. Repeating this cycle several times, he was finally able to free his knife and open the bag of cotton balls with it.

Although his vision was beginning to blur, he was also starting to warm up. Beyond exhausted, he wanted so badly to lie down for just for a minute. Suddenly, his eyes flared open. Deep in the recesses of his brain he knew that would be the wrong thing to do. No one would ever find him here, and in the spring the sand and gravel would churn his bones into a fine dust. He swayed like a drunken man, placing his hands inside his pants again and then shaking them vigorously.

On the fourth attempt, a spark touched the cotton, and it flamed up. Almost crying with pain Lance pulled some of the sticks closer and they caught with the telltale crack. The fire took hold, he toppled over, and darkness seized him again. Outside, the river made a dull noise as it raced past. The wind howled, and the sky grew dark threatening more snow. The fire took hold for only a few precious minutes but then sputtered out, and the silent figure lay where it had fallen.

———— • ————

They were carrying him again, the old ones, in that blanket. Where are they taking me? He could hear their subdued murmurs—they were talking about him, he was sure of that. But he couldn't make out the language—the language was foreign and indistinct … definitely a Native American tongue. He could smell their bodies—sweat mixed with pine and wood smoke.

The blanket was warm, and his body melted into it; he could feel himself drifting off as he was gently carried along. Suddenly, there was a shout and the sound of a rifle shot. He was once again standing at the edge of the river. He saw the bullet leaving his body as if through a high-powered camera lens zooming in, and followed the bullet back to the barrel. As clear as day, he saw the shooter's eye in the scope, the other wide, glinting in the morning light. Then, his whole face, as his head came away from the rifle, his cheek resting in its place, momentarily, then firing, all in one smooth motion.

The scene was reversing itself again and the bullet came rushing towards him. This time it was faster than his gaze could follow. He moved his head sharply to avoid it and it came up against something hard and his eyes fluttered open. There was the tunnel right there in front of him—Is it the one people claim to see just before their death? Lance felt panic. Am I wrong about life after death? Is there something on the other side? Am I ready?

He stared at the light for a long time and his mind slowly came into focus. He was lying on his back, looking up at the entrance to his small cave. He lifted a feeble hand towards the light—a terrible weakness was upon him. His teeth were chattering, and the little fire had gone out. How long had he been lying here? Hours? Days? He knew not. The fire had been almost smokeless, and the little smoke it produced swirled up to the entrance of the cave and was caught and dispersed by the constant breeze and the river mist.

———— • ————

Several hours after Lance lost consciousness, Brad had taken a long look down into the cove. From his vantage point, the cove was empty except for a few bits of debris here and there. But the cliff walls looked smooth and unassailable. Through his binoculars, he studied the water for any evidence of the body. There was a moment when a wisp of smoke drifted past the lens. Brad moved the binoculars back and forth, momentarily excited. There was a good bit of mist swirled around this spot and as he adjusted the focus, Brad realized he'd mistaken it for smoke, or so he thought. It's the little things.

For the moment, Lance was safe. The ashes that had been his fire were near his head, so he rolled on his side, hoping to blow the embers back to life. A stab of pain from his wound made itself known as he blew feebly on the coals, but there were no embers left. He had to get the fire going again. His clothes were damp and one of the legs of his wool pants had frozen to the ground. He managed to pull it free. How many times would he be thankful for wool? While still wet and frozen it retained some of his body heat. He found one of the cotton balls that had fallen out of the baggie and dragged some small pieces of wood closer. As earlier, it took him several tries to drop a spark into it and a tiny flame snaked up. Dropping some slivers on, when they took, he added larger pieces as well. Reaching around the cave, he gathered a small bundle of wood. Had it not been within reach, there was no way he could have mustered the strength to stand or even crawl. He gingerly fed the fire, before passing out again.

When next he awoke, it was pitch-dark, and he was in the grip of a panic attack. Even in the cold, he was sweating, and his breathing was shallow. In the darkness, a tiny glow, a minute ember still clung to life. Lance blew on it frantically, and it glowed brighter. His hands felt around for his bundle, and he was able to easily rekindle the fire this time. Once the fire was burning brightly again and his momentary panic was gone, he noticed he was warm. This little cave retained a phenomenal amount of heat.

He thought of the Anasazi peoples from the Four Corners country. He had climbed high up into those houses that they called "cliff dwellings". Long ago, in a forgotten time, they had carved deep circles into the cave floors. These "kivas" as they were called were a marvel of sixth or seventh century engineering. These ancients built a technical and complicated "machine", as his tour guide had called it. At an elevation of eight thousand feet, on cold winter nights, the kiva would hold the heat from a one-hour fire until morning. This saved the precious and dwindling resource of wood. Perhaps the rock that this cave had been naturally carved from had those same properties.

In the flickering firelight, Lance began to undress slowly. He needed to determine how badly he'd been injured and administer some first aid as best he could.

He first set aside the still damp Abolition of Man. Struggling, he managed to get his jacket off. It didn't appear that his limbs had been affected but the pain was intense. The downside to being warm was that the numbing effect was gone, and the shock had worn off. The full weight of pain hit him. The cloth from his shirt, sweater, and merino wool underlayer had been forced into the wound by the bullet. On his first attempt to pull it away, he realized there was a lot of cloth in the wound.

It might work as a sort of bandage, but he knew better—the cloth needed to come out, or infection could set in. He managed to get his shirt off. Unbuttoning his long underwear, he was able slip them down to his waist. He added a few more sticks to the fire so he could see better.

He was bleeding again, the warm blood trickling down his chest and back. That was a good sign. It meant that most likely, the bullet had gone clean through. In the dim light, he could only see blood on his left side and what appeared to be the wound high up, just under his collar bone. He prodded, gingerly finding bits of cloth and pulling them out. This caused even more bleeding, but he persisted until he found no more. He then felt for the exit wound. It was higher up tearing through the flesh of his trapezius muscle, because the shooter had been slightly below him and he'd made that quick drop to his knees. The trajectory of the bullet angled upward, missing the bone, and exiting at an even higher point. He ascertained that it hadn't broken any bones or clipped his lung.

His major concern was blood loss and infection. He had nothing with which to bathe the wound, so he tore out a couple of pages of the book and used them as a cloth. Once he had wiped the area down, he stuffed some of the paper into the wound and applied pressure, first the front and then the back, by pushing himself against the wall of the cave. Within a few minutes, the bleeding slowed. Making more wadding, he began stuffing the entrance wound. When he was too exhausted to do more, he lay down, pulled his jacket over himself, and, using his sweater for a pillow, fell asleep.

When he awoke, a grey light filtered through the cave opening. The fire had gone out again, but his clothes were dry. Somewhere in his delirium he had put his shirt back on. He carefully removed his shirt, feeling the bite of cold air against his bare skin. He checked his wound; the wading appeared to be holding. He pulled his underwear up, buttoning it and then his shirt. The sweater and jacket took more time to struggle into.

His thirst was desperate now. He needed to somehow get to the river. Twice he tried to stand up but both times his head swam, and he felt like he was going to vomit, so he crawled.

Peering out into the storm at the swirling snow, he withdrew a condom from his pocket. Tearing open the package, he tossed the wrapper aside. When he pushed forward into the cold, he realized just how fortunate he had been. It was bitterly cold.

It was roughly midday, but which day? He couldn't be sure; factoring in his wound and judging by his thirst, he had probably been in the cave for two days. Even in his compromised state, years of conditioning forced him to methodically survey his environment as soon as his head cleared the cave. He quickly realized the cave was a few feet inside the crack and the crack itself was obscured by a jut of the cliff wall. It would be impossible to see from above. Due to the slickness of the walls, the position of the overhang and the slight right angle provided an optical illusion that the wall was unbroken. In fact, from the far side of the little cove, it had appeared as no more than a tiny spot to get out of the wind.

After a few minutes looking around to be sure he was unseen, Lance crawled out onto the slippery shelf. Snow had built up on the back cliff wall where the constant splashing of the river hadn't melted it away. Crawling the few feet to the river, he blew the condom open like a balloon, filling it with water. He tied it shut and scavenged sticks, pushing them ahead of him, as he crawled towards the shelter of his cave.

He knew that if he was caught out here, there would be no way he could fight back. Hiding was his best option. He needed time to heal and recover enough strength to make his way out. And he could leave no tracks for his pursuers to follow.

Even this small task fatigued him. He was shivering again and knew that his core temperature had dropped from the frigid plunge in the river. It would take a few days for his body to reset its internal thermostat—and that was with care, fluids, and nutrition. Between his body temperature and significant blood loss, he was incredibly weak.

Part of a small evergreen tree had been snapped by the current and tossed up on the shore. The two remaining branches looked like the out-stretched arms of a dead man. The thought and the cold made him shudder. He knew the tree was too green to burn, and if it did, all it would generate was smoke and a lot of it. He had crawled a few feet before his mind made a connection—it was from a pine tree! He contemplated retrieving it, but he was so fatigued, he swayed on all fours, calculating its value versus the energy it would take to salvage it.

His hands were getting heavy again and he dared not stay out in this cold much longer. Laying down the water-condom, he crawled to where the pine tree remnant was, the wind picking up. The branch was a bit longer and thicker than he had thought, and part of it was stuck in the snow. On his first attempt, it held fast, and for a moment he considered abandoning the idea. But he gave another good pull, and it came free.

His head was swimming again. There would be signs of its dislodging, but he trusted the falling snow to cover it. It took him well over twenty minutes to push the sticks, the condom and the log back to the cave. He tumbled back into his warm little shelter, thoroughly exhausted.

He squeezed some water from the condom into his mouth. It trickled down his throat, quenching the fire of his thirst. The condom held a pint of water, and he drank half of it. Finally satisfied, he tied it off and placed it away from the fire against the wall. He lay down again, and this time, rather than passing out, he relaxed and fell asleep. This became his cycle throughout the rest of the day and into the night—sleep heavily, drink, and sleep some more.

———— • ————

By the following morning, he was feeling less foggy and even a little stronger, but he still didn't want to chance standing up. A ravenous hunger was upon him. This was a good sign. Pulling the pine branch closer, he removed some of the pine needles and placed them inside one of the condoms. When he had a good number, he put it aside. With his knife, he peeled the bark back and scraped the mantle underneath and began eating the fibrous strands. It was full of precious nutrients, and he decided the effort to bring the log in had been worth it. Taking time to chew thoroughly before swallowing, he followed each with a sip of water.

Cutting three small branches off, he squared off the ends and fashioned a crude tripod, lashing them together with a piece of paracord from his knife handle. He then cut and peeled three sticks about three inches long with varying circumferences, none more than half an inch. After carefully pouring the remaining water into the condom with the pine needles, he pushed the sticks into the top, leaving the ends sticking out. This would allow steam to pass through. Using another strip of paracord, he tied the top of the condom tightly under the lip and around the sticks. He then made another pass with the cord around the top of the condom and tied it to the center of the tripod so it hung down between the braces.

Lance added small bits of wood to the fire and placed the tripod over it with the condom about a foot above the flames. If he could keep the flames from reaching the condom itself, the heat would slowly boil the water, releasing much needed vitamins into the pine needle tea. At this high elevation, water came to a boil slowly, so he settled in to wait, nibbling on more of the mantle, while focusing on keeping the fire burning.

After a few minutes he began anticipating the warm drink, and it dawned on him that it would be too hot to handle.

Removing his boot, he took off his thick wool sock. The smell was strong, so he removed both boots to give his feet some air. He folded the sock down and placed it with its mate next to the fire. He reached for the book, hoping to read a little, but it had been exposed to too much water, and there wasn't much he could make out.

He would have to find a way to climb out of this place, avoid his enemy or enemies, whoever they were, and make it to safety. The problem was that his wound was in a place where he couldn't bind it. Putting it in a sling was out of the question because he would need his arm to climb and fight if necessary. That was tomorrow's problem. For now, he would rest.

He had eaten a little something and when his pine needle tea was boiling lightly, he gingerly removed it from the tripod, slid it into the sock, and enjoyed his warm drink. A friendly fire was there for comfort. These small luxuries gave him hope—hope that he would survive, hope that he would see Lynette, his mother, and Uncle Joseph again …. But a dark hope stirred in him as well—the hope that he would come face to face with the enemy that had attacked him without warning or provocation.

He sipped the tea until it was all gone. Evening came quickly and the silent figure in the cave next to a raging river slept silently, as the wind blew and the snow piled up outside. Tomorrow would mark the fourth day since he'd been shot.

———— • ————

The snow continued to come down, and the little corner of wilderness was beginning to fill up with people. The two SEAL teams were stirring, Lynette and Daryl had arrived at their main line cabin, and Ben and Wes were closing the distance fast, expecting to be at Lance's main camp by the end of the day.

In the cave, Lance was mentally preparing for the day and the days ahead. He ate what little of the pine mantle was left, gathered up his meager belongings, and slowly lifted himself to a standing position. He was still weak, but he didn't feel nauseated, and for that he was thankful. Stacking the few remaining pieces of wood, he had the makings of a fire ready in case he needed to return.

He arranged it so he would only need to drop a few sparks into the kindling to get it going.

Remembering the light and tunnel he had seen during his first day in the cave, he did something he had not done since childhood. He lifted a feeble prayer towards heaven. "God, Lord, whoever you are … if you're real, I could sure use some help here." He felt a little better and a little silly.

For a moment, the light at the entrance to the cave dimmed slightly and his head snapped up, but no one was there.

"Okay," he said, nodding his head in affirmation. "Okay, let's go."

As soon as he stepped out of the cave, he noticed that it was maybe six or seven degrees warmer; still below freezing but not nearly as bad.

He carefully looked about before going down to the water to drink as much as he could. A lot of people think you can eat snow, but the truth is you need to melt it first, or it will speed up hypothermia. The energy it takes the body to convert it to liquid is a wash. At the water's edge he filled another condom to carry in one of his large front pockets.

Looking for an escape from the cove, he decided that the water was too great a risk and therefore not an option at this point. The walls were sheer and slick, although the angle above the little overhang held some promise. It was a broken cliff wall and could be climbable: if you could get up the first fifteen feet, the final fifty feet or so were doable. But as far as he could see, there was no humanly possible way to get there. There has to be a way.

Trying to find a handhold, he felt his way along the wall—thinking maybe there was something he couldn't see but could feel. He gave up after a while; it was smooth like marble, and his fingers found nothing. Guarding his left arm, he focused on preserving the little strength he had, as well as keeping the wound from bleeding again. After pacing back and forth like a caged wolf, examining the cliff from every angle, he began to get frustrated. It seemed a cruel joke to have lived this long only to be trapped by the very thing that had saved him.

He went to the river for another drink. Scooping the water up with his hands, leaning in close to the river, he was able to see around the corner downstream. Just around the corner, about eight feet up, was a broken lip of rock that hung out over the water. What lay beyond it or above it he had no idea. What lay beneath was the terrible churning monster that roared at him constantly. The river narrowed there even more and appeared to go through several more chutes. He was certain he could not survive the water again, and there was zero chance he would be lucky enough to find another sheltered spot that had all the ingredients for survival.

Looking to the heavens again, he whispered a silent prayer for help. No response.

Lance could see what he had to do—run fifteen feet across the cove and launch himself around that blind corner. It wasn't just the distance that was so challenging—he also had to propel himself upwards to reach the lip of the cliff. That meant make a slight turn in the air, grab on, and pull himself up. To miss would almost certainly mean death. Had he been in perfect health on a clear day, with dry ground, he was confident he could make that jump. But here, now, wounded—it was a long shot at best, and he knew it.

He looked around a last time, hoping another option would present itself.

He walked to the place he would launch from. His foot would need to go slightly into the water. He poked the spot with a stick—it was solid. How am I going to make this work? He was fatigued just walking around. He had to act or miss this window of opportunity, as he was growing weaker with each moment. Taking one last look to ensure his knife was tight in its sheath, he did several squats to limber up his legs.

His first few steps were a stumbling run, but he dug his toes in and pushed himself forward. Because of those first few missteps he was hardly at top speed when he drove his foot hard into the spot just inside the waterline and jumped. He tried to make the slight turn in the air but realized he was going to miss. Instinctively his left arm reached out, and at the last second, his fingers caught the edge of the lip. They slid a few inches before his grip held, and his body swung around, coming up hard against the canyon wall.

For a long moment, he dangled above the river, holding on with his wounded arm, every tendon straining. The wound tore open again as he hung there. Flinging his good arm up, he was able to grab on with both hands. Scrambling, pulling, and pushing with his feet, he lifted himself onto the ledge.

There he lay on his back panting and gasping for air. His hands and arms were numb, but he was alive. He knew now that he would not be returning to the cave.

As his breathing began to settle, he sat up and looked around. The slope was steep but spotted here and there with trees, and he knew he could make it to the top. With a momentary pang, he realized he couldn't see the cove from here. It was always hard leaving a place that had offered safety and security, but that is the nature of life. We move on into the unknown and trust in the gods or fate or whatever it is.

He nodded and looked up into the sky as a few flakes fell into his eyes. "I guess I owe you one."

The slope was steeper than he had expected, and he needed to rest every few feet. His plan was to reach the top, find another place to rest, and check his wound. The slope had several patches of snow and places where grass had been exposed by the wind.

He spotted a whitish plant off to his right among some dried grass. Recognizing it, he gathered some up. It was yarrow, easily mistaken for a weed, as it grows wild just about everywhere. It was an old-world plant that flourished in the new and had several medicinal uses, good for both fever and infection. Yarrow had been used as a coagulant for battlefield injuries since the days of Alexander the Great.

When he finally made the top, there wasn't much to see, except more trees and forest and a long way to go. He looked back. It had taken him almost an hour to make a short distance. His gaze followed the trail he had taken. There was a fair bit of sign from his climb, but there was nothing he could do about it.

A cold shiver of awareness came over him—in his weakness and desperation he had completely forgotten to check the far bank. It was a sheer cliff on that side and heavily treed on the top. It was an unlikely place to approach but had someone been there he would have been within range of their gun the whole time.

He still had no clue as to who had shot him or why, although he could still picture the face from his dream, but that was nonsense, just a figment of his imagination. Still, it was clear and distinct—he'd watch for that face, this he knew.

Lance moved away from the edge and made his way into the trees to rest. How long he had been in the cave he couldn't be sure, but he guessed two or maybe three days.

Who shot me?

If the shot was an accident by a trigger-happy hunter, he'll be long gone.

Should I head back to camp, since everything I need is there?

Lance knew if it was a deliberate attempt on his life, he could not go back to his camp.

Although it had stopped snowing briefly during his ascent, the snow was falling again. Calculating the distance, he guessed that in his current condition it would take a day or two to get to the road. Pushing the logistics out of his mind, he took a few tentative steps forward, thinking only of his next small goal. It's the small things that make the big things happen, he told himself.

The rocky outcropping about forty yards away would be his first goal. Taking a long drink of water before he moved, he chose his route with care, leaving as few tracks as possible and weaving among the trees for cover. Pausing regularly to listen and look around, he was skirting the edge of a low outcropping when he saw impressions under the snow! The snow had filled in the tracks, but it was a clear zigzag pattern. He recognized it for what it was—a search.

You can tell a lot about man or beast by the trail they leave, and this one was familiar. It was the kind of route he would have taken, had he been on the same task. He estimated that the tracks had been made yesterday. Whoever the searcher was, he was making his way downstream. The cave had been on the opposite side of the stream from where he had gone in, and now Lance was going upstream, working his way back to that spot. Alert for danger, he walked on the edge of a low rocky outcropping, leaving no tracks. It was only about twenty yards across. Hunched over, it was high enough to obscure his passing from the far rim. When he rounded the far side, he had a perfect view of his little cove.

He located the spot where Brad had knelt and watched the area on that first day. The tracks were sheltered here, the outcropping acting like a wind-break. That he had remained there for some time watching was obvious. He had shifted his position several times and Lance counted his lucky stars once again. The crack and the cave were concealed perfectly. One would have to be considerably lower down to see it and even then, it would not be obvious. How long have the wind and the water been preparing the perfect place just for me?

The snow was deeper farther away from the cliff, and he could make out what looked like another trail of tracks approaching from a different angle. Apparently, there had been a concentrated effort to find him. Lance abandoned his accidental hunter scenario, assuming the worst and knowing he needed to avoid another encounter.

Did someone follow me, or did they know where I was going to be? I was only specific at the sheriff's office. He remembered his wild dream and the sound of a helicopter. Could it have been more than a dream? What am I actually up against? Still incredibly weak, now more than ever he had to think—to figure out how to get back without being seen and how to attend to his wound. He needed water and if possible, something to eat along the way. Familiar with most of the vegetation in these woods, he was confident he could sustain himself if his strength held.

What he needed now was another hole to crawl into until dark. Hopefully, he could gather something to eat and travel only at night to avoid detection. He would also need a weapon.

Staying concealed had served him well—his enemies had probably presumed he'd drowned. Will my pursuers become complacent as the days wear on? He would behave as though it was the first day.

———— • ————

Lance was fifty yards farther up the canyon edge when he found what he was looking for—a small stream only a few inches wide, originating in the forest and dribbling slowly over the cliff edge. He took a few steps in the stream and had only gone a few yards when in a sheltered spot, he found a distinct boot print. It was a size ten or eleven and judging by the tread, military issue. These days you could order something similar online, so he didn't want to read too much into it. Nevertheless, he looked warily in the direction the tracks took.

His own tracks could not be seen—the stream was just wide enough to conceal them in the slow-moving water.

After another forty yards, he emerged warily on the edge of a small clearing. It was only twenty yards across, but it meant being exposed for a time, and that didn't sit well with him. He couldn't move quickly, so he would need to be hyperalert about his foot placement. The small spark of adrenalin in response to potential danger was wearing off now. It felt like his boots were full of cement. He estimated that the crossing would take ten minutes with tension building in his system as he braced for a shout or a shot.

Once inside the trees on the far side, he started hunting for a place to rest. When he found it, it wasn't much—a small log across the stream created a bridge. He leaned against the tree from which the log had broken. Several rosebushes with shriveled hips on them grew along the banks, and he picked several handfuls and ate them, seeds and all, storing more in his pocket.

He was hoping that the little stream wound back up towards the lake he had seen, sending him in the correct direction. But so far it hadn't played out that way. He had travelled approximately a hundred yards from the cliffs' edge. He wanted to check his wound but decided to find a secure place where he could take time to dress it again. After permitting himself fifteen minutes to rest, he began working his way upstream once again. There were places where it was choked with vegetation, and he had to push his way through. Here and there he collected a few more rose hips. He was drinking constantly from the stream and had filled another condom with water. He knew that streams could hold bacteria, because they often flowed out of beaver ponds with muskrats and ducks. He certainly couldn't afford to get sick on top of everything else, but he needed to stay hydrated, so he took his chances.

The stream wound in and out of small open areas and he crossed each one with care. Suddenly he came upon tracks again. These were different—same boot tread design but a much larger track. This was one big man and that made two—both wearing similar footwear. He had no illusions now. He had been tracked by a group of men who might still be on his trail. But how many? These tracks had been made around the same time as the last ones and if they were moving in a skirmish line, he could expect another set out another hundred yards.

Ten yards on, he found another set of tracks—two sets really. He found where a man had gone out at a fast pace and back on his excursion in the direction of Lance's camp. This was a much smaller track, but the stride had been steady in both directions. He could not make out any details of the tread in these tracks as they were filled with snow.

Checking his back trail, Lance was relieved to see there was little evidence of his passing. He found a couple of Oregon grape bushes with some berries still on them. He ate some and stored some. Farther along he came across some velvet dock, or great mullein, as some people called it. It was a heavily leafed plant with a fuzzy top that looked like an anorexic stalk of corn. He gathered the seeds, storing them in a different pocket. Tossed into a body of water, they would stun any fish nearby, and you could gather them by hand. It was illegal, but he wouldn't let that minor technicality prevent him from eating. The native girls also used it as rouge, rubbing it on their cheeks, keeping them red and irritated for a time. The leaves had medicinal and nutritional properties, so Lance picked a few handfuls, stuffing them into a pocket.

Three men, all working together!

He was in deep trouble. His objective for today was to get beyond the skirmish line and find a place to wait out the rest of the day. He would make a wide circle that would take him to the lake. From there, he would push towards the trailhead where he had been shot, cross the river just where he had intended to that first morning. He could avoid his camp but hopefully strike the logging road and make his way out.

He estimated that he'd make it to the lake by tonight and after another day reach the vicinity of his camp.

———— • ————

It was midday, and Lance knew he needed to keep moving. At times, the world spun, and he had to stop and steady himself. Keeping his footprints in the stream, he found the next set of prints where he expected—a hundred yards out. Again, there was no distinct pattern, as the tracks were half full of snow. He found the fourth set at about two in the afternoon. He had covered the four hundred yards slowly and methodically.

His experience and instinct told him this four-man team had been sent to kill him. He was sure of it. When he had gone another two hundred yards with no more tracks, his suspicions were confirmed. Now beyond their perimeter, he could get some rest. He chose a spot where several trees had blown down across some large boulders left over from the ice age. They formed a natural lean-to, which would keep him out of the wind. He went to work, using boughs and branches to fill the cracks. He finished it by piling snow on, which sealed it up tight.

Once inside, he brushed away the snow that had filtered in. He had gathered some birch bark while walking. Snapping off several branches from the underside of the roof, he soon had a small stack of firewood. It was mid-afternoon by the time the shelter was complete. It wasn't as good as the cave, but at least he would be out of the wind. He would chance a small fire at dusk before striking out.

His wound throbbed steadily but hadn't bled for several hours. He decided it would have to wait. As he thought about it, the story of the yarrow came back to him. As the fable goes, Achilles's mother had dipped him in a potion made from yarrow as an infant making him immortal. Like all myths, it had some basis in truth. He took the time to remove his coat, shirt, and long underwear and after chewing some of the bitter yarrow into a poultice, he applied it to his wound.

He was whittling a short spear when weariness overcame him, and sleep came unbidden.

19

Preach was glad this was their last day. There was absolutely no way Coolidge could have survived this long. He knew Brad was relentless, but he had had enough. Four days of searching and not a trace. Still, he was a professional and focused his attention on staying strong and alert. He was out at the five-hundred-meter mark, carefully working his way back up the river.

As he was crossing a small stream, something alerted his subconscious but he took a few more steps before pausing to look around. Over the years, he had learned to trust these nagging notifications. Nothing seemed out of place. He heard nothing, smelled nothing, yet still he waited. What is it? He was looking back in the direction he had come from when he spotted it—a glimmer just on the edge of the stream. He had almost missed it. Something had caused water to splash up on the snow. It was as small as a dime. Sliding off his glove, he reached down and flicked it loose. No tracks, so maybe a bird had caused it and then taken off.

The stream continued through the trees, and he traced its pattern, but the bush was thick, and he couldn't see far. He followed the stream for a few more meters, but there were no more signs. There was almost no chance a person or beast could cover frozen ground without leaving some kind of sign. He turned to resume his original course when he realized that every time he had stepped into the water, his tracks were invisible. Could a wounded man, four days after leaving no sign, appear here in the deepest, darkest part of the forest out of nowhere?

He recalled the stories he'd heard about Lance Coolidge. In the service, few stories need to be embellished. Often truth is stranger than fiction and there was no doubt a mystique surrounded Lance. Preach had sloughed off the stories about Lance, but Brad continued to present them as reality to the men. He clearly both hated and respected the man at the same time. Maybe it was his desire for glory—not wanting to miss the chance to be the one to take Lance's scalp.

Preach decided to search farther upstream. He had only gone a few more steps when he spotted another splash—this one a little more distinct and a little larger. Then just a hint of a track—the edge of a boot. It was fresh—no more than an hour old. He found himself noisily brushing up against trees with his pack as the forest closed in around the stream and he decided to remove it.

When he found a spot in the stream where he could stand and leave no tracks of his own, he hung his pack and his rifle quietly from a branch on the far side of a tree. He then slid his pistol from its holster.

In another hundred meters, the tracks went up a slight embankment, as though a ghost had suddenly materialized.

He shuddered, and a foreboding swept over him. Arwa-Rue—the Ghost Spirit.

"Get out!" A voice rang in his head. For a moment he considered ducking back the way he had come, but he caught himself and smiled.

You gotta stop listening to those stories, he thought to himself.

Just ahead was a crude shelter.

So, this is how he's been surviving! But how did he avoid detection for so long?

Preach's confidence returned as he considered the situation. He decided not to radio the others, as it could alert Lance. He would most likely have a gun. Anticipation came over him—he would be known as the man who killed Lance Coolidge, and even better, he would snatch the glory from Beats.

It gave him a queer delight, picturing himself reporting it to the group and seeing the look on Brad's face. The shelter itself would keep him out of sight and muffle his approach. He could see the edge of the small access opening to the shelter. If he angled up on it carefully, he could be at the entrance and with luck catch Lance by surprise. He looked beyond the shelter for tracks. There were none, and he was certain Lance was still inside. Nightfall was coming, and he wanted to catch that bird out of here. He took a gentle step forward.

———— • ————

"Lance!" An urgent voice echoed inside his head. He snapped awake, disoriented, thinking he was still in the cave. Then the jump, the climb, the traverse along the stream, all came together in his brain in an instant. What, who awakened me? How long have I slept? It was darker out. Listening intently, he could hear only the gurgling stream. He waited a few more moments, then grabbed the little spear he'd made and leaned it beside the entrance. He decided to have a quick look around and get some more water before dark.

He was down on all fours when his head cleared the opening. Preach had closed the gap and was only feet away. He lunged forward and swung a vicious kick. Lance saw it coming and tried rolling away, but the boot thudded off his skull. He sprawled on his back, half in and out of the shelter. Preach was on him instantly, knee on his chest and gun pointed at his face.

"Where is it?" Preach demanded.

Lance was puzzled and said nothing, anger boiling up inside him.

Roughly, Preach started patting him down. Finding the knife, he tossed it aside. Dragging him free of the shelter, he riffled through his pockets, finding remnants of the book. He tucked it back into his pocket and patted it gently.

"I'll leave that for you to read later."

Then he jerked him around onto his stomach and Lance grunted with pain. Preach paused his work.

"So Beats did get one into you." His malignant nature taking over, he started pressing here and there, and when he got to his shoulder, Lance gasped.

"Ah, there she is." Preach could see the roughed-up area of the jacket where the bullet had penetrated. "Lucky ... well, you were lucky!" With that he chuckled manically.

Emptying Lance's pockets, Preach tossed the mullein, yarrow, and berries aside.

"Big medicine?" he asked condescendingly, using the native term.

He flipped Lance over onto his back again, but this time Lance didn't give him the satisfaction of showing his pain.

Keeping the pistol trained on him, Preach peered into the shelter. There was nothing in there.

"No gun? Lose it in the river, did ya?"

Lance said nothing.

"Just you and that knife for four days? Damn, boy! They train us good, don't they?" He was animated. "You know, you done us proud. Being as how you're such a good man, I'll give you a couple of options. You tell me what happened to that envelope, and I'll go easy on you. What say ye, heathen?"

"Envelope?" Lance was genuinely confused.

Preach slapped him, a stinging blow across the face.

Lance struck out feebly but Preach brushed his arm aside and slapped him again. His nasty, sadistic streak bubbled to the surface, inflicting as much pain as possible.

"Seems like you Coolidge boys all die the same way—clueless and defenseless."

A strange light of awareness crept into Lance's eyes as he tried to understand what Preach was saying.

"Oh, that's right, you thought it was an accident. Oh, oh, I forgot. Shhh ... it's a secret." He laughed his sadistic laugh again. "If it wasn't for your brother, none of this would have happened. I'll ask you again: where is that damn envelope? We know that Cathy woman put it in your Jeep. Where is it?"

Cold fury consumed Lance, but he was helpless.

"You killed Kyle?" He was incredulous.

"Nah, that was Bellamy ... pretty slick work that's for sure. No one suspected a thing. Killed that Cathy woman as well. He screwed that one up, though. But thankfully we had you there to take the fall"—he paused for effect—"and here we are." Then quickly he pointed the gun in Lance's face again.

"I tell you where it is, and you kill me anyway, so what's the difference?"

"The difference is how you die." With that he slammed his boot against Lance's shoulder.

"Ahhhh!" Lance cried out. "Okay, okay! It's in the river; go get it yourself."

It was a double bluff since he had no idea what Preach was talking about. He was hoping Preach would realize he was unlikely to give in easily. What he desperately needed now was to buy some time. Keeping this guy talking was the best way.

"Hmm ... I don't know. 'Lying lips are an abomination to the Lord.'" With that he stepped on Lance again, pressing hard on his wound. Their eyes locked. Sensing the man's evil nature, Lance goaded him with his stare.

"You're a pussy!" Lance hissed. "You dishonor yourself, your country, and that uniform. You're as good as dead." He finished with a biblical quote of his own: "You lie in wait for your own blood."

His eyes were wide, and his teeth were bared against the pain, daring the other to break his will.

Enraged, Preach stomped down harder, and Lance made as if trying to escape. He rolled away from the shelter, but Preach viciously kicked him in the kidney. Lance gasped as pain shot through him. He rolled the other way, his head near the entrance to the shelter.

"Pussy!" Weakening, he was barely able to breathe out the word.

Preach stepped forward, raising his foot to find its mark on the shoulder again.

Lance weakly brushed his foot aside and gave a little laugh of his own as Preach stumbled slightly.

"Girly ...." Lance forced a smile, stretching his arms wide in a mock embrace. "Come on," he taunted. "You hit like a girl." His voice was thick with contempt.

Berserk now, Preach rushed forward, intent on maiming Lance, kicking hard at his head.

In one fluid motion, Lance struck out with his own leg, sweeping Preach's anchor leg.

The momentum carried him toward Lance. As Preach fell, Lance reached up and grabbing his handmade spear, drove it upwards with all the strength he had left. The spear pierced Preach's throat, lodging itself into his spinal cord, impaling him there. For a moment, they were eye to eye, a look of shock and horror on Preach's face. His body jerked convulsively once, and then the crazy light went out of his eyes forever.

Lance rolled him off and lay gasping, once again all his strength and energy spent.

After a few moments he was able to sit up. His body couldn't take much more.

When this man doesn't report in, a hornet's nest will erupt, and they will have my position narrowed down considerably. I need to move now!

But where to go?

They would have been all over his camp, so he was cut off from his supplies. Lance crawled over to Preach's body. His arms were sprawled out in both directions, his body ironically forming a cross, the spear protruding from his neck. It was such a crude weapon, reminding him that men had killed each other long before firearms were invented.

Searching his pockets, Lance found several energy bars, some dried fruit, magazines for his handgun and rifle, as well as a small first-aid and survival kit. He stripped him of his jacket and gloves as well. He immediately ate one of the energy bars while removing the knife from Preach's belt. One of his pants pockets contained a radio, which Lance recovered, turning it off for the time being.

It was almost dark now, and he was sure time was running out. Preach would have left his gear nearby, and it would make the difference between life and death if he could find it. Lance recovered his own knife and started casting about for Preach's pistol. It had landed in the snow, but he couldn't find it in the dim light. He decided to scramble about on his belly.

In the distance was the sound of a chopper. They could be here in moments! Did Preach signal them while he waited outside the shelter? He decided it was likely. The chopper was definitely coming closer. If it was equipped with infrared optics, he would be in big trouble. He could hide inside the shelter, but he didn't have the strength to move Preach and the body would already be increasing in temperature. He held still as the helicopter passed over, letting out a sigh of relief when it kept on going.

Hearing it circling in the distance, he was sure it would make another pass. He now had a sense of what he was dealing with and reluctantly decided to move deeper into the forest. He needed time to rest and think, but no such luxury would be afforded him now. First, he would simply try to make some distance, and after that he would start thinking in terms of concealment.

Remembering an uprooted evergreen tree, Lance backtracked down the stream, a hundred yards or so. He was going to try a "death jump" as they called it. It was a trick he had seen deer use. When they were wounded and being pushed, they would sometimes backtrack and jump into an uprooted tree. Concealing their tracks, they would jump again to the far side of the tree, costing the hunter valuable time trying to locate them. Keeping his steps in the water, he made his way carefully downstream.

With only the ambient light of the snow on this cloudy, dark evening, he passed right by the camouflaged pack and the rifle twice in a vain attempt to locate them. Exhaustion and fatigue wreaked havoc on his mind, and he focused only on escape. With a clearer mind he would have taken more time. He would always sacrifice stealth for gear.

Finding the spot, he made the jump. It was only four feet but when he landed, he took a few stumbling steps and managed not to fall. Then he made the second jump, landing clear of the tree on the far side. Walking downstream, keeping close to the tree, he stepped onto a birch log lying perpendicular to the evergreen and made another twenty yards before stepping into a small patch of spruce. Pushing his way through these, he began a wide sweep deeper into the forest, away from the river.

He was able to squeeze on the gloves, but the jacket was too small. It would be an extra layer of protection at night. He was munching on another energy bar now, his mind beginning to settle into the task at hand. Evade, escape, and survive.

From some unknown well of strength, he used the pain to focus on what needed to be done. He now had an even deeper motivation to live. He would find this Bellamy and kill him. He would kill everyone involved in this conspiracy! He would live, and they would die.

———— • ————

When you strip a man down, he's pretty fragile—no claws or teeth with which to devour his prey. But what that man still possesses is the powerful mind. It is the body's function to protect the mind, to sacrifice parts of itself if need be. But the mind, set upon a course of action, gifted with creativity and intuition, is what makes man the dominant species on the planet. Not just a little above the animals but towering above them. The crowning creation, endowed with a uniqueness that allows him to consider, explore, and create a thing before it is. The other side of that coin is that, as Bruce Lee said, "the body must be conditioned to do what the mind requires of it." Lance understood this. He also knew it wouldn't do to run aimlessly about. He would need to find a place to rest, think, and plan.

Several times he stopped, caught his breath, and waited for the veils that danced across the moon to lift—providing him with enough light to gain his bearings. He didn't want to walk in circles and end up back where he'd started or worse, end up trapped against the river. He had heard the helicopter leaving the area, and it gave him a general direction that helped. They would never leave a team member behind. By tomorrow morning at the latest, they would be on his trail. His plan was to push deep into the woods, hide when he could, run when that wasn't an option, and fight if need be.

For all his anger and desire to retaliate, he knew how lucky he'd been with this last attacker. He couldn't count on luck again, and he didn't have the strength to withstand another encounter. Now they would be more cautious and would probably kill him on sight. After all, they had originally shot him on sight without warning.

Lance had never pursued reputation, but he had natural skills that his uncle had trained and honed to maturity. They would find their man, and when they did, they would be angry. Then it would sink in that he had killed a SEAL team member with a stick—a home-made spear, the crudest of weapons. This would make them cautious. They knew who he was, and that was to his advantage. Their caution would make them careful, and careful meant slow. He would use the advantage to put some distance between them.

When he had made a few miles, he found a nest of boulders with a blown-down tree whose roots were exposed. In the glow of the moonlight, they looked like long, bony fingers stretching outwards. The place was out of the wind, with a slight hollow where the ground had been ripped up by the roots of the tree. These places often collected water and made for poor campsites. In this case, it was dry. He needed to warm up and would chance a fire, which would be hard to see except from the air. The breeze was blowing away from his last camp, where the rest of the team was likely to soon be, so the smoke wouldn't drift in that direction.

He quickly gathered some firewood and soon had a comfortable, friendly fire going. Within a few moments, his little nest of boulders was warming up. He chewed on some of the dried fruit. After taking a good half hour to rest, he built a crude lean-to in case it started to snow. He also put down some evergreen boughs to keep himself off the ground. It wasn't much, but he was utilizing the natural environment. His campsites were getting worse—a troubling trend. He was completely exhausted, and after feeding a few more sticks into the fire, he nestled under his small roof and covered his legs with the extra jacket, and within moments was asleep.

Lance slept a solid hour before the chill born of the flagging fire woke him. He fed it a few more sticks and dozed off again. The fire, sleep, and bit of food had really helped his morale. It would be a long night, but he would permit himself only three or four hours of rest and move out long before morning. Near the end of the third watch, he awoke.

He found himself fantasizing about his bed back home. With the fire going strong, he began shedding layers of clothing. Sitting bare-chested next to a fire in the middle of the woods, he imagined he must be quite the sight. A wild man pitted against a deadly enemy, wounded with his back to the wall, ready to snap and snarl. He imagined zooming in on Google Earth, locating this exact spot. In his mind's eye, the coordinates and elevation were in the bottom right of the screen. Similar to God's view, he reflected.

He had sensed a presence with him since first tumbling into the river—the voices, the sensation of being carried, the warnings and the shadow at the cave mouth. Lance frowned. If there is a creator, what interest would he have in me? Just one of billions of living beings, and how many billions or trillions have gone on before me?—including Kyle and Rachel. His mood darkened. Strangely, he didn't feel alone. Yet he had killed again—a wisp of guilt filtered into his conscience. Doesn't the Bible say, "Thou shalt not kill"? Are there exceptions for war and self-defense? He decided if there weren't, the system wasn't fair. The feeling lingered until he forced the dilemma from his mind.

His fingers went to his wound. It had scabbed up a little in the back but had bled again after the fight. There was no paper there. He found some of the wadding in his shirt pocket and extracted pieces from the wound itself. He sniffed them—the odor was a combination of old and fresh blood, but he could detect no infection thankfully.

He rotated his arm slowly and although it was sore, he had full rotation in the shoulder.

A rogue breeze found a devious path through the boulders, and he shivered, drawing closer to the flames. It hurt like a bugger when he cleaned the wound with alcohol pads. He then applied a generous amount of disinfecting ointment. Applying a large bandage where the bullet had gone in under his collarbone, he secured it with tape. He did a much sloppier job with the exit wound, as it was hard to reach. Donning his clothing, he restocked the fire and slept once more. The wind danced lightly around the boulders, wafting the smoke away as it rose above the rocks.

A few hundred yards away, an old coyote lifted his nose to the wind. The smoke disturbed him, but the other smell on the breeze permeating his sensitive nostrils was frightening. He had never encountered a man during the eleven winters he had been alive. A deep instinct warned him that this scent brought with it a much greater danger than fire.

Well before dawn, Lance was on the move. He had slept longer than planned. Warming himself, he ate one of the last energy bars before extinguishing the fire. "You want me, boys?" he asked under his breath. "You're going to have to pay to play."

20

An hour after dark, Brad pretty much knew.

Both teams had made the rendezvous with the men arriving within minutes of each other. Truck came in last because he had been the farthest out. The chopper was waiting, and the pilots were getting antsy.

"We can't spend the night," one of them was saying.

Brad nodded and gave the signal for them to take off. He had tried to raise Preach on the radio several times. When the sound of the helicopter had faded, seven men stood in the darkness.

"Make camp," he ordered. "I want to be ready to go at first light. Make a big fire. If he can see it, he will head toward us."

Within minutes they had a fire going, and the men were preparing their individual tents.

"I'll take the first watch, Romey—you pick one of your men for the second, and Beats will take the last."

"Watch?" Romey was surprised by the order.

"We have a man missing on a kill-or-capture mission. And we have achieved neither. We are also tracking a dangerous man—so yeah, I think a rotation is in order, don't you?" He was testy. Preach was a friend and a key member of his outfit.

"Makes perfect sense to me, sir; I'll take the second watch myself."

Romey went about getting ready for their fifth cold night. He was hopeful that they could catch up with Preach in the morning, radio for the chopper, and be back in town by noon. It was worrisome when a man didn't show and couldn't be reached on the radio. In the bush, anything can happen; it wasn't hard to get in trouble and have to spend the night. Eventually, it happens to everyone.

Romey glanced over at Brad, who was circulating around the men with a word of encouragement here and there. He wasn't buying the sincerity of it. Brad was a cold, calculating man. He suspected that he wanted to speak to his own men without being too obvious. He was careful and thorough; that was a fact.

Setting up a watch was a good idea. It meant added security and more importantly, a set of ears listening all night long, in case there was a call or signal from Preach. Just before ducking into his tent, he located Brad's position again; he had moved off ten feet, his back to the fire. Romey appreciated the training and understood the importance of not polluting your night vision with firelight.

Brad had spoken to both Beats and Truck, and they agreed something catastrophic must have happened to Preach. He would crawl in if he had to. They were all anxious to get moving, but traipsing around in the dark could mess up signs or tracks. They also ran the risk of injuring themselves. They had night vision equipment but needed a point from which to start looking. No, they would wait until first light, then move out. Truck had seen no tracks on his way in, so there was zero chance Preach had overshot the rendezvous point. The search area was narrow, and he expected the morning would bring some answers.

———— • ————

The temperature had increased slightly when Romey rolled out of his sleeping bag. The air was heavy with a familiar feeling that indicated snow was on the way. Although it was a few minutes before his watch, his internal alarm had been tripped, and he was ready. He had trained himself to sleep in exacting intervals. His grandfather had taught him to concentrate on a time to wake up, and after some practice, he was able to get it to within minutes. On many occasions, he had hit it dead on. The subconscious mind was more powerful than most people realized.

He stretched and looked to where he had last seen Brad, who was nowhere in sight. Puzzled, Romey made a wide circle around the camp away from the fire. When he had almost covered the circumference, he thought he heard a hushed whisper. Straining his ears, he heard more muffled whispers ... then a clear "Yup". Brad filtered in through the darkness. He was buttoning down the front pocket of his jacket and was brought up short at the sight of Romey.

"Surprised me there," Brad said.

"Talking to yourself?"

"Talkin' to the wind really," he explained.

Romey looked past him into the darkness. "Takin' a chance with a killer on the loose."

Brad had no way of avoiding it; Romey was too cagey for that. "Made a sat call to see if we can get the chopper up in the air for some recon at first light. They said, 'No go.' Another storm's brewing, and it may be another day or two before she clears."

Brad had made that call, but he'd also given Wallace an update. He checked his watch and headed for his tent.

The fire was burning strong, meaning Brad had kept it going. He would do the same. He wondered what had happened to Preach. Could he have come out on the short end of an encounter with Coolidge? The odds of that were unlikely, after four days without a sign. It was more likely that Preach had fallen or encountered a grizzly. Still, they had to behave like both men were still alive—one needing help and the other dangerous and on the loose.

If it had been Romey's call, they would have pulled the pin after two days. They wanted Coolidge badly, that was for sure, and Romey sensed there was more to this manhunt than met the eye. He hated being out of the loop—it was tough enough worrying about what was out there without having to worry about what was going on inside the camp. And now this late-night private call.'

After his watch, he caught another couple hours of sleep. When he awoke, it was snowing, and the camp was coming to life under darkness with dancing headlamps and as the men packed their gear and prepared breakfast.

Brad's men had some nongovernment-issued gear, and he wondered at that. He had met some of the Blackwater crew in Iraq, and they had better equipment—or at least they were given more flexibility in what they chose for themselves. Romey decided he would be happy when this one was over. There was little chance they would have to work together again. Brad and his men were mercenaries; of this he was confident. Whatever else they were, he didn't want to know.

Teddy came up with two cups of coffee and handed him one. "Leadbeater's a strange one," he volunteered. "I saw him marking his bullets with a felt pen last night by firelight. When I asked him about it, he said, 'Load my own.'"

"What's his mark?"

"B ... his initial."

"Figures."

They drank in silence, both men alone with his thoughts. After breakfast, they geared up, as the grey light of morning approached.

Brad was talking and drawing in the snow with a stick. "We made our way upriver approximately 250 yards apart. I was along the river, and Beats was three hundred yards out, which puts Preach here in this line. We will spread out between Beats's line of travel and Truck's. There are seven of us ... so a man every seventy-five metres. We have no idea how far back he is ... could be a day's walk. I tried calling for a chopper to scout ahead, but that's a no go due to the weather. We'd best plan for another night or two."

In most groups, that comment would have solicited a groan, but there wasn't a hint of disappointment from any of them. They all wanted to go home but had long ago stopped putting personal desires above the mission. Besides, no one wanted to leave without finding one of their own.

Brad took the route that Preach would have been on. Beats would follow his own route but out another hundred yards. Truck took his lane again, the outer limit of the search area. The other four were positioned in the gaps.

They had walked for an hour, with a radio check every fifteen minutes. It was snowing heavily, and yesterday's tracks were already filling in. Brad missed the line that Preach had taken by about twenty yards and as a result didn't see where he had veered off along the stream.

He was another five hundred metres past it and almost two hours into the morning before he spotted tracks on the far edge of a small clearing. They were just indentations now, but his keen eye recognized them for what they were. Backing under the boughs of a nearby fir tree, he got on the radio.

"I have tracks … hold your positions."

Brad looked warily about. The snow reduced visibility considerably. Rifle at the ready, he skirted the clearing, coming up on the tracks in a narrow gap. The stride was even and strong, no stumbling or erratic movements. Preach's tracks.

Brad radioed again. "I have a direction leading towards the rendezvous. Continue to hold."

Each man waited with anticipation. After twenty minutes, he crossed the creek and saw how Preach had gone on a few paces, then circled back. He had started upstream—what caught Preach's attention? Had he heard something? Again, he radioed, "Tracks leading north."

He followed the tracks with care—here and there a print remained where the snow couldn't get at it. He almost missed the pack and rifle. Noting with satisfaction that although snow had collected on the stock, the barrel was facing down to prevent moisture from accumulating in it.

A little farther along the trail, an extra set of tracks appeared. It was as though they had materialized from nowhere and it gave him a queer feeling. Lance was dangerous prey! The tracks had also circled back to the stream … for a drink, perhaps? After a few more steps, he saw the outstretched form and knew right away it was Preach.

———— • ————

The men gathered around in disbelief. The snow had partially covered his corpse, with the spear lodged in his throat sticking up towards the sky. His frozen-open eyes had partially filled with snow and looked even more ghastly. Brad had made a quick search of the shelter before the others arrived but found nothing. By chance, he found the sidearm in the snow and tucked it behind his waistband.

"Looks like quite a struggle." Strong rarely said much.

"Coolidge!" Beats was incensed. "How in the hell?"

"His ghost's come back to mock us all BA!" Leadbeater spoke out his superstition.

"Beats!" Brad shook his head in warning.

Truck retrieved the pack and rifle and said, "I figure he kept on going upstream and slipped by me somehow."

"How's that?" Brad asked.

"If he had gone downstream, he would have grabbed this," he said, holding up the pack.

"Ghosts don't need gear." Teddy was mocking Leadbeater—a grim prospect on any day, but today with the loss of Preach, he was spoiling for a fight.

"What's that?" Beats stepped forward aggressively.

At Brad's sharp rebuke, Beats stopped, glaring at Teddy.

"Romey, keep your man in line. We don't need trouble among ourselves."

Romey jerked his head at Teddy, indicating he needed to back off.

Red spoke up to break the tension. "It looks like his radio is gone."

Brad swore, "He's probably been listening to us this whole morning, damn it! We will need to limit our radio time."

"We could use Morse," Truck suggested.

"He's no civilian," Red spoke again.

"He's right," Brad said. "We need a different plan. We move out together but if we need to separate, we do it in groups of two. I'm the odd man out, so I will be alone. Set your radios to vibrate. We make contact every fifteen minutes. Your team number is the number of buzzes you give to indicate you're good ... if you have eyes on and you can't talk; it's your team number and then a long buzz." He demonstrated. "The rest of us will close on your position. If you find tracks or any indication of his passing, it's your number and two long buzzes. Are we clear?"

Everyone nodded.

Brad was team one. Beats and Truck team two. Red and Romey team three. And team four was Strongman and Teddy.

They wrapped Preach in his sleeping bag and tent before sliding his body inside the shelter. They could retrieve him later, and this would hopefully keep the animals off until then.

They stretched out in another skirmish line, this time in sight of one another. Brad sent Romey and Red downstream even though they all agreed that had Lance gone upstream, ghost or not, he would have retrieved the pack.

———— • ————

The sudden appearance of Lance's tracks out of nowhere and his ability to get the best of Preach, while apparently unarmed, made Brad both angry and cautious. He had tried to make everyone aware of the caliber of the man they faced. He had warned them not to let their guard down. He himself had accepted that Coolidge was dead. At that distance, Beats would not have missed. This played on his psyche. Did he really think that a ghost had killed Preach?

In the regular army, superstitions made their way through the ranks quickly. The story would grow in the telling, but these men generally knew better.

These men were all selected specifically for their mental toughness.

Bzzt, bzzt, bzzt.

It was team three checking in.

When they had walked for over an hour and not found a single track, Brad grew concerned but did not share his unease with the group. By now team three would have made the river and started back. He halted the men and waved them in.

"No tracks, nothing," Beats said.

Brad gave him a sideways look, but he no longer looked rattled.

"There's almost no chance he could have gone this far without leaving sign. Ideas?" He opened the floor for discussion.

Truck spoke first. "I think he has left the stream and made his way east. He would have heard the chopper, so he wouldn't have headed towards his camp. My guess is he's going to run for it. We should start thinking about where he's going rather than where he might be."

"Why now, though?" Brad asked. "He's had four days."

No one had an answer to that.

Brad pulled out his map and pointed at it. "There is nothing in that direction for a hundred miles … where would he be going?"

"Red said he's an old Lobo," Strongman volunteered.

"I think that's the point: he's going nowhere and plans on leading us on a chase."

Brad consulted the map again. What would I do if the situation were reversed? Guerrilla tactics—I would run, hide and fight—in that order.

"Okay," Brad agreed. "We rendezvous with team three back at the shelter, and then we head east. He has to have left some sign somewhere."

Teddy almost made another ghost comment, but Beats didn't appear to appreciate his humor, so he kept it to himself.

They had burned up valuable time looking for Preach, dealing with his corpse, and continuing the fruitless search. They had only hours left in this day, and it had continued to lightly snow.

Romey and Red were at the shelter when they approached. Red spoke up. "We could sure use that chopper. I wish this damn weather would clear."

"I had the same thought myself," Romey agreed.

After Brad filled them in on the new plan, he pulled out the sat phone. "I'll send a report," he said, walking off a hundred yards, out of earshot.

They lined up along the creek, about fifty yards apart after the short break. Moving out again at a methodical pace, Brad reminded them to stay sharp, but the advice was unnecessary—everyone was ready.

A few minutes out, fists in the air accompanied by two short buzzes, then two more brought them to a halt. They had found tracks.

They were undoubtedly from last evening now and no more than a dim outline.

Red was impressed. "Neat trick."

Truck spoke in his slow, deliberate tone. "I've seen deer do that a time or two, usually when they are wounded and running out of steam."

"You think he's wounded?" Romey asked.

Truck moved closer. He was the tracker in the group, and they knew it. He had guessed the direction Lance had taken before the group came to a consensus.

"You can see here, he stumbled a little when he made that first jump."

The snow had almost concealed it, and none of the others could make it out.

"He's either wounded or exhausted, maybe both." Truck was confident.

Taking the lead, he found where Lance had stepped carefully onto the birch tree, concealing his tracks.

There was a grove of small trees at the end of the log. He brought his rifle to the ready position, and everyone else followed suit. What a group they were! The two men in the rear spun around, rifles up. The two men on the outer edges covered the sides. No one had to bark out an order, each man simply did as he'd been trained. Brad, Romey, and Truck pushed into the little grove of trees. Beyond were distinct tracks. No effort had been made to conceal them here. They waved the rest of the team forward.

"Yup. He's going to take us for a run!" Strong was definitive.

Brad was feeling better now that they had found the tracks and a direction. "Well, let's not keep him waiting."

With that, they were off. Brad winked at Beats, who had a bland look on his face. His pride had been wounded, and he desperately wanted another go at Lance. The men were strung out twenty yards apart with Truck in the lead. They needed to make sure he hadn't employed another trick.

Truck paused, waiting for Romey and Brad. "He's hurt, I'd say. He's dragging his feet and stopping to catch his breath, even on flat ground."

"You think Preach did some damage?" Brad asked.

Truck shrugged. "Maybe Beats got one into Lance, who knows. I'd say he hasn't gone much farther. He's draggin' his ass pretty bad."

They reached the little nest of boulders just before dark. Approaching with care, the troop filtered into the branches that formed the lean-to. They found the energy bar wrapper, the blood-caked wadding, and remnants of the bandage and adhesive.

"He's wounded, all right." Brad was emphatic. "An old wound at that. Looks like you made your shot, Beats." If Brad thought that would cheer Beats up, he was wrong. Beats was seething. He had the guy dead to rights; why was Lance not dead? Beats'd seen bullets do strange things, but he practiced constantly, and his hand loads were precise, making sure to match performance with the harmonic of the barrel.

It was like him to be more concerned with his shooting prowess than the loss of one of their own.

———— • ————

The makings of a fire and some extra wood stacked neatly seemed to indicate Lance would be back any minute. Romey had stepped away from the group to relieve himself.

"Guys," he called quietly to the group, "you're gonna wanna to see this!"

They all looked at each other and trooped out to Romey. There, a crude arrow formed from tree branches leaned against a rock, pointing northeast.

Beats swore bitterly. "You're a dead man! A dead man, you hear me? You son-of-a-bitch!" He screamed into the night.

Brad slapped him roughly on the shoulder. "Looks like he's feeling better. Let's get some sleep. Tomorrow will be a long day. He's a whole day ahead of us." With that they dissipated into the rocks to make camp.

Brad had held his cool, but inside anger was bubbling up. He wanted to kill Lance in a way he had never wanted to kill before. They would catch up to Lance, even if it took all winter—and when they did, Lance Coolidge would suffer.

21

Doug Hallward was at his desk, taking a much-needed break from the Coolidge case. It had consumed most of their resources and all of their energy. He was working on some paperwork for a couple of upcoming court appearances.

Geraldine was on a call at her desk. She had a peculiar look on her face. She was nodding, asking questions, and taking notes. After hanging up, she made a beeline for his office.

"What's up?" he asked.

"That was the lab. They were able to lift three sets of prints from the vic—" She corrected herself, remembering the sheriff's relationship with her. "From Cathy's place."

"They get a hit?"

"Yes and no."

"What does that mean?"

"They ran the prints through the database, but there was no match. However, I had them compared to the prints from the John Doe you found at the pull-out."

"You're kidding?"

"Yup, John Doe was in the house. You can confidently say that these two murders are linked."

Hallward whistled his surprise.

"There's more! The second set of prints does not belong to Lance Coolidge."

The sheriff had been leaning back in his chair, but with this news, he dropped the front legs back on the ground hard. "That's damn good police work!"

"Thank you ... the FBI does have its uses." She wagged her pen at him.

He glanced at the notepad with the scribbles she had made. "Those old-fashioned notepads help you concentrate, don't they?" At that, she just smirked.

Hallward summoned Barton into the office and shared this new information.

Barton was thoughtful. "If we add all this into your timeline, it looks less and less likely that Lance did this. But what about the necklace?"

"A plant, maybe? You said yourself it looked a little too obvious."

Barton responded with a nod. "What now? We have a dead suspect and another on the loose. And we are further away from the truth than ever."

"Now, we call off the wolves! That's why we follow the evidence," Hallward said dryly, clapping his hands together. "We can get to the bottom of this later. Right now we need to put an end to the chase!—if it's not too late."

Geraldine was testing theories in her mind: What about this phony FBI agent? Was he the second person in the house? Although she doubted the business card still had any prints, she would send it to the lab anyway.

The sheriff picked up his phone and called Joseph.

———— • ————

Joseph listened carefully, taking notes. Over and over again, he circled the words, LANCE IS INNOCENT. When he hung up with the sheriff, Joseph called Peter Ashgrave and gave him a concise report, enduring his sighs of frustration.

The last thing Ashgrave wanted was another conversation with Joseph Coolidge.

"My assistant is typing it up as we speak. There is an email on the way documenting where the investigation is at. Peter, I implore you, call off your dogs!" He heard the email ping over the phone. "That's probably it now."

Ashgrave gave it a quick scan. "Okay, Joseph, I will make the call. However, the team leader makes a sat call each evening, so if they are maintaining radio silence, we may have to wait until then."

Joseph called Katherine to relay the news, and she breathed a sigh of relief. "He has to be alive; he just has to be."

"He will need to hold on a bit longer. Keep praying, Katherine. This is going to be close. I will be on a flight in the morning."

———— • ————

Geraldine put in her daily report, and Crown received it with some serious misgivings. Should I cash out now? This thing is unraveling. He was torn. His stock options and the cash he was receiving on the side were not enough for him to disappear in the manner he had planned on. On the other hand, he couldn't spend money from jail.

He could see that Wallace was cleaning up loose ends—and he might be one of them. At this thought, the blood drained from his face, and he had to sit down. What to do, what to do? When do you cash in your chips and leave the table? Soon. This much he was sure of. He needed to decide soon.

He delayed his decision, chancing a call on the burner phone instead.

Wallace was stone cold as he relayed the news, which was further confirmation of the information that had just been leaked from the Armed Services Committee.

"Try to relax, Byron." He tried to sound reassuring. "You've done your job, and no one can fault you for that. It's important that there are no pattern changes that will alert anyone. You understand?"

Crown nodded as though Wallace could see him through the phone.

"Crown! You understand?" He repeated.

"Yeah … yeah." He let out a breath. "Understood. You're right, of course." He felt a bit better.

"Good. And, Byron, dispose of that phone. No more calls. I will contact you when we're in the clear."

———— • ————

After hanging up, Wallace looked thoughtfully at the receiver for a minute. Byron had guessed right—no matter how this thing played out over the next 48 to 72 hours, Byron Crown was marked for death.

Bellamy! A thought came to him, and he was immediately pleased. Bellamy may prove useful one more time. Can I bring him back into the fold? Of course I can—Bellamy has nowhere else to turn and he will be eager to re-establish his loyalty.

Wallace tried his phone, but it was out of the service area. He'd try again later.

No matter what the orders were, Wallace knew that Brad would not pull out right away and would wait for instructions. They need to kill Lance and retrieve the envelope, or at least establish that it is gone for good. This thing can still blow over. Then it will be back to business as usual. He had received the news about Preach with misgivings but based on the last report, they were closing in on Lance, and he might be dead already. He could only hope.

———— • ————

The team was well into the morning and, unbelievably, had lost the trail again. They were discussing the possibilities when the sat phone buzzed. It was not protocol, so there had to be a significant reason for the call.

What the hell? Brad thought to himself. They knew his reports came each night. Each night, he talked with Wallace as well.

At present, they had no idea where Lance had gone. Even Truck was stumped. For all they knew, Lance was watching and listening to them right now. They desperately needed that chopper, but the weather was still too volatile. Brad decided to let the call go to voicemail. That way, he could evaluate the message before having a live conversation.

After several minutes, he moved off from the group and listened to the message. It was an order to stand down. A medical and recovery team would replace them when the weather cleared. An explanation was not provided with the order, but that was not unusual.

This shortened their window of opportunity significantly. He would, of course, ignore the order and not tell the men about it either. They would need to catch up with Lance soon.

The team had carefully followed the trail, and it was as plain as could be, stretching out before them across a five-hundred-yard clear-cut, where it disappeared over a small knoll. Beyond the knoll, the trail went on for another couple hundred meters—at which point he had entered a blowdown.

Anyone who has never traversed one of these cannot fully appreciate the difficulty. Trees thrown on top of each other in a snarled mess, piled as high as a two-story building. To cross one, you must scramble through, under, and over. Often on the edge of a clear-cut, blowdowns might only be forty or fifty yards deep. This one stretched out for hundreds of yards.

Brad dispatched two men in different directions to see if there was a way around. Both came back with the report that it stretched out for several kilometres in both directions. There was little chance Lance had come back out on this side because neither had found tracks.

Their little band spread out, making their way through the maze with minimal progress. For the first few yards, the tracks were plain enough but then they began to thin out. He had stepped on a log here, crawled under several there and then they were gone—as though he had opened his wings and flown away. They cast about for tracks, but it was almost impossible to create a grid, and after half an hour of intensive searching, Brad ordered everyone back. Gathered in a loose circle, they were sharing ideas and strategies.

"In there you can get close and with a pistol, have the advantage," Romey pointed out. "We need to be doubly alert pushing through that shit."

The rest nodded in agreement.

Brad gave orders. "We will need to stay close together. I want two men stationed back here in the clearing, a hundred metres out and five hundred metres apart. And make sure you can see each other. He's likely to come back out this side. I agree it's hell in there, but it is for him too. And he's wounded, don't forget that."

Truck responded, "His stride was steady and strong this morning. I'd say he's making a recovery."

Brad had noted that as well, not liking it much. "Maybe; we'll see."

The fog and swirling snow stirred up by the wind had produced fluctuating visibility going from good to bad, moment by moment.

After a quick meal, they set out again. The helicopter crew had given them their rations, but they would need more in two days.

In two days, this thing will be settled one way or the other. Brad was scowling at the thought, and Romey was watching him—trying to figure him out.

The two pickets took their positions in the field. Brad had intentionally put the two biggest and strongest men—Strong and Truck—on guard in the clearing. He wanted the most agile men with him.

Within moments, a fog blew in, and they were invisible to the group making their way into the blowdown. Like magic, they faded from sight. Truck looked over towards Strongman, but he too was invisible.

———— • ————

Lance was still in deep trouble. He had feigned strength with the expectation of making the treeline and keeping them cautious. But loss of blood, hunger, and thirst were wearing him down. There was no way he could hide his tracks, so he left the arrow for psychological purposes. He thought he had heard a shout last night just before dark. Sound flattened out quickly in this country, with its trees, boulders, and folds in the ground.

When he discovered the blowdown and saw the magnitude of it, he immediately recognized the opportunity it presented. He had spent his entire life in these woods or ones like them. He could feel his way through these mazes. Like a mental and physical algorithm, with practice you came to understand their nature. It was really about that innate sixth sense we all possess but few develop.

He would walk the maze like a bridge, but first he must deal with his tracks. He made them plain where it was difficult to follow: Brushing over logs heavily to leave marks, then stepping carefully in the open, placing his feet on dry branches or ducking under low logs. He would sometimes straddle a wind-swept log and shimmy himself along, leaving a definitive track pointing in the wrong direction.

Finally, he found what he was looking for—a windswept log hung up, providing a steep path to the top of the jumble. Before trying it, he left a track here and there. He planned his approach carefully and was able to hop from log to log and then onto the one he'd chosen.

Normally he would have enjoyed himself, but with his strength so low, every step was dangerous. If he fell from such a height, his wound would tear open, and he'd likely be impaled on the branches below.

He slipped on his first step up the log and almost fell. Leaning forward, he steadied himself but was still dizzy. Gingerly, he made his way to the top and looked back to where his camp had been. No one was in sight. His plan was to make his way across the blowdown, leading them farther into the wilderness. From his vantage point, there appeared to be a cove among the trees—on the far side of the blowdown. It was a long way; he put the distance out of his mind and pressed on. He needed to find food and shelter, but for now he thought only of escape and creating distance between himself and those who pursued him.

He had been listening to their communications on the radio, which gave him a good estimate of their numbers. After they found the body, they had gone to radio silence, obviously finding another way to communicate. He had wondered if they would resort to Morse code, but they were a resourceful crew, and had he been on the other end of this, he would not have given himself much of a chance.

Pushing the danger out of his mind, he began to find his rhythm and was soon moving well from log to log and tree to tree. The morning wore on, and with his need to concentrate, he did not notice the time passing. He slipped several times but caught himself and avoided logs with accumulated snow. When this wasn't possible, he slowed his pace and crawled and shimmied in places. He was on a particularly narrow log when it cracked under his weight, bringing him up short against another log. He lunged for the top of a nearby tree, holding on for dear life.

After gathering himself again, he continued. He had gone a few more yards when he heard a loud snap! He held very still. The sound had come from the direction he was going. Had they gotten ahead of him somehow? Just then, there was a quiet, high-pitched call. It was a cow moose! She was just ahead, her dark bulk visible as she moved in and out of the trees. She called several times before he saw her calf, feeding on some willows. His heart leapt for joy! He had made the other side! He didn't want to startle them and draw attention to his presence, so he waited until they had moved on. Only then did he find his way to the ground.

———— • ————

As the crow flies, he had gone only about four hundred yards, but it had taken him half a day. They would have to work hard if they were going to catch up to him now. Don't become overconfident, he told himself. These men were as skilled as he was, and besides, he was outnumbered. Still, he found assurance in this small victory.

The moose had gone in the general direction he was going as well, so he followed them. If there was a trail for them, there would be one for him as well. An added bonus was that moose never strayed far from water.

At a sudden flurry of sound, his hands came up instinctively to the fighting position. A grouse had flown up from underfoot, and he'd almost stepped on it. It lit on a branch just a few feet above his head. He was staring at its blinking eyes when he noticed the others. A small covey was perched in the same tree. Fool's hens the old-timers called them. They thought everything was a coyote or a wolf, and if they just got into a tree, they'd be safe. Their survival strategies were limited, and he had often killed them with rocks or sticks. When a rock came close, they would jump to another branch rather than flying off.

Uncle Joseph had told him that God made some animals just for food—and fool's hens were just that.

Lance killed three before they finally flew far enough that the effort outweighed the reward. After tying them to his belt, he carried on. At one point, he found a small juniper tree and gathered some of the needles for seasoning. He would feast tonight!

Resisting the urge to stop and eat one immediately, he kept moving. He would find a place to rest and eat. For now, he was safe. He was tempted to stay in the blowdown, but they would eventually make their way through. If he lit a fire in there, they would smell the smoke. He needed more separation.

———— • ————

At the same time Lance was killing the grouse, they found his death jump tracks.

———— • ————

The snow had not accumulated as much as Lance had expected, but it was still tough going in places. The moose cow and calf had cut a trail that made the going slightly easier. The forest was sparse in patches, and so it was windier on this side. Lance made every effort to mingle his tracks with those of the moose.

Another set of partially filled-in tracks appeared. Upon examination, Lance determined that these had been made by a domesticated cow—probably an old steer gone wild. They could be extremely ornery, and few predators would tackle a full-grown bull. Even a pack of wolves would think twice. He realized he must be close to the north end of the Craig ranch. Little help that would be. No one works the ranges this time of year.

He managed another mile before he was forced to stop and rest. He was following the tracks of the cow now as they skirted a small lake. He had been attempting to make a slow arc back toward the original lake he had spotted from the river that first day. This certainly wasn't it, and he suspected he was well east of there by now when he came to a tiny stream flowing into a lake.

As he passed yet another tree, marred by horns, he realized the bull was a monster! The scrape was a good three and a half feet from where it had stood. God help the predator that tackled him! He had taken a drink from the stream and then moved out to where it entered the lake. The weight of the bull had broken the thinner ice here as he passed over.

Lance filled a condom with the clear water, after drinking his fill. He checked for droppings before filling it up. E. coli poisoning was not an option. He should have taken the socks from the man he'd killed. He could have used one as a canteen, with the condom acting as a bladder. But the idea came too late, and he remembered one of his instructors saying, "Front-end thinking is ten times more valuable than back-end thinking."

Just then, something in the water caught his eye—a sliver of silver. As he looked, the shape of a fresh-water mussel became apparent. He reached down and gathered it up. It was sealed shut and very much alive. Putting it in his pocket and ignoring the strong smell, he made his way downstream to the lake where he gathered more. Fresh-water mussels can carry bacteria and toxins as they are constantly filtering the murky water through their systems. Unless it's an emergency, one should refrain from them, but Lance didn't give it a second thought. If ever there was a time to take a chance, this was it.

With most of the day gone, he knew he must rest. Surveying his back-trail for several minutes, he saw that all was still and quiet.

He pushed into a grove of small pine trees, where he made a shelter by pulling several saplings together above his head. Using the dead man's belt, he lashed them together. This provided the framework, and by weaving other branches in and out, he created a snug dry spot.

Gathering firewood and with the birch bark he'd collected during his trek, he started a fire. It took only a few sparks to ignite the resin-filled bark.

He placed a couple of extra boughs above the hole in the shelter to help dissipate the smoke. He had read about this in a western novel but had never tested out the theory.

Although his fire was hidden, he worried that the smoke, carried on the wind, would reach his pursuers. The smell of woodsmoke can carry for miles.

His stomach growled as he prepared the grouse. Skewering it on a green willow branch, he pressed the juniper needles into the meat and seared it to seal in the juices. Then he roasted it slowly over the fire. Even though he knew full well poultry should always be cooked completely before eating, he devoured some as soon as it was hot. He placed the mussels in the coals so they would open face down, keeping the ashes out.

Before re-dressing his wound, he ate the second grouse. By then, the shelter had warmed up. Removing the old bandages, he was concerned by the slightly foul odor. Cleaning it with a couple of antiseptic wipes, he undressed completely to allow the sweat to evaporate from his body. Placing his clothes on top of several tree boughs to dry, he lay down, using the dead man's jacket as a pillow. For the first time in days, he was comfortable and soon drifted off to sleep.

He woke at intervals to add fuel to the fire or quash the odd ember before it caught on the hanging boughs. Sometime in the night, he woke and put aside a mussel out of the ashes to cool. It was bland and chewy, but he gulped it down. He would have the rest for breakfast. Savoring the last grouse, he rubbed it thoroughly with the juniper and slow-roasted it over the hot coals. He wasted none of it, even toasting the heart and liver and eating them like delicacies.

"Consider the birds of the air. They neither sow nor reap, yet your Heavenly Father feeds them." He considered this quote from Matthew with amazement. Those same birds had become his meal. A strange irony indeed, he thought and smiled.

For the first time he had time to think. He'd now heard a voice warning him of danger twice, yet no one was nearby. He'd also sensed a presence—a guiding hand these last few days. Is it just the lonely wish of a desperate man? He assumed so, but the feeling persisted. Why are all these Bible passages coming to mind? He wanted to be honest with himself. Am I desperately trying to find common ground with Lynette? He didn't think so. He believed she would accept him regardless.

Has she heard about my plight? Probably not—and even if she did, undoubtedly there is some ruse, some story they are using to justify hunting me down. What are they looking for? Something they think I have? What did the fighter ask? "Where is the envelope?" What envelope? Whatever it is, it's important enough to kill me for.

They had shot him without warning, and that was just bad form on home soil, in peacetime. He reviewed the last few days and weeks, but there seemed to be nothing unusual or out of the regular pattern of life that pointed to anything he could isolate that provided answers.

Then he remembered the fight in the parking lot. Had they been looking for this something in my Jeep? That would mean they thought he was in possession of it before the fight … Or were they trying to plant something? He reviewed the encounter in his mind, recounting the day. Nothing made sense. Did they mistake the garage paperwork for something else?

The sheriff's department shared my location with these pursuers. This must mean I've been accused of something. Perhaps his past had come back to haunt him. No, it is something else—something they think I have. Either way, he would use this information to stay alive. If captured, he would withstand torture and refuse to reveal where he'd hidden the envelope. At the very least, it would buy him some time.

Putting all the unanswered questions out of his mind, he got dressed and fed the fire. He was fast asleep when a spark kicked up, landing on a tree bough. It settled there for a moment, glowed brightly and then died out. A drop of water trickled from the roof and hissed as it landed in the fire.

Lance awoke to the sound of the wind. The fire was still radiating a little heat. But what was that? Someone is sitting at my feet! He listened, straining his ears. Keeping his eyes closed and his breathing steady, he pretended to be asleep.

There was no movement and no sound—just an awareness that someone was there. But there wasn't room in the shelter for a second person. His eyes fluttered open. The flames cast strange shadows on the roof of the shelter. He was warm—very warm, too warm. Was he sweating? Fear swept over him. Fever! He swept his brow with the back of his hand, and it came away wet. His wound was infected!

Prior to the First World War, when men discovered how to kill each other en masse, more soldiers died of infection than at the hands of the enemy. He dug into the first-aid kit and found some aspirin and Tylenol, chewing and swallowing one of each, not much caring for the chalky taste and the difficulty of swallowing the pills.

He had checked and redressed his wound earlier, but he checked it again, gently pulling the bandage back, trying to see it in his peripheral vision. Was it the firelight that made it appear red?

He drank some of the water he'd collected, washing down the residue of the pills. He wished he had the yarrow he'd collected to make a tea with. The Tylenol would keep the fever at bay but wouldn't help the infection itself. Was it delirium that made me think someone was with me in the shelter? He didn't feel that sick.

Lance hated running and hiding; it went against his fighting nature. But he knew that outnumbered and unarmed, he had no chance against these men. He understood how lucky he'd been in his hand-to-hand fight but knew they would not be careless again. Of this he was certain, and the death of a comrade would provide them added motivation in the fight. He tried to relax, and sleep soon claimed him again.

22

A fter a frustrating day, the insertion teams were camped on the far side of the blowdown, less than a kilometre from their camp of the night before. One of their number was not with them, and this provided some hope.

The moose was there. A moment ago, it was not. Truck had been studying the border between the clearing and the blowdown. The moose had come out from the blowdown five hundred yards from his position.

With his binoculars, he tracked it as it fed on the vegetation along the edge. It probably had just bedded down inside the tree line but what if it had found a way through?

The fog had been drifting in and out for most of the day, and at the moment, Strong was lost in its haze.

Truck checked his watch—it was just after four p.m. He thought briefly of communicating that there might be a way through the blowdown, but he'd learned infinite patience over a lifetime of battles. It never paid to move too quickly or jump to conclusions.

When finally the fog briefly lifted, he turned his binoculars towards Strong's position, glassing the entire area. Only when he was certain they were alone did he stand up to get Strong's attention, waving his arms. The other saw his movements and brought him under his glass. Truck was making the walking and looking signs and saluting in the direction he was intending to look. Strong acknowledged this with a wave.

The moose was feeding away from him, keeping the wind in its face. It was a magnificent creature, a bull with a massive rack, weighing in at close to a thousand pounds. Truck kept his pace slow so as not to spook the old boy, but eventually it spotted him and trotted off. There were plenty of old tracks here in the snow and nothing fresh, lending credence to his idea that maybe the moose had worked its way through the blowdown.

He found the spot where the moose had emerged and followed the tracks. He climbed over several logs that the long-limbed animal had easily navigated. Almost immediately, he found the bed where it had rested, watching the clearing. The tracks from the bed led deeper into the blowdown. Following them for a hundred yards, he made slow progress through the thick mess. It looked promising, although he knew the tracks could just weave in, out, and around, ending up back in the clear-cut. His instincts told him the moose had come from the other side. It was late, and he decided to chance the radio. He buzzed once and within a few moments a buzzing came in response.

"May have found a way through. Permission to proceed?"

"Granted."

That was the whole conversation, but it was enough. If he could make his way through before dark, he would have the advantage come morning.

Several times, the trail wound back within sight of the clear-cut, but eventually the serpentine route the animal had taken led him to the far side, just as darkness was closing in.

He radioed again. "Through. Will bivouac till morning."

"Roger."

——— • ———

In a moment of uncharacteristic carelessness, Lance had left the radio in the shelter while stepping out to collect firewood, and he missed the first exchange. He missed the second in his deep sleep. The food, the warmth, and his overwhelming fatigue had done the trick. His eyes did flutter momentarily, but then his breathing steadied again.

——— • ———

Brad and his team made difficult progress, and he was still concerned by the lack of tracks. He made the decision to pull everyone back before dark and try another tack in the morning. They had just rendezvoused with Strongman when Truck radioed his last message. Strong filled them in on Truck's movements.

Brad considered a sprint to meet up with Truck but dismissed the idea. There was too great a chance of getting turned around in there in the dark or, worse, an injury. They would camp here tonight and push through first thing in the morning. The weather was clearing, and that meant the rescue team would be here to replace them. When they caught up with Coolidge, they would secure the envelope. Then he would personally make sure Lance did not leave this wilderness alive.

Brad had always been honest in his evaluation of himself and others. He held a supreme belief in his superior abilities—a confidence born of an unbroken string of victories, tempered by caution and logic. They hadn't been able to pick up Lance's trail even after an exhaustive search. This was an almost impossible feat in the snow. But somehow, he'd accomplished it. He knew this was having a psychological effect on the team and himself as well.

Wounded, Lance had killed Preach with a crude homemade spear. Brad would not have thought that possible. Lance's ultimate victory was making his tracks disappear.

Brad was beginning to have doubts of his own. What if Lance slips out of our grasp and gets away? He kept that nagging little voice to himself. His respect for Lance grew with each day that the manhunt dragged on. Imagine what we could accomplish together. We would be almost unstoppable. Could I recruit Lance? No; Brad knew that if Lance ever discovered that his brother's death was no accident, he would turn on a dime. Besides, from all accounts, he was a principled man, and they can be the most troubling of men—but also predictable, and therefore usable and detrimental to their own cause. Brad was ruthless and, when possible, exploited these characteristics.

He walked away from the group for his usual parlay on the sat phone. This time his only call was to Wallace. There was nothing he could do; the rescue team would be coming in the morning, and they would be ordered out. Wallace emphasized the importance of finding Lance first.

After the call, Brad used his multitool to remove the back of the phone. He traced the main power wire from the battery supply, gave it a tug, and the phone went dead. Then he tossed the wire into the snow. He made a show of shaking it and slapping it against his palm as he came back to the team.

"Dead," he said. "Damn thing's dead, dropped my call. Must be made in China."

Several in the group laughed.

"Let me have a look." Red held out his hand.

Brad tossed it to him. "Sure, be great if you can figure out what's wrong with it."

Red nodded, wagging it in the air. "If I get it fixed, I'll order Chinese."

———— • ————

At first light, Truck was on the move. He had made camp just inside the treeline, where he had slept well. His provisions were more than adequate for the weather. Deciding against a fire, he used his Sterno gel instead, warming up his tent, making a cup of tea and some instant oatmeal ration. After reusing the teabag for a second cup, he swished the dregs and tossed them out. He then dipped the aluminum cup in the snow, giving it a quick wipe with his fingers before putting it back in his kit.

There were no tracks, so he followed the treeline until he could discover if Lance had made it out of the blowdown. He reminded himself not to let his guard down. Lance was a dangerous man and most likely armed.

He felt no sadness for Preach in the traditional sense, as he had never really liked him. However, the hole his death had left in the team would make his life more difficult. For this reason alone, he would kill Lance Coolidge without a second thought. He could read the signs and chalked Preach's mistake up to overconfidence, a mistake he would not make. If he saw Lance Coolidge, he would shoot on sight. It's a queer feeling knowing you will soon encounter the man who has taken the life of a team member with a homemade spear. Preach had been a vibrant, capable veteran.

———— • ————

Brad and the other five were moving at the same time as Truck.

Red handed the radio back to Brad. "I can't figure it out. She's hooped for sure."

Brad shrugged, putting it in his pack.

Red caught Romey's eye, and they drifted together as they did every morning.

"Today's the day, I think," Romey volunteered. "Has that feel."

Red quietly said, "Sat phone's been sabotaged. This gets weirder every day, boss."

Romey frowned. "Keep that between us for now. I've got to hand it to Coolidge; he's a ghost in these woods. Now I know why he's been able to evade us this long. This is more his element than ours. And he's had the same training."

"Truck's pretty good too," Red added.

———— • ————

Lance awoke as the first bit of grey leaked into the eastern sky. This was his second morning in the pine tree shelter. He was going through the cycle of hot sweats and cold chills a fever brings.

His best bet was to stay right here and try to gather his strength. If that had been an option, he would have taken it, but it wasn't. His pursuers would be on his trail, and he must move. How long can I hang on? How long until my strength plays out and they finish me? He decided he wasn't going to make it easy for them. After eating the remaining mussels, he gathered his meager belongings and popped two aspirin and two Tylenol. After just a few steps, his legs almost buckled under him. He was so thirsty; he broke a cardinal rule and ate some snow. Catching himself, he downed the last of his water.

He had bought himself some time with his deft trip through the blowdown but had squandered the advantage with his prolonged rest. By midmorning, he was standing on a low-ridged ravine that cut across his direction of travel. There were steep snowy slopes in places and frozen clay cliffs everywhere else. Below, groves of poplar trees reached up to the lip of the cliff. None were close enough that he could climb down, but he had an idea. Lance walked another three hundred yards and turned left into a grove of trees. From here he backtracked to the cliff edge. Several poplars were within jumping range. As a boy he had practiced this. The trick was to jump to a slender one, let it bend under his weight, taking him gracefully to the ground.

Choosing a likely tree, he took two quick steps, careful to place his feet in his original tracks, and jumped. He grabbed for the top of the tree he wanted and held fast. The tree did bend but not in the slow graceful arc he had expected. It barely slowed his descent, and just before his feet were about to hit the ground, he heard a crack. He let go, and the tree sprang back to its original position, and he came up hard against the ground. His tuck and roll lacked finesse, and he lay there looking up through the spindly winter canopy, now devoid of leaves. He had successfully bought himself a little more time. It wouldn't stop them, but every minute would help.

———— • ————

Truck set a brisk pace, picking up yesterday's tracks and following them to the shelter. It was abandoned. He picked up the trail again, less than an hour after Lance had made his jump into the poplars. He was in a small grove of trees when the trail disappeared. Hands on his hips, he studied the ground in every direction, but nothing. He walked twenty yards out in a circle. Nothing! He did the same at forty yards. Still nothing. He went back to the grove and examined the tracks again, cursing himself for wasting time. It was now obvious that Lance had backtracked. He gazed down the back trail, trying to imagine where Lance had gotten off. Nothing provided much of an opportunity besides the shallow ravine, so that must be it.

Not wanting to corrupt the tracks, he followed in a path running parallel to the others. It was easy to find the spot. Deep impressions clearly indicated where Lance had jumped. He approached the cliff slowly and carefully, not wanting to be shot at while looking over the edge.

It was obvious that Lance had jumped into the trees and shimmied down. Truck was a big man and dared not try that trick. How far did this lip go before he could make his way down? He had bought himself some time, but Truck could see that Lance had slowed—there was a drag to his step again, and his stride was shorter. He was weakening and the gap between them was closing. If he could find his way down, he could narrow the gap. He was confident that he would catch up with Lance today.

Truck was now also confident that Lance was unarmed. There had been several places that would have provided a perfect ambush position. Truck had approached them with extreme caution and knew that Lance would have set an ambush—if he could have. Truck picked up his pace now, excited with anticipation. The rest of the team was coming but he would finish this himself. And then, retirement—white sandy beaches and beautiful women. He found a steep but navigable slope down less than twenty minutes later.

———————— • ————————

Lance, ever diligent, watching his back trail, spotted Truck as he crested a small knoll among the trees. One man! Where were the rest? His eyes scanned the woods. There was no one else.

He scanned the ground, looking for something he could use as a weapon. A frozen branch had snapped from a birch tree and was hanging loosely. He would swing it like a club. He didn't have the strength to run so his only chance was to ambush this lone combatant. If he could take him out and collect his weapons and gear, it would be a whole new ball game. He would need the element of surprise, and of course there was the blade.

He found a small thicket of willows to hide in. It was out in the open and might be overlooked. He left tracks right alongside the thicket, then made a circle over a small rise in order to approach the spot from the opposite side where his tracks could not be seen by the pursuer. He would need the man in close enough to use his knife.

Lance had barely completed the maneuver, squirming into the low brush and squatting down, when Truck appeared. He was looking around cautiously but approaching at a good clip. He was being careful not to step in Lance's tracks but just off to the side. This created a problem for Lance. He needed to use the club—wait until Truck passed, and take a full step before swinging. Lance rehearsed the movements in his mind, imagining each one in advance. When he saw how big Truck was, he knew there would be a fight. There was no way Truck would go down with just one blow unless Lance could catch him right above the ear. Lance knew that this was where he must aim.

Truck moved smoothly and quietly for a big man, pausing every few steps to look around. Lance knew his position was well concealed and more importantly, an unlikely spot.

As he had hoped, Truck was not focusing on it.

Lance's heart was beating in long, slow thuds, and his breathing was shallow. Sucking air through his dry mouth, he was able to keep quiet and still. As Truck came alongside his position, Lance tensed, ready to strike. Truck hesitated, looking around. The tracks told him he was close. Lance could hear Truck's breathing and watched him shift from foot to foot, silhouetted just a few feet away. Lance tried to relax—his muscles were tightening up.

Without warning, Truck moved out again: one step … two … three steps!

Lance lunged forward, swinging the club in a wicked arc. At the sound, Truck whirled like a cat, and the blow caught him just above the eye. Lance leaped forward, swinging the club again. Truck managed to raise his left arm, taking the blow on his forearm. The force of the blow rendered the arm useless. Truck let out a desperate roar and heaved himself to the side.

Lance struck again, catching Truck on the back, to no effect. He was relentless, striking again and again. It was now or never. He simply didn't have the strength for a long fight. He was landing blow after blow on Truck, getting weaker while Truck seemed to be getting stronger—rising to his feet only to be struck down again and again.

Lance was at the end of his strength. The big man would not stay down! Bloody and bruised but apparently indomitable, he charged forward, head-butting Lance under the chin, sending him sprawling backwards into the snow. Truck's momentum carried him forward on top of Lance in the full mount position. His bulk pinned Lance to the ground—with snow closing in all around him, his arms were pressed against his sides, and he was unable to pull his knife. With practiced precision, Truck's knife slid from its scabbard into his hand. Lance saw what was coming and, in the moment, accepted this was the end. It was as it should be; he—Lance Coolidge—would die in a bitter fight to the death.

Suddenly, Truck's body was lifted off Lance, like a miracle. Relief washed over him. There was a flurry of movement. Someone else was here—another big man was viciously punching Truck. Who is it?

Daryl Craig lifted Truck to his feet and drove a mighty blow into his midsection and a final devastating blow to his jaw, snapping his head back. Truck dropped into the snow, and this time, he didn't move.

Lance fought to understand what was happening. "What? Uh … how?" His voice faltered.

Daryl shushed him, holding up seven fingers and indicated two different directions. "Can you walk, man?" he whispered urgently.

Lance nodded. "I think so."

Daryl moved out, and Lance followed him, stumbling past and looking down in awe at Truck's motionless form.

What a magnificent fighting man, Lance thought. His admiration, however, didn't stop him from picking up Truck's M4 carbine as he went by, working the action subconsciously.

They had made no more than fifty yards when a bullet whined overhead, clipping a nearby branch. In the same instant, they heard the report. Both men lunged over a knoll, bullets whistling all around. Daryl was running low and hard, with Lance on his heels, hurried along by the hail of gunfire.

There was fire coming from their left. Lance sprawled prone in the snow, rifle at the ready. It took him a moment to realize the fire from the right was friendly—they were laying down a wicked barrage from a concealed position.

This gave Daryl and Lance the opportunity to move again. This time, Daryl was putting distance between them and their pursuers. He looked back and saw Lance was flagging. He slowed his pace so Lance could catch up.

"Sorry," Lance said between great gasps, his hands on both knees and his head hanging low.

Clearly worried at Lance's weakness, Daryl caught him. Holding him up with one arm, he pointed with the other. "I have a snow machine a couple hundred yards away. I promise if you can make the sled, I can get you out of here and get you somewhere safe."

"Lead the way, I'll … make it."

As they ran, an occasional shot rang out behind them. The few hundred yards to the snow machine took what seemed like an eternity to Lance. When they finally made it, Daryl pushed Lance forward onto the seat and fired it up. Within seconds, they were racing away.

The ride was only about a mile, but in that short time, Lance lost consciousness. They came out on a spruce covered bench and there, next to a small stream, was one of the Craigs' line cabins.

Daryl pulled up to the door, managed to prop Lance up, and half dragged him as they stumbled into the cabin.

The cabin was warm, and the smell of bacon and coffee filled the air.

"Coffee," Lance mumbled as he tried to take a chair.

Instead, Daryl led him to the bunk and sat him down.

"Let's start with some water and work our way up to coffee. How does that sound?" Lance only had the strength to nod. The water was cold and went down nicely—from a cup, to boot! How wonderful these little treasures were in the moment.

"I hate to abandon your friends out there. If you're strong enough, I'll go back and help."

Lance was dumbfounded. "No friends." He managed to force the words out.

"Then who the hell were they?" Daryl asked.

Lance shrugged.

Daryl went to the stove, poured a cup of coffee and handed it to Lance. It was black, strong, and far and away the best cup of coffee he'd ever tasted. He was hungry and exhausted. He was only able to take a few sips before placing it on the stump that doubled as a nightstand next to the bed.

He lay back in the bunk, while Daryl checked Truck's M-4. He extracted the magazine. It was full so he slid it back in, then checked his semi-automatic

.308 hunting rifle. It was a little old, but he could hit a silver dollar at two hundred metres. It still had the 3x9 Bausch and Lomb scope it had come with.

Daryl glanced over at Lance. He had fallen asleep or passed out. Daryl was taking off Lance's jacket when he noticed the bullet hole. Upon closer examination, he observed the angry wound, swollen with infection. Daryl couldn't imagine how Lance had survived all these days—with no supplies and that nasty wound—being hunted like a dog.

He was all man!

Daryl bathed the wound, applied disinfectant, and replaced the bandage with a clean one from the first-aid kit.

After undressing Lance down to his long underwear, Daryl found the extra magazines in his jacket pockets. Placing them on the nightstand, he leaned the rifle within arm's reach of the bunk. He restocked the woodstove and covered Lance with several heavy blankets. Daryl knew sleep was the best doctor, so he let Lance rest. Then he went outside to look around. If they wanted Lance, they would have to come through Daryl first.

———— • ————

Brad had been the first to spot Lance. He saw the brief struggle between Truck and Daryl, mistaking Daryl through the brush for Lance. At first light, Brad had the team waiting to enter the blowdown and they'd pushed hard and made excellent time. There was no opportunity for clear identification, let alone a clear shot. Making the knoll, he hazarded a quick shot; Beats was at his right, and the rest were only moments behind. When they opened up on that position, all hell broke loose. Their fire was being returned from off to the left, and damn effective fire at that.

"I'm hit!" Beats called out in a relatively calm voice. Brad ducked low into the snow and raised his head slightly chancing a look. Beats was holding his left arm at the triceps with his right hand. His back was against a tree facing the fight, rifle swung over his back. Red was down. Romey was calling for a ceasefire. Then they heard the distant whine of the snow machine before it faded into the distance. They had been stopped in their tracks.

Their position was fair. There were trees for cover, and they were able to drop out of sight. If they stayed put, they were relatively safe. Staying low, Brad was able to get to Beats, but not without attracting a few more bullets. They weren't wasting ammo, whoever they were. Beats would be all right—a bullet had burned his arm drawing some blood, but it wasn't serious. He would be sore for a week or so, but that was about it. Red had fared a little worse—a bullet had grazed his skull, just above his right ear, knocking him out cold. Teddy was attending to the profusely bleeding wound with steady hands.

"S.o.b." Romey was pissed and cursing. "What the hell is this?" His anger was directed at Brad.

"How the hell should I know this was going to happen?" Brad snapped. "It was supposed to be a simple op!"

"This has been personal for you from the beginning, and now we have one dead man and two wounded, one seriously," Romey shouted.

"Red will be okay," Teddy said.

"Four wounded," Strong corrected. "I can see Truck, and he ain't movin'."

Romey cursed bitterly again. "I swear, B.A., if you get these men killed by withholding valuable intel ...."

Brad stared hard at Romey. "You'll remember your place, or I'll have you court-martialled."

"Fill your boots, but these men are my responsibility. No more secrets!"

Brad ignored Romey's threat; he had no answers. They now faced four able-bodied men, as best he could figure, instead of one wounded man. And now to compound their problems, they had wounded men of their own. A wounded man is always more trouble than a dead one, as it takes at least one to care for him. Beats wasn't out of it, though—one bright spot. But how had Lance gotten help after all this time? The radio he'd taken from Preach didn't have the range to reach the outside.

"Truck's moving." Strong had the only eyes on him. Truck rose from the ground like a huge grizzly waking up from hibernation. He wagged his head slowly back and forth, trying to clear his mind. Strong whistled, and Truck looked up lazily. On the third whistle, he found its direction and swung that big head around. Even at that distance Truck looked a sight.

"Over here," Strong called out, anticipating a shot that didn't come. Truck began slowly, methodically making his way towards them like a man in a trance. Several rifles were now trained on the position where the shooters had been. But all was quiet.

"Cover me." Strong took a chance and rushed to Truck's aid. Despite his size, Strong hefted him to his shoulder as the others probed the woods with intermittent gunfire.

Truck was a bloody mess. How he was still conscious was a mystery. The beating had left him unrecognizable. Several deep cuts were bleeding profusely, leaving a significant amount of blood on the snow. His jaw was swollen and appeared to be broken. Strong placed him down gently in the snow. Teddy had bandaged Red up and began administering first aid to Truck.

"We will need to get the wounded to care. Too bad that sat phone is broken." Romey's tone was accusatory and caustic.

Brad was thinking the same thing. "When we don't report in, they'll send the chopper," he assured them. "Let's stabilize them as best as we can, and then all we can do is wait. Beats, let's you and I look around if you're up to it."

"Yeah, I'm good."

Finding where the shooters had nested, Brad was able to confirm that there had been two men, as he'd suspected. It looked as though everyone had come together at the same moment. These two must have been on the move and spotted the I-teams only moments before the fight. Their position was concealed and slightly elevated—this was the luck of the draw. They had also had the element of surprise. Had they not been a trained group, they could have been wiped out. He could only assume that these men were trained special forces. Perhaps with the decision to pull them out, a support team had been sent in to aid Lance. But a team of only two men? Unlikely, but if so, they would need to activate their exit strategy.

"Time to cut the apron strings," he said to Beats.

"What about Truck?"

"He would do the same thing himself. They are sending a rescue and recovery team in to replace us … somebody knows something."

Beats considered that. It was like him to not to worry about the fact that this information was just coming out now. In the past, he had made a point of just doing his job, collecting his money, and keeping his mouth shut. This had been a great gig, and he was, by most accounts, a rich man. He wanted to enjoy some of that money, and besides, he had always trusted Brad's judgement. In that moment, they made the decision—they were getting out!

"What about the rest of them?" Beats indicated the group.

"They'll make out. Chopper'll be here today."

They found tracks of the enemy combatants heading in the same direction Lance and the other man had gone. Brad surveyed the vast wilderness before them with his binoculars and found the snowmobile tracks. This would be their ride out. If not, they would circle back and commandeer Lance's Jeep. Brad checked to make sure he still had the coil wire.

23

"Hello! The cabin!"

Whatever Daryl was expecting, this wasn't it. A rush attack maybe? Or something to that effect. Lance was sleeping soundly on the bunk. His eyes fluttered at the call, but he didn't wake.

"Lance! Wake up!" Daryl raised his voice just enough.

Lance's eyes flared open, and he was momentarily disoriented. Then the fight with Truck, the scrambled gun battle, and the race back on the snow machine all found context in the moment.

"We've got company," Daryl announced while peeking out the window. A lone figure stood in plain sight, wearing winter camo.

"We come in peace," the voice called out again. "Is Lance Coolidge in there? It's an old friend asking …."

Daryl called back. "State your purpose. Friends have been hard to come by lately!"

Ben Thompson laughed through his nose at that. "Tell him it's his old buddy Ben from the border. We spent some time together trying to understand that ol' unlucky number thirteen."

Daryl glanced over at Lance, who nodded. What is Ben doing here? None of this makes any sense.

Daryl was still cautious. Without a word, he pushed the cabin door open and stepped back into the corner, rifle at the ready.

Another man shadowed the doorway. He had been up against the wall outside the door. He held his empty hands high, and his rifle was slung over his back.

Lance had come to a sitting position and was covering the small window, trusting Daryl with the front door.

Wes Bass stepped into the cabin. "Is that coffee I smell?" With that he scooped up a cup, poured himself some, and took a slurp. "Lyin' abed when there's work to do … Just like you Americans! Nine to fivers, the Germans used to say. Fight you hard, from nine to five."

"Ben!" he called out to his buddy, "Coffee's on!"

Ben Thompson entered the cabin, taking in the scene in one sweeping glance.

"No me mates." The Spanish for "don't kill me" was not lost on Daryl, who was still covering him with the rifle.

Wes's eyes came to rest on Lance. "Looks like you got your tail in a crack, old friend." It was a hearty, good-natured statement, but there was relief in his voice as well. "I was a bit worried you would have salted all the hides before I got here."

"I just about had mine stretched before y'all came along," Lance replied, genuinely happy to see them.

Ben smiled at that and refilled Lance's cup. His tone turned serious. "We found it easy going on the snowmobile tracks, and I suspect they will as well. We slowed them down some, but as you know, they're a tough group and likely to keep coming. We trimmed the odds a little, but I would say they are still a strong force. It would be best if we could move if you're up to it."

Daryl stepped in. "He's got a fever, so it would be best not to move him. Who are you guys?"

"I will have to keep you guessing on that one, friend. Sorry," Ben replied.

Daryl was guessing special forces, but they had no identifying insignias, and there was something different about them that he couldn't put his finger on.

"We need to make this happen—these pine walls will be little protection from gunfire."

"I only have one snow machine. We have a main line cabin about ten miles away. It's easier to defend and its better supplied. There's a truck there so we can get him to a hospital."

"Good, take him there then, and we'll trail along behind and watch your six." Ben took out a radio and handed it to Daryl. "This is good for six klicks, if you have line of sight. Let us know when you're safely at the cabin and again when you are in the truck and moving. We will give you the affirmative with three squelches. Once you are safe, we are out of it."

Six klicks? They're Canadians! That's the difference, that slight accent—especially Wes. JTF-2 maybe; bad dudes for the most part. Excellent training, and pit bulls in a fight. Why are they here?

Daryl helped Lance into his clothes. He was shaky and weak but determined. He finished his coffee and they each ate a can of salmon.

The seat on the sled was only built for one, so they put a couple of blankets down for Lance to sit on. Ben and Wes had been at the cabin for half an hour, and they were now ready to move.

Before they set out, Lance asked Daryl how he'd found him. "Lynette. She told me to check here. She'd been praying, and she saw you in a dream—"

"A dream?"

Daryl shrugged. "Makes a man consider, doesn't it? It's a long, cold ride to the main cabin. You'll need to let me know if you need to stop along the way."

They started off well and made the first mile at a good clip. Ben and Wes followed along in the tracks laid down by the machine. After that first mile it was rough going, and as darkness closed in, they were still only about halfway to the main cabin.

Lance held on for all he was worth but finally he had to put his hand up, and Daryl stopped the sled on a flat spot. Lance was shaking and shivering. "Need a break." His voice was weak.

Daryl poured some coffee for Lance, who accepted it with trembling hands.

"It's another few miles … Do you think you can make it? Or should I make us a camp for the night?"

Lance dearly longed for the warmth and comfort of the cabin. He was shocked by his own weakness. It's a terrible thing when you've relied on strength your whole life, and now you find yourself weak and vulnerable. "I'd like to try for the cabin."

After a few minutes out of the wind he began to warm up. He ate some more salmon, but he was feeling queasy and suspected he wouldn't be able to hold it down. Daryl fired up the machine, and soon they were bumping along the twisted trail once again. Lance was in and out of consciousness, vaguely aware of Daryl stopping now and again to shake him out of his semi-conscious state. He'd gulp down a mouthful of water and then coffee, and they'd be off again. Daryl wondered if he was making a mistake by pushing someone this sick, but he kept on.

———— • ————

The single headlight of the snow machine pointed the way in the darkness. It was well after eight p.m. when they finally pulled up to the cabin.

Lynette swung the door open, casting them in its shaft of light. She came running out without a coat.

"He's alive," Daryl said huskily, "but wounded and sick."

"Thank you, Jesus!" she cried out.

Lynette took one arm and Daryl the other as they half carried him into the cabin. The main room housed a crude kitchen, woodstove, and bunk bed. There was a double bed in the second room. They helped him to the bottom bunk and started to remove his outer clothes, which were covered in snow and ice particles. He was shaking uncontrollably, and Lynette rubbed his shoulders, trying to warm him up. Suddenly, he cried out, and she recoiled.

"He's been shot in the left shoulder," Daryl explained. "The fever is on him, sis."

While she was attending to Lance, Daryl went to the woodstove, extending his hands towards it. He was ice-cold himself. Once he had warmed up his hands, he took the radio from his pocket and pressed the call button. "At the main cabin. I repeat, at the main cabin." There was no response.

Lynette gave him an inquiring look. To this, he raised his hand. "Give me a minute." He pressed the call button down three times. Still nothing.

Without a word, Lynette went back to working on Lance. She had him stripped down to his long underwear and was continuing to rub his arms and chest, carefully avoiding the wound. After a few minutes, she covered him with a heavy blanket, leaving his upper chest and shoulders exposed.

Daryl went outside, moving the sled to a lean-to shed and bringing the blankets inside. They had lost one somewhere along the trail. Before coming back inside, he moved away from the cabin and tried the radio again. Still nothing.

Lynette pulled the top of Lance's long underwear down, exposing the angry wound and the crude bandage. She was boiling water; their first-aid kit was laid out neatly on the table. The wound was worse—ugly and red with telltale signs of blood poisoning setting in.

"Looks bad," she mumbled under her breath. "What happened out there?"

Daryl was warming up, working on a bowl of stew. "He was close to the line cabin just as you thought, but I still came upon him by chance. I was scouting for tracks when I came across Satan's prints."

She hated the name he'd given that old bull but didn't say anything.

He continued, "It was rough going, so I parked the sled and followed his tracks on foot. I spotted movement and thought I'd seen the old boy. I figured I'd sneak up on him, only it wasn't the old bull I'd seen. It was Lance Coolidge sneaking into some brush. I was going to call out to him, but then a big guy came into view." He recounted the rest of the day's events for her, not glossing over any details.

"We may have jumped into a hornet's nest here, and may even have run afoul of the law, not to mention aiding a foreign military. I could be up for treason, but I couldn't leave him to the wolves. I just couldn't, not a man like that."

Are his eyes misty? Lynette turned away so as not to embarrass her brother. Removing Lance's bandage by the light of the lanterns, she could see that the wound was indeed in bad shape. It was still quite dirty, and bits of fabric and paper had fused into it. Using the tweezers, she began carefully removing the debris. Thoroughly cleaning the exit wound, she found remnants of the book.

When she was confident all foreign material had been removed, she washed the wound with the sterilized warm water.

From time to time, Lance moaned or mumbled but never regained consciousness. She worked carefully and methodically, knowing that the wound would not heal while still infected. The final bit of business before dressing the wound was to apply alcohol. There are few things more effective against infection. But it would sting like a bugger, so she asked Daryl to hold him down if need be. She put some on a clean cloth and dabbed the entrance wound. Immediately, Lance's eyes flared open, a wild and crazy look in them.

"Shhhh …," she soothed him. "You're okay, you're safe."

His eyes were still wild as he looked into hers, but something stilled within him. Slowly he relaxed, closing his eyes again. The pattern was repeated several times until the wound had been thoroughly treated. Daryl had been ready, but in the end, he wasn't needed.

"Tough guy," he said.

Finally, Lynette applied disinfectant and bandages and pulled the blankets over him. Taking some penicillin out of the kit, she ground up two pills. They had prescriptions for the animals, and she guessed at his weight and what his need would be.

"Hope he's not allergic." Daryl's brow was furrowed.

"We need to chance it. I didn't notice a bracelet or a tattoo," Lynette responded.

His ghostly pallor was most concerning, and when Daryl suggested the hospital, she stopped him.

"He's lucky to be alive. We need to stabilize him before we move him again."

Daryl didn't argue. He knew better. Instead, he set about preparing a defense. They had a 30-30 and a twelve-gauge Defender shotgun with plenty of ammunition. He checked the loads and made them ready. He double-checked his .308 and the M-4. Digging out his Glock, he set it on a chair beside the bed for Lance.

There was an old double-barrelled shotgun hanging above the door that had belonged to his father. He broke it open and loaded it with buckshot.

On a whim, he took it out to the lean-to and hid it within arm's reach, resting it butt down against the inside of one of the upright poles.

He tried the radio again, and still there was no response, so he went back in the cabin, locking the door behind him. Lynette had put the first-aid kit back together.

"He drank some water with the penicillin; he got it all down, so that will help. Now we wait. Why don't you catch a couple hours' sleep? I will keep an eye on him for a while."

Daryl hesitated, not wanting to leave her alone, but he was dead tired and knew she'd wake him if there was a problem. He made his way to the back room, removed his boots, and lay down. He'd barely covered himself with the heavy blanket before he was fast asleep.

———— • ————

Lynette noted where each of the firearms were. She retrieved the 30-30 and rested it on her knees as she sat in a chair next to Lance. Turning the lantern down, she listened to the hum and crackle of the fire. She imagined she was a sight, like one of those pioneer women of old. Standing over my man, ready to defend him to the death. My man? Yes, from the moment we met in the bistro, I knew. This is the man I have waited for my entire life! God heard my prayers and has kept him alive. She had even known, deep within her spirit, where he would be. She couldn't explain it logically—but he was where she'd imagined, dreamt, or been told ....

She had to believe it wouldn't end with him dying here tonight. She'd petitioned God for his survival, and here he was. They would make it through this trouble, and then they would build a life together. She thought of Daryl as well; his strength seemed endless. She knew the toll the day had taken on him, but he hardly showed it. He was marvellous, and his loyalty was without measure. She was in a wilderness cabin with enemies all around, but there was nowhere she'd rather be. The two men she loved the most were with her, and nothing else mattered.

These two strong men who put everything on the line for their country and their families. And what of the two mysterious Canadian soldiers? She shuddered at the thought of them still out there in the cold. Why did such men exist? Men who place the cause, the mission, above their own lives? Fighting men who would stand up against injustice and oppression. She was grateful for them, even though she didn't understand why they had come. She got up quietly, went to the door, opened it a sliver, and peered out. All was quiet except for the river a few yards away.

Stepping out into the night, she raised the radio, pushed the call button, and spoke, "They made it safely to the cabin." There was no reply. She turned to go inside when the radio sprang to life. Three squelches and that was all. It was enough. Her heart leapt, and she whispered a silent thank you to the strangers who had saved Lance's life. She locked the door behind her, stoked the woodstove, and returned to his bedside. Tomorrow would be a pivotal day.

———— • ————

Before dark, Romey knew they wouldn't be coming back. He'd buzzed them several times on the radio with no response. There were forces at play here he didn't understand.

Red was stable. They had sutured the wound on his scalp, and while it had bled a lot, it was superficial. Truck, however, was a mess.

They made camp just inside the trees, and he ordered an adequate fire to keep the men warm. They created a reflecting wall and built a comfortable shelter. An ugly anger was beginning to rise in Romey. It was unforgivable for Brad to abandon his command and even one of his own men.

Calling Teddy over, he instructed him: "In the morning, I'll need you to head back to the landing zone, get the chopper's attention, and let them know where we are."

"Yes sir. I'll be ready at first light."

He was walking away when Romey called him back. "Don't trust anyone, and if you spot Brad or Beats, steer clear of them, and radio me right away. Is that understood?"

"Absolutely clear, sir." Teddy was having his own bitter thoughts as well.

The moon was coming up, bathing their wintry world in its ghostly light. Tomorrow was shaping up to be a clear day. The chopper crew would be looking for them by first light. He might be able to save Teddy the walk. He would order a signal fire with a load of green boughs ready in case they heard the chopper. As the crow flies, they were only a few miles from the LZ, and a good smoke would surely be noticed. Romey took a cue from Brad's playbook: he would place a sentry that night and take the first watch himself.

He positioned himself about a hundred yards outside the camp, once everyone had settled in. His thoughts went to Lance Coolidge. He had evaded them for a week—an impressive feat indeed. He began to doubt the premise of this pursuit. Now that Lance had made good his escape, Brad and Beats had abandoned the field. What was that about? And who were the men who came to Lance's aid? He suspected by this time tomorrow he would have some answers.

———— • ————

Lynette kept a close eye on her patient. She managed to get a few sips of water laced with Tylenol and Advil into him. This would help with the fever. His breathing had steadied, and he was now resting quietly. When she found herself unable to keep her eyes open anymore, she climbed into the top bunk, bringing the gun with her, barrel pointed at the door, and allowed herself a catnap.

It was 1:35 a.m. when she heard Daryl moving around in the bedroom. He came into the main room, his massive frame filling the doorway. He could see her peering at him from the top bunk even though the lantern had been trimmed low. Stretching, he went to the pitcher and poured himself a cup of water. Soundlessly, the big man placed his hand gently on her shoulder, then stooped low to examine Lance.

"I'll be back soon to take a shift," he whispered and traded her the Glock for the rifle.

———— • ————

As he stepped out the door, the cold hit him. The temperature had dropped again. A bright three-quarter moon hung in the sky surrounded by a moon dog. The river gurgled pleasantly. As his eyes adjusted to the pale light, he took a good look around. All was quiet. He didn't waste time outside.

Pondering how Lance had survived almost a week in these conditions, Daryl realized it was a testament to his strength and endurance. Hopefully we can move him tomorrow.

They had plenty of supplies, and Lynette had filled the forty-five-gallon water barrel while he was away. That was a lot of trips to the river, but a well-spent effort now that they might need to make a stand. He was thankful they had made it to the cabin. Lance might not have survived another night in the cold.

It was a long drive to get into cell range. Daryl hoped that the telecom company would keep the towers up even after the switch to 5G. Too many hills and trees for those shorter waves to reach these remote areas.

Lynette was sitting in the rocking chair with a shawl wrapped around her shoulders when he returned. She had restocked the woodstove. "Three squelches came in on the walkie talkie a few hours ago."

Daryl nodded. "Go get some sleep; you'll need your energy tomorrow. I'll keep an eye him."

"Okay. If he wakes up, try to get some stew into him." She slipped into the bedroom but left the door open. The bed was still warm; she snuggled under the heavy blankets and was soon fast asleep.

Lance spoke weakly. "In the movies, when you wake up, there is a beautiful woman sitting in a rocking chair worrying about you."

"Sorry to disappoint you." Daryl smiled wryly, relief in his voice. "If it's any consolation, the beautiful girl is getting some sleep in the next room." He indicated the direction with a sideways jerk of his head.

He raised Lance's head slightly and propped him up with another pillow. Then he raised a cup to his lips, and Lance managed a good drink of water before letting his head rest back on the pillow.

After filling a bowl with stew, Daryl came back to the bedside. Lance's breathing had steadied. Daryl scooped a small spoonful and placed it against Lance's lips. His eyes didn't open, but Daryl managed to get three spoonfuls down the patient before he lost consciousness once again. He was still very warm, and that worried Daryl. The infection was serious, and the best course of action was to get him to a hospital.

———— • ————

Lynette was on the morning shift as a few rays of sunlight filtered in through the shuttered windows. Daryl had been up for about an hour and looked fit enough to tackle hell with a water gun.

"How's the fever?" he asked her.

She replied without looking up, "Not good, it may have dropped a degree or so, but it's still too high. I've given him another dose of penicillin. Hopefully it will help clear up the infection."

Daryl was by the door, gun in hand. He had shrugged into his heavy jacket. "I'll go take a look around and see what's what."

All was still outside. The creek kept up its ongoing conversation. Moving off a hundred yards where its influence was less, Daryl listened carefully. He waited a full ten minutes and was just ready to move to another position when a subtle movement stopped him. It was just a flicker, but he held himself still, waiting. There it was again—just a slight movement of a tree bough. Is that a bird or some other animal? Like a ghost, a silhouette materialized, and now a man stood in winter camo where a moment ago there was nothing. He recognised Wes Bass immediately.

Wes was looking straight at him. Uncertain as to who had seen who first, Daryl lifted a hand in silent greeting. Wes returned the greeting and strode forward. It wasn't until he was within a few feet that Daryl heard the faint sound of his footfalls. He was the elite of the elite, and in that moment, Daryl was grateful this man was on his side.

Wes flashed a devilish grin. "You get the drop on me, man?"

"Not likely," Daryl replied. "Where's your partner?"

At that the grin widened into a smile. "Why, he's been here the whole time."

There was a purposeful crunching of snow behind him. Daryl was appalled at his foolishness—they had played him like a child. Looking over his shoulder casually, he hid his surprise so well, there was even doubt in Ben's eyes. "Let's get you men some breakfast." He marched back to the cabin with the men in tow.

"I brought some friends with me," he announced, as he pushed the door open.

When they entered, they were covered by the Glock. Daryl knew his sister and was not even slightly surprised by this move. Meanwhile, both Canadians paid the pistol almost no mind. Ben, last through the door, closed and locked it behind him.

Indicating Lance, he said, "Looks like he made it through the night. I wouldn't have bet against that feller, but the odds looked to be against him last night."

"How can I ever thank you?" Lynette said earnestly. "You saved his life."

"The truth is, Miss …?" Ben hesitated, not knowing her name.

"Lynette Craig," she volunteered.

"Lynette," he continued, "it was the fast action of this gent that saved him. We just slowed them down by throwing some lead downrange." The crow's feet near his eyes deepened, attesting to the humour he found in the situation.

The three men were seated around the table, and Lynette poured each a cup of scalding hot coffee. She also ladled generous portions of stew into bowls and served a plate of liberally buttered bread. The men leaned into the food, and for the moment, silence filled the room.

She had eaten earlier and sat at the table with them, cradling a warm cup of coffee with both hands. Her hair hung loosely, the sun tinting the honey-coloured highlights.

Ben pushed his chair back. "Is he up to travelling?"

She shook her head. "His fever is still high, and I'm not sure we should chance it."

"You need to chance it!" Ben replied firmly. "That sunshine out there means reinforcements are coming."

They shared intel about the two SEAL teams, the apparent wounding or killing of Lance, and their covert mission directed from high up in the US government.

"We must assume that they will come with a full force today, and your best bet is to get him to the hospital in town. There is reason to believe he may get some 'official' help if you can get him there."

"Not to be selfish," Ben added, "but this gets dicey for us from here on out. We won't be able to explain our presence here, and no one will vouch for us if we are captured, killed, or wounded."

"You've done so much already … how can we ask you to risk more?" Lynette said.

Ben hesitated. "The mission is not complete until he is safely away. But we must consider the consequences. We are Canadian soldiers on a military incursion into the United States of America. And the last time I checked, militarily Canada would last about two weeks in all-out conflict. It would never come to that, of course, but politically, heads would roll. And our friend in Washington would not be able to help," he concluded, looking at Lance resting peacefully.

Then he asked, "You been feeding him that stew?"

"Yes, and I've given him two doses of antibiotic," Lynnette replied.

"What about coffee?"

"What about coffee?" she replied, somewhat confused by the question. She looked at each of them, trying to understand.

Wes spoke up. "Aren't you … his girlfriend?"

She hesitated, not sure how to respond.

"Well, anybody that knows Coolidge, knows he needs a coffee." He rose to his feet and filled a cup.

"Coffee!" Wes used his nickname. "You up for a cup of java, my friend?"

Lance's eyes fluttered open. It took him a minute to remember where he was as Wes loomed above him, brew in hand.

"Give us a hand," Wes said, looking over his shoulder at the others.

They propped several pillows behind Lance, and Wes offered the coffee. Lance's hands trembled slightly as he eagerly accepted it. They were all gathered around him now, which brought a smile to his face. His gaze went from one to the other as he blew gently on the coffee before taking a sip. "Is it my birthday?" he quipped.

"No, but you narrowly missed the celebration on the other end. Had this big galoot here not gotten to you when he did, she'd have been all over, my friend."

"It wasn't just me," Daryl added to Ben's narrative. "These boys here covered our retreat. The truth is, they saved both of us."

"I guess that makes us even then. Eh?" Lance attempted the Canadian suffix, fumbling it horribly.

"Hmm, I think I'm still down one." Ben grew more serious now as he explained the situation they were in.

Lance knew who the friend in Washington was, of course. He filled in the blanks based on his "interaction" with Preach. They were clearly looking for something they thought Lance possessed; what that might be he couldn't guess. He told them about Preach's claim that someone named "Bellamy" had run his brother and family off the road and that this manhunt was somehow connected.

Based on Lance's description, Daryl knew Preach was the same soldier he had run into at the main camp.

"Struck me as a mean, vindictive little bugger, that's for sure."

"That he was," Lance said quietly. "That he was."

Each of them understood the import of his words.

"We need to move you," Daryl stated emphatically. "We have our truck, but if the road is blocked or we run into any trouble …."

Lance took a big sip of coffee. It was the best cup he could ever remember drinking. To a man back from the edge, every cup was better and better.

"Pack up some of that stew and a thermos of coffee, and I'll make it," Lance said, with a wink at Lynette.

She was about to protest, but they were all in motion, and the decision had been made.

———— • ————

They loaded the back of the old F150 SuperCab with several blankets and pillows and warmed it up before they brought Lance out to it. He was shaky on his feet, but he squeezed behind the seat and stretched out, his head on a pillow in Lynette's lap. Before securing the cabin and removing the key from the sled, Daryl retrieved the old shotgun and set it back above the door. Ben took note of the shotgun's location and nodded his approval.

It was a cold, crisp morning. Daryl was driving, and the three men filled the front seat, their weapons on their laps and their gear in the truck box.

24

The chopper arrived late in the morning, carrying the search and rescue team, a couple of paramedics, and Sheriff Hallward. While one of the paramedics was administering aid to Truck, Romey had a brief conversation with Hallward. The conversation helped explain the disappearance of Brad and Beats, but Romey was shocked that they'd risked life and limb on a false premise. Brad clearly had an agenda of his own, and Romey swore to himself then and there, that the next time he crossed paths with Brad Akron ....

The chopper swung in a wide search pattern, but the sled tracks led into the trees and disappeared. Not wanting to spook Lance or those helping him, they debated deploying the search and rescue team but decided not to risk any more lives. They had to trust that whoever was helping Lance would provide the aid he needed.

Romey cursed himself for having been a fool. He was thankful that Lance had managed to elude them all these long days, surviving in seemingly impossible conditions.

Reading his thoughts, Red sat down beside him and yelled above the roaring chopper motor and blades. "It's not your fault, boss. We were just following orders, and there's no shame in that."

Romey understood this, but new-found doubts about his career path were nagging again. Maybe it is time to hang it up.

The flight path of the chopper missed the truck moving down the main road. The pickup wound its way along a snow-covered road, disappearing and reappearing amidst the thick forest.

———— • ————

They had driven for about an hour before reaching the hunting camp Lance had set up. The flagging tape was still there, cold and brittle—flashing in the brisk morning wind that had whipped up again. The trailer and wall tent were there, but the Jeep was gone. It had been driven off in the night, judging by the partially filled tracks.

"That's weird," Daryl said. "Why would they take the Jeep and not secure the area?"

"Not much time to stop here." Ben looked back at Lance. "Anything you really need?"

"There is some water in the tent under the bunk." It was like him to think only of the necessities.

Without a word, Ben got out of the truck, and after a quick glance around assured him that the place was abandoned, he went into the tent. A moment later, he came out with the case of water under his arm. He glanced into the trailer where the quad sat idle, covered by a blanket of snow. He tossed the case of water into the back of the truck. They were frozen solid. Retrieving several bottles, he put them behind the seat on the floor to melt.

"Looks like you had a couple of gas cans in the trailer?"

Lance nodded.

Ben continued. "Whoever took the Jeep took those as well. Two men. They broke off from the main group. They must have pushed hard to get here. They were tired, but they didn't waste any time lingering about. They opened the hood for some reason. Maybe they were having trouble starting it in the cold."

He had read the sign on the ground the way some men read an instruction manual. There had been no attempt to hide anything, so it had been easy to see, even in the few brief moments of his walk to the tent. The tracks of the Jeep were plain enough. They were heading in the only logical direction—down towards the highway. They followed the tracks for a solid hour, watching for possible ambush locations as they went. The road made a sharp right, but the Jeep had turned left onto a narrower road. Daryl stopped at the road.

"One of our smaller line cabins is up that way."

They knew what was on his mind.

"Our mission is defensive from here on out," Ben reminded him. "We need to get him to the hospital. That's the priority."

Daryl nodded, rolled up the window, and drove off. It went against the grain, letting them hide out at the line cabin. He never refused its use to a hunter or hiker who came across it. In fact, that had happened more than once, and most left it better than they found it.

Another hour and they made their way past the sour gas plant, which, as usual, they smelled long before they saw it.

"Who the hell works here? Nobody that I know." Daryl's quip was one of those offhand comments you get on a long drive.

It had started to snow again, and Daryl slowed, taking every turn with caution. They were a silent group, none given to small talk.

Wes had been checking his GPS occasionally, and when they were on a long straight stretch, he finally broke the silence. "Our stop is about a klick ahead—a winding section, and when she straightens out again, stop without pulling over. That will leave less tracks."

"You're getting out in this?" Lynette was incredulous.

"You should be fine from here. You're only a few hours from the hospital. If you hand me your phone, I'll add a contact called 'A Friend'. You can text me the word 'safe' when you make it to the hospital."

She gave him her phone; he added the contact and handed it back.

The truck rolled to a stop. When Ben opened the door, the wind whipped up, drawing a few flakes of snow into the cab. He took two of the thawed water bottles and then reached out his hand, and Lance shook it heartily.

"Coffee, be well, my friend, and try and stay out of the drink. We have farms to attend to."

"And don't take no shit!" Wes added.

Lynette had tears in her eyes. "You both have a place here with us, if you ever need it."

Both men turned and saluted Daryl, and he returned the gesture.

"Get a move on," Wes said, slamming the door.

A moment later, they had their packs on and were moving towards the treeline.

Daryl brought the truck up to speed. Lynette looked out the back window, trying to catch sight of them, but the snow being kicked up by the truck obscured any view she might have had of them.

"Strange men," she said, thinking out loud.

"The best," Lance echoed her sentiment, his head resting back on her lap.

Lynette looked at the contact in her phone—+222. She had not seen that prefix before, and the plus meant it was an overseas number. On an impulse, she tried to take a screen shot of the number, but nothing happened. She tried again with the same result. Assuming it was an issue with her phone, she pulled up a different contact and tried again. This time the screenshot formed a thumbnail on the bottom left of her screen as usual. She pulled "A friend" contact back up and attempted another screenshot; still nothing. She glanced back to where Ben and Wes had gotten out, but they were long gone. Just how far ahead is military technology?

———— • ————

Lance was fully alert and Lynette filled him in on the situation, explaining that he would most likely be arrested for Cathy Short's murder. Lance remembered who she was and the strange behaviour she had displayed. It was her strange behaviour that had prompted him to ask questions about her. There were so many things he didn't understand. Had they asked him, he would have come in immediately to clear things up. Instead, they had shot him without provocation and sent the military after him. Since he was retired, this was a gross violation of his rights as an American citizen.

What he couldn't wrap his mind around was that somehow all of this was tied to his brother's murder. It seemed implausible.

Such is the nature of evil—it consumes everything in its path until it swallows even itself. Had they left him alone, nothing would have come of his nagging doubts about the accident. Now, he would not rest until he found Bellamy. A slow-burning anger had been lit within him, and he would push and prod him until the truth was revealed.

The concept of truth persisted in his mind. Without truth there can be no justice, and there can be no truth if there was not a bedrock standard that can be applied to determine what truth is. We are living in a time when people, for selfish reasons, want to deny anything that is absolute—that is, until they need justice themselves. Then, when they have proselytized the entire world to make converts to their philosophy, at the end of it all, truth is the victim, and the prophet is thrown upon the heap of corpses. Let them have their time. Lance would patiently endure and eventually the truth would be made known.

"I don't want to go straight to the hospital," he said suddenly. "I want you to turn me in. They will arrest me, but you need to be in the clear in order to continue to help me."

In response to their protests, he said, "Don't worry. Unless they shoot me on the spot, I will still get medical attention."

The plan made sense, and despite their feeble protests they knew it was their best course of action.

The sheriff's station parking lot was full when they pulled up to the front door. Lance set his teeth and pulled himself out from the back seat, momentarily leaning against the side of the truck.

They entered the station, Daryl first, then Lance, and Lynette bringing up the rear. The room, awash with conversation and activity grew immediately silent. All eyes were fixed on the trio as they entered. Hallward was there and two of his deputies, but also Geraldine, Romey, and Red. Lance pushed himself forward, his hard gaze resting on Romey and Red. He recognized them for who they were.

Romey looked into those hard green eyes, and something went cold inside him. This was a dangerous man!

Lance's gaze swung to the sheriff, and he spoke in a strong, clear voice that belied his weakened state. "Sheriff, I guess because of these two, I'm your prisoner now."

Hallward hesitated a moment, struggling to come to grips with this new reality. Standing before him was a man they had falsely accused and inadvertently hounded almost to death—a man who by all accounts could have gone full Rambo—yet here he stood, even more formidable in this meek posture.

"There will be no arrests here today, son. This has been a tragic series of mistakes."

Lance couldn't believe what he was hearing. As the tension left his shoulders, the release reached his knees, weakening them considerably.

Romey was quickly at his side to lend support. "I've got you, man," he said in a husky voice. And then, in a tone that was more commanding and sharper than he intended, he barked out, "Let's get this man to the hospital!"

They loaded him back into the truck and within a few short minutes were carrying him into the emergency ward, a posse of armed men and women that overwhelmed the nursing staff.

The head nurse was able to block most of them from the examining room by pulling the curtain shut in their faces, but there was no budging Romey or Lynette.

"I'll get us all some coffee," Daryl volunteered.

"Red," Romey called through the curtain, "nobody comes in here without passing you! Is that clear?"

Lance looked at Romey questioningly.

They removed Lance's jacket and boots and unbuttoned his shirt. The nurse inspected the bandage. "Nice work," she said to Lynette.

"I gave him a dose of penicillin last night and another this morning." Lynette held her interlocked fingers under her chin in hopeful anticipation.

The nurse scratched a note on the chart. "Mr. Coolidge, do you know where you are?" she asked.

"I do," Lance replied.

"Do you know what day it is?"

At this he hesitated, "No ma'am, I can't say that I do."

"Hmm." She took her flashlight and scanned his eyes. "What's your birthdate?"

"July seventh. And I am trained to resist anything beyond my rank and serial number. Will that be all?"

At that she scrunched her nose. "With that sense of humour, you'll probably be all right. Let's check out that wound, shall we?" She carefully pulled the bandage back and examined it. "Infected for sure. I'll clean that out, and the doctor can have a look. He should be here soon."

On cue, Red said, "Romey, I've got the doc here."

"Send him in."

Doc Currie had been serving Lone Prairie for over twenty years and was not given to nonsense. He pulled the curtain back and came to Lance's bedside. Taking a moment to read the chart, he asked, "Do we all understand how the chain of command works?

Romey nodded.

"Great, in here I am in charge. So you can leave and give us room to work. I want the firearms out of the hospital as well. If you feel it's necessary to provide security, post your man at the front door. Is that understood?"

"Yes sir." Romey was polite. He looked at Lynette. "Let me know if you need anything," he said before ducking out.

Doc Currie came around opposite Lynette. He knew who she was and shrewdly judged that she would not be leaving his side, so didn't press the issue with her. He had been briefed as to the nature of the wound and the condition of the patient. He examined both the entrance and exit wounds.

"Looks like you're still maintaining a fever. We will continue the antibiotic treatment and prep you for surgery so I can flush that wound properly. We should be able to stitch you up just fine. The bullet didn't hit anything vital, but it would have been less trouble if I could have seen you a week ago," he added.

"I was busy."

"Yes, so I hear. Well, don't you worry; we'll take good care of you. If we can keep the infection at bay, you should make a full recovery. I'll give you two a minute, and then we'll get you down there, asap."

When Doc Currie had gone, Lynette took Lance's hand. A soft light glistened in her eyes. "I'll be here when you're out of surgery."

Lance squeezed her hand. "I was never alone out there, Lynette. In this life I've seen people in pain and dying, and I'm telling you now, someone was with me ... some of the ancestors maybe; I don't know, but someone else too. By the way, how did you know where to send Daryl?"

"I was praying for you, and somehow I just knew ... I felt it."

Lance leaned back into the bed. "I'm scared, Lynette."

This surprised her. "Lance, you're here now. You heard the doctor. You're going to be all right."

"It's not the surgery I'm scared of ... I'm scared of losing my edge. I'm a warrior."

The surgical team lifted Lance onto the gurney, despite his assurances he could transfer himself, and wheeled him away.

"Surgery OR-7," he heard someone say. That figures, he thought to himself. He then gave one last squeeze before letting go of Lynette's hand.

She walked out into the waiting room as Daryl was coming in, a coffee and sandwich in hand for each of them. "He's in surgery."

He put his arm around her and gave her a squeeze. "I'm sure he'll be all right." There was genuine confidence in his voice.

The woman from the sheriff's station was there, just a few chairs away from her. She was checking her phone, and that reminded Lynette of her promise.

Pulling her phone out, she brought up "A Friend" and began to text, "Made it to ..." The words disappeared. She started again. "We have ..." Again, the words disappeared from the screen. "Text one word," Ben had said. She typed the word "SAFE". This time the word remained on the screen, and she hesitated only a second before pressing send. The message bubble popped up, indicating it had gone through successfully. It was only there for a moment when the screen went dark. Her battery had died.

She reached into her purse, hoping she had a charging cord. Suddenly, her phone screen lit up. It was rebooting. She entered her passcode, and the power was still at 47 percent. Perplexed, she pulled up her messages. The last one to "A Friend" was gone. She went into her contacts and "A Friend" was missing.

Sighing, she thought that there are some things you just don't want to know.

Her next call was to Katherine, who picked up on the first ring. "How is he?"

"He's in surgery, but the doctor thinks he will be okay."

Katherine let out a tremendous sigh. "I'm on my way."

———— • ————

The surgery did go well. Lance was placed in a private room with an IV drip that failed to tether him to the bed. He had a succession of visitors. Geraldine came to take an extensive statement. His mother and Lynette kept a constant vigil, and Uncle Joseph popped in for a short visit.

When they were alone, he shared some of his suspicions and the facts as he knew them. He was convinced that if he applied pressure in the right places, the truth would come out.

Before Joseph left, he said. "I'm better served with my ear to the ground in Washington. When you're feeling up to it, meet me there."

Romey visited him early on the third day. He relayed as much information as he could, including the disappearance of Brad and Beats. He was convinced that Truck knew more than he was letting on, but he'd remained tight-lipped and had been reassigned.

"Any idea what the talk of an envelope is all about?" Lance asked. "Cross kept asking me about it."

"No, but whatever it is, you had best keep your head on a swivel."

Lance was reluctant to ask about his brother or how his death could be connected to this. It was obvious now that Kyle had seen or heard something related to this plot, and they had killed him to cover it up.

Why run them off the road? Were they eliminating a witness with first-hand information or information they thought he possessed? Why did they take such extreme measures in coming after him? Why were they so convinced that he was in possession of something valuable or incriminating?

———— • ————

Lance's Jeep had been abandoned at the line cabin, and other than the damage they had done to the ignition, it was in working order. The assumption was they had another vehicle waiting. Brad and Beats had disappeared as though the earth had swallowed them up.

Truck had been arrested, but he claimed that he had just followed orders and had no idea where the other two had gone. He had been released from the hospital after just two days and had returned to base.

———— • ————

Clarence had retrieved the Jeep. It was drivable, so the mechanic drove it back to town. He took the liberty of ordering the parts to repair the ignition.

After the FBI and the sheriff's office had completed their investigation, Daryl went in and packed up the camp and brought Lance's gear back to the ranch. He put it out to dry in one of the barns.

On the morning of the fourth day, the Doc released Lance into Lynette's care, exacting a promise to make sure he finished the full cycle of antibiotics.

The Craigs set up rooms for Lance and Katherine in the big ranch house. It was south facing, on a knoll overlooking the pastures and river snaking down the valley. The area was now covered with snow and dotted with cattle. It had a huge veranda that wrapped around all but the north side of the house. The yard was always manicured. In the spring and summer, a series of perennial plants and flowers bloomed consecutively. The house itself had been built only a decade earlier. While it held all the charm of a country rancher, it was brightly furnished and had all the modern amenities. The centerpiece of the main living area was a massive river-stone fireplace that warmed the entire house.

Lance made a miraculously quick recovery in that big, peaceful house. He was able to relax, as he did in his mother's home. It dawned on him that there was nowhere else he experienced that sense of comfort. Is it because Lynette is here?

After two weeks on the ranch, they found him doing odd jobs early one morning and decided they could hold him no longer. A steady diet of protein, spring water, fresh air, and gallons of coffee had allowed him to regain most of his weight.

They were never sure if he was having shoulder pain, as he never mentioned it, although there were occasions where he would stop what he was doing and give it a rest or stretch it, but that was all.

The morning they found him doing chores, Lynette called him for breakfast. She and Katherine were sitting at the table, waiting for him. As had become their custom, one of them would pray before the meal. This morning it was Katherine's turn, but Lance stopped her and bowed his head.

"God, for what we are about to receive, may we be truly grateful, and may we learn your ways, the way of the truth, Amen."

"Amen," Katherine whispered and for a few moments, they ate in silence.

When Lance finally spoke, his voice was calm and assured. "I will be leaving soon. I spoke with Uncle Joseph, and we need to pick up the trail before it gets cold. We have several leads to work on, and promised myself that I will get to the bottom of Kyle's death."

Both women knew what it meant to be Lance Coolidge, and they loved him for it. Even though they longed for him to be near, to stay and live in peace, they knew he would have no peace while his brother's murderers breathed free air. They knew that they could not ask him to deny who he was, and they also knew he had the skill set to do what needed to be done.

"Miss Katherine, you are welcome to stay here while Lance is away," Lynette offered.

"I was thinking you might want to see where Lance grew up and stay with me for a while," Katherine replied.

In the end, that was what was decided. They would leave in the morning.

———— • ————

Daryl drove them into town in the old truck, and Katherine followed in her Jeep Grand Cherokee. When they pulled up to the garage, Lance's Jeep was parked outside, all washed and clean. All three service bays were full. Two of the trucks were from the Sukunka Sour Gas Plant.

Lance smiled. "Got a fleet account?" he asked, indicating the gas plant trucks.

"Yeah, but I'm the only game in town." Clarence laughed heartily. "You look good as new, Lance."

"Don't tell the ladies—it still hurts like a bugger sometimes, but every day it gets a little better."

"That's the right direction at least."

"Agreed. Jeep's ready, I see."

"Yup, fixed, fueled, and ready to go." Clarence handed him the keys.

Lance tossed the keys up in the air, caught them deftly, and shook them with gratitude. "Can't thank you enough."

"You're family," said the other sincerely.

Lance turned to go. "Thanks again."

"Oh hey, I wanted to mention something to you. Do you remember me telling you about the thermostat I found in the garbage can the morning after …." Clarence paused. "After Kyle?"

"Yes, I remember." Lance's curiosity was piqued.

"Well, a guy came in a couple days back. Said his heater wasn't working—that he'd been up in the woods one night and just about froze to death. He said Kyle had removed the thermostat in the spring and had forgotten to replace it."

"Really?" Lance's sixth sense was stirred.

"Yup, a Chevy 350, just as I suspected. Found out why there wasn't no paperwork. Kyle did it at the end of the night and didn't charge the guy."

"That sounds like Kyle," Lance agreed. It dawned on him that this could have been the last person to see Kyle alive. He would have gone straight home before starting out for their mother's. That was the plan and why they were on the road that evening. He said as much to Clarence.

"What colour was the truck?"

"Dark blue extended cab … hang on."

Clarence went inside and came back out with an invoice. "Here's his info … 2005 Chevy half-ton. Customer was Clifford Bellamy; paid cash." He was smiling, proud of himself, but something in Lance's expression caused the smile on his face to drop.

Lance went cold inside. He snatched the invoice out of Clarence's hand. "Can I keep this?"

"Sure, I'll go photocopy it. What's the deal, Lance?"

"I'm not sure." Lance was intentionally vague. "I would just like to talk with the guy, that's all. Did you notice if it had out-of-state plates?"

"No, in fact they were Montana plates."

That didn't fit, but he could have stolen the plates.

"Any chance you remember the number?"

"No, sorry."

Lance didn't share his discovery as he said goodbye to his mother and Lynette. Katherine gave him one of her big hugs. "You make sure you're careful; we don't need our hearts broken."

"I will," he lied.

He had filled Lynette in as much as he could the night before, so now his short stroll with her was more intimate. "Lynette, you know how I feel, and I'm trying to learn how to say what's on my mind."

She waited patiently for him to get it out.

"I will never want another woman now that I've met you. I knew it that first day when I saw you at the garage. When I return, we'll make permanent plans. You will be safe at my mom's house. I am glad you will get to spend some time getting to know each other."

"Your mother is a special woman, Lance. I have fallen in love with her already."

Nothing could have pleased him more than this. "She has warned me several times to make sure I hang on to you. She's never said that about anyone before."

Lynette smiled her approval.

After a lingering kiss by the Grand Cherokee and a few whispered good-byes, Lynette drove off with Miss Katherine.

Lance shook Daryl's hand, thanking him again for everything he had done, especially for saving his life. "I'm not sure how long I will be gone."

Daryl produced a cell phone and charger and put them in Lance's jacket pocket. "Use this until you can sort out one of your own. It's a spare; keep in touch. I will check on the ladies from time to time."

"Again, thanks," Lance said sincerely.

Daryl brushed it off and climbed in the front seat of his truck. "Adios, amigo."

———— • ————

The Jeep started up with a roar. It was warm from sitting in the shop, and the heater was cranked. He took the cell phone out of his pocket and took a snapshot of the invoice. This had to be the Bellamy that Preach had tormented him about. There was little chance he was still around, but Lance would check the hotels just in case.

Neither the Harvest Moon nor the other hotels had a blue Chevy truck in the parking lot, and the clerks confirmed that no such vehicle had been registered.

Barton was at the counter when Lance strode into the sheriff's station. A slight hush fell over the room, but business continued.

Barton was congenial. "Lance, you look good."

"A couple of weeks ago, you would have shot me on sight."

Barton's head bowed slightly in shame. "I was just doing my job, he offered.

"I know. Actually, that's why I came by … to let you all know I have no hard feelings." Before Barton could respond, he continued. "Can I speak to the sheriff?"

When Barton looked over his shoulder, Hallward was waving Lance into his office.

Lance sat down, and the sheriff eyed him quizzically. "How are you doing, son?" he asked with genuine concern.

"I'm doing very well," Lance replied honestly. "I will be leaving town soon, and I am curious about how your investigation is coming along."

"I've been sending your uncle regular updates." The sheriff paused. "He's a demanding man," he added. "We are at a standstill; no new leads, no new suspects, but the investigation is ongoing. We just don't have a lot to go on."

Lance shared the story about Clifford Bellamy and his encounter at the garage with Kyle and subsequently with Clarence. He then relayed the story about the things Lee Cross, aka Preach, had said.

He pulled the invoice out of his shirt pocket and placed it on the desk.

Hallward would have made an excellent professional card player—his expression was bland. He reached into his desk and tossed a business card towards Lance. "FBI Clifford Bellamy."

Lance was disappointed. "He's an FBI agent?"

"Not so's you'd notice. The number goes to a voicemail on a burner phone that's been deactivated. Geraldine, the FBI agent that was here, checked it out. No such agent exists. The card is a phony, and I suspect the name is as well. If he stole plates, he'd blend in easily. There are tons of those trucks in this area."

This had to be the man who had killed Kyle and Rachel. The problem was he didn't know where to start looking for him. He didn't even know what he looked like.

Hallward's description was detailed. It sounded an awful lot like the man he'd encountered in the parking lot of the Harvest Moon, and he said so. Had I been that close to Kyle's killer and let him slip away?

The sheriff picked up the phone and dialed. As he did so, he was muttering, "I have an idea. —Mark. It's Sheriff Hallward. How's business?"

Lance could only hear Hallward's end of the conversation.

"Oh yeah, it's almost winter. You still have some older beaters for rent? I'm thinking like an older Chev or GMC? ... Would you mind going out back and making sure both of them still have their plates? ... I can wait."

After a couple of minutes, the voice came back on the line.

"Aha! I see. What colour is it, and what's the plate number?" Hallward was scribbling on his notepad. "Yes, I'll keep you posted." With that he gently hung up the phone.

"It's a trick some car thieves use. They steal a car and to deflect suspicion, find a similar vehicle in a rental compound, in the back forty where no one will notice, and steal the plates. This one is a black 2000 Chevy half-ton."

Lance was impressed, and he spun the notepad around. He entrusted the plate number to memory.

The sheriff didn't say a word. He just turned the notepad back around and slipped it and Bellamy's business card into his desk drawer. "We ran the card for prints, but no luck."

Lance rose to his feet. "Looks like a new lead. I'm going to DC tomorrow. I have a borrowed phone. Mine ended up in the drink. Please let me know if anything develops, Sheriff."

"You'll be the second to know," Hallward promised.

Lance thought of his uncle Joseph and knew what he said was true.

25

Silence is often difficult to interpret, and for Byron Crown it was excruciating. He had called Wallace's secure line and got an "out of service" message. He knew the last thing he should do was panic. However, he believed the time to wrap things up was now. He had a place picked out in Panama and had made up his mind: he would leave his stocks with the proxy they'd set up for a worst-case scenario.

For now, he was confident he could still access them at arm's length and set a deadline for himself. He would wait seven days. If there was no communication from Wallace in that time, he would assume he had been left in the wind. He sent a memo to his staff explaining that he would be taking a few weeks off and that they needed to keep him up to date on all current cases. He purchased a ticket to Europe online. His contact in Brussels would put him on a private jet and then fly him to Panama.

———•———

Joseph was notified of Byron's flight plan within the hour. He understood exactly what this meant and knew he needed to prevent Crown from disappearing completely. He was certain he was a weak link and that under pressure he would crack. This could give them full access to the entire network. He would need to get some indictments and move the investigation forward quickly.

———•———

Wallace had made the same assessment of Crown, but his solution was decidedly more direct. Unable to reach Bellamy, he would have BA take care of Crown.

———•———

Byron looked sourly at the incoming call on his phone. Damn that Joseph Coolidge! He was relentless! He gathered himself together and answered, "Senator Coolidge, what can I do for you today, sir?"

"Planning a vacation, are you?" A casual but cutting reply.

Byron was unnerved and realized he should have been more prepared. "Yes I am," he snapped. "Perhaps you can get to the point. I have lots of work to do."

Joseph ignored his terseness. "I'd like your written update on the investigation within the hour. As you can see, things are not at all what they seem." Joseph kept his tone conciliatory. "Byron, I suspect you're not completely evil. Just corrupt. I'd like to make you an offer. You provide testimony and evidence of this scheme, and I will ask the court to go easy on you." He paused.

"Testi—what are you talking about?" he sputtered. "Is that an accusation?"

"We are well past accusations Byron, and your window of opportunity is closing. Do you really think they are going to let you walk away from all of this?" Joseph reminded him of the lack of honour among thieves. He wanted him to think about how much might have already been revealed, and he wanted Byron to think about his own safety.

"You have nothing I need, Senator," Crown said and hung up. He was angry and scared but hoped he had sounded indignant.

A desperate urge to get out rose up in him. He was glad now that he had made the move to book his vacation. It was going to take tremendous patience to wait, but his only chance of a clean escape lay in keeping to an unsuspicious pattern.

For a moment, the thought occurred to him that he would be made a fall guy, but he quickly dismissed the idea. Still, it wouldn't pay to be naive. He opened his desk and pulled out his revolver, flipped open the cylinder, checked the load, and snapped it back in place. It rolled smoothly, giving him a momentary sense of security. They probably wouldn't dare, but if they did, he would be ready.

———— • ————

The ego is the image or narrative we create about ourselves. It is a construct, really—usually a reflection or manifestation of who we think we are or who we want to be. If we are never really challenged or tested, we never truly know who we are or what we are made of. It is challenging to truly do a self-assessment because we may not like some of the things that are revealed about ourselves in such moments of clarity. This is especially true when the revelations are contrary to characteristics that we attach great value to. Or worse when they reveal obvious flaws in character or ability. This is why most men think they are above-average lovers, drivers, and fighters. This is also why some people have to be told they can't sing or dance. They legitimately didn't know.

When you encounter someone who is elite in their field, an expert or professional, you truly experience the gap between your skill and theirs. This can provide a sobering reality check. Play a sport against even an aging professional, and you will understand. So many people, unchallenged, will venture in over their heads as a result.

Perhaps if he had thought it through, Byron would have connected the dots—the Panama connection was not his idea. In fact, he used the same system to cover his tracks both financially and in subterfuge travel as they all did. And this was purposefully planned to accomplish the stated purpose: to eventually retreat and disappear. But it served a secondary purpose as well—direction and control. Byron was now being funnelled in a direction that had been predetermined for him.

His ego, even though warned by his survival instinct, would not permit him to believe he wasn't smart enough or strong enough to withstand the cunning of the senator. Mark Twain once wrote, "The problem isn't what you don't know. It's what you know for sure that just ain't so." This was also the reason he brushed aside Joseph's offer. Booking a flight was the first domino falling. It set in motion a chain of events he was powerless to stop.

The first indication that something was wrong was his credit card; it had been declined at lunch. When his bank card worked, his immediate suspicions were dispelled. That evening on his way home from work, he stopped for fuel, and his bank card didn't work either. He paid cash and resolved to call his bank in the morning. He had received an electronic coupon earlier in the day for his favourite restaurant. It was customer appreciation day, and he had won first prize—a two-hundred-and-fifty-dollar gift certificate. Given the challenges with his cards, he decided to take advantage of the win and stop there for dinner. He didn't feel like cooking anyway.

Intersections was a fine dining experience, and the place was just starting to get busy with the dinner rush when he pulled up. The valet made the usual offer to park his car, and without so much as an acknowledgment, Byron handed him the keys and in turn received his ticket. The place was warm and alive with delicious aromas that made his stomach growl. He was getting hungry.

"Hello, Mr. Crown, how are you this evening?" The pretty young hostess greeted him in her usual friendly manner. "I didn't see your name on the reservation list."

"I wasn't planning on coming in, but I received this email." He held up his phone with the prizewinning message open on the screen. "Do you have room for one more?"

"Ah, I'm sorry, that's the third one of those we've seen tonight. It looks like we've been punked. We had no such contest. I'm sorry," she said, pouting dramatically.

Byron was visibly disappointed; he was about to ask for a table anyway but remembered the trouble with his cards. "Another time, then," he said, a strained smile on his face. What an awful day, he thought to himself.

He handed the ticket to the young valet and slumped into the driver's seat in frustration. He had driven less than a mile when he heard a distinctive bang and the low tire pressure indicator flashed up on the dash. The car was wobbling. Swearing loudly, he pulled over. It was a warehouse area, dark and deserted. He got out to have a look, and sure enough the left rear tire was flat. He was using the light on his phone to examine the damage when a truck pulled in behind him.

Reaching into his jacket, he slid the gun from its holster, concealing it next to his leg.

A friendly voice called out from behind the lights. "Looks like you've got car troubles. Do you need a hand?"

Byron hesitated a second. "No, I think I'm all right, I can call the auto service."

"I'm an off-duty police officer. What's the trouble?"

He had opened the door and stepped out. The officer was shining his flashlight at himself, illuminating his own features.

Crown had never met Brad and didn't recognize him.

Keeping the flashlight on himself, Brad offered to show his ID. As he reached into his pocket, Byron adjusted his grip on the pistol. Brad pulled out a wallet and shone the light on the badge.

"I'm with the FBI myself," Byron said. "I wasn't sure who you were or what to expect."

Brad laughed. "Yeah, I don't blame you." He covered the distance between them in a few short steps. "Nice suit, just coming from the office?"

"Uh huh, this has been quite the day."

Brad walked around to the flat tire. "Do you have a spare? Let's get you on the road. This isn't the best area of town. Don't mess up your suit. I can swap it for you in a couple minutes. Consider it a professional courtesy."

When Byron didn't move, he spoke again.

"Pop the trunk … unless you're loaded down with drugs or something."

"Sure, thanks." Byron put his gun back in its holster, and Brad chuckled. "Like I said, I can't blame ya."

In a few minutes, the tire was off, the donut spare was on and secure. Brad checked the tire and the area carefully to see if there was any evidence of the charge that had blown the tire. It was all clear. He purposely didn't put the blown tire in the trunk but left it leaning against the back of the car.

They made some small talk, and Brad made as if to leave, checking his watch. "I've gotta run. You okay getting that tire in the trunk?" He had intentionally closed it after retrieving the spare.

"Oh yeah, of course … thanks for your help."

"No problem." Brad jumped back in his truck and drove off with a couple of light taps on the horn to say goodbye.

Byron waved as he went by.

The car was still running so he popped the manual lever inside the driver's door and went to the back of the car again, carefully lifting the tire back into the trunk. He was going to be happy to get home and put his feet up.

Some instinct warned him a moment too late. The gunman had snuck in close behind him. He intended to turn when he felt his head slam forward as the bullet entered the back of his skull just above his spinal cord. There was a moment of awful realization and then he was sliding down the trunk, landing heavily on the pavement. The light closed in like a tunnel, followed by a dreadful darkness.

Beats turned the body over, taking his pistol and wallet. He then rifled through the car, quickly checking the console and glovebox to make it look like a robbery. A minute only, and he was done. Lights flashed from up the road a few hundred yards. He in turn flashed the lights on Byron's car then turned them off along with the engine.

A moment later they were crossing the river, and as Brad slowed down, Beats tossed the gun and wallet over the rail. He then deleted the prize emails he had sent from his own computer and slapped it shut as they drove on in silence.

26

Ross was waiting for Lance when his plane touched down in DC. They shook hands and Ross simply said, "You've been through it." He looked at him intently to get a read on his condition.

"I'm about eighty percent recovered," Lance told him.

"That's plenty good," Ross said as he scooped up one of his bags. Then he led the way through the airport to the waiting car.

Lance had not expected to be back in DC so soon. The town always seemed to suck the life out of him. How his uncle had tolerated it so long was a mystery. The saying about all roads leading to Rome was accurate; these days, Rome was Washington, DC. And the statement "Power corrupts, and absolute power corrupts absolutely" was never truer than in DC. The electorate would fire someone only to discover that their influence carried on. The replacement who arrived bright-eyed and idealistic was soon crushed and consumed by the system, their resolve worn down, their lofty ideals sacrificed on the altar of compromise or outright capitulation.

He supposed there were more men and women like his uncle, unwavering in their love of God and country. But most were not. He knew this and accepted it as bitter medicine, realizing that, in many cases, it was these very politicians who marched young men off to endless wars: The old men bickering and the young men bleeding. Good governance. Lance decided it was like waste management. You know the trash is going to keep coming, but if you don't pick it up every week, it just keeps piling up—not an option in any civilized society.

Lance followed Ross down the marble Senate corridor to Uncle Joseph's office. These days you had to have permission to enter these hallowed halls, complete with a tracking lanyard. Between the cameras and facial recognition software, there wasn't a moment that someone or some AI tool wasn't tracking your every move.

Uncle Joseph was standing by his desk to receive Lance and when he arrived, Joseph grabbed Lance's hand tightly and pulled him in close. There was still some strength in Joseph's old frame. Although the years were taking their toll, he stood straight and dignified as always. His office was palatial, with an extensive floor-to-ceiling library bulging with books. The shelves wrapped around behind the ornate cherrywood desk. To the left were a coffeemaker, photocopier, and paper shredder; to the right, a whiteboard wiped clean. Scattered about the room were several stiff leather chairs. Lance knew Joseph didn't want his guests getting too comfortable or they might stay too long.

Lance dropped himself into one of them, admiring the comfortable old office chair his uncle had had for years.

"Good flight?" Joseph asked, while pouring coffee.

"All right," Lance replied as he accepted the hot brew. After tasting it, he placed the cup gently on its saucer. It clinked, china on china, and for the moment, it was just them: two gentlemen sharing a coffee in the most sophisticated manner, in the halls of ultimate man-made power.

"That's a great cup of coffee."

"Guatemalan. It's grown high in that rich volcanic soil. I went down last year as part of a diplomatic visit, and this was a personal gift from Cheryl, Carlos Vargas's daughter at Hope of Life. I thought you'd like it."

"Very good." Lance took another sip.

Joseph retrieved four files marked CLASSIFIED. "You pick your enemies well."

Lance snorted at that. "They picked me."

It was the personnel files of IT-1. It turned out they had been a unit for years—all highly-skilled and decorated.

There was a killed-in-action notice in Lee Cross's file.

"The three amigos are now considered deserters. I suspect they've been running a private operation for a while. They would have needed a contact way further up the food chain."

"Three? I thought Van Rhymes was reassigned."

"He was." Joseph pushed the file forward and opened it up, revealing the word AWOL in big, bold letters. Joseph went to the whiteboard and started writing out the timeline. They logged every individual involved and when they entered the picture. Relying heavily on Hallward's notes, they added the new information about Bellamy's thermostat repair and ended with Lance's hospital visits with Romey and the Craigs. His uncle had done most of the work, but this was Lance's chance to fill in some gaps. An unnamed person above the timeline was identified by a circled question mark. Someone had to be behind this, and they suspected that someone would also be the key to why all this was happening.

"Okay, let's assume that Kyle saw something he shouldn't have while repairing Bellamy's truck. Bellamy panics and kills him. But then everything goes cold for months. Why? In our timeline, you are a new dynamic infused into the situation … between these two points." Joseph indicated the gap between Kyle's death and Lance's arrival. "At the same time, Cathy Short and our John Doe are killed." Joseph drew another circled question mark at this juncture.

"Apparently," Lance said, "they were looking for an envelope, probably the same thing Kyle had seen and that's why they killed him. If he'd had it on him, they would have retrieved it."

"Yes!" Uncle Joseph was emphatic. "They think you have the envelope, so they frame you for murder as a ruse to get it back. You continue your hunting trip as planned. So, they come after you in the bush."

Seeing the timeline drawn out visually helped Lance to put it in perspective.

"I had signed the paperwork for the garage with Clarence and the Freemonts. I wonder if they saw me with the envelope and mistook it for whatever they were after."

"Where is that paperwork now?"

"At the lawyer's, and there's probably a copy at mother's house by now." Lance was thinking out loud.

"Hmm. Okay. I'll request a copy from the lawyer and see if there is anything about the sale that was unusual."

"I'm guessing not," Lance said. "Everything was pretty straightforward."

"Still, we need to eliminate the possibility." Joseph was being his usual methodical self. "We know the unknown male from the rest stop was in Cathy Short's house and probably killed her. I had his picture sent over."

Joseph shook it out of a yellow envelope onto his desk. "The guy had been shot in the head," he warned.

The bullet had messed up Roger's face, but Lance recognized him right away. "That's the second man from the scrape in the hotel parking lot!" he exclaimed. "I'll be damned!"

"It's a damn good thing they didn't know about that, or the manhunt would have been that much more intense—if that were possible. Someone planted that necklace in your Jeep ... as part of the incriminating evidence against you and—"

"Hold on." Lance raised his hand. "If this guy and his accomplice put the necklace in the truck, that means they killed Cathy Short for sure! It's how they were going to frame me! But I catch him in the act, thinking he was stealing the stereo. In fact, he wasn't taking something, he was putting something in there—the necklace!"

"That still doesn't tell us why they wanted you out of the way." Joseph paused, tapping the dry erase marker against his temple again as though trying to force an idea forward.

"Whatever this thing is, it is important enough to kill five people over," Lance said.

"Six! They found Crown this morning. He'd been shot in the back of the head. His wallet and pistol were missing. It's being ruled a mugging."

Lance whistled his surprise.

"He was my weak link and I'm trying not to let my prejudice get in the way, but the Armed Services Committee approved the SEAL teams. Can you guess who pushed them in that direction?"

Lance drew a blank.

"Our own Senator Wallace."

Lance was stunned. "You think this goes that deep? What on earth could his stake in this be? How would Wallace know about Cathy Short's murder?"

"It's Washington. There are ears everywhere, and as it's in his home state, he has cover."

"Another dead end." It was all beginning to wear on Lance.

"Not exactly, but our freeway has definitely turned into an overgrown trail." Uncle Joseph was keeping him on track. "We just need to keep going. It could just be our old rivalry and a chance to flip my seat with bad press. I've been digging into any connection Wallace may have had with Crown. It's best I don't share the source of my information."

"And?" Lance leaned forward.

"And there was clearly communication between the two, but it's easily explained by the investigation into you." After a moment he continued, "There is another connection, albeit a tenuous one. Wallace had purchased a few thousand shares in a multinational company called ComCorp, and it turns out our friend Crown had bought several thousand shares as well around the same time."

"What's ComCorp?" Lance asked.

"It turns out they are a lot of things. Resource development, mostly. Lumber, mining, fracking, oil, and gas, with holdings all around the world. Canada, Indonesia, the Middle East—and Montana."

"Montana?" Lance sat up straighter.

"Yes, it would have taken some digging had I not done due diligence on them in the past, but they own this." Joseph pointed to a circled spot on the electoral map of Montana. "The Sukunka River Valley Sour Gas Plant."

Lance was stunned again. "Isn't that a conflict for Wallace?"

"It would be, but he cited it in his financial disclosure the year after the plant opened and sold the shares at a slight loss, claiming he was unaware of the connection. We both voted in favour of the plant at the time."

Lance relaxed back into his chair. "Illegal drilling you think?"

"Their audits show everything was on the up-and-up. The yields are close to the original estimates; no issues that I can find. But I have come to hate coincidences, Lance. Crown sold his shares around the same time! With his death, the trail goes cold, and our list of suspects grows even colder."

"Something has been bothering me, Uncle. Why did they kill Cathy Short? The only person who knew I had asked questions about her was Deputy Barton. And why had she acted so strangely?"

"Barton's a lifer at the sheriff's office and squeaky clean. I don't think there is anything there with him."

Recalling their interactions, Lance agreed.

Joseph continued, "We need to think outside the square or in this case, the timeline. I did some more checking, and it turns out that Cathy worked at the assay office, prior to the sheriff's department, where she'd only been for a few weeks. I called her old supervisor, and you'll never guess what I discovered."

Lance raised his eyebrows. "Don't tell me … he's dead?"

"Heart attack while running on his treadmill. Another coincidence?" Joseph erased the circled question mark next to Cathy Short's name and replaced it with the name, Gerald Mackenzie.

"Why does that name sound familiar?" Lance dug for a fuzzy memory.

"He was an old friend of your dad's; they hunted and fished together as young men."

At that, Lance recalled some vague stories.

Joseph went on, "Nothing recorded in the assay office connected to Com-Corp. I've had all the records checked."

Lance ran his fingers through his hair and rubbed his cheeks vigorously, struggling to get his thoughts in order. "Okay," he said. "Let's assume all these dots connect. What's our theory? Cathy is involved in something at the assay office—something her boss was involved in or becomes aware of. The boss is murdered; she gets scared and pulls the plug on her job? It's an assay office, so the connection is minerals. ComCorp discovered gold or silver, and they are keeping it to themselves … maybe even developing it? They pay Wallace off to approve the site and convince you to vote the same. Why not just get a permit to put in a mine?"

Joseph was listening carefully. "It was hard enough getting the gas plant approved near the park. A gold mine would take years of environmental reviews before possible approval."

"With millions of dollars of gold, it does seem like a logical motive, but what did Kyle see or hear that caused them to go after him?"

Joseph circled Bellamy's name on the timeline. "This is where Kyle's life intersects. This is where he must have seen or overheard something, but Kyle was no dummy. He would have reported whatever it was right away."

Lance interrupted him. "What if, like me, he didn't immediately recognize the importance of what he had seen?"

Joseph picked up the thought in earnest. "Ahh. So they kill him before he can put two and two together!"

Both men stared at the timeline, and Lance said, "Maybe Cathy made the connection to Kyle's death, and that's why she was so nervous when she saw me. They killed her later that same day—but why then? Months had passed. Did they believe she was going to talk to me?"

Lance tried to rub away an ache in the back of his neck. "Bah. This is too complicated. We could be way off track here." Lance was frustrated with all the talk. After all, he was a man who preferred action and knowing who and where the enemy was.

Joseph was not prepared to stop the flow of ideas and ignored Lance's frustration. He pulled his pipe from the desk drawer and lit it before continuing. "Cross asked you about an envelope." He circled their fight on the timeline. "What if they thought she had passed some vital information on to you?"

"Why would they think that?" Lance asked, genuinely curious.

"Maybe she told them she gave it to you?"

That stopped Lance in his tracks. "Possible, if she was bargaining for her life, I suppose. But they killed her anyway and then came after me to retrieve it, under the ruse of her murder …."

Smiling, Joseph refilled their coffee cups, squinting through the smoke curling up into his eyes. "You end up in the river, and they assume that whatever it was is lost forever. However, it's been a few weeks, and you haven't produced anything incriminating. So life goes back to normal, and they start wrapping up loose ends, like Crown."

"We need to get inside that plant," Lance suggested, "and see what's going on."

"It is private property. No judge is going to give us a warrant based on this." Joseph nodded at the whiteboard and tossed the marker onto his desk.

"I'll go. With or without a warrant. My gut tells me the answers to our questions are inside that plant."

"In time," Joseph cautioned him. "Let's get as much intel as we can first. I'll get some real-time satellite photos of the area. If they are mining out there, there will be evidence—equipment, that sort of thing. You get some rest and meet me back here tomorrow at nine a.m."

Lance knew his uncle was right. He'd flown across the country and needed a meal, a hot shower, and some sleep. He caught a cab back to his hotel and flopped onto the bed. He still tired more quickly than he would like, but every day he was getting stronger.

———— • ————

That evening Lance ate his meal in the hotel restaurant. He had just ordered when he caught the eye of an attractive brunette. She gave him an inviting smile, but he looked quickly away. What a strange change had come over him!

There was a time, not too long ago, that he would have gone over to say hello, and …. He blushed in embarrassment. Thinking of Lynette now, he realized he had outgrown his old lifestyle. He'd never been overly promiscuous, but the presence and the voice in the cave had brought a new awareness—a deepening sense of right and wrong. Strangely, though, his warrior nature seemed unchanged, and this both encouraged and concerned him.

The next morning, he found himself in Joseph's office again. When he entered, his uncle was looking at some satellite photos. The lines on his face were drawn deeper this morning. Through his teeth, past the unlit pipe, he spoke.

"Not much to see here, Lance. A few open pits with equipment but nothing that could be considered a large operation. They look like aggregate pits, for roads or construction, I would guess."

Lance was disappointed. "You think we are off the mark then?"

"No, I'm trusting your gut on this one. We need to see what's going on in that plant. I'm thinking we go through the front door."

"Oh really?" Lance was surprised.

"Part of the agreement to build was occasional environmental inspections. It's been a couple of years, and I think they are due." He winked at Lance. "We only have to give them seventy-two hours' notice, but I'm thinking forty-eight should suffice. I've made the arrangements, and an environmental team will be on the ground tomorrow."

"I'll be on a plane today." Lance was excited. Uncle Joseph was indeed thorough. He must have worked late into the night. Where did he get the energy?

"Lance, whether you like it or not, you're something of a local celebrity there now. You could be recognized right away. We need to let the environmental team do their work and make a determination from there. We want a completely unfettered opportunity to lay charges, if we find anything. I'm sorry, but you have no standing as an environmental professional or as a law enforcement officer."

For the first time in his life, Lance found himself at odds with Uncle Joseph. But before he could say anything, Joseph picked up the phone. "Lorraine, is he here yet? Good, send him in."

Joseph rose to his feet. The door opened, and Romey stepped into the room. He was clean-shaven and wore khaki pants, a dress shirt, and matching brown belt and shoes. Lance recognized him for what he was—the broad shoulders; steady, confident gaze: military bearing. But to the untrained eye, he looked the part just fine.

"Lance, may I introduce you to Jerome Manning. He has recently been appointed to the president's energy council. He will be going to the Sukunka plant with the environmental team as an observer."

Lance was taken back. He had not seen this coming.

Romey stuck out his hand. "Nice to see you again, sir. You look well."

Lance took his hand. "I'm retired … you don't need to call me sir."

At that Romey shrugged. "It's meant with all due respect." He turned to Joseph Coolidge. "Nice to see you again as well, sir."

Joseph bowed slightly and gestured Romey to a seat; then he sat back in his worn leather chair.

"I've made the arrangements; the inspection is the day after tomorrow.

Diverting his gaze to Lance, Joseph continued, "I gave Captain Manning a full debrief this morning. He will go in with the environmental team and take a good look around to discover what's going on in there besides gas. They'll take photos of anything suspicious, and any fortifications, in case we order a breach.

"Lance, you will be ready to respond if there is trouble. Your plane tickets are ready, and the rest of Romey's team is en route via an earlier flight."

Even Lance was impressed by his uncle's planning and efficiency.

Joseph asked Romey if he had any questions, to which he replied, "Plenty but I understand the plan, yes."

After Romey had left, Joseph looked intently at Lance. "Are you sure you're feeling strong enough?"

"Absolutely. Any guess on what we will find in there?"

"I'm hoping we'll be able to flush out some grouse. I'll keep an eye on our friend down the hall. You may not be able to see the wind, but you can see exactly which direction the vane is pointing."

Lance was thoughtful. "I know you probably don't need me to tell you this, but be careful. Whatever this thing is they won't hesitate to murder to cover it up. And if it's as deep as we think it is—"

"Ross is always nearby," Joseph reminded him.

Lance got up to leave. "We need to find Brad Akron and/or Leadbeater; not knowing where those two are is most disturbing."

"I'll keep working on it from here. You keep your eyes open, and be careful." Uncle Joseph came around the desk and embraced Lance in a great bear hug. "Love you, son."

He handed Lance a phone. It didn't have a logo, but it looked a whole lot like an iPhone. "This is the latest and greatest sat phone. Here is the antenna," he said, reaching over and sliding it up to demonstrate, then pushing it back down.

"Just like a phone from the early two thousands," Lance quipped.

"GPS tracker, altimeter, location beacon, thirty-yard signal scrambler, two USB drives—and a battery that lasts a week even with regular use." Joseph reached into his pocket and handed Lance a portable charger. "This has capacity for three charges and a multiport adapter for all the outlets in the world."

He was almost out the door when Joseph stopped him. "Lance, do you know who Jubal was in the Old Testament?"

"Never heard of him," he responded, knowing a lesson was coming.

"How about Tubal-cain or Bezaleel?"

Lance shook his head.

"Each of them had a special and unique talent that was a part of who they were. Lance, you are a warrior. It's who you are, but you are more than that— you are also a man of understanding and contemplation. The gazelle lives another day because it outruns the lion. And the lion eats because it outruns the gazelle." He balled his fists and brought them up to the boxing position, clenching them firmly. "Don't be afraid to be who you were created to be. Live with confidence today, because today you are the lion."

———— • ————

Lance started to fall asleep as the plane was taxied down the runway. The next few days would be pivotal, and he wanted to be as rested as possible. He would be returning to those mountains, but this time, with even more confidence. They had tested him once and might do so again, but he would persevere and overcome. He knew their secrets and understood their ways. In a sense, he was as much a part of the mountains as the trees, the grass, and the rocks. He hadn't gotten to any real hunting, but next year, he thought—next year. When this business is finished and the warm south winds blow into the valleys and the streams begin to flow again and the meadows come alive with new birth, I will walk the old paths. I will watch the hawk catch the thermals and glide on its graceful wings, up, up towards the heavens. This spring will be different—I will have Lynette by my side. He meditated on this picture as he drifted off to sleep.

Jostled awake by turbulence, he heard the captain announced, "Ladies and gentlemen, we've started our decent into Helena and should be at the gate in about twenty minutes."

He hadn't realized how tired he'd been—sleeping for most of the flight. He hadn't told his mother or Lynette that he was returning. The task in front of him didn't allow for any visiting, and he must stay focused.

He called Daryl on the phone he'd given him. He wanted his own gear, and Daryl assured him it was dried out and ready to go.

There was no sign of Romey on the other end, as he'd arranged his own ride.

Lance took a room in Helena. In the morning, when he entered the foyer, Daryl was sitting in a booth at the hotel restaurant eating breakfast. Lance slid into the vinyl seat across from him.

Daryl scooped a couple forkfuls of eggs before looking up. "You look good, Lance."

Lance scoffed. "Everyone's been telling me that."

"Your Jeep and trailer are at the house. You want some company?"

Lance instinctively started to decline and then reconsidered; after all, this was his future brother-in-law. "Sure. I may need rescuing again. I'll fill you in along the way." He reached over and took a piece of fruit from Daryl's bowl.

"We'd better order you your own meal. I've seen you eat, and I'm still hungry," Daryl said. They were sharing a moment of comradery, as men will.

The drive back to the ranch was filled with conversation about what they suspected, with Daryl listening carefully, throwing the odd question in here and there. It was a long drive, and the dialogue drifted between the military, the ranch itself, and their childhoods. There were long gaps when neither man said much. One of those gaps was preceded by Lance sharing his experience in the cave and the voice that spoke to him. Daryl listened carefully and pondered quietly.

Lance was surprised to learn that Daryl wasn't planning on ranching forever. He planned on using it as his home base but would build another house farther down the valley, on a bench with a great view of the mountains and beyond.

His specialty in the military had been winter warfare. This had led him to invest in a small company that manufactured high-end outdoor gear. It had been started by several of his military buddies, and he'd been lending ideas and cash and was planning on working at it full-time. Currently, it was just a part-time gig, and he was working from home while helping Lynette with the day-to-day operations of the ranch.

Daryl was a quiet man, and at times, his demeanour was brooding. When he asserted himself in a conversation or a situation, he dominated the moment. It wasn't just because of his size; there was something indomitable in his character. He was fiercely loyal, and Lance knew he must not betray that trust by putting Daryl in a situation where he would feel the need to sacrifice himself. He had already proven that he was willing to take risks during the encounter with Truck. Lance didn't want any harm to come to Daryl, which could also have a negative impact on his relationship with Lynette. There is a saying: "You can't make old friends out of new friends." But it felt to Lance as if they had known each other all their lives.

After arriving at the ranch early in the afternoon, a bite to eat, and some of that fantastic Guatemalan coffee, they headed out to the barn to pack Lance's gear. It was completely dry, and they stacked it in the trailer with the quad. Daryl put the wall tent back into its bag. While they were loading a few things into the Jeep, Lance found the Slim-Jim, which had fallen between the seats.

"I saw that," Daryl volunteered. "Wondered about it."

Lance relayed the story about the fight in the parking lot and his discovery of it the next morning.

"Might explain the necklace I found in your glovebox," Daryl said.

"Yeah, I figured that's what they were up to. They must have needed me to take the fall pretty bad to go to all that trouble. I will never forget that man's face. He may be responsible for Kyle's death."

At Daryl's questioning expression, Lance said, "I'll have to leave that for another time."

Daryl shook his head in dismay. "No end to the evil in human nature."

Lance couldn't argue with that. He'd seen enough of it, that was for sure. But he had seen the other side as well: People willing to make extraordinary sacrifices for others—sometimes for people they didn't even know.

When he had a moment alone, Lance checked the sat phone. It was still fully charged as promised, and the network connection had three bars. There was a second icon—radio waves for the satellite connection. It showed full bars as well. It didn't come with instructions, but none were needed, as it was intuitively designed.

He called Joseph's private line. His uncle answered on the first ring.

"Made it back safe?"

"Yes, we still on for the inspection tomorrow?"

"It was bumped a day; they exercised their right to seventy-two hours' notice."

"Okay," Lance responded. "We'll head in that direction in the morning and be in the backup position. What time is the inspection?"

"First thing in the morning, ten a.m. —We?"

"Daryl Craig. He's already proven his loyalty and frankly, his ability."

Joseph was relieved. "I'd like to get to know the man who saved your life."

"Something tells me you will get that chance soon enough," he was thinking about a future with Lynette. Joseph read the statement for what it was.

"I just had a visit from a friend, and there were definitely several calls between Wallace and Crown." Joseph let that information hang for a moment.

Lance waited. He had an inkling who the friend was but knew better than to ask. "A smoking gun?"

"More circumstantial evidence, unfortunately. Wallace will claim he was just keeping abreast of the investigation in an official capacity. What we really need is direct evidence. Whatever they were into needs to be exposed."

"Whatever it is must be tied to that gas plant. Maybe something will turn up in the inspection." Lance was hopeful. "We need to catch a break somewhere here. We are due."

"Luck is the residue of hard work," Joseph reminded him. "I'll buzz you if anything comes up."

———— • ————

That night Lance retired early. It dawned on him that it had been weeks since he'd had a panic attack. Some said they would get better with time. Others disagreed; he hoped the former were correct. He had been so busy trying to stay alive that the subconscious fear had abandoned him, perhaps replaced by a clear and present danger. He was feeling more peaceful; this house had that effect on him. He drifted off, meditating on positive things, focusing his mind on some of his exquisite memories. He had been visualizing the moment he'd pulled off the road, on the way to his hunting camp. He had imagined the sun filtering through the trees as the doe stepped daintily out of the woods.

Suddenly, he snapped awake. *The Slim-Jim! I used it to fish the garbage out from underneath the seats. What if … what if whatever they thought I had was in that pile of garbage? Cathy Short left the sheriff's office just before me. She could have slipped something into my Jeep!*

Lance knew the feeling you get when you just know something intuitively in your gut but you can't explain why. He had that feeling now. *I didn't lock the Jeep—it was broad daylight outside the sheriff's station in sleepy Lone Prairie.*

He got out of bed and started to get dressed, then thought better of it. They were leaving tomorrow, and he could put the hustle on Daryl to leave early. He imagined an envelope sitting at the bottom of the rest stop garbage can. It could be the one piece of the puzzle that would unravel this mystery. Would the Park Service have emptied it by now? His heart sank at the thought, but he reassured himself that it was unlikely they were working this late in the year. Still, the thought nagged at him, and he was unable to sleep.

———— • ————

They left early, into the bleak and dreary cold. Winter was asserting itself again, and the wind was howling and spinning the snow around. The plan was to get to the rest stop early, find the envelope, and see where things led from there. They would spend the night at the same line cabin Brad and Leadbeater had used during their escape, and move out early the next morning, positioning themselves in a backup posture to await orders.

Lance was beginning to get that ol' lustful desire for action. Daryl could sense the slow change that was overcoming Lance. He became more intense and sharper; even his body language and speech changed. His voice assumed the ring of command; the phrases were shorter, sharper, and more concise. The air in the truck became electric, not because of an increase in frenetic energy. Quite the opposite; there was a cooling, and a hardening. Like the stiffening of white-hot iron when it is dipped into frigid water; in that moment, it is tempered and transformed.

Daryl was almost shocked by the transition—this man was deadly. Surely the stories about him were not exaggerated. As formidable and confident as he was, Daryl decided he would not want Lance Coolidge as an enemy.

"Here!" Lance said, indicating the pullout. The sun was up, but the sky was threatening yet another winter storm.

A small lock held the lid on the garbage can. Prepared, Lance made short work of it with the back of his hatchet. When they brushed the snow off the wind carried it away into the trees. It was half full of garbage.

Over the howling wind, Daryl yelled. "Let's just throw the whole can in the back seat, take it to the cabin and sort through it there!"

Providing comic relief, the can wouldn't fit into the back seat.

"Hang on!" Lance barked. "I have a garbage bag in my gear." He found it in his pack, and they carefully scooped the contents into it and tied it up tight. The freezing temperatures had moderated the smell of the garbage, but still it lingered a little.

Within a couple of hours, the smell was overtaken by that of the sour gas plant. They maintained a slow pace as they drove by. There wasn't anything to see from the outside; just a series of grey and blue buildings and stacks that emanated the foul odor. The several access roads were gated but unmanned, except for the security guard at the main entrance.

Lance had the itch to sneak inside and look around for himself but knew that could scuttle their carefully laid plans. He would be patient. By this time tomorrow, they would have a better idea about what was going on in there.

It was midafternoon when they reached the line cabin. The snow had drifted on the road, and it was obvious that no one had been here recently. Once inside, Daryl lit a lamp and started a fire in the potbellied stove, and within a few minutes the place warmed up. It was a one-room cabin with two bunks, both of which were made, complete with sheets and wool blankets. The wood crib was also full.

"Well, they left it better than they found it at least," Daryl said.

"Doesn't surprise me. Old habits die hard," Lance reminded him. "You never know when you yourself will be needing the comfort and protection of a good shelter; if you deny your enemy, you deny yourself."

Lance had brought in the M4 and their gear, including sleeping bags. He tossed them onto the bunks and rolled them out so they'd be ready. Daryl put water on the potbellied stove for coffee and started heating some canned stew.

"Let's see what we've recovered," he said, indicating the garbage bag.

Lance was slightly reluctant; there was so much riding on the contents. He didn't want to have his hopes dashed. He dumped the contents onto the floor and saw that everything was still mostly frozen. Wrappers, cups, tissues, chicken bones—all of it covered in coffee stains.

Not seeing an envelope, he was in disbelief; he had been so sure. "Nothing. It's not here." He groaned, unable to hide his disappointment. He sifted through the material several times, trying to conjure up an envelope. He started stuffing everything back into the bag when something caught his eye.

"You are invited …." The rest of the words were blotted out by a stain. He picked up the small red envelope slowly—it was a five-by-eight wedding invitation style card. It's always the little things ….

He had been looking for something official—a large brown manila envelope or even a legal-sized one. How many times do we miss what is right in front of us because it's not what we expect to see?

Daryl stopped stirring the stew, holding the spoon quietly in anticipation. Lance put the envelope aside and placed each item, one by one, back in the garbage bag and placed the bag outside the door. Retrieving the envelope, he sat at the small table and placed the envelope in front of himself. Daryl went back to stirring. Lance carefully tore it open and poured the contents into his hand. A flash drive—an intact flash drive that appeared to be none the worse for wear!

He turned it over repeatedly. This was not at all what he had been expecting to find.

Remembering that the sat phone had a USB drive, he pulled it out of his jacket pocket. The battery still showed full power and there was one radio wave icon. He pulled up the antenna and a second one appeared. The reception was strong. On the bottom of the phone next to the charging port were two USB ports—one micro-USB and the other a traditional one. He slid the flash drive in, and the screen lit up orange with the word "loading" flashing every second or so. Then "File size 2G" flashed on and off twice before opening. There was one file only, called "C-CUD." He touched the icon, and the file opened.

Lance caught his breath and looked up at Daryl. "Holy shit!" Lance almost dropped the phone like it was hot.

"What is it, Lance?" Daryl came around the table to look. There on the screen were the words "ComCorp Uranium Deposit."

There was a lot of documentation, but the first part was an assay, showing a high concentration of uranium. Lance knew from some of his classes at the academy that this was an unusually high concentration; similar to those found in Canada. Deposits of this density required minimal enrichment and produced high-quality medical isotopes.

The original assay samples had been sent in by an individual prospector—Kal Rollins. An erroneous report was sent back to Mr. Rollins showing low amounts of copper, zinc, and gold—in other words, nothing promising. There was also a record of the Sukunka Gas Corp staking a claim a year later, after Rollins had let his claim expire without renewing it. There was too much here to decipher on the small screen.

"How had Gerald Mackenzie allowed himself to get caught up in this?" Lance wondered aloud. Maybe they had paid him off and when he started getting nervous, he passed the flash drive off. Was his plan to get it to me or to Kyle? He must have been confident we would recognize its worth and turn it in. Instead, it falls into Cathy Short's possession somehow—she finds it, or he gives it to her. Most likely he gave it to her, and she had put it in my Jeep. The original assay was eight years old; a full year before the application for construction of the gas plant. He paused and looked up.

"So they have been mining uranium right here at the plant?" Daryl asked.

"The real question being, who is the customer?" Lance said.

"It may be a clandestine operation by our own government," Daryl speculated.

"That wouldn't explain the frame-up or Brad's team going AWOL. No, this is something far more diabolical. My brother and his family were killed because of this, and as cynical as I may be, I won't believe that of my own government. Besides, our family are patriots. I'm sure at a minimum I would have been trusted with this information. I think it's the bad guys."

"Who are the bad guys?" Daryl asked.

"Everybody else."

Lance hit the redial button. This time, it rang three times before Joseph answered it. Lance explained everything to his uncle and could hear him scratching away on his pad.

Joseph waited until Lance had given his full report. "Send the file to my email; it's the only contact on that phone. I don't need to tell you that this has just become a matter of national security. We are going to need to act quickly. Is Daryl Craig with you?"

"Yes, he's here."

"Good. Put me on speaker."

"Okay, go ahead," Lance said.

"Gentlemen, this is much worse than we thought. If uranium is being produced in that plant, we will need to act quickly to secure the site. We have Romey's team on the ground, with you two that makes six. Can I ask the DOD to reinstate you both? We need to have legal cover on this."

As one, both men replied, "Yes!"

"Good. Send that file and wait for your orders."

Joseph hung up and checked his email. The files were already being down-loaded.

He hit the intercom button. "Lorraine, get me a meeting with Peter Ash-grave and Max Sandor. Tell them it's a Level 1 National Security issue. Remind them that in all the years since 9/11, I have never invoked this protocol. This meeting under the article is non-negotiable."

Within the hour, both men were sitting in front of his desk. As usual, Max looked the most relaxed. Ashgrave wore his usual annoyed demeanor—the muscles on the sides of his square jaw flexing in and out. Joseph had created a basic dossier from the email. It included Lance's preliminary observations as well as schematics of the plant, pipelines, roads, electrical grid, and the low-er levels of the plant—electricity, HVAC, elevators, and emergency stairwell access.

While they were skimming through this information, Joseph filled them in on their suspicions. He also advised them that there was a SEAL team on the ground and two retired military personnel.

"Shit on a stick, man! We need to find out what the hell is going on in there and put a stop to it." Ashgrave was animated and only rhymed his cuss words under extreme circumstances.

"Consider those two men reinstated at the rank they held at retirement."

"Gentlemen," Joseph continued, "I have reason to believe we have trea-sonous elements right here in some of our highest elected offices in the land. We need to keep this information between us." Then, looking Ashgrave direct-ly in the eye, Joseph warned: "If ever there was a time to put partisan politics aside, it's now."

"Don't tell me—Wallace, right?" Ashgrave's voice was thick with con-tempt. "You two have been at each other for years. I swear, Coolidge, if this is a vendetta because of your nephew—"

Max cut Ashgrave off politely. "Sir, the Agency shares Joseph's concerns in this regard. The sour gas plant is owned by a multinational company of which Senator Wallace was a shareholder. He divested himself of the stocks a few years ago but purchased a larger number through a proxy firm. He slid a file forward. It's a complicated web, but it's all there—the money transfers, the stock holdings, the whole thing run out of a bank in Panama."

Both Joseph and Ashgrave were stunned.

"Guess who else had holdings there?" Max asked.

"Crown." Joseph breathed out the name.

"Crown, yes, but also one deceased Lee Cross, Brad Akron, Ian Leadbeat-er, and Gary Van Rhymes." He tossed their pictures one by one onto the desk.

"Where is the money coming from?" Peter asked.

"Well, it's not … not yet anyway … the company's legitimate holdings keep the stock strong. It's gained 11 percent this year alone. I'm thinking that leadership will slowly filter the money into the company to deflect suspicion, making everyone rich along the way. Which may mean the uranium is still to be delivered."

Ashgrave looked back and forth between the two. "You two have been working this angle for a while on your own, I see."

Max grinned. "Even a satellite needs to know what tree out of a trillion it should look under."

"Who is the likely buyer?" Joseph asked, keeping his suspicions to himself.

"Who isn't? Iran, North Korea, or some wannabe caliphate somewhere. I'll notify the president and the Joint Chiefs," Ashgrave said, suddenly springing into action. "Have your men stand by, Coolidge. I'll organize an insertion team to lend support, but we may need them to go in early. Thank God we discovered this now; hopefully we're not too late. Max, get me as much information as possible. I will need to have my powder dry when I meet with the president. I want to know where the gas gets shipped and who buys it—tanker manifests—anything and everything."

Max interjected. "This isn't about chain of command. I would like to point out that I too serve at the pleasure of the president, and we will have more influence if we meet with him together."

"Fair enough, I'll set it up," Ashgrave said, getting up. Addressing Joseph, he said, "Tell your nephew good work for me, and let him know we have his back!" With that, he hurried from the room.

"Tough and smart—they have the right man in that job." Max was developing a grudging respect for Peter Ashgrave. He winked at Joseph and on the way out the door, Max said, "Stay tuned, boss. Told you it was a cool phone."

After he left, Joseph took the pipe out of his drawer and lit it, drawing deeply, the smoke swirling around his weathered brow. Cool? What's the world coming to when the director of the NSA uses that word? Ah well, my time will soon be over, but just maybe I can do one last patriotic act for this country I love so much. He shook the match out and dropped it in the metal garbage can beside his desk.

Then he called Lance and updated him. He passed along the news that they'd been reinstated to their rank at retirement. This meant that Lance was commanding officer on the ground.

27

It was relatively easy for Brad and Beats to make good their exit from the arena. What was that old saying? "Discretion is the better part of valour." Brad was a realist and knew the situation had become untenable.

They hoofed it back to Lance's camp and commandeered the Jeep. Brad replaced the coil wire and made short work of the ignition. They already knew where they were going—the line cabin was a perfect place to hole up for a night. They had hoped that finding the abandoned Jeep, everyone would believe they had another vehicle waiting there. And it worked—everyone accepted that as the most likely scenario. After a night's rest, they made their way across country towards the gas plant. There were living quarters on site where they could wait for things to blow over.

Security at the plant consisted of men that Brad had handpicked—vets loyal to him. They were earning double the going rate and kept their mouths shut. He assumed they had few or no suspicions—and if they did, they kept them quiet. Everyone who worked at the plant was from out of state. When their shifts were over, most went straight home. This was especially easy since they were shuttled back and forth to an airstrip on site.

When Wallace had approached Brad about this operation, he had immediately seized upon it. They were way beyond subtleties, and the offer would net him millions. At first, the plan was to ship the rough ore to the coast and then through friendly third-party companies to the coast of Iran in the Persian Gulf. From there, it would be sent up a similar pipeline to a subsurface nuclear plant. But that meant moving tons of material; logistics was a nightmare and shipping a daunting challenge. It was later decided that they would break the ore down on site, process it into slurry, and then compress the slurry into pellets and ship it.

Two pipes were laid to the coast—one for natural gas and the other a conveyor belt of sorts, with stops along the way where the slurry could be offloaded and transported by truck or rail as a redundancy.

Then came SUSNEX2, as the Iranians were calling it. "The computer virus from the future", some said. But it was actually a joint project by Israel and the US, utilizing German components from Siemens. The virus was designed to infiltrate and infect the Iranian nuclear facilities—it would assume control of their computers and adjust everything from the rate of centrifuge spin to the temperature of the water. It was also designed to send back false data showing everything operating correctly. Once these changes were made, the virus deleted itself.

After the first such attack, Iran eliminated disk and thumb drives from their entire military network. They realized the virus had been uploaded by a staff member. A disk labelled "employee salaries" had been left lying around.

Despite the new protocols, somehow, Israel and the US found a way to perform the same trick. Speculation was that it was some sort of virus pre-loaded into the software somewhere along the line, but they could never figure out where the breach was. All this undetected sabotage went on for months before the Iranians again realized something was wrong and shut it down. This, combined with the systematic assassinations of their most elite physicists, set the Iranian nuclear program back years.

They were desperately looking for a way to get back in the game quickly when Wallace approached them with the offer to supply uranium pellets. It was extremely appealing because they were taking it from under the noses of the Americans. A little Trojan Horse payback of their own!

The other appeal was the internet. There was little chance the Americans would attack with another virus as the plant was on their own grid. There was too great a risk it would infect their own infrastructure. The pellets would take time to enrich further, and Iran's capacity to do so had been severely hampered by the attacks.

That's when Wallace made them a bold new offer. They would receive U-235 uranium rods ready to be used in their reactors. This would increase the price tag by billions, but it was a workable solution. ComCorp went to work creating a nuclear mining operation beneath the gas plant right where the best deposits had been discovered.

Years of planning and work were now almost complete, and they were only days away from final delivery. Several shipments had already been sent to the coast—down the dry pipe on three-wheeled electric carts. These were an adaptation of the "Leak Detection Robots" developed at MIT Saudi Arabia. The design had been scaled to size, and they were powered by a contact in an electrical groove at the base of the pipe, much like an old toy car track. They were designed to carry cargo, but in a pinch, they could also carry personnel. However, personnel needed an oxygen pack, as there was no airflow in the pipe.

For Brad and Beats, travel back and forth from the plant was simple: They dressed up like workers and drove one of the company trucks. No one looked at them twice. The gas plant trucks were in town frequently for repairs or to pick up supplies. In fact, they had used a company truck to find and deal with Crown.

They picked up Truck, and the team was back together again—almost. Brad's eyes narrowed as he remembered Preach stretched out in the snow— that crude spear lodged in his neck. Preach always was a bit reckless, but he was a first-class fighter. Brad would never have believed Coolidge could have killed him while wounded and Preach with the drop on him. There was a part of Brad that still wanted to take Lance on—one on one, despite the cold wind of caution that blew through Brad's psyche. But that wouldn't happen now.

They would deliver the product, the company would get rich, their stocks would soar, and they would all live out their days in a tropical paradise. This was the plan Wallace had set forth for them. However, Brad had been making plans of his own. When this was all done, he had no intention of running with the herd.

It never bothered Brad that he was betraying his own country, or that he would be assisting a hostile regime in developing a weapon with which to bully its neighbors and the world. He reasoned that if it was good enough for the executive branch, it was good enough for him. He had seen many of these deals over the years and knew he was just a pawn in their game.

He glanced unconsciously towards Truck and Leadbeater idly playing cards. Truck had healed up completely and was once again the powerhouse he always was. Brad thought now about the intelligence of the big man. Brad had never underestimated Truck and suspected he had plans of his own as well. Good, he thought—one less person to break away from. As for Beats, he is like a bear cub refusing to leave its mother. I will need to chase Beats up a tree. Another couple of days and the balance of the orders will be filled. We will seal off the lower floors and it will be years before anyone discovers what happened here. By then, we will be long gone.

Brad donned his hard hat as he walked to the main floor security control room. It had become his practice to check the perimeter sensors and cameras several times a day. He had opted for high tech instead of leathernecks, partly to reduce manpower. They also had more confidence in a system that didn't sleep. The sensors were well spaced in circles fanning out from the plant for several hundred meters. There were also laser tripwires that activated HD video cameras and thermal cameras whose fisheye lenses overlapped one another, covering the entire perimeter. Remote-controlled gas-powered Gatling guns with thirty-round bursts per second were spaced strategically around the circumference of the plant, and dozens of security cameras were strategically positioned inside the brightly lit building.

The plant was on the grid, but the primary power source was boilers, fueled with gas produced on site. Like many modern plants, they were energy independent, which disguised the heat signature that satellites might pick up from their work below ground. This was a stroke of engineering genius. The boilers were overkill for a plant this size but not completely unprecedented.

The cameras and munitions were manually operated from the control room or from an app on Brad's phone and pad. The place was far from impenetrable, but it wouldn't be easy to attack.

"Still awake?" Brad nodded at the control room operator as he entered the room. "What's the word?"

"Nothing much. A couple of deer wandered through the web this morning, but that was all. I had one of them dead in my sights, a nice big buck. We could all be enjoying venison right now."

"I'm glad you resisted the urge." Brad patted him on the shoulder. He had a way of endearing himself to other men.

Taking control of the toggle, he shifted from camera to camera, looking carefully around until he was satisfied the area was clear. He then cross-referenced the images with those on his phone, spot-checking several cameras at different intervals throughout the web. All systems checked out.

"Environmental inspection tomorrow," Brad reminded him. "This room is off limits to them!" Brad did not care for the timing of the inspection but knew it was overdue. A rep from the president's Energy Council would be on hand, so there would be no monkeying around. There were several areas they would deem off limits due to hydrogen sulfide gas concerns but would yield to the pressure that was sure to follow. This would give the inspectors the feeling that they had applied their authority to access everything they wanted. They would huff and puff and make a display of handing out sensors and airpacks to the inspectors as though they were only concerned for their personal safety. Once the plant demonstrated that all environmental protocols were being followed, they would be given a clean bill of health and left to finish their work.

A few more days and all our work will yield dividends beyond our wildest dreams. If only my mother could see me now. Brad was already well established financially, but the coming payday was the one he had been waiting for. They had successfully evaded detection, and the sheer audacity of a project of this magnitude was almost unbelievable. What an adrenaline rush it had been!

———— • ————

Brad had planned his disappearance carefully. As a lad, he had two good friends, and he combined their names into the alias "Clayton Delorme". An expert forger created a Canadian passport and a British Columbia driver's license. He had never used either name as a password or associated them to himself in any way.

When he assumed his new identity, he would cease to be Brad Akron or even BA. Otherwise, he was certain Wallace would always have just one more job for him to do. I will leave this life forever and retire in style. It was with some bitterness that he accepted there was not a single person in this world who would miss him. The trade-off was that he would be an independently wealthy retired businessman in a new land of his choosing.

———— • ————

It was an excruciatingly long wait at the line cabin for orders. Both Daryl and Lance understood the need to be patient and wait for orders, but they also knew that every minute counted. They could only speculate how much uranium had already been shipped. Even thirty to fifty pounds was enough for a rogue actor to create a bomb and potentially deliver the payload via a missile warhead. An attack of that nature aimed at the US would be devastating and would turn the world upside down.

They ate, checked their gear, and cleaned their rifles. Daryl was sporting his own clothing line. It was warm, comfortable, and offered freedom of movement.

Suddenly, they heard the low hum of an engine in the distance, and both men grabbed their rifles. Lance looked out the small window to the road leading from the cabin. Only a moment passed before a truck came into view.

"Visitors!" Lance said. Daryl didn't say anything, but he was frowning as he came alongside Lance, peering out the window. The truck was still a few hundred yards away, approaching slowly on the rough road.

"I'll check the back," Daryl offered, going to the opposite window. Nothing appeared to be out of order.

The truck pulled up alongside the Jeep. Lance recognized the driver even before he stepped out of the truck. "Daryl, it's Red and the team," he said with relief.

Lance swung the door wide open and stepped out onto the narrow porch so they would get a clear view of him. He waved them inside and without waiting went back inside.

Romey was the first one through the door. He was in civilian clothes and didn't appear to be armed. The rest of the men trooped in after him. They were belted up and ready to go.

"Now you can salute," Lance said. They all stiffened, but he added, "At ease, gentlemen."

"We just got word that the situation has changed," Romey said, "and our orders were to rendezvous here with you and await orders, Major." He emphasised the rank.

Lance gave them the lead-up to finding the memory stick and filled in some significant gaps in the story.

"Any idea what's on the stick?" Teddy asked.

"Yes, and as soon as we have clearance to tell you, I will."

Just then the phone rang. It sounded like submarine sonar. Lance answered it. He was surprised it wasn't his uncle Joseph.

Without a preamble, Ashgrave jumped right in. "I see by the GPS you are all together. Can you turn on the video?"

Lance complied, snapping out the built-in leg and placing it on the table in front of them. Uncle Joseph was there, in a white-walled featureless room.

"I am Peter Ashgrave, chairman of the Armed Services Committee. We have assigned operational control of this op to General Gus Gonzales, who I will introduce to you in a moment. This has become the top priority for national security. We have briefed the president and the Joint Chiefs, and we are a go! Major Coolidge, have you briefed the team?"

"I have not, sir; I was awaiting authorization."

Ashgrave summarized the situation and then called on the general.

The general came on-screen immediately. He was younger than they expected—definitely under forty. His hands were folded on a desk in front of him. He had a shock of grey around the temples but little else that would designate him as a mature general.

"We have three more SEAL teams on their way, as well as naval and coast guard assets being moved into position near the port as we speak. The thermal reading from the plant confirms that there are no more than fifty-five personnel inside. The plant produces gas, so many of these are legitimate workers. However, that does not mean they won't be hostile. You need to be diligent. Take nothing for granted; a guy in coveralls can be just as dangerous as a guy in fatigues."

He continued, "We have activated four battle carrier groups to a heightened defense condition, in different places around the world. We strongly believe it's the Iranians." He swiped his iPad before continuing. "According to the building schematics, the forty-eight-inch pipe is the anomaly; it simply doesn't have a functional purpose. We believe it's a transportation route for the slurry. It may also provide concealed in-and-out access. We suspect the nuclear facility is underground. Infrared isn't picking up personnel, but they may be undetectable in a hardened area. Also, we could end up with a nuclear nightmare should they scuttle the plant. Stealth and swiftness are called for if we are going to catch them flatfooted. Your team needs to make a silent approach and entry. Assess the situation, and if necessary, engage them. Our analyst has come up with two potential entry points. I'll send the layout to your phone. Move out within the hour; this op is green for go. Questions?"

The team looked at Lance. He took a moment to collect his thoughts. "General, what do we know about their defenses?"

"That will be in your download. Keep in mind there are several laser tripwires and HD cameras. We have a contingency to knock those out prior to your approach. They will be blind; I can guarantee that."

"Munitions and or armed defense?" Lance asked.

"I suspect you may meet with small arms resistance."

"With all due respect, sir, they have carried out an audacious plan on our own soil for years without detection. If I were them, I would have planned for detection and attack, and therefore defense. There will be guns."

Gonzalez wasn't a general because he was rash. "What's on your mind, Major?"

"I suggest we wait until tomorrow; you find a reason to delay all shipping—a bad weather warning, an oil spill, anything to buy us some time. We make a few changes to the Environmental Team. Daryl and I go in with Romey and Red. We take a look around and can be inside when the action starts. When the other teams are in place, you text me. We hit them hard and fast and secure the site before they know what hit them. They will most likely have a redundant power source, so we may not be able to knock the cameras out. They will have a protocol for blackouts that will be bad for us."

The general took a deep breath. "I like your assessment, but I will need a stand-down order from the boss."

Red spoke up. "I have no civilian clothes, sir."

Lance pivoted back to the general. "How many on an environmental team, typically?"

Someone off to the side spoke, and he repeated what they said. "Six or seven."

Lance thought for a moment. "They may have workers who are oblivious to what's going on below. Let's use their own trick. We meet with the team of environmental inspectors as planned; we don't need to prep them. Let them believe we are from the Energy Council. That way if we don't know what we are talking about, they will chalk it up to politics."

Again, someone spoke from off to the side.

"Stand by for authorization," Gonzales said, and the screen went black.

"I like the idea," Strong said. "Where do you want us?"

"I want you close by. That place looks benign, but there is no way it's not guarded and fortified. You will need to stay inside the treeline until you're needed. There is a flat dead zone of about four hundred metres on all sides. My suggestion is you go in through the front gate. It's two hundred metres, and the lanes have been slightly beautified with a few trees lining the route. Approach with caution; perhaps from inside we can neutralize their defenses."

"Any motes and alligators?" Teddy asked, and they all laughed.

"Let's be ready to move out. Orders rarely get changed," Lance reminded them.

His words sobered their mood, and they set about checking their gear, cycling their weapons, and checking their loads.

Daryl looked around at the group of men, the best of the best. He would do his best to give a good accounting of himself.

The phone rang again. It had only been about fifteen minutes. Tension filled the room as the video came on.

"Major." The general's voice was strong. "The chief has agreed to your plan."

Romey exhaled a long cleansing breath and as one, the men relaxed for the moment.

The general continued, "We have no way of protecting you from a radiation leak, accidental or otherwise. There will probably be gear inside; we will send you the protocols in the event of poisoning, but I think we know that stuff is all bullshit! Just get in and secure the place as quickly as you can. If there is a meltdown or explosion, you won't be able to drive away fast enough. The plant is isolated, but the communities for a hundred miles around will be uninhabitable for centuries, and prevailing winds could contaminate five states and two Canadian provinces. So don't let that happen!"

The general concluded, "We have a nuclear team standing by to assume control once you have secured the site. I have one reservation though, and that is Corporal Craig."

"Me?" Daryl was surprised but squared himself to the camera.

"Yes. Unfortunately, you're not trained for this—"

Lance cut him off. "Sir, I'm sure you have been briefed about my ordeal? Permission to speak freely?"

"Of course."

"Corporal Craig came to my aid under fire, putting himself on the line. These men will attest to his tenacity, ferocity, and ability. After all, it was this very group of men that were pursing me at the time. I vouch for him; I trust him, and I need him, sir."

"Major, the irony of this situation is not lost on me. It's the stuff of legends. The access points and safety protocols will be sent to you shortly. In the morning, we deliver hell! Three more SEAL teams, three entry points, and two choppers with a boatload of marines are standing by. You have command on the ground, so we will await your go. If there is no word from you, we go at eleven regardless. Understood?"

"Yes sir."

"Good. Corporal, welcome to your baptism of fire." The screen went black again, and moments later a file was downloaded.

Strong walked over to Lance and rested a big paw on his shoulder. "It feels good to be back on the right team, sir." He looked around at the group. "You gotta love these guys." Nodding at the sat phone, he continued, "Tomorrow, we deliver hell!" He exaggerated the mimic. "If I have to tackle hell with a garden hose, it might as well be with you gents."

Romey smiled. "Strongman, I think that was the most words you've ever said at one time."

Strong gave a half shrug and reached for another cup of coffee.

———— • ————

If the line cabin was a point on Google Earth and you zoomed way out, you would see a flurry of activity—four aircraft carrier battle groups at various places around the globe as well as the coast guard and other vessels moving into position around the port.

Chinese and Russian military commands raised their own alarms as American warships moved to battle posture. Some well-placed spies reported that NATO was on high alert due to an unidentified threat. No one on this side of the globe would be getting much sleep tonight, and on the other, tensions would be running high as well. Chains of command were being checked to ensure that there had been no provocation or orders that could have been misinterpreted by the Americans. Foreign generals and admirals were wondering if the Americans were planning a pre-emptive strike somewhere, and if so, where?

All of this was unseen by the six men resting in a small cabin in the northern Montana wilderness. It was hard to believe that such a great fire could be ignited by such a small spark. Yet here it was, a suspicious world on edge, waiting for someone somewhere to light the fuse.

———— • ————

At six a.m., the cabin was astir with movement. As there were only the two beds, several of the men had slept on the floor. On Lance's orders, the bedrolls were rolled up and stored on a bunk. All unnecessary equipment was stowed; this would be a light and fast-moving operation. The plan was to have Strong, Teddy, and Red drive the Jeep past the plant, on alert for anything unusual. Lance, Romey, and Daryl would follow suit a half hour later in the pickup. They would then intercept the "Green team"—as they had taken to calling the environmental inspectors—at a preselected intersection and follow them into the plant.

At seven a.m., the Jeep pulled away from the cabin.

A half hour later, Romey drove the truck out, with Lance riding shotgun and Daryl in the back. It was chilly, but their bulky jackets compensated for the civilian clothing worn by Lance and Daryl. They each had a pistol tucked inside their belt; Lance had his knife scabbard on the back of his belt along with extra magazines. Each had a second pistol inside their jacket pocket. There was no way they could waltz in there with rifles.

They had been at the intersection for almost thirty minutes when a flicker of headlights appeared through the trees. Although they had radioed the all-clear, the Jeep was nowhere to be seen. When the ironically green-coloured pickup with three men and one woman pulled up alongside them, the sky was greying; it would be full light soon.

The passenger window came down. The driver was frowning, as he had been expecting only one person.

Before he could say anything, Romey blurted out. "How come you're late? We have been waiting for almost an hour!" He intended to put them on the defensive.

The passenger looked at his watch nervously. "Late?" He was rattled. "The inspection's at nine, no?"

"We were told eight thirty." Romey's tone was bland. "Oh well, no harm done. I'm Jeremy Manning, and these are my colleagues, Daryl and Lance." Both men nodded a greeting.

They had turned on their interior light, and the driver patted his chest. "I'm Alex; this is Kevin," he said, indicating the passenger. "In the back seat are Susan and Reg." Susan gave a nerdy expressive wave—she was clearly the extrovert of the group.

"Someone have a thorn in their ass?" Alex asked. "Why the snap inspection?"

"I'm not sure; probably someone in Washington scoring some political points. Let's get this done and get out of this godforsaken back country." Romey was smooth, you had to give him that. "You guys take the lead—we barely know what we're doing here ourselves."

"Sure," Alex said, putting the pickup in gear.

———— • ————

When they pulled up to the main gate, the guardhouse was lit up with two men inside. The barrier was down as always. A pole camera pointed in the direction of approaching vehicles.

Lance watched one of the guards approach the first truck and the interior light flip on. They could hear only a word or two of the conversation.

Lance took out his knife, quickly breaking the dome light and brushing the shards onto the floor. The guard passed a few items through the driver's window ahead of them and then lifted the barrier, waving the first vehicle through.

When it was their turn, the guard raised his hand. He was wearing a side-arm. "You're all together? We were told five people." Shining his flashlight into the cab, he was clearly trying to light up their faces for the camera. Daryl had slid over to the driver's side in the back, drawing his gun and concealing it between his legs.

Romey answered while producing his ID. "You heard wrong, I guess. We are here on behalf of the president's Council on Energy." He spoke with an air of authority.

The guard looked at each of them with a knowing eye. "Can you turn on your interior light so I can get a look at y'all?"

"Sorry, man, it's busted—crappy rental."

The guard aimed his flashlight at the broken fixture. "Wait here," he said and went back to the guardhouse.

"No rent-a-cop," Romey mumbled.

"Steady, guys." Lance was completely relaxed.

The guard returned with hard hats, visitor lanyards, safety glasses, and earplugs. "The hard hats and lanyards must be worn at all times. Keep the glasses on your person; you may end up in areas where they are needed. Drop them off here on your way out. Have a good visit." With that he waved them through.

Alex and his team moved out down the lane.

"Keep an eye out for any more guards or any other defenses," Lance said while texting his first message: "Two guards at the main gate—both armed. We are approaching the plant."

A second gate led to a parking area, but it was open and secured—most likely because of the wind.

"Second gate—chain link. Open," Lance typed.

Several plant representatives were out front waiting for them. As they approached, Lance went live on the sat phone.

They all put their hard hats and safety glasses on and stepped out of the truck as one man. Alex and his team were already making introductions and getting the pleasantries out of the way.

Lance took several pictures of the plant and surrounding area, and by the expressions on their faces, he could see they weren't liking that very much.

One of the greeting party stepped forward. "Hello, I am the plant manager, and you are?"

"I'm Jeremy Manning, the president's liaison. You don't mind if we take a few pictures, do you?" Romey's smile was warm, friendly, and naive.

The plant manager didn't like it, not one bit, but he forced a smile anyway. "Of course not, but there's not much to see out here. Won't you come inside?" He gestured for them to go.

"After you, sir," Lance insisted.

As he went into the building, he clipped the phone onto his shirt pocket with the fisheye lens peeking out. The view was concealed by the jacket occasionally, but he was now live streaming.

Past a set of large double doors, they entered an office area with a plexiglass divider that went from counter to roof. It looked out of place in an office environment. The manager tapped it with his knuckles. "Sound barrier."

He then stepped through another door off to the right and they all followed. "You won't need your safety glasses for a while if you'd like to remove them," he advised. "It's a bit noisier in here, so use your own judgement on the earplugs."

"I'll leave my glasses on," Romey said. "I have a slight light sensitivity."

There was a row of hooks with jackets on them. Lance took off his jacket and hung it on a hook, his lead was followed by everyone on the team, even the Greens.

The phone's camera was now fully exposed, and their every move was being watched by the president, the vice president, and several top aides, as well as the general and Joseph, who had received a special invitation.

Alex worked through his checklist as they continued the tour. There were cameras everywhere. There were also too many people loitering about, casually keeping an eye on the proceedings. Lance's team rightfully comprehended that these people were security. They looked like workers, but they weren't working on anything. Perhaps the untrained eye might have been fooled by them—carrying clipboards and pointing at things, but Lance was marking positions and counting bodies. They were an hour into the inspection when they came across a narrow, downward stairwell.

"Where does this go?" Alex asked.

"To a generator room, but for today we will avoid it because we've had an H2S leak and we're still getting readings," the manager said.

Alex wasn't satisfied. "Let's have a look," he insisted. "We can wear airpacks."

Susan didn't look too pleased with that idea but said nothing.

"Fine. I'll have some gear brought up," the plant manager said.

As they were being fitted with the packs and the plant manager was warning them to be careful, Lance made a play. "Hey, you guys don't need me down there, do you? I need a loo ... drank too much coffee."

Susan saw this as her out as well. "Yeah, me too. Where's the ladies' room?"

The manager looked around, not wanting the group separated, but everyone else was almost completely suited up.

"Down this corridor, first right—you'll see the sign on the left. We will be back here in a few minutes. Don't wander around without an escort. There are some dangers."

Lance gave an enthusiastic thumbs up. He was hoping to look around on his own and found Susan's chatter distracting as they went down the hall.

"Did he say the first right or the first left?" Lance asked.

"First right, I think," Susan said.

"I thought he said left, I'm always getting turned around. You're sure?"

"Yeah, I'm sure," she said, laughing at him a little.

When they came to the hallway that turned right, the bathrooms were off to the left. Lance was relieved the men's room was first.

"BRB!" she said and pushed the swinging door into the ladies' room.

Lance stayed in the empty washroom for a few seconds before retreating quickly back down the hall, working his way out of sight within moments. He knew the cameras were tracking him, so he made sure to look confused from time to time, as though he was lost.

The plant was clean and bright. He was looking for access to the lower levels, but they were hidden. He saw a main control room and made a beeline for it.

The controllers saw him coming but realized too late that he was about to enter the room.

His wave was friendly. "Hey, guys, I'm a bit lost … this place is bigger than it looks."

They were borderline hostile. "Who are you, and what are you doing here?" one of them barked.

"Jeez, man, chill. I'm with the environmental inspectors. I went to take a piss and got separated from the group. —Oh, hey, I see you've got cameras." He leaned in close to the screens, taking them all in. He spotted Susan standing at the end of the hallway. *Is she waiting for me to come out of the bathroom?* He saw several areas where workers were congregating. He pointed to one group on the screen. "That's them! How do I get there?"

The controllers were clearly annoyed but at a loss as to what to do with him. "Sir, this is a classified area. I'm going to call for an escort to get you back to your group." He lifted the receiver on the phone.

"Classified area!" Lance echoed in surprise. "I'm here as a member of the president's Energy Council—you're making me think you have something to hide."

The controller hesitated and then put the receiver back. His attitude did a one-eighty. They had been given strict orders to not make any waves with the inspection team. "No disrespect intended. I … we are just trying to follow proper protocol."

Lance looked at the screens again. He could see Susan was back with the team, and there was a discussion going on.

"The main concern we have is potential leaks, so where is the main gas line?" he asked in a more serious tone.

The second controller came forward and pointed to a camera facing a large metal door. "Through that door is the first access port to the main line."

"Is there a camera in there?"

"No, but we have sensors every five hundred metres. Look here." He pointed to a flat screen with digital read-outs and animations showing flow to every pipe. He touched the screen and zoomed in. "Here is that pipe. You can see there is an elbow and a valve, so in the event of a leak we can shut the pipe off in sections and stop the flow." The animation showed the gas flowing normally through the pipe.

"These sensors are all the way along the pipe, is that correct?"

"Yes, all the way to the coast. We've never had a leak or an event of any kind. This is a state-of-the-art facility."

"Where is that in relation to where we are?" Lance asked.

"That would be sublevel A, one floor down on the north end. There is a green line that leads to it, from the elevator here," the controller answered, pointing to another screen. "Or there is stairwell access here."

Lance didn't want to ask more questions that might raise further suspicions. Controller one had shut up in a hurry.

"And where are the tailing ponds?"

"No cameras there, sir. There is a high fence, and only a few birds have ever strayed into them." He was doing his part to defend their environmental record.

Lance noted that at least one SEAL team would be approaching unobserved. The inspection team was working their way towards Lance, no doubt looking for him.

"Is there a closer stairwell to the lower levels?" Lance asked.

Controller one looked like he was about to have a coronary.

"Level," controller two corrected. "Not levels. I know, sublevel A sounds like there should be others, but this plant is built from a generic design. Some of the bigger plants have several sublevels."

"Ah." Lance looked him straight in the eye. This guy was telling the truth, although he had his doubts about the other controller. How many workers are completely in the dark about the sinister goings-on below?

He needed to get them safely out of the building before the yogurt hit the fan. His watch read 10:05, and the plant manager was approaching with the environment team. Time was running out.

Lance stepped out of the control room. "Sorry, guys, I got turned around. Let's look at sublevel A, shall we? I understand that's where the main gas line is."

Alex could see no purpose in that and started to protest.

"Humour me, gentlemen. I want to be able to tell the president we looked at everything."

"Why the hell not? I never voted for the guy, but he's still the boss," Romey said.

———— • ————

General Gonzales winced at the comment, but the president didn't let on he'd heard it and continued staring intently at the screen.

———— • ————

Before the team crammed into the tiny elevator, Lance made note of the stairwell just beyond it. The elevator lurched to a halt at the bottom, and Lance took a few more pictures. While doing so, he checked that there was still reception.

"What's the key in the elevator for?" he asked casually.

"Oh, if you are loading the elevator, it can be locked in place, with the door open." The manager's answer seemed rehearsed.

They made their way down a causeway, the sound of machinery growing louder. Pausing to put in their earplugs, they opened the door to the main gas line access. It had that stale smell of a place long sealed up. The weak fluorescent light took a moment to flicker on. Lance knew from the schematic that the second pipeline was here as well, but there was no evidence of it; only a tool crib with several airpacks for emergencies.

The team seemed anxious to leave, but Lance was sure this was the access point they'd used to smuggle out the nuclear material. How they had concealed it so well was beyond him. Reluctantly, he followed them, flipping out the light as he left.

"Satisfied?" the manager yelled over the din of the machinery.

Lance nodded.

When they made it back to the elevator, Daryl announced he was going to take the stairs since the elevator was too crowded.

The manager detached a ring of keys from his belt and unlocked the door.

"See you at the top," Daryl said pleasantly.

Lance was impressed! Just like that, one of their team would be able to check out the stairwell.

Back on the main floor, Daryl was looking through a small, screened window on the door. When he emerged, he caught Lance's eye and gave a slight shake of his head. Nothing. Lance looked at his watch—10:24.

———— • ————

Brad made sure he was in the secret control room as the environmental team arrived. There was not enough light to make out their faces and the audio was not clear. With Romey clean-shaven and wearing a hard hat and safety glasses,

Brad didn't recognize him. His attention was on the guy trailing behind the group, who seemed to avoid the cameras.

When Lance headed towards the control room, Brad became even more alert. There are no cameras watching the guys who are watching the cameras—it's a dead spot. Did this visitor figure this out? Brad was about to confront Lance, when the inspection team reached him. What are they doing? The obvious thing is to have a look around sublevel A. There isn't much for them to see—the pipe hasn't been accessed from there in a couple of years, and the hatch is now concealed behind a concrete wall.

He watched them emerge from the room and once again was suspicious of Lance. He grabbed an overcoat. "Truck, Beats, I need to go topside. One of those guys could be a problem. It's probably nothing, but you'd better join me in case."

He had a red key and a black key on a small chain with a fern-like emblem on it. He put the red key into the elevator key slot, turned it to the right, and heard the elevator making its way down to their level. Keeping his eye on the iPad screen, he was able to make sure no one would stumble upon them as they made their way up.

As Brad and his group reached the main floor, the environmental team was passing the control room again. Lance glanced over and saw the screen that showed the elevator with three men coming out of it.

Lance removed the phone from his pocket and typed: GO!

"Guys, it's time to go—now!" He barked the last word as an order.

Daryl had snaked his pistol out first. This didn't go unnoticed by Lance. Daryl will do all right; he surely will, Lance thought proudly.

Romey's gun was pressed into the manager's ribs as they herded them down the hall towards the restrooms.

"What the hell is this?" Alex was startled.

"US military special operations. This is going to get dangerous—stay in the restroom until one of us comes to get you."

"But—" Susan started.

Lance cut her off: "Non-negotiable."

They turned the corner and made it to the restroom. Daryl ducked into the men's room, gun up and ready. A moment later, he was out and waving them in.

"Stay here and stay together," Lance ordered. "Not you, partner." He grabbed the manager by the scruff of his neck and pulled him back. He was pale, and Lance was certain he was party to the operation. "Frisk him."

Daryl found the manager's sling holster under his lab coat. Daryl slid the gun out and held it up to the manager's face. "What's this for?"

"None of your damn—"

Daryl slapped the manager open-handed, knocking him hard against the wall. A full search revealed no other weapons.

"Grab his keys," Lance instructed.

Daryl tossed them to Lance.

He waited, covering the hall as they gagged and zip tied the manager to the handicapped armrest in the women's washroom.

As they emerged into the main hallway, an explosion rocked the plant.

At the same moment, Brad, Beats, and Truck rounded the corner fifty metres away.

Because Lance and his team had their guns out, they had a slight advantage in the moment. Not hesitating for even a split second, Lance got the first round off—the man under his gun was Beats. As Lance fired, the sensation that everything was happening in slow motion overtook him, a sensation he had never experienced in battle. In that moment, his dream of being shot came back to him—the bullet going in reverse out from him and back to the shooter. The shooter! The same face Lance had seen in his dream—how odd! All of this detail in a split second! How is it possible? He saw the man flinch when the bullet hit him, but everyone was moving, and someone on their end had gotten a gun out almighty fast and fired.

Lance, feeling the whirr of a bullet pass his head, lunged back into the restroom hallway—and all was quiet for a moment. Both Daryl and Jerome had retreated there as well. Lance glanced back towards the restrooms. There was no movement. The environmental team appeared to be following orders.

"Lance, buddy, is that you?" Brad's voice came from down the hall. "Damn me, man, you just start shooting? Whatever happened to foreplay?"

Lance called back, "BA, if Leadbeater is still alive, you tell him we are almost even."

"Screw you, Coolidge! We'll ante up again in a minute." It was Leadbeater's voice this time.

The rattle of automatic gunfire was coming from somewhere else. Lance pulled the phone out and pressed the scramble icon. "You're not going to surrender, Brad? And I thought you were a smart guy. That shooting you hear is the cavalry."

Silence. Had they moved?

Daryl was shaking his head. "That was some fast action and out of my league. Brad was shooting before I could get a round off. I've heard of a quick draw, but he pulled that gun out cold. Had Beats not fallen against him from your shot, Brad surely would have gotten one of us."

Lance got down on the floor and slid towards the main hall. At the same time, Romey stuck his gun out at chest level. A quick peek indicated that no one was there.

They moved out after Brad and his team.

———— • ————

Brad's group were passing another hall off to their right and had ducked down it as soon as the shooting started.

Unfortunately, that hall was empty as well, and where it led was anybody's guess. They followed drops and smudges of blood down the hallway that ended in a T. There the blood trail ended, leaving no indication the direction they had gone.

Lance took a chance and darted his head in and out again. He had been looking right but a bullet from the left hit the wall where his head had been for that split second.

Lance indicated to Romey he was to go right, and Daryl was to follow him left. They both moved on the silent count of three.

The hall was empty, but there was sporadic shooting in the distance.

"Blood," Romey whispered, pointing at a stain a few feet down the hall.

Lance nodded for him to follow and indicated with a sideways jerk of his head that they would carry on pursuing the shooter.

The hall to the right had many doors, and Romey tested each one as he worked his way down. His vast experience warned him not to trust the blood trail entirely because Beats could have backtracked to one of the rooms and locked himself in. If that was the case, he would end up behind Romey, and that could prove deadly. Whatever this area was, the doors were all locked, and the hall ended at a set of double doors.

Brad had divided the team to increase their odds of escape. Presumably, they would meet at a predetermined location.

Romey suspected Brad had purely selfish motives. After all, he had abandoned Truck in the wilderness, since a wounded man would have slowed them down. Brad might have done the same again.

The doors were just slightly narrower than the hallway. Romney, leaning his shoulder against the end wall, pushed the door open with his foot, expecting a shot. Nothing! The doors opened into a spacious area that was part of the plant, with pipes, scaffolding, and tool storage.

There was a significant amount of blood on the floor where Beats must have pushed through the doors, falling hard. Wounded and trapped, he would be even more dangerous.

Several people were rapidly making their way towards Romney. His vision was obstructed by shelving and equipment, but a few seconds later, Red came into view followed by Strong and Teddy. He let out a low whistle, and Red's rifle came around quickly even as Strong and Teddy covered forward and side positions. Romey waved them over and explained what was happening.

"The surprise was complete," Teddy said. "Most of the building is secure. We found the Green team in the restrooms and assumed that the guy you tied up should be in custody."

"I'm a bit turned around," Romey admitted. "These halls are a maze. Clearly Beats didn't go out the way you came in. He's wounded." He indicated the blood smear on the floor.

"He probably crawled in a hole somewhere," Teddy commented.

"The main control room and the elevator to the second level are behind us."

They looked around. There were no doors besides the ones they had come through, so where had Beats gone? Moving in a circular pattern, they tried to pick up the blood trail, with no luck. They went over the entire area, checking behind equipment and in garbage containers, and even examined the causeway above them, before Strong spotted a retractable ladder hanging down. In this case, it had been retracted from the top. There was no way to reach it from where they were. The causeway only went in one direction—towards the control room.

Guns up, they followed it. There on the floor was a telltale drop of blood. It had splattered, indicating it had fallen from above.

"Right above us," Strong whispered. "He could have gotten a couple of us."

They had little doubt that for a time they had been under the gun of a deadly marksman.

"Running …." Romey wagged his head. "He must be heading somewhere."

Suddenly, there was gunfire from the direction they were going.

—————— • ——————

Lance and Daryl had made their way slowly through the maze of hallways. Checking a couple of dead ends and a dozen doors, they found two unlocked rooms, but both were empty. When they emerged, they were back in the main part of the plant but in a different area than where Romey and his team had met up.

Their pursuit had led in the same general direction, as the plan was for Beats to meet Brad and Truck at the elevator.

Beats had been advancing along the scaffolding and had just managed to duck into a shadow as Red, Strong, and Teddy passed beneath him. Beats was pressing hard on his wound, trying desperately not to spill any blood that might alert others to his presence. He wanted to chance a shot but dared not release his pressure on the wound. All he could think of was escape, even though it went against his nature to run. The bullet had gone in above his right hip and at first, he was concerned it had nicked his liver. However, if that had been the case, he would no longer be walking around. Since there was no exit wound, he was able to contain the bleeding with his right hand and brace himself with his left as he worked his way down the metal causeway. His head was swimming, and his eyes were beginning to blur.

He was still several hundred metres from the elevator when he spotted more movement below. It was Brad and Truck. They would make it to the rendezvous point before him. He climbed over a flat-roofed false wall that was part of a line of makeshift storage rooms and offices. Several hundred metres back, he could see Lance and a big guy he didn't recognize.

Beats realized they would reach the elevator at about the same time as he would. Would Brad leave without him? He had always been loyal with an all-for-one attitude. However, he was remembering abandoning Truck. Brad had assured him that they had no other choice, but now wounded, he wasn't willing to take a chance. He slid the rifle, which he'd recovered from a stash, off his back. Squinting from the pain, he brought the scope inline. This was his chance to right a wrong that had been plaguing him. Damn it! He'd had Lance dead to rights there at the river. He had never missed before, but his mistake had led to this. And then the long, improbable chase through the wilderness. He didn't like to admit it, but he was a bit superstitious and recalled the stories of the Afghan villagers calling him the "Arwa-Rue." And now here he was, being relentlessly pursued.

"Arwa-Rue," he scoffed to himself. I'll exorcise this demon right here and now and send him back to hell. Gritting his teeth, he moved the scope from Daryl to Lance and started to squeeze off a shot just as they disappeared behind the wall. Those walls were just drywall so he kept the rifle moving, confident he was pacing Lance accurately.

At that very moment, Lance and Daryl stepped into an open doorway, rather than continuing their course. A bullet passed harmlessly between them, tearing through the drywall and showering them with bits and powder. They threw themselves inside the room, expecting the gunman to be there; now they were unsure of where the shot had come from.

Several more shots probed the same area, creating a cloud of dust and debris as Beats continued to fire, but no shots found their mark. It took Lance and Daryl only seconds to perceive that the bullets were coming from above, angling down through the wall, narrowly missing them. The shooter was back on the causeway that crisscrossed most of the building. For the moment, they were unseen but still pinned down.

Instinctively, believing those shots were meant for them, Brad swung his gun up towards Beats and fired two quick shots. The first bullet ricocheted off the metal platform and cut an angry path along Beats's calf. The second clanked hard against the scaffolding, changed direction making an angry whine as it and whistled past his ear.

"For God's sake, man," Beats cried out.

Brad was looking down the barrel at Beats, and for a moment, Beats thought he was going to shoot at him again. Instead, he slowly lowered the gun, glaring at him. Beats began waving and pointing wildly in the direction from which Lance and Daryl had come.

Daryl was working his way along the wall, bent down in an erratic run that made pacing him difficult. Beats fired several rounds, hoping to slow Daryl down. Daryl ducked inside a room, feeling something tug at his shirt.

Too late, Beats realized he'd been tricked. Lance had crawled along the wall, closing the distance between them. He'd forced one of the doors open as a ready retreat and popped up seventy metres away. The distraction Daryl had provided gave Lance the opportunity to set himself and fire.

The bullet caught Beats dead center, knocking the wind out of him and driving him back. He couldn't believe it. Shot at that range with a pistol while he had a rifle and the high ground. Why didn't I trust my instincts? This whole op was cursed from the beginning. Through the fog, he could see movement and swung his rifle around.

"Go, Brad!" he shouted and started firing.

When Romey and his group opened up on Beats's position, Brad immediately knew that his own was untenable.

Truck had been working his way along the wall towards Lance and Daryl when suddenly there was a tremendous crash. Drywall sprayed in every direction. Daryl had spotted Truck as he passed a small window, and charged through the wall, knocking him flying in a whirlwind of dust and debris. Even Lance was caught off guard by the ferocity and suddenness of the move. The two big men were rolling on the ground in a colossal struggle.

Brad threw an indiscriminate shot their way, as he bolted towards the elevator with Lance charging after him.

Lance wouldn't let Brad escape. This needed to end here! As Lance rounded the last corner, he could still hear gunfire from his right and knew that at least one of his men was engaging Beats. Lance would need to trust them—he was certain he had hit Beats hard.

Brad had the lead and was able to make the elevator and within seconds descend to sublevel A. He took his key chain out of his pocket, inserted the red key, and turned it to the right. The elevator started down to the secret level below. He flipped his iPad open and touched the camera icon above the elevator.

Had his reception not been scrambled earlier, he would have seen the SEAL teams approaching, and he would have engaged them with the Gatling guns. He had been unable to respond to the laser tripwire alarms, and apparently, the controller had been unable to as well. He wasn't sure, of course, without a surveillance camera in there.

Lance was frantically pushing the elevator button, but it couldn't be summoned to the main floor with the red key engaged. Had Beats not opened fire when he did, Brad and Truck's ambush would have eliminated Lance and Daryl or at least put them out of the fight.

Brad's eyes narrowed as he looked at the screen. Lance was at the stairwell, taking a set of keys from his pocket.

Brad couldn't believe it. There was only one other set of keys that could access these lower levels, and Lance had them. It was definitely time to get the hell out.

Lance raced down the stairs, two at a time. He unlocked the door at the bottom and emerged in the hallway next to the elevator, gun up and ready. He had a pretty good idea what that red key would do. He inserted it in the slot next to the button, and turning it, he could hear the elevator coming up.

The elevator lurched to a stop, and Lance had his gun ready when the door opened. It was empty. He stepped inside and saw Brad's key still in the slot. Lance knew he would be in a profoundly vulnerable position when that door opened on the lower level. Lying flat on the floor, when the door opened, he was fully expecting a shot that didn't come. The area was empty.

Stepping from the elevator, Lance found himself in a relatively comfortable living space, with a pool table, a bar, several couches, and a big-screen TV. So this is where they have been hiding. They must have come here after leaving the line cabin.

Lance pocketed Brad's key. Then he remembered the sat phone; it had fallen out somewhere along the way. The other teams had body cams, so the president and Joint Chiefs would know how things were progressing up top.

A wall to his left forced Lance to work his way to the right. There were several rooms with beds, TVs, and computers, as well as a common area. Farther down, there was a fully stocked kitchen and beyond that a workout room with free weights and treadmills. The entire area was like a sprawling warehouse and the rooms, while comfortable, were uniform in design.

Lance took his time, making sure every room was clear. He was beginning to believe that Brad had left, but Lance hoped Brad wasn't on the mining level. Lance definitely didn't want to go down there without a nuclear team.

At the far end of the room was one last door. It turned out to be a storage room that held cleaning supplies and toiletries; it was slightly cooler than the other rooms.

Lance concluded there was nothing here; he would need to go lower.

Leaving the room, he flicked out the light and remembered the storage closet on sublevel A. Both rooms were laid out the same way and both had a slightly cool feel to them. He turned the light switch back on and cast about the room—looking for what, he had no idea.

A vent on the left-side about shin height was blowing warm air. Why is this room cool? It should be as warm or warmer than the rest of the building. Lance touched the left wall—it was warm. He then moved around the room to the back wall—it was cold! He tried moving the shelves, but they were fastened to the wall. He shook them here and there, but they didn't budge.

He guessed the concrete wall was exposed to the earth on the other side, but that didn't make sense—this room was far enough underground that the temperature should be moderate. He wanted to take a closer look, but the room had the same weak fluorescent lights, and he didn't have a flashlight. Too bad he'd lost the sat phone with its powerful light.

He was about to give up when he noticed something—a wall plug that wasn't sitting flush. The edge was slightly raised, and it looked like there was a smudge on it. In the dim lighting, he couldn't be sure. Getting down on his knees he noticed some dust on the floor underneath it. He held the back of his hand over it but there was no noticeable change in the temperature. When he touched the plate, it gave way under his hand. With a slight pull, it swung open on a small hinge, and there, hidden behind it, was a small plunger-like button.

In the old Indiana Jones movies, a button like this might release any number of horrors, but here he was, and it was his job to press that button. He pushed it down and heard a distinctive click off to his right and then felt a cool rush of air. Had he not been on his knees he would have missed it—under the shelves a small door had popped open. A dim light emanated from around its edges.

Lance pulled his gun from his belt. The opening was two feet high and maybe six feet long. He would have to lie down and shrimp or roll his way in. The prospect did not appeal to him. Not knowing what was on the other side was spooky.

Taking a deep breath, he pushed the door open, swinging it away from him easily and quietly. He couldn't make out anything distinguishable on the other side. His eyes needed to adjust, so he crawled back out and turned the light off. The eerie glow was more pronounced now, coming out of the dark hole.

He was just about to slide into the space when everything went pitch black. Reflexively, he lifted his head, and it came up hard against the bottom shelf. For a moment, he felt as if he was back in the cave. Instead of panicking, he remembered the warm presence he had experienced there, and he felt it again now. And there in the darkness, Lance smiled. "I have nothing to fear but fear itself," he whispered, remembering the quote.

All was quiet on the other side. He squirmed out of the space and felt around for the outlet with the hidden plug. Groping, he found the light and turned it on again. Blinking in the light, he pushed the hidden button. The click was quieter without the door being released. The light came on—as he suspected, it was on a timer.

He crawled into the eight-by-eight room beyond. There was a small, yellow emergency light wrapped in wire mesh but nothing else. They had simply put up a wall to divide the room and disguised the wall by placing the shelf on it, top to bottom. The concrete was only an inch thick. A service ladder led up to the next level. Knowing that the light would soon go out, he started to climb immediately.

———— • ————

Brad had a good lead on Lance—and was moving at a brisk pace. This was a last-ditch escape route, with a basic hatch leading up to a darkened room.

Lance had just cleared the ladder, and his eyes were barely adjusting when the light below went out. The slight glow that remained would prevent him from falling into the hole, but that was it. He reasoned that the light switch would be close to the access hatch and after a few minutes, his search was rewarded. Turning it on, he was stunned—the room was encircled by a bank of bright lights.

28

R ows of three-wheeled carts sat in a half pipe. They were connected to electrical tracks that were an extension of similar track within the pipe. The presence of two freight elevators led Lance to believe that this was the point from which the uranium was smuggled out.

Several airpacks hung from the wall and there was a gap where one had been removed. Attached to each of the airpacks was a digital Geiger counter. They would sound an alert if the radiation exceeded a certain number of millisieverts. Lance turned one on and it was nearly ten times the normal reading. As he walked towards the elevators, it increased considerably. The reading was also high at the mouth of the pipe. While the readings weren't dangerously high in the short term, Lance didn't want to be in this environment for an extended period.

It was clear that the robo-carts had been designed to carry a small amount of cargo. It takes approximately thirty pounds or thirteen kilos of uranium to produce a bomb. Depending on the richness of the ore, they could smuggle out enough uranium to make dozens of bombs. Several of the robo-carts had harnessed seats for a single passenger.

Lance took one of the airpacks off the wall and checked the pressure gauge; the tank was full. He shrugged into it and Velcroed the Geiger counter in place on the shoulder strap. Sitting in the harness, he located the main power switch on the right side. When he turned it on, it activated an LED headlight next to each of the three wheels.

Lance grasped the situation with his keen mind.

It was unlikely that the carts were used to transport personnel to the coast. It would take too long, and the oxygen supply would run out long before arrival. Lance concluded that Brad was simply taking it to a jumping-off point where he had a vehicle waiting. If that was the case, Lance might be too late to catch him.

Lance pushed the cart down the track to the head of the pipe. There was probably a way to ride it there, but he'd never seen one of these, let alone driven one, and navigating it down the half pipe with the third wheel free looked like it could lead to disaster. It was surprisingly light and moved easily. Once he had it in position, he strapped on the airpack mouthpiece, turned on the regulator, and climbed into the harness. There were stirrups for his feet and a seat belt. Once he was buckled in, he moved the joystick slowly forward, then in reverse. It was a simple, intuitive design. The speed was controlled by how far forward you pushed the joystick. He rode at a slow pace for several hundred metres before speeding up.

There was a slight thump between each length of pipe, which allowed him to estimate his speed by how often he heard the telltale thump-thump of the transition. Soon, he was flying down the pipe, the LED lights shining just far enough ahead to illuminate the pitch-black pipe. Both exhilarating and terrifying, it was like a controlled descent into a black hole! At times, he was pitching downward with increased speed, and he would have to back off on the toggle. Other times, he would be climbing, and progress would be painfully slow. He wished he had his jacket now as the temperature had plunged.

At the last second, Lance saw something rushing towards him out of the darkness—a metallic object that flashed for a split second in his headlights. He heard and felt the collision at the same time, as he was sent spinning in the darkness. The cart lost connection to the track, and when at last he came to rest, he was hanging upside down in the harness. Not able to make out a thing in the pitch black, he was breathing heavily through the airpack.

It took all the self-control he could muster to remain calm. Locating the Geiger counter, he was able to tear it off his pack, but almost dropped it. Turning it on, it lit up orange with a reading of 2.4. Tolerable. Using the light from the counter, he found his seat belt and unbuckled it. By bracing himself on the frame, he gracefully fell out of the robo-cart. Leaning against it, he ended up pushing it back a few feet. There wasn't enough room stand up, but he was able to maneuver around in a crouched position.

He checked his air supply; he had just over twelve minutes left. What was it Neil Armstrong had said? "If I had a problem with only ten seconds to react, I would spend nine seconds thinking." Lance sat down on the floor of the pipe and thought. He had twelve minutes; that meant Brad had planned on getting out somewhere within that same amount of time. There had to be a place for him to get off and resupply or bug out.

Lance tried to put himself in the mind of the other. Brad would have allowed for a hiccup; he would allow five extra minutes, Lance decided, at least that's what he himself would do. That meant that at top speed, Lance could travel about two more kilometres. But how far could he go, crouched in a pitch-black pipe on foot? He knew he couldn't make two klicks in twelve minutes—but then again, this was a lot of guesswork. Finally, he decided to dedicate two minutes to fixing the robot. If that didn't work, he would start down the pipe and hope for a miracle. He would have five minutes ….

Wait, he thought, I don't just hope anymore, and he burned up another few seconds of his precious air with a prayer. It's been said there is a time for prayer and a time for action, but Lance decided to pray.

"Lord, I ask for your help and guidance to get me out of this pipe and to catch this criminal and bring him to justice!"

Pulling the robo-cart, Lance slowly spun it toward the upright position. In the glow of the screen light, he could see that one of the wheels was bent. He was able to push it back into position, but the bearing was seized. It would no longer glide smoothly but he would have to be content with that. When he finally got the robot turned halfway around, he examined the contact and it appeared to be intact. If he could force it back into the track, maybe, just maybe it would work. He spun it the rest of the way around as the contact lightly scraped the wall. He must take care not to damage it further. It came up against the lip of the track and hung up. But no matter how much he pushed and pulled; it would not jump back into the track. He looked at his air supply. Nine minutes and thirty-eight seconds. He had already surpassed the time he'd allotted himself.

Then Lance noticed the tire was seized. Finding the valve and using Brad's keys, Lance was able to release a little air. He pushed again—still nothing. He released more air and this time he was able to wrestle the power contact into the track. But still nothing. He pushed the power button, and the LED lights came on, blinding him momentarily. He slapped the Geiger counter against his arm and wriggled awkwardly back into the harness. Dispensing with the seat belt and stirrups, he moved the toggle slowly forward. His heart leapt as it began to move. He hit a transition—thump! The lights flickered on and off. He wouldn't be able to go fast, but he was moving forward. He rode for several minutes before checking the air gauge: Five minutes, twenty seconds.

The next few minutes in the black tunnel dragged like hours. He didn't know what he was looking for, but suddenly, there it was—something shining in the distance. As he got closer, he recognized it as reflective tape. There was a strip on the top of each piece of pipe now—he had to be getting close. The robo-cart was slowing down and eventually rolled to a complete stop. He couldn't make it move forward. It was dead. The motor must have taken too much abuse in the collision. Lance crouched down and scurried down the pipe.

After a few minutes, the robo-cart's lights ceased to be of any use, fading to a tiny point behind him. His legs were cramping, and he bumped his head several times. Holding the switch down on the counter provided a tiny bit of light. He moved urgently, crawling and scurrying, running out of time. He didn't bother wasting precious seconds looking at the gauge—it didn't matter what the reading was. He just needed to keep moving forward.

Another hundred yards, and the air ran out. It was still pitch black except for the reflector tape catching a bit of ambient light from the Geiger counter.

Lance tossed off the apparatus and held his breath. It wouldn't do to breathe in carbon dioxide. He could hold his breath for three minutes, two under physical activity.

Turning sideways now, he was doing a sort of scurry-shuffle. Falling forward, he reflexively sucked in a breath, but there was no air. He rose up again, a dark panic closing in on him. Rounding another corner, he could see a dot of light, but consciousness was beginning to slip away. A hand reached down out of the light, waving him on. He gave one last heave forward and his lungs filled with the sweet air of life. Coughing violently, he managed the next few steps and reached up to grab the hand. It was cold and hard—the first rung of a short ladder. Lance pulled himself up the three rungs and rolled out onto the snow. He lay on his back gasping, a strange giddiness upon him.

He lay there not minding the cold, just happy to have survived the long, black hole. Resting now on the event horizon, he was safe. When he stood up, the first thing he saw were the snowmobile tracks. Brad had gotten out and ridden away. He was long gone. All of this effort and Brad had still gotten away.

———— • ————

Lance moved off into the trees, collecting wood for a fire as he went. He had it burning bright and had warmed himself up before adding some green boughs to create a smoke signal. Even with all that smoke, it took over an hour for a chopper to arrive.

After kicking snow onto the fire, he ran to an open door and jumped inside. He was looking directly into the barrel of an M-4. A serious young marine held the gun steady. Lance gave him a genuinely friendly smile.

"Relax, son, I am Major Lance Coolidge. Point that rifle in another direction, will you?" Lance relaxed into the seat and enjoyed the ride.

———— • ————

Brad had escaped into the trees on the snow machine with a significant head start. Even though the chopper and a drone had circled the area, there was no sign of him or the machine. He had made a clean escape.

When they flew over the plant, there was a flurry of activity on the ground. It had primarily been an air assault due to the remote area and the attention a land incursion would have drawn.

They landed on the plant's helipad. The fight inside was over, and several people were being escorted to the waiting choppers, handcuffed, their heads hooded in dark cloth sacks.

The SEAL teams had coordinated the breach from two directions and from the roof into the main area of the plant.

A small group of nuclear personnel were gearing up to go in. Their suits reminded Lance of just how dangerous the situation had been. If the plant had been scuttled, the whole area would have been destroyed, killing everyone as well as creating an ecological disaster unparalleled in American history.

Two marines were posted at the front door. As Lance approached, both men snapped a salute. He returned the gesture and went inside.

Lance retrieved his jacket from its hook. Several handcuffed people were seated in the hall beyond the lobby area, including the environment team, with several marines standing guard. The fact that those in handcuffs had not been hooded indicated that their status was still in question. On Lance's order, the environmental team were uncuffed.

"You will need to stay and be debriefed, so don't stray far." Without waiting for a response, he inspected the other detainees.

One of the men looked up. "What about us?"

"What about you?" Lance's voice was hard and flat.

The other swallowed hard. "I'd sure like to know what the hell this all about." He was trying to sound tough but was clearly frightened.

"If you've done nothing wrong, you have nothing to worry about." Lance suspected he was a worker who truly didn't know anything about the scheme. However, that was not up to Lance to determine.

A small band approached from down the hall. Romey and his team walked towards Lance with a prisoner of their own. It was Truck, and he had taken yet another vicious beating. Just behind him, stumbling slightly, was Daryl, who didn't look much better. There was a nasty gash along his cheek, and both his eyes were swollen—the left one almost shut. He had a cracked lip, and his nose appeared to be broken. Truck's head was hanging low as they came abreast of Lance.

Before Lance could say anything, Strong spoke up. "Daryl asked us to stay out of it. I can assure you; it was a world-class tilt. Even I would think twice about tackling either one of these boys. It went back and forth and was nip and tuck there for a bit as to who would come out on top. But our boy here just wouldn't quit." He slapped Daryl on the shoulder.

"Sorry, boss," Red added. "We just couldn't interfere."

Lance understood their sentiment; they were fighting men, and it must have been quite the fight! He would have liked to have seen it himself.

"Never thought a man could beat me with his fists," Truck mumbled, struggling with the loss, his head hanging from both fatigue and shame. The last time these two had met, it had been different. Truck had already taken a clubbing and was not able to give a proper accounting of himself.

"Put a hood on him, and get him into a chopper," Lance ordered.

He placed a gentle hand on Daryl's shoulder who looked at Lance through the slits that were now his eyes and managed a grin through cracked lips, revealing a chipped incisor.

"Your sister will have my hide for this."

"If you believe that, you have a lot to learn about my sister." Daryl smiled, then winced.

"Come on then, let's get you home." Lance took his arm and put it over his own shoulder, and they walked out to the chopper.

"Sir!" A marine handed him a sat phone as they cleared the doorway. It was General Gonzales.

"Hell of a job, son. Looks like we achieved complete surprise and secured the plant. I know you probably understand the magnitude of the service you've done for your country here. Well done!" He repeated the acclamation.

"Thank you, sir. Akron escaped."

"Yes, I heard." There was regret in his voice. "We've got the place buttoned down. We'll find him."

Lance wasn't so sure but kept that to himself.

"We'll get a full debrief tomorrow. For now, get some rest and enjoy your ride home."

"Thank you, sir. Will do."

Lance helped Daryl into the medical chopper.

"I've got him, sir." The medic took over.

"I'll catch the next bus. There's something I need to check."

Daryl had given up trying to talk, opting instead for a thumbs up. The medic slammed the door, and they were off.

Lance wandered through the plant. One of the SEAL team leaders showed him the secondary surveillance room.

"Lucky, they didn't get a chance to use those," he said, indicating the perimeter guns.

"They were busy," Lance replied.

"Yup, things would have been a lot different if your team hadn't made it inside. We didn't lose a man."

Lance took the stairs down to the lower levels. Both access doors were wide open. He made his way slowly through the living quarters, looking for a clue that might help him figure out what Brad would do next.

His room was neat, and the bed was made. Old habits die hard.

There was a copy of The Art of War by Sun Tzu, other books on military strategy, and novels—John Grisham, Tom Clancy, and the like. Several casual shirts, jeans, two sets of coveralls, and jackets with the plant logo hung in the armoire, as well as several suits. Lance frowned. There didn't seem to be anything in the room that was helpful.

It wasn't until much later that Lance remembered seeing something important.

———— • ————

Lance had barely hit the ground back at the Craig ranch when he received another congratulatory phone call, this time from the president. It was a private call, and Lance appreciated that, especially because he hadn't voted for him and wasn't interested in being used as a political prop. However, he respected the office and was honoured by the call.

There was also an urgent text and voicemail message from FBI Agent Lombard. On the way to the hospital to check in on Daryl, Lance called back, but there was no answer.

Daryl was doing well. As Lance had expected, the man was a beast. He was badly bruised, and the doctor thought there was a cracked rib or two. They'd cleaned up and butterfly-stitched the gash on Daryl's cheek. He asked to go home, but the doc insisted that he stay at least one night for observation over concerns about a concussion. Knowing Doc Currie, Lance wasn't surprised that the doc had won the argument.

As Lance was leaving, the doctor caught Lance's eye. "I've been busy since you've come to town."

"Think of it as job security." Lance gave an absent-minded wave as he made his way to the front door. Doc Currie had a sour look on his face as he watched Lance go.

Lance was planning on borrowing a car from Clarence for the afternoon, and the garage was only a five-minute walk from the hospital.

As he was leaving, Sheriff Hallward was coming in the front door. "Lance, I heard there has been some sort of accident involving Daryl. Thought I'd check in and see how he's doing." There was concern in his voice.

"He's doing great," Lance reassured the sheriff. "You wanna grab a coffee? I'll fill you in."

Hallward seemed to be studying Lance, looking for something in his face. "I take it you haven't heard from the FBI?"

That brought Lance to a standstill. "There was a message on my phone but no answer when I called back. What's happening?"

"Let's get that coffee. It sounds like we both have something to share."

"Sheriff, I don't like waiting for bad news. If something has happened, I'd like to get it straight."

"This isn't bad news—well, not for you at least."

When they had seated themselves at the bistro, Kelly poured them a coffee and dropped off two menus. Lance suddenly realized how hungry he was and ordered a meal.

"We got your man," Hallward said as they started in on the coffees.

"My man?"

"Clifford Bellamy!" There was triumph in his voice.

"What? How?" Lance started to get up. But the sheriff gestured for to sit back down, which he reluctantly did.

"He's not in my jail, but he is in custody."

"The FBI?"

"Uh huh. That's what the FBI was calling you about, I'm sure. We caught him with good ol'-fashioned police work, and then they swoop in with federal warrants and scoop him up. He was running on the stolen plates from the rental place. One of my deputies spotted the truck. We boxed him in just outside town, and he had nowhere to run. I thought he might try to shoot it out, but he came in cool and casual. Better to live and fight another day, I suspect."

Lance couldn't believe it. For weeks now, everything had gone against them, and now things were snowballing in the right direction.

Out of respect and trust for Hallward, Lance provided a full accounting of the events on his end. Hallward listened intently with little expression, chewing on the side of his mustache from time to time.

When he was through, the sheriff sat silently for a few moments. "Damn, that's more than a few gaps. The area is secure now?"

Lance nodded affirmatively.

"What now?"

"That depends on what happens up the food chain." Lance was thoughtful. "Your department may have provided the link to whoever is ultimately responsible for all of this. I doubt you'll get much credit though. I don't need to tell you—this conversation never happened, and you don't know anything."

This pleased Sheriff Hallward. As a pure-hearted law enforcement officer, he believed the reward was in doing the right thing and making a difference.

They had finished their meal and were quietly comparing notes when Lance's cell rang. It was Agent Lombard. They would pick him up within the hour. Another night with no sleep—how many had he missed over the years? He'd lost count, but he wouldn't mind missing sleep on this night. He would finally come face to face with his brother's killer.

———— • ————

Lance entered the barren interrogation room with an ice cold feeling in his stomach. The room was brightly lit with fluorescent lights surrounded in metal mesh. The bare white walls reflected and intensified the light. There was only a single piece of furniture in the room—a metal table and chair, fashioned as a single piece, like the old schoolhouse desks. It was bolted firmly to the concrete floor with a microphone just out of reach in a fixed position.

Several loudspeakers were mounted in the four corners of the ceiling.

Clifford was chained hand and foot to a metal loop on top of the table. His hands were held in place with approximately six inches of play. A dark hood lay on the table in front of him.

He was calm, but his eyes were alert to the others' intentions. Lance's face was bland as he came face-to-face with his brother's killer at long last. He had fantasized about what he would do to this man if they ever met. And now here he was. Seeing the man in chains, trapped by his own evil, Lance felt something more akin to pity. Scratching and scraping, fighting and killing one's way through life couldn't have been pleasant. Bellamy was like a mad, wounded dog, lashing out in a desperate attempt to survive.

Lance dropped a small metal object roughly the shape of a top on the table. Due to its odd shape, it rocked back and forth, against the metal desk, before coming to rest. Bellamy looked down at the thermostat, unable to comprehend its purpose.

After a long moment he looked up at Lance. "You probably don't remember, but I saw you in Washington once."

Lance didn't respond.

"You had just finished testifying before the Senate, and we passed in the hall. I remember taking a long look at you because word was you were a dangerous man."

Lance remained expressionless, but his voice carried that menacing tone that caused men to look up and pay attention. "Been awhile since we put someone to death here in Montana. So unless you have something you'd like to share with me, we are going to get the paperwork started."

Clifford ignored that, knowing he still had a card to play. "That brother of yours …"

Lance stepped forward; jaw clenched. Bellamy leaned back in his chair, less frightened than cautious. "There was something familiar about him, but I just couldn't put my finger on it. Figured it out too late."

"You figured everything out too late, Bellamy. You're a psychopathic killer, and you will be put down like a rabid dog."

Clifford thought about that and supposed it was true, but the label didn't bother him. "I'm small potatoes in this whole operation, and you know it. You cut me a deal, and I'll spill my guts. Bastard tried to have me killed. I don't owe him a damn thing."

Lance stayed quiet, waiting for more.

Clifford leaned back farther in his chair until the chain tightened against the loop. "Ahhh—you don't have the whole story then." He was pleased with himself.

"If you're talking about BA and his team, you're wrong. We also know about your man in Washington. I'm not sure you have anything left to bargain with, friend."

Bellamy stayed relaxed. He needed to be careful not to agitate Lance. They hadn't read Bellamy his rights or offered him counsel, so he suspected correctly that if he didn't have something to offer, no trial awaited him.

"I have emails, text messages, and a recording. But if I'm going to die here anyway or get shivved in prison—hell, I'll just keep my mouth shut."

"That's fine." Lance's voice was cool. "I'm sure there's an extra cell in Gitmo we can borrow." He picked up the thermostat and turned to leave the room but paused at the door. "This is a thermostat for a 2005 Chevy 350 engine. The truth is, Bellamy, I just don't care what you choose. Either way, you'll never see the light of day again. I suggest you do spill them guts of yours and make a deal." The heavy metal door slammed shut behind him.

In that moment, Clifford knew he had played out his hand. There was no two-way mirror in this room, no video camera, nothing. They had brought him here blindfolded, wherever here was. For the first time, he was scared. Prison he could deal with, as long as it wasn't death row. Maybe he had overplayed his hand. The lights went out, and the room was pitch black. He instinctively pulled against his chains, but they held fast, rattling in the darkness.

Time passed slowly. He called out several times, but all was silent. At first, his calls were defiant, but when there was no response for what seemed like hours, he finally yielded and attempted negotiation. He made the offer again and again to provide evidence but still no one came. Why?

Many hours, perhaps a whole day passed, and finally, he heard the door open. The sound of leather shoes creaked against the floor as someone walked around him. He jumped at a hand on his shoulder, then a hiss of a whisper.

"Write. Write it all!" Something slapped against the table, then the footsteps retreated, and the door slammed shut. Again, he was alone in the darkness.

After what seemed like an eternity, the lights flashed on, and he was forced to cover his eyes to shield them from the brightness. In front of him was a pad of paper and a pen. He hesitated only a moment before pulling the pad and pen towards him, his chains rattling against the fasteners as he scribbled on the page.

———— • ————

It was all there: A staggering plot to undermine the safety and security of the United States and her allies. Names, text messages, and emails—a treasure trove of intel. Bellamy had kept it in a safety deposit box and now disclosed the key's location, the same key he thought Kyle had taken. Bellamy had been a fool—that grease monkey never did know or suspect a thing. All Bellamy's plotting had come to nothing. I will never see the light of day again.

Those words echoed in his mind. He would make a deal all right, and maybe he would end up in a maximum-security prison. Despite all his bluster and tough talk, Bellamy wanted to live. He was confident an opportunity for freedom would come. But for now, he was a key witness and would be protected.

29

Captain Leslie Shapiro was sleeping in the cockpit of her F-35 along with the rest of her squad. They had been on high alert for the last six hours. It was two in the morning. She was one of the few Israelis who had stayed in after the mandatory stint. She loved to fly and had an even deeper love for her country. She had been raised on the stories, told over and over, about her great-grandparents who had perished in Auschwitz. Duty, honour, and sacrifice had been pounded into her from an early age. She was programmed to take orders, and she had just been woken up and given hers: They were to provide air support for a bombing mission into Iran.

———— • ————

Meanwhile in the Persian Gulf, a freighter was steaming towards Iranian waters. Its cargo meant the difference between the survival of their nation or its imminent decline. Her captain, a veteran seaman, had been part of the youth movement that had ousted the Shah. With pride, he had witnessed the glorious revolution and the establishment of a long-awaited Islamic theocratic state. He too, was a patriot who loved his country. The contents of his cargo had not been disclosed to him.

They were running under a United Arab Emirates flag and were only a hundred kilometres from Iranian waters. He was on the bridge when the transmission came in to scuttle the ship. He read the instructions over several times, his mouth growing drier by the second. He swallowed hard before raising the alarm and giving the command to abandon ship.

They were at full stop in the water. The master alarm was buzzing its long, echoing strains, and sailors were rushing to prepare the lifeboats. Twenty-nine souls. Will we be rescued? He had no way of knowing.

The explosives had been set ahead of time. Only he and the first officer had been instructed in the scuttling procedure. When the men were clear of the ship by a couple of kilometres, they would trip the charges by remote control. There was also a timer that needed to be set manually, just in case.

The captain caught the eye of the first officer. Waving him over, the captain read the communication from Tehran. "I'll set the timer and then you and I will get in the last boat. Make sure the engine is running when I get there."

With that, the captain made his way into the hold. Opening the locker that held the timer, he set it for ten minutes and grabbed the remote detonator from a small briefcase. Out of habit, he began locking everything back up and then, realizing what he was doing, he shook his head, slammed the locker door, and quickly climbing to the deck. The lifeboats, still lashed to the ship, were bobbling furiously on the six-foot swells, but they were seaworthy craft and if necessary could make it to the mainland on their own.

The captain accepted a hand as he climbed into the stern of the last lifeboat, holding the detonator close to his chest.

His first order was a single file retreat from the ship. Her lights became ghostly against the starless night as they slipped away. When they had made the recommended distance, he called for a halt. Taking out the small briefcase, he opened it. A tiny green light was blinking that would go solid when he flipped the toggle switch.

The captain heard three loud, distinct clicks. The sounds seemed to come from everywhere and nowhere at the same time. Suddenly, high above, the sky lit up with a blinding flash, followed almost immediately by a tremendous boom that echoed and reverberated all around them, until it rolled away like distant thunder.

Everything went dark. The men were speechless. The engine was silent, and the freighter had disappeared, its lights extinguished by the pulse. The light on the detonator had gone out as well. The captain's heart sank. They had failed. He had failed! Had they been attacked by an EMP? Had the dreaded nuclear war come upon the earth?

After a few moments, the men started calling out to one another frantically. A few headlamps came on. The first officer was at his captain's side, handing him a flashlight.

"Man the oars!" he shouted. "Lash the lifeboats together!" He was a good captain, and he wanted to keep his men together. They would all make it or none of them would. There was safety in numbers.

Low on the horizon, a light appeared, and then another. The searchlights swung back and forth like lanterns in a coal mine. Within a few moments, they found the freighter, bathed in a pale light. In the darkness, they had drifted back towards it and were within a couple hundred metres of the stern.

There was a distant hum, but there were no engine sounds. The captain had heard American drones patrolling the night skies above the Pakistani border, and he recognized the familiar sound now. One drone was holding position above the ship. The other was circling around it, scanning in every direction. Bitterness rose in his throat. The Americans would seize the ship and confiscate the cargo. He pulled out his sidearm and fired several useless bullets at the drone. The wind was picking up and swirling around them.

Suddenly, a bright light appeared above them, and the captain realized he was feeling the downdraft of propeller blades. The craft itself was completely silent. How is that possible?

A loud voice rang out in flawless Farsi. "This is the US Navy. Throw down your weapons, and prepare to be boarded."

In a moment of frustration and anger, the captain considered shooting at the light emanating from the silent helicopter. But then he thought of his men. Whatever this American technology was, they had muskets compared to machine guns, and he knew it. Any aggressive move would most likely result in a significant loss of life. In a final act of defiance, he tossed his gun into the sea.

———— • ————

The Speaker of the House called an emergency session of Congress. Peter Ashgrave likewise called the Senate Armed Services Committee together, and the president was in the situation room with the Joint Chiefs. Joining them was Max from the NSA and the director of the CIA. The US military had been placed on the highest level of alert.

The Israelis had offered to strike Iranian nuclear facilities. What the world did not know was that the intel for these strikes had come from the Americans themselves, and in fact the first bombers in had been American stealth B-2s.

Pictures were beginning to emerge from Iran's official news agency, showing destruction at various locations around the country. The Ayatollah was vowing revenge for these "cowardly" acts of aggression by the Israelis and Americans. Thousands of Iranians were marching in the streets chanting, "Death to Israel! Death to America!" Lines were being drawn, and several Middle Eastern countries were aligning with Iran. Most troubling of all was the fact that even Jordan was leaning that way.

Turkey had come out aggressively condemning the attacks as "destabilizing and provocative" and had removed use of their airspace and military bases. This created a crisis within NATO.

Tensions were running high, and both the Chinese and Russian militaries were on high alert.

Diplomatic efforts were already under way. The Canadian consulate in Iran had requested an audience with the Iranian president, hoping to open a backdoor communication channel. The US ambassadors in Russia and Beijing were awaiting orders from the president, with appointments scheduled as well.

The president was preparing to address the nation at noon on all the major networks, and the speech-writers were scrambling.

In his office, Uncle Joseph was waiting for Lance, thoughtful as always. The information they now had was devastating. Joseph was keeping a close eye on developments in the Capitol. When he spoke directly with the president, they decided to neutralize the foreign crisis before tackling the domestic threat. When Lance entered Joseph's office, he looked fitter and healthier that Lance had ever seen him.

Over coffee, Uncle Joseph shared the intel they had gleaned from plant personnel, files, and ship manifests. They had also gotten invaluable information from Clifford Bellamy, leading directly to the big fish at the top of the operation.

The Iranians had fronted the entire operation, paying off officials and infiltrating key positions on regulatory boards. Using the pipeline to smuggle the uranium out, they had taken delivery of several shipments. The early morning attack had occurred with the cooperation of Israel precisely for that reason. After all, they had enough uranium to build at least two nuclear bombs. The decision was made to neutralize their facilities before they could arm a warhead.

An elaborate system had been developed using a series of ships, much like getaway cars in a bank heist. One ship was left in a foreign port, and the uranium was transferred to another. As cover, the ships flew the flags of a neutral state without that country's knowledge or approval. Once in Iranian waters, they simply hoisted their own colours and sailed on in with no one the wiser.

The ships were all owned and operated by ComCorp. The company was set to make billions from the deal, and in turn, so would its shareholders. The Securities and Exchange Commission had halted trading that morning, pending an investigation. The RCMP were conducting a raid at ComCorp's head office in Calgary, and word was that the CEO was on the run.

Lance listened with rapt attention to the details. Had Clifford Bellamy not been such a homicidal maniac, the entire plot might have gone undetected for years. President Kennedy had warned before the Bay of Pigs raid that "somebody always jumps the gun." He had been proven right once again.

"All enemies," Joseph said. He slid another file across his desk towards Lance. "Foreign and domestic."

Lance flipped through the file. "I take it this will be handled privately?"

Joseph tapped his index finger on the desk. "That, my boy, remains to be seen. Let's go watch the show. The president is set to speak."

The set off down the hall and came to a common room packed with spectators. There was a massive screen on the wall, and people were milling about, chattering excitedly. This was a who's who of the legislative branch. Security was tight, and tension was high as everyone waited to hear what the president had to say. When he came on, he wasn't in the Oval Office but an undisclosed location. He was flanked by the vice president as well as the director of the CIA and General Gonzales.

Wearing a suit and tie, he sat at a desk with the presidential seal on the wall behind him. Lance had to admit the optics were fantastic. He looked presidential and in charge.

The room became subdued.

———— • ————

"My fellow Americans," the president began, "today I come before you at a moment of great peril for our country. One week ago today, on my orders, several special forces personnel took control of a sour gas plant in northern Montana." There was a startled murmuring from the crowd.

"This plant, while only in operation for a few short years, was being used as a front for a clandestine uranium mining and enrichment operation. I am pleased to report to you today that the plant was secured without a breach and without risk to the communities nearby.

"I want to thank those specialists for their service to our country, for their exemplary abilities, courage, and dedication. And indeed, for their service to the broader human family. I have sent an attaché to both the Russian and Chinese governments with the evidence we discovered at the plant and evidence from our subsequent investigations. I want to assure their people and the American people: We do not have any evidence that would implicate either of these nations. I have asked them to lower their respective military postures. Upon review of this evidence, both countries have agreed to stand down.

"This plot was clearly planned and perpetrated by the aggressive and evil regime that is Iran today. I want to make it clear that this fight is with that regime and not its citizens. Nor is this a fight with the religion of Islam. America is welcoming to all religions and beliefs. All have added to the tapestry of freedom and the sharing of thoughts and ideas that have made America the great nation it is.

"This morning as commander-in-chief, and with the cooperation of the Israeli Air Force, I ordered a predawn raid, an air strike to destroy strategic nuclear facilities in Iran.

"Iran had assured the world that its nuclear ambitions were friendly and nonmilitary. This incident has exposed that narrative to be a lie. With a nuclear bomb in its arsenal, Iran would not only be a regional threat but a global one as well.

"We also interdicted and captured an Iranian freighter and its crew. That freighter was being used to transport the uranium that was mined at the plant in Montana. It was en route to Iran. The freighter is owned by a Canadian-based global company called ComCorp. The same company owns the sour gas plant and as such has become suspect. Canadian officials are cooperating complete-ly with our investigation.

"I am pleased to report that all this morning's missions were successful. And all our personnel have returned safely!"

A cheer went up from the group.

"Furthermore, Congress has informed me that later today 'a state of war' will be declared between our two countries. This is an important legal require-ment of our constitution, as America continues its commitment to the rule of law. This allows us to bring to bear the full weight of our military to aggres-sively confront this ongoing threat.

"Finally, to the people of Iran, let me say this. As I speak today, an ambas-sador from the Canadian consulate is presenting an offer of peace to Tehran on our behalf. This war can be over before it begins, should they choose to stand down their military, agree to nuclear inspectors, and make good on their promises to stop sponsoring terror around the world.

"America will always exercise its sovereign right to defend itself.

"We will have more information for you as it becomes available. I am here with the vice president and General Gonzales, whom I have placed in charge of ongoing military operations, as well as the directors of the NSA and the CIA.

"Several reporters are standing by online, and we will answer as many of your questions as is prudent under the current circumstances. With that I will yield to them. God bless America!"

The room exploded into conversation and activity, and Joseph and Lance slipped out the way they had come in.

"I know you're not a fan of his, but that was a great speech," Lance said with a mischievous glint in his eye.

"Yeah, he will probably get re-elected, and I'll have to put up with his crackpot policies for a few more years." They both chuckled at that. Then Joseph grew serious. "Now for the domestic enemies …."

30

For the first time ever, Senator Wallace was unsure of his next move. He could take that trip to Belgium and then Panama. The problem was, he wasn't just some obscure individual that hardly anyone would miss. The deal had come undone, pieces were falling off the board, and his options were now limited.

A cunning and intelligent man, he was in his office brainstorming to find an angle that he could work. He felt like he was in the dark and dared not interject himself into the situation for fear that he would draw suspicion upon himself. He had no idea about Clifford's arrest and detention. In Wallace's mind, the weak link was ComCorp's CEO. Will he talk? Eventually they all did. It would take longer now that "enhanced" interrogation techniques had been suspended. Can I get to him first?

Brad had disappeared, and the senator couldn't blame Brad. Damn it! He is the surgical instrument I could use right now. Wallace had made several attempts to contact him by encrypted email and even attempted a "dead drop" at a pre-disclosed location. Nothing!

The phone rang. Taking a deep breath, he picked it up, answering in his usual way: "Wallace." It was Peter Ashgrave. The senator's heart was pounding, and his mouth was suddenly dry. "What's up?"

Peter jumped right in. "We've got a hornet's nest here, and frankly I can't keep up with everything—information is coming in fast and furious." Ashgrave paused. "I know you're up to your eyeballs, but I could really use some help on this. I need someone with experience. What do you say? Your country needs you."

Just like that, the clouds were rolling away, and an opportunity was presenting itself.

Wallace was coy. "I don't know. These things always end up a political nightmare, and if you're not careful, it's often the oversight committees that bear the blame."

"Yeah, but when it goes well, you can ride the wave of political capital. Besides, everyone is rallying around the flag. The president's approval rating is through the roof."

"Okay, okay. I'm in." Wallace knew better than to hold out too long.

"Great, there's a committee meeting in two hours. We need to get ahead of this, so it's going to mean some long days."

Wallace responded honestly. "I've never been afraid of hard work, Peter. You know that."

"Good, see you shortly."

Wallace hung up the phone deliberately with renewed confidence. Better to be pissing out than pissing in. He often reminded himself of this political truth. He would be walking a tightrope here, but as an active member of the committee, he wouldn't be in the dark. And maybe, just maybe, he could deflect attention away from himself.

He clapped his hands together. "Ha! Here we go, boy. Buckle up."

Wallace never permitted himself a drink while at the office, but today he would make an exception. He opened the bottom drawer of his desk and retrieved a bottle of brandy and a tumbler. He poured a couple of ounces and tasted it, feeling the warm, smooth liquid slide down his throat. He swirled the brandy around in the glass a few times before taking another drink. He would find a way out of this; he always did.

———— • ————

As Wallace entered the meeting room, the first person he saw was Joseph Coolidge. What is he doing here? The old guy looks like he could drop dead at any moment. In all honesty, he looked healthy enough ... and Wallace knew it was his prejudice for the man that made him wish Coolidge would drop dead.

Joseph glanced Wallace's way but made no acknowledgement of his presence. Several members of the committee approached Joseph, shook his hand, and said thanks.

Thanks for what? Wallace wondered.

The tables had been arranged in a rectangle with places for perhaps thirty people. Each position had a name tag and a microphone. A large-screen TV was situated on the wall where everyone could see it. After working the room briefly and avoiding Joseph, who was busy flipping through files and notes, Wallace found his spot.

Ashgrave called the meeting to order. "Before I introduce General Gonzales, I want to remind all the members that very shortly, Congress will be declaring that a state of war exists between the US and Iran. Each of you has been selected for your experience, judgement, and loyalty. This is a bipartisan effort, and we must put our political differences aside for the sake of our country."

Someone spoke up in a good-natured tone. "Then how come there are more members from your side of the house?"

"Because we still control the chamber," Ashgrave quipped back, bringing laughter to the room, a welcome reprieve amidst the serious situation they faced. "Let's get down to business, shall we?" The group became silent and sober.

He spent the next few minutes bringing everyone up to speed, providing intel on the raid at the sour gas plant. The conversation turned to the source of the intel, and this led to Lance's ordeal in the wilderness and subsequent rescue.

There were several questions for Joseph regarding the well-being of his nephew.

One of the senators asked the obvious question, "Who ordered the SEAL teams in after Lance?"

"I did ... well, the committee did," Ashgrave responded.

"Why did you send SEAL teams in? Shouldn't that have been a police matter?"

Ashgrave glanced in Joseph's direction, but his expression remained bland. "Because we knew that the police ... even a SWAT unit would be out-classed under the circumstances. Notwithstanding his innocence, our assessment of his abilities was accurate."

The same senator continued to press the issue. "Am I the only one who is confused here? How did this issue come to the attention of the Armed Services Committee?"

Wallace held himself very still. He had been taking notes and listening intently.

"Senator Wallace brought it to our attention." As Ashgrave spoke, all eyes turned to Wallace.

He cleared his throat. "Yes, as you all know, this is my home state, and I have served here for many years. In that time, I have had the privilege of get-ting to know many of our law enforcement people in the state. I was contacted by the FBI supervisor in Helena, a Mr."—he glanced down at his notes—"Crown. Byron Crown. He made me aware of the situation, and I passed the information along."

"Did you know the suspect was Lance Coolidge, Joseph's nephew?" another member inquired. Everyone in the room was aware of the animosity between the two.

"I did not, not right away, but I put two and two together pretty quick."

Peter raised an eyebrow. "How come I had to hear about the connection from Joseph himself?"

"It was an ongoing operation, and it wouldn't have been prudent to pro-vide information to the family member of a suspect." He looked across the table at Joseph. "Sorry, but I was just doing my job."

Joseph maintained his poker face. It was slightly unnerving.

Peter spoke again. "That doesn't make a lot of sense. You could have at least informed the committee. The whole reason we went in with the SEAL teams is because of who Lance is."

Wallace was uncomfortable with the conversation's direction. A master negotiator, he decided to be self-deprecating to elicit empathy. "It's possible that competitiveness and my feelings towards Joseph clouded my judgement, but at the end of the day, any one of us probably would have done the same."

The room was full of politicians who understood that the nature of the game was to use any and all advantages, but this was extreme, and while they understood it, most of them didn't respect it.

Another committee member spoke up: "It turns out that one of the teams was completely corrupt and was given inside info that Lance had damning evidence in his possession. Am I understanding that correctly?'

"Yes, that is correct," Wallace answered.

"How the hell did they weasel that detail to the team? They must have had someone on the inside. Two dead, one missing, and one captured …. What does the captured man have to say for himself?"

Ashgrave looked in Gonzales's direction. "General?"

"As quiet as Jesus before Pilate."

Wallace exhaled some air. Truck would keep quiet; he was sure of that. He would do what he could to get him out, but he needed to be in a position of power to do that.

The room fell silent, and it seemed natural to adjourn the meeting for a short break.

————— • —————

Wallace was bothered that during all the hours of deliberation and conversation, Joseph had said little. They both mingled, with Joseph getting the lion's share of the attention. Everyone was curious, and there were lots of nonofficial questions. Joseph dropped a thought here and a question there, casually mentioning inconsistencies in the way things had unfolded.

When they reconvened, a young senator posed the question that most had probably been thinking: "It occurs to me that someone in a position of influence pulled some strings to get that particular SEAL team deployed. Whose idea was that?"

There it was—the question Wallace knew was coming. The break had afforded him a few moments to think about how to deal with it, and he had decided to tackle it head on. "It was me," he admitted.

Several of his peers turned hard, suspicious eyes on him now.

"Hold on," he said, raising his hand. "This team was the most decorated SEAL team in history. They have been the tip of the spear in countless operations that this very Senate has overseen. I knew they were not deployed, which is why I recommended them. It had nothing to do with my relationship with Senator Coolidge." It was a masterful stroke; it filled in the gaps and gave everything an air of legitimacy. Even some of the hardest eyes softened a little.

The young senator was not satisfied, however. "And they just happened to be corrupt?" The question was more of an accusation.

"Now see here!" Wallace bellowed, and several other voices from his side of the aisle jumped to his defense, creating a free-for-all.

Joseph alone remained calm, scribbling on his notepad, not even bothering to look up.

Ashgrave brought the meeting back to order. "Do any of us really believe Senator Wallace is culpable in this? Really? Let's get back to business; we need to work together at times like these!"

The room quieted, but tension still hung in the air.

"Do we have a statement from the FBI supervisor?" a member asked.

"This is the first I've heard of this agent," Ashgrave said.

For a moment, no one spoke.

"He's dead!" Joseph dropped the statement like a bomb, breaking his silence.

A chorus of murmurs went up, and a cold realization swept over Wallace. How did Joseph know that, and how would he have perceived its importance? Wallace sensed a trap but could not pinpoint where it was coming from. If Truck or the CEO has talked, I wouldn't be sitting here right now. What is Joseph up to?

Joseph was speaking again. He nodded towards the back of the room, and the lights dimmed. Ashgrave looked surprised but said nothing.

Joseph had a slideshow clicker, and he put it into action. The first picture to appear on the wall-mounted TV was of Crown crumpled on the ground next to his car.

"It was a suspected carjacking; however, we have reason to believe he was assassinated."

More murmurs arose.

"He was killed on a deserted street in one of the few spots without cell service, drawn there by a free meal offering from one of his favorite restaurants. His credit and debit cards had been disabled. In fact"—he brought up the next slide—"here are several shots of him fueling up and paying cash." The surveillance pictures were very clear. "With a few keystrokes, a bank employee put Crown out of business that night."

He had everyone's attention.

"The employee is on holidays. I hope for his sake, whoever is behind this plot doesn't find him before we do."

Ashgrave spoke up. "Joseph, what makes you think this potential assassination is linked to this case? Crown probably made a lot of enemies over the years."

Joseph advanced to the next slide. It was a bank statement. "If you notice, he made a stock purchase a few years ago, in his 401(k)." Another slide. "Several thousand shares of ComCorp. He sold them a year later."

Somebody whistled and said, "Boy howdy!"

"Damn!" Ashgrave cursed. "We have an Iranian asset somewhere in a position of influence. Lights!" he called out and the area brightened again. "This doesn't leave this room, is that clear? No damn leaks. This is national security!" He was emphatic.

The lights dimmed again, and Joseph brought up another document. "This is a purchase he made the day after he sold those shares. He made this purchase through a numbered company in Panama for the exact same number of shares. Our friends at the NSA traced it all back to Crown. Whoever killed him did it to shut him up. He was dirty."

Wallace was relieved that he had used a more sophisticated strategy himself. He had set this up for them, so the trail would never lead to him.

"We pulled up all his communications and could not find a pattern that might lead us to his accomplice."

The next slide was a list of phone numbers, with several of them circled. "Here are the calls Crown made to Senator Wallace," Joseph said, looking directly at Wallace. "So that clears up the concerns of my colleagues. You did in fact have three calls with Crown that day; you will note the time stamp here." He indicated it with the laser pointer.

Wallace was shocked by this corroboration from Joseph and stared triumphantly at the young senator who had accused him. The senator looked away in disgust.

"You had to refer to your notes when we asked you about Crown even though you'd had three conversations and had met him previously. I thought that was odd at first, but we meet a lot of people in our work."

Wallace just shrugged.

Joseph put another slide up. It was more phone records, with over a dozen circled numbers. "Then we found this. It turns out that over the last five years, you have spoken to each other on more than a dozen occasions. That does seem odd."

"Does it?" Wallace asked, beginning to sweat.

"Yes. You couldn't remember his name, you—a man who is admired for his ability to meet someone once and remember their name. How is it you can't remember the name of someone you spoke to sixteen times in the last five years?"

"What is this?" Wallace was looking into the faces of his peers and found no friendliness in any of them.

Ashgrave was glaring at him now. "That's a really good question, Wallace. What is this?"

He started to get up, but Ashgrave held up his hand. "You stay put until this is over." Wallace slumped back in his seat.

Joseph brought up another bank record, and it belonged to Wallace. It showed his purchase and sale of ComCorp stock.

"That's already a matter of public record," he snapped.

"It's curious that you sold your stock within forty-eight hours of Crown selling his." He circled the date stamp again with the laser pointer. "And within forty-eight hours of this conversation." He flipped to a slide showing the phone record. "You had him killed, didn't you?" Joseph's rich, deep voice boomed, filling the room. "Wallace, you are a traitor to your country, a murderer, a thief, and a liar!" Joseph threw the accusations right into his teeth.

Wallace rose to his feet, shaking with fear and rage. "That … that doesn't prove a damn thing and you know it. This is a political hit job, and you …." He wagged his finger around the room. "You are all culpable." The accusation rang hollow as did his feeble defense.

Two more slides came up, showing text messages between him and Bellamy. Wallace sat down hard, his lower lip trembling. Then most damning of all, the audio system came to life.

"What?"

"Sir, we've run into some problems here."

"Problems? What the hell is that supposed to mean?" It was Wallace speaking, followed by a shuffling sound and a new voice.

They heard the story from Clifford's own mouth, about stopping to get the truck fixed and the events that unfolded, up to the point that he had made the decision to eliminate Kyle.

Wallace was speaking again: "Put me on speaker phone. I need to know right now, is there anything else that you two are not telling me?"

"This is the first I've heard about this other stuff." Roger was speaking.

"Is there anything else?"

"No sir."

"Okay, then this whole thing is salvageable. I want you to get that envelope back. Shoot that hick if you must, but I want this thing done, is that clear? Or do I need to send someone to help you?"

"No sir, we've got this under control. I owe that Coolidge one for tonight anyway."

"Control?" Wallace was almost shouting. "You call this control? Uh, what did you just say? What name was that?"

"Coolidge, the guy that owns the Jeep."

The recording ended, and all eyes were on Wallace. His head was flung to one side, like a petulant child. He pushed against the arms of his chair in an effort to rise but the general stepped forward, halting his progress.

Joseph placed the clicker down gently and spoke. "The capitol police are waiting outside."

A few minutes later, Wallace was escorted away, a broken and defeated man, trapped in the pit he had dug for someone else.

Ashgrave was at Joseph's side. "I was wondering about your change of heart where Wallace was concerned and why you suggested he be in the meeting." He laughed heartily. "Coolidge, you're an old campaigner. I hope I never get on your bad side." He shook his head and took a few steps before turning around. "Well done," he said and hurried off.

———— • ————

Lance was waiting for Joseph when he got back to his office. A flat-screen TV was broadcasting a presidential press conference. Their eyes locked for a moment, and Joseph nodded.

Indicating the TV, Lance asked, "How much coverage do you think this will get?"

Joseph shrugged. "It's like the old adage—If a tree falls in the forest and CNN refuses to report it, does that mean it didn't happen?"

"What now?' Lance asked.

"Retirement! I'm never going to top this." Joseph stretched his long frame, reaching for the sky. "Which means … there will be a vacant senate seat in Montana—a seat that has been held by the Coolidge name for forty years." He had that youthful glint in his eye again. "Something to ponder."

Lance smiled. "I'd better call Miss Katherine."

31

The Starbucks on Queen Street in Auckland, New Zealand, always had a lineup because it was one of only a few in the downtown area. Brad hadn't made a habit of coming here, as he didn't want to establish a pattern of behaviour in his first few months as Clayton Delorme. As always, he sat where he could watch the door and, in this case, both doors. The crush of customers waiting for their orders caused him to lose his line of sight from time to time, but it was sunny and warm, and he was relaxed.

He had been smart with both his money and his planning. Making a small fortune before the ComCorp deal, he could live comfortably for the rest of his days. He had purchased a nice place in the countryside near the beautiful tourist town of Tauranga. It was a private setting with rolling hills, and a short jaunt to the beach. He spent most of his time in a rented apartment here in the city, however, preferring the hustle and bustle and the opportunities to meet Kiwi women.

He had seen the Sky News report about the arrest of Wallace and several others within his inner circle. Although the reporting was sparse, this was a matter of national security, and the news would trickle out, but only to the degree that the powers that be permitted.

Truck had disappeared—arrested, no doubt—and Beats was dead, so he was alone. He had always been alone, but he wasn't one to wallow in self-pity. His ComCorp stocks had tanked since the arrest of its CEO.

There should have been a long and expensive extradition process, since the company was based out of Calgary and its CEO was a Canadian. The mogul had a large estate nestled against the eastern slope of the Rockies, and if he had any sense he would have stayed put. Suspiciously, he had been arrested by the FBI in a Vegas hotel, and they were holding him in an American jail.

Brad had met the man once and seriously doubted that he would make such a fatal error in judgement. JTF-2 was behind it—Brad was certain of that. They had probably made it look like the CEO was on a pleasure trip, flying him secretly into the country and setting him up in a Vegas hotel room. They had probably even used his own private jet. Then, they had tipped off the FBI, and bam! He was done. It was all illegal, but Brad guessed that, as usual, they would get away with it. This fact and his own proclivity for larceny further justified in his mind everything he had done. Why not take care of myself first? In the Darwinian paradigm, it was logical.

ComCorp itself was still more than viable with vast holdings. It would bounce back in the long term. Brad would wait.

He was sipping on an Americano, enjoying the buzz of the morning and the attention he was receiving from some of the women. His handsome face was accentuated by his fine grooming and impeccable attire, and women found him attractive. Of course, some were more intuitive, feeling his vibe and steering clear of him. Those he simply wrote off. He didn't mind playing the odds, even where women were concerned.

Just that morning he had picked up some new clothes from RJB designs. He had become a regular client, and Roger, the owner, was always cool and helpful. He was probably in his early fifties, but you'd never know it. He looked much younger.

Amidst his daydream, Brad sensed someone at his side. A set of keys was gently placed on the table in front of him. He recoiled inwardly, instantly recognizing the black key tag with a silver fern symbol and a red key attached. Brad stayed cool, taking another sip of coffee as Lance slid into the chair across from the table, a coffee of his own in hand. Brad looked past Lance to see who was with him, but it appeared he had come alone.

"It's just me," Lance said. "As far as anyone is concerned, I'm here on vacation." Lance held the coffee in his left hand and his right was out of sight below the table.

The coffee was in a generic cup. "No outside food or drink allowed in here," Brad noted.

Lance smirked. "Stickler for the rules, are ya? Good, me too. I'd never drink this swill."

"You fly all the way over here because of that key tag?"

"That, and I found a shirt in one of the closets on sublevel A. It had an interesting label."

"RJB designs." Brad made more of a statement than a question.

"Have you noticed that it's the little things in life that often matter the most?" Lance looked at his watch as he was speaking. "Look at that—morning of the third day. Almost prophetic, wouldn't you say? For the last few days, I've been watching that clothing store, and suddenly there you are! Almost like it was meant to be."

"How do you want to handle this, Coolidge?" Brad sounded like he was bored with the conversation.

In that moment, Lance thought Brad looked like a panther—steady and calm but coiled up, ready to pounce. You could just feel his deadly nature.

"I'll leave that to you, Brad." Lance was staring him dead in the eye.

Brad shrugged and leaned forward. "You know what I think? I think you want some of the money. I think you don't have much of a plan and now here we are in a crowded coffee shop with innocent people all around. What are you going to do, pull that gun your hand is resting on and shoot me down in cold blood?" He was almost sneering.

"You would think that! I could have confronted you anywhere," Lance replied calmly.

Brad had to admit that he was right, but he was stumped as to what Lance was up to. Brad glanced over Lance's shoulder again.

Lance's lips formed a half smile when he saw the other's eyes flicker away again.

Although this irritated Brad, he showed no outward sign of the inward feeling.

"I just wanted to personally tell you it's over. Truck is broken and in prison. Your diabolical plot has been exposed, and the plant is secured. Your freedom here was short-lived, and all your plans have come to nothing. You lost, Brad!"

Brad's face contorted with anger. The words had hit their mark, just as Lance suspected they might. He had wanted to throw Brad off balance and keep him there.

Brad's face went cold again. "Whatever, man. Everyone wants something. You wouldn't have given me this chance if you were going to kill me." He was a cool one, all right.

"You're right," Lance countered. "I'm going to give you one chance. Hand over your gun now, and we will settle this by knife and fist like men. That way, no one else will get hurt."

Brad was surprised, not expecting a way out. Knowing Lance still had his gun trained on him under the table, Brad stood up slowly and pulled out his pistol, concealing it alongside his hip. Gently, he dropped it into a nearby wastebasket.

"Your turn," Brad said calmly, his manner concealing his intentions.

A young Asian woman had just picked up her order and was about to pass beside him. Brad moved as if he was giving her more room. Then in one motion, he swept the coffee out of her hand, splashing the hot beverage on Lance. In the same motion, he rose and spun her around, pushing her on top of Lance, throwing him off balance. Brad's knife was out in a flash, and he struck out wildly. The young woman screamed in shock and pain—she had been cut badly across her bare shoulder, showering them both with blood. Brad hit the side door and lunged into the street.

Lance had not anticipated such a brutal, calculated attack. It had accomplished what Brad knew it would—time to get away while Lance helped the poor woman.

"Someone help this girl!" Lance shouted. The last thing he needed was citizens holding him up. Doing some fast thinking of his own, he shouted, "Does anyone know who that guy was?"

The bystanders were shocked into inaction. Just then a woman rushed forward, knelt and applied pressure to the wound. "I'm a nurse," she told the young woman.

It wasn't clear if she couldn't speak English or if she was just in shock. She remained mute. Suddenly, the place erupted with activity, everyone talking and shouting at once. Several people rushed out into the street.

One bystander asked Lance, "Are you all right, mate? You're bleeding."

It wasn't his blood. "I'm all right," Lance assured the man.

As the crowd milled about, Lance took the opportunity to exit the coffee shop through the same side door. Once outside, he noticed that several people were looking up the street at something that had caught their attention.

He had been a fool to think he could appeal to Brad's pride and goad him into a fight. For a minute, Lance thought it had worked. Brad Akron was a ruthless and cunning enemy. Lance would not underestimate him again. This needed to end now!

Lance sprinted up the street. He had completely recovered from his ordeal in the northern woods and had been training for an eventuality like this. His wind was better than he expected, but they were at sea level, and the air was clear. Still, running up even a slight grade can be taxing.

He had gone a block when he saw what had happened. A cyclist had collided with a pedestrian and been sent flying. The chain had come off his bike and the man was banged up. Several citizens were trying to help him, but he wasn't cooperating. Instead, he was laying into them with a string of colourful expletives. Lance took all this in, slowing his pace only a little.

Brad was about a block ahead. Is he limping? The road intersected another with a green belt beyond—some sort of park. Lance spotted a sign indicating that this was the University of Auckland campus.

Emergency vehicles whined behind him, and he wanted to end this before the police converged on their position. Brad crossed the road at a dead run and disappeared into the wooded park beyond. Lance was only seconds behind, and he came to a stop, listening. The traffic sounds were muffled, and the air was cooler here under the canopy. He took several long cleansing breaths and moved forward, spying an open space about seventy yards beyond. What would Brad do? Like a deer, he would probably keep to the treeline. Was it pure luck or divine intervention, that had brought them to the same place this morning? Lance had been watching for a few days, but how often does one buy clothes? He had no idea what alias Brad was using or where he was living. All Lance knew was that Brad had the ability to disappear, and if he did, Lance might never find him again.

The many tracks of people who had walked through this area meant that finding a distinguishable one seemed unlikely. Then just like that, there it was—a print in the soft ground! It was fresh, and the person had been walking at a good pace. A good tracker doesn't forget a track—this one was toed out slightly, just like the ones Lance had studied in the snowy Montana canyon.

In that moment, Lance realized again that the world is profoundly connected and that there are consequences to everything we do and everywhere we go.

The track provided Lance with a direction. As suspected, Brad had stayed in the green belt. Lance had the advantage of a gun, but he couldn't be certain Brad didn't have another. And Lance knew for sure that Brad had a knife. In the hands of a skilled practitioner, a knife was just as deadly as a gun.

While moving at a good clip, Lance cautiously searched the trees, the shrubs, anywhere that could provide an ambush or hiding spot. Then he saw his adversary: in a gap in the trees, a hundred yards away, he caught a glimpse of Brad approaching a police officer, pointing in Lance's direction.

"No, watch out!" Lance yelled.

Too late! When the policeman looked where Brad was pointing, his knife flashed and struck the officer above the ear with the handle, and he fell like he'd been hit with a bat.

Lance raced forward, trying to close the distance, knowing what Brad had in mind. Lance had gone no more than thirty yards before Brad had the officer's sidearm clear of the holster. At a dead run, Lance squeezed off a shot. Brad jumped back like he had touched something hot and snapped off a shot of his own. Lance felt a hot iron laid across his ribs. The man could shoot! Lance took two steps sideways and fired another shot. A piece of the fountain just beyond Brad splintered off. Lance had missed. He took two more running steps to the left as Brad dove behind the fountain, chased by more bullets from Lance's gun.

Lance continued left and was able to see around the fountain. Brad was leaning against it. The first shot must have hit the mark. Seeing Lance, Brad lurched from his position, and headed towards the trees on the other side of the park. As he went, he threw a hail of bullets back, and all Lance could do was hit the ground, in a low spot in the grass.

After rolling over several times, Lance sprang back to his feet and fired. Brad was just entering the trees when another bullet found him. He stumbled and disappeared into the trees.

The place was empty now, as everyone had gotten the hell out of there. Somehow the injured policeman had disappeared as well.

"Lance," Brad called, his voice surprisingly strong. "You hit?"

It was a surreal moment, two men hell-bent on killing each other, and now they were having a conversation.

"Yeah, I'm hit. Not bad … burned my ribs some. You?"

"You clipped me along the forearm with that first one, and the second one walloped me in the back. Hang on …." A couple of seconds went by. "Hit my belt, but must have hit a branch or something along the way. All good!"

"Ah," was all Lance could muster. What a strange conversation this was, like old buddies talking it up.

"How many rounds you got left?" Brad asked.

Lance slid the magazine out to look. "Two and one up the pipe." He jammed the magazine back in place.

"Damn," said the other. "Me, too! Looks like we're even with the pistolas. I'd like to take you up on your original offer and go to the knives now. What do you say?"

That old battle lust ran hot in Lance's blood. "How do I know you don't have another gun?"

Brad laughed. "Because I would have used it instead of borrowing one from the cop."

"Throw out your gun then, and come on," Lance commanded.

During the conversation, Lance had taken up a position behind the fountain.

Brad emerged from the woods, solid on his feet, the gun hanging from his index finger. When he was in full view, he threw it far off to the side.

The man had courage and confidence! In spite of himself, Lance felt a measure of respect and kinship with this evil man. They had been trained to do inhuman things, and that always changed a man. Still, Brad was a magnificent fighting man—with strength, courage, stamina, and heart. Had the circumstances been different, they might have been friends.

When Brad slid a knife out from beneath his collar, however, all bets were off. Moving forward, he deftly tossed the knife back and forth between his hands, without looking at it. His eyes were fixed on Lance, and once again, Brad had become a predator.

——— • ———

"Today, you are the lion." Joseph's voice echoed in Lance's mind. Tossing his gun away, he pulled his knife out from its scabbard. He reflected on all the years of training and conditioning that had brought him to this place and accepted this fight, even as he accepted the reality of his own mortality. He wanted to live, marry Lynette, and have children, but even that would not, could not deter him from this destiny. He looked again at the handcrafted knife. Its deadly design would be put to the ultimate test now.

Lance called out one final offer, knowing the other would never accept it: "You could drop that knife and live."

"I'd rather die here than spend the rest of my life in a cage. I'd make you the same offer, but we both know we'd just have to do this at some other place and time."

Lance acknowledged that by bringing the blade to his forehead and bowing slightly. "To the end, then."

"To the end!" said the other.

Both men held their blades low, cutting edges up. They circled each other warily, each evaluating the other's style, posture, and movements.

Brad suddenly shifted direction, going against the grain of their movement and closed the distance.

Lance slashed up and to the side, a flicking movement that caught Brad on the wrist with the back side of the blade, drawing blood.

As Lance brought the blade back into line, Brad threw a front leg kick. He didn't telegraph the kick at all, and there was power behind it.

Catching Lance in his midsection, the kick forced him off balance. Brad followed up with a spinning back kick that clipped Lance's knife hand, and he almost lost his grip.

The man moved with the grace of a ballet dancer, resourcefully utilizing his martial arts to augment his blade.

Lance set himself, hoping the numbness in his wrist wasn't obvious.

Brad was silent and menacing as he scanned for any weakness he could exploit, his eyes darting back and forth. His blade flashed straight out, attempting a direct hit, but Lance could parry those all day long and did so, smoothly.

As Lance countered, he kept the forward movement and tried a thrust of his own, but Brad slapped his arm, pushing the knife out of line. This usually creates an opening to thrust your knife into the opponent's belly, but Lance rolled to the right. Spinning all the way around, he caught Brad with a back fist. Lance couldn't generate a lot of power with this move, but it was enough to push Brad off balance, leaving him vulnerable.

As Lance's knife came around in a sweeping arc, Brad athletically jumped back out of the way.

It seemed that neither man had found an advantage.

As they circled each other again and again, it was Brad who usually made the first move. Lance was just as comfortable counterpunching as the other took the initiative.

Brad flicked a quick inside-to-outside arc kick, trying to catch his knife hand again, but Lance easily avoided the move. In fact, it seemed a little slow. Did Brad's collision with the cyclist slow him down slightly?

Lance struck out again. This time, the back of his blade bit deeper into Brad's forearm.

Brad brought his knife up in an amazingly quick motion, turning his hand slightly in an attempt to slide between Lance's guard and hinder his parries.

Again, Lance parried the attempt, spinning Brad slightly with a push-slap against his shoulder.

Brad was continuously trying to create an opening. Lunging forward on agile feet, he feigned a jab and slashed left and then right, all in one fluid motion.

Lance parried the jab, but the blade drew a fleck of blood from his cheek. That one had been close.

Another front kick, followed by an inside arc kick, forced Lance to step back again. It had been a bit slow. Something was definitely hampering Brad's movements, but whatever it was, Brad was hiding it well.

Back and forth they sparred—a flick here, a slash there. Both men were bleeding with Brad receiving the worst of it.

Lance noticed a pattern as the fight took on a rhythm. Brad was generally smooth and strong on his feet—his conditioning was equal to Lance's own. They were evenly matched in ability, but there was a slight weakness when Brad stepped right or kicked inside out.

Lance knew if he could time it right, there might be an opportunity.

Vaguely aware that a small group had silently gathered around them, Lance didn't dare take his eyes off Brad. Whoever lost this battle would do so because of an unforced error.

Brad yielded momentarily, stepping back and taking a deep breath, giving them both the opportunity to look around.

Several heavily tattooed Maori men were watching with keen interest. None spoke. They watched in awe and amazement. This was knife fighting at the highest level—they knew they were watching something special, and as vicious and nasty as it was, it was a rare spectacle.

Lance initiated the next clash. He decided to press Brad and test his theory that something was wrong with the other's adductor.

Moving in close, Lance shifted left, creating an opening for Brad to throw another arc kick. The opening came and went without Brad making the attempt.

They circled again and Lance jabbed once more. This time, Brad barely made the parry.

Lance picked up the pace, drawing Brad in again. Shifting right and then left, using lots of head movements, Lance forced Brad to increase his lateral movements. First right, then left, jabbing and slicing, Lance's blade found Brad's forearm yet again.

His arm was beginning to flag slightly but not enough to present a clear opening.

Lance shifted to his left, forcing Brad left. This time the opening was a little wider, and Brad took the bait. He flicked the arc kick with plenty of space and time to make it count.

Lance would use a slicing motion to catch the leg and then, with an upward movement, slide past it and plunge the knife low and hard.

That was the plan, but as the kick came up, it did so with incredible speed and then instantly changed direction. Brad brought his leg up high, and it dropped hard. It was a wicked axe kick!

Lance realized with stark clarity that he had been masterfully baited; the weakness was a ruse. All he could do was fall straight back. The kick dropped with full force on Lance's wrist, knocking the blade from his hand.

The spectators let out a collective "Whoa ...!"

As Lance rolled backwards, he used the momentum to push off the ground to his feet in a reverse handspring.

Coming up with a handful of dirt, as Brad sprang towards him, all Lance had time for was an underhanded throw.

Some of the dirt caught Brad in the eyes. He blinked in disbelief—that was the oldest trick in the book.

Lance bowled forward, catching Brad on the shoulder and spinning him around. Lance then dove and rolled, his hand closing around his knife. As he completed the roll, he was back on his feet. Brad's eyes were watering, but his vision had returned.

Lance shifted his knife to his left hand in a flash and threw a right jab. The blow landed with a thud, square on Brad's forehead. He was knocked backwards, but instinctively, he kept his blade up, maintaining the guard position. The jab was like a piston and as it snapped back, there was no chance to catch it with the knife.

Brad had been momentarily stunned and wasn't able to adjust to the fact that Lance now held his knife in his left hand.

Lance stepped left and feigned another jab with his right hand. Brad swiped at it, not wanting to miss the chance again.

This pulled his blade out of line, and Lance timed it perfectly. He rolled his hand against Brad's knife-hand wrist in a Wing Chun manoeuvre. Westerners call this "sticky hands". Curling from the inside out, Lance positioned the back of his hand against Brad's, forcing it out of line.

Following through with momentum, Lance took a small step forward. Then, rolling his hips, he swung the blade under Brad's knife arm. It struck home and sank deep between his ribs.

Lance thrust in and out three more times—rapid, brutal movements. Then with his right palm on his breast, he pushed Brad away and down.

As he fell, his knife slipped from his fingers and clanked to the ground, a shocked look on his face.

The spectators were silent.

Lance deftly tossed his knife back to his right hand and kicked Brad's away.

Brad was half sitting, propped against the fountain.

Lance's breath was coming in great gasps and tears were forming in his eyes.

Frothy blood was beginning to gather on the edges of Brad's mouth, as his right lung filled with blood.

"I'll just rest here a bit, if that's all right?" Lance whispered leaning against the fountain himself.

Brad tried mouthing a word, swallowed hard and tried again. What came out was a gargled whisper.

"Goo … good job … thought I had you there." Brad's head fell to his chest, and he was gone.

One of the Maoris stepped forward. "Cops comin', mate." He peeled off his T-shirt, displaying a billboard of tattoos and handed it to Lance.

Pulling off what was left of his own, he dipped it in the fountain, and used it to wipe off as much blood as he could. After dousing his face and hair, he slipped on the borrowed shirt and walked away towards the university.

When he glanced back, the Maoris were gone, and a pool of blood had settled in around Brad's body.

———— • ————

Lance would never forget that scene. The sun shining, the birds singing, and a warm, sweet fragrance on the breeze. Feeling lost and alone, he was deeply sorrowful for having taken yet another life—the life of a kinsman, so that others, not of their breed, good people, kind people, could live. He hoped it would be the last for him. He had seen too much death and destruction. There was nothing he wanted more than to live out the rest of his days in peace and quiet. He turned on his heels, faded into the trees, and was gone.

———— • ————

In the afternoon sun, as the shadows began to stretch, there among the great trees, in a small clearing, a young man sat silently on a tattered old blanket. Drawing deeply on an ancient pipe, his eyes squinted against the swirling smoke. He stirred the remaining coals of a dying campfire and watched as hungry fingers clutched at the pieces of wood. Sparking up, it instantly brightened the small space, illuminating his serious face—a study in concentration, alert to the slightest sound or movement. It wouldn't be long now.

Behind him, there was a slight scuff of moccasin feet on the loose sand. Lance whirled around with the speed and agility of a great cat and let out a tremendous roar, catching the woman and child in midstride lunging towards him.

The young boy let out a squeal as Lynette tackled Lance. The boy struggled in vain at the man's legs, pushing and straining until finally Lance gave way, falling backwards to the ground.

"Uncle! Uncle!" Lance was slapping the ground trying to tap out as Lynette choked him mercilessly.

She released him and started cheering and dancing around with her arms in the air while the boy laughed hysterically.

"She got you, Dad!" The boy was jubilant in his mother's triumph.

It was one of those perfect moments, full of grace and peace. Lance looked down at the small boy, scooped him up, and held him close.

"That she did, Joey," he whispered, "that she did!"

THE FIELDS OF
Gomorrah

A GRIPPING STORY
EXPOSING THE DARK WORLD
OF HUMAN TRAFFICKING

STACEY HERRING

CASTLE QUAY BOOKS

WINNER OF THE WORD GUILD
BEST NEW MANUSCRIPT AWARD

UNIVERSITY OF
LOST
CAUSES

ST. JUDES
EST. 1867

LARRY J. M^c CLOSKEY

CASTLE QUAY BOOKS

WE ARE THE SOLUTION
TO POVERTY

JUST
ACT

ANGIE PETERS

CASTLE QUAY BOOKS